I0771152

NEW WORLD CITY

HYPERARCANA
BOOK 1

SPENCER HEY

Copyright © 2025 by Spencer Hey

All rights reserved.

No part of this book may be reproduced in any form or by any electronic or mechanical means, including information storage and retrieval systems, without written permission from the author, except for the use of brief quotations in a book review.

ISBN: 978-1-968066-00-0 (Paperback)
ISBN: 978-1-968066-01-7 (Ebook)

Contact: spencer@heyspencerhey.com

Visit: www.heyspencerhey.com

The story, all names, characters, and incidents portrayed in this work are fictitious. No identification with actual persons (living or deceased), places, buildings, and products is intended or should be inferred.

Version 1.1

Cover art and design by Ryan Mulford

PROLOGUE

Two truths of the watch in New World City. First: Don't buy into the lies. The State wants you to believe they see everything and have it all under control. They don't. Drugs. Weapons. Murder. Magic. Mayhem. Anything is possible. Second: Heroes are needed. But heroes die like everyone else.

Two hard truths of the neon-soaked sprawl. Two hard truths that Constable Shuwen Li had to learn the hard way.

Go back five turns of the wheel. She was working the security detail when Mayor Eli Strauss Sr. bit the dust. During a speech. He was cut down mid-sentence. In broad daylight. On live TV.

Shuwen was right there. Only age twenty-one at the time, but already a decorated officer. She stood in front of the stage. In her crisp, blue uniform. Shoulder to shoulder with her elite team. Right next to her old partner, Tomas Sterling. They looked out over the crowd, watching for any sign of trouble.

But the trouble came from behind. A cyber-synth monster with four arms wielding the big katanas.

The State insists that monsters like that aren't real. But it was real enough for Old Man Strauss. It burst through the curtains at the back. Cut through two officers like butter. Turned the podium into a butcher's block. Decapitation. Dismemberment. Blood spattered the faces of the onlookers. Wet slap of limbs falling dead to the ground. A moment of horrified, shocked silence.

Then total chaos. Thousands screaming. Panic. Wild gunfire. People running in all directions.

Several officers were trampled to death as they tried to control the mob. Tomas Sterling was one of them. He was built solid. Like a brick wall. But that didn't matter. An anarchist got lucky and kicked out his leg. Tomas fell to one knee. That was all it took. The frenzied mob rushed over him. He was crushed. Shuwen right there beside him. She had taken down two anarchists. Was binding the hands of a third when she saw Tomas fall. Their eyes met, shared the recognition of doom in that moment before he disappeared. Under the wave of bodies.

She was never the same after that day. Seeing the people she had sworn to protect trample her partner. Consume him like a mindless mass of flesh-eating bacteria. Whatever youthful optimism she might have had—it bled out right there on the street, along with Tomas.

One hard truth chiseled into Shuwen's brain.

Heroes die.

Ever since then, she saw the city and its people differently. She saw the ugliness. The corruption. Always there. Bubbling beneath the surface. Waiting to boil. Waiting for her to bring the cold fist of justice.

PART ONE

BULLET

CHAPTER 1
SHUWEN

...RACES TO THE SCENE

Constable Shuwen Li is on the last few rounds of her patrol when the emergency call for backup comes in over the radio. Mayor Eli Strauss Jr. has been shot. At a political rally in the Downtown Plaza. In the middle of a speech.

«Nine officers down. Civilian casualties. Gangs and anarchists active in the area. All available officers respond.»

Without hesitation, Shuwen turns on the sirens and heads for the highway. Her beat is Lucky Precinct 13. That's Ring 1. Just outside the downtown. The highway should get her to the plaza fast.

Hopefully fast enough.

More information trickles in as she cuts through the evening traffic. Her car a guided missile flying toward the polished steel and black stone towers of The Core.

«Mayor is alive and secured.»

Good. Junior is luckier than his old man.

«Assassin identity and whereabouts unknown.»

She picks up the handset. "This is Constable Li. Requesting detail and update on the situation at the plaza?"

«Anarchists control the plaza. Well-armed. Do not engage without backup.»

She sees smoke rising above the buildings. Hears the sound of explosions.

«Repeat: Do not engage without backup.»

She shuts off the radio. Her pulse quickens.

This time will be different.

———

After Old Strauss Sr.'s assassination back in '95, there was a thorough Stasi investigation. It dug deep. What it found was rot. Several precincts had a hand in the hit, and the corruption trail led all the way to the Chief Inspector's door.

The old mayor was hated by most of the NWPD, and he probably deserved it. But for Shuwen, that was no excuse. A cop's duty was to the law. Absolute and unwavering.

Even in this godless age, duty had to remain sacred. Without it, the world was a wild, violent mess. The law brought order. Made things clean. Simple. You didn't have to like the rules, but if you played by them, your choices and your conscience stayed clear.

That was how you best served justice on the streets of New World City. You had to be hard. Principled. Unyielding. Anything less and you would be eaten alive.

———

The wheels scream as Shuwen swerves into the exit lane. She pulls a nifty power slide at the bottom of the ramp, drifting onto 10th Avenue. Then floors the accelerator.

Still a few blocks from the Downtown Plaza, the chaos

is everywhere. People running in terror, fleeing the scene. The sounds of riot. The smell of burning.

Traffic becomes a solid wall. No way through. Shuwen slams on the brakes, out of the car in a flash, moving on foot. She leaves the sirens wailing behind her.

The sounds of chaos grow louder. Pyro grenades exploding, close enough to taste. The air thickens with smoke.

She ducks into an alley, taking quick cover behind a dumpster. Staying low, she adjusts the silver bracers on her wrists. The metal plating vibrates at her touch, the engravings of her family's crest—a tiger rampant, holding a three-pointed star—glowing pale blue. She closes her eyes. Breathes deep. Waiting for the familiar rush of the ancestral magic...

There it is.

She feels the mystic eyes of her father. Her grandfather. Great-grandmother. And more. The strength and wisdom of ten generations. They will be her guide. Her protection.

In half a tick, she is back out on the street. The smoke is thickening, but she can see right through it. Her breathing is easy and clean.

Gunfire erupts a few blocks over, coming from the wrong direction. She must stay focused. She sprints ahead, toward the plaza. Moving faster than should be possible, vaulting over cars, rushing upstream through the river of panicked citizens. To any onlookers, she's a blur of graceful movement.

———

At the end of the Stasi investigation, ninety-nine officers were found guilty. They were shipped to prison camps, implanted with docility circuits, and worked to death.

Twenty-two of the one hundred eighty-five NWPD precincts were dissolved completely. The Chief Inspector was given a choice: exile or execution. He chose execution.

Shuwen came out clean, of course. Not a hint of involvement. She even got a special commendation. Sixteen gangsters apprehended at the scene, seven officers rescued, dozens of citizens shepherded to safety. Yet she felt no pride. She was just doing her job.

But what was her job? She wasn't so sure anymore. The NWPD was not the institution she thought it was. Many of her colleagues had broken their oaths. Failed in their duty. Betrayed themselves.

If the law was not absolute, then Tomas had died for nothing. Her father's sacrifice and his father's sacrifice; her family's long line of service—if the rule of law was not iron-clad, then it all meant nothing.

After the commendation ceremony, Shuwen was ordered to take a halfspan off to recover. She used that time to draft a resignation letter.

She never submitted it.

———

Three blocks away from the Downtown Plaza. It's quieter than Shuwen expected. Seems like most of the citizens have cleared the zone. And she's seen no anarchists or gangsters yet. Most of the action must have moved elsewhere.

She passes under the elevated tracks that snake around The Core and its adjoining districts. The trains have been shut down, but there is still an occasional spark from the old wiring overhead. Flashes of electric blue in the clouds of riot smoke.

At two blocks away, she slows her run to a brisk walk. More cautious. There could be creeps hiding anywhere.

She hears shouting from what must be the plaza. And then the soft jangle of sleigh bells. A sound that means trouble.

A lanky, hunched figure emerges from the smoke directly in front of her. Puffy shirt, tattered white cloak, and derby hat.

Charlies.

One of New World City's so-called "Big Six" gangs, The Charlies are the oddest of the bunch. They dress like an old-world theater troupe. Paint their faces white. Load themselves up with every street drug you can imagine. They seem to have no purpose other than wanton destruction.

"Stop, in the name of the law! Hands above your head!" Shuwen shouts. The magic in her silver bracers amplifies her voice. Their pale blue glows a little brighter.

The Charlie lazily lifts its head, fixing her with a deranged gaze. A sickly, brown-toothed grin spreads across its painted-clown face. Shuwen knows that look.

This junker is completely whacked out. They will not listen to reason.

There is a loud mechanical click as a knife springs from the Charlie's puffy-shirt sleeve into its right hand. A neat, stage-magician's trick. But before he can brandish it, Shuwen closes in. She delivers a fierce, left-handed back-fist, shattering his jaw with a gnarly crunch.

Her strike sends a shock-wave through the Charlie's skeleton. The knife slips from his fingers and clatters on the ground as he stumbles backward. Shuwen steps forward and follows with a roundhouse. The clown goes flying, splats against the side of a parked delivery van, then crumples to the ground.

———

"Resign? What will you do if you leave the force?" Her mother's words were more accusation than question.

During her recovery after The Strauss Sr. Assassination, Shuwen traveled out to the country to stay with her mother in their family's cottage.

They sat together on the porch. It was quiet. Cloudy with a slight breeze. The soft sound of wind through the trees. Occasional bird songs. Pleasant. Peaceful.

"I don't know," Shuwen replied, her eyes fixed on the horizon, trying to empty her mind and let it drift to a vision of life outside the NWPD. "I could become a teacher. Open a dojo." It sounded silly, but the thought sparked a flicker of hope.

"A dojo?" Her mother scoffed. "Don't be ridiculous."

"I'm serious," Shuwen protested. "I could start a dojo. Help people train, learn how to protect themselves. Teach them some of our family's fighting style. Teach them how to become... better versions of themselves."

"You would hate that. You know it." Her mother's words hit home. "That's too far removed from the action. Not making a real difference."

"I don't know..." Shuwen was tired. Yet she felt an urge to argue. "Running a school would give me more control over my life. The people I train—I could show them the freedom in strict discipline. It could be nice."

"Nice."

Her mother repeated the word, dripping with disdain. She let it hang in the air before following it up with a long, loud sigh.

Shuwen knew that sound well. It was the same sigh her mother had given her father a thousand times. He had been a constable, worked for the NWPD his entire life. Decorated and respected. Retired with the highest honors. But some scandal had marred his precinct at the end of his career. He hadn't chosen to retire. He was forced to. He was angry. Shuwen had been very young then. Her parents never gave her the whole story, but she remembered the arguments. The sighs from her mother.

"Yes, the police are corrupt," her mother began. "Yes, the State is corrupt. But the Li Family is not. We are pure. You are the last of us still serving. The city needs you. It is your duty, Shuwen. You do not have a choice."

———

Shuwen squeezes the cuffs tight. Binding the Charlie's hands behind its back.

She activates her com. "This is Constable Li. Hostile subdued, ready for pick-up. Intersection of Argyle and South Street."

There is an immediate, robotic response:

Acknowledged. Sending collection. ETA 10.

The automated police drones will arrive shortly to take the defeated gangster away. To be interrogated. Then, most likely, implanted and sent off to the work camps. Never to be seen on the streets of New World City again.

Shuwen takes a moment to dust herself off, towering over the shuddering pile of white clothing. The Charlie's hat has blown off in the fight, revealing a mess of filthy, tangled hair, dyed in a patchwork of bright colors. The painted white face misshapen and smeared with blood. He wriggles around on the ground, just managing to lift and turn his head. Eyes wide. The drug-addled brain struggling to grasp what has happened.

Shuwen frowns with disgust. She's not keeping count, but the number of Charlie's she's dispatched must be close to three dozen.

So disappointing that it has come to this. An endless stream of junkers...

She adjusts her bracers. Waits for the rush. Another deep breath. Then she is off and running again. Into the smoke.

The plaza is just ahead.

This time will be different.

CHAPTER 2
TY

...UPSTAGES HIS COMPETITION

"I will never forget that day, when our great city lost one of its greatest leaders—my father."

Mayor Eli Strauss Jr. stands tall at the podium. A crisp, baby blue suit with a soft, white pinstripe. Quaffed silver hair. Pearl teeth. A perfect picture of New World City's political power and respectability. Spotlit and center stage, he is the focal point of the Downtown Plaza, a charming, historic square nestled among the old banks and skyscrapers of The Core.

A line of NWPD officers stand behind him. With another line on the ground at the front of the stage. Several more throughout the grandstands. This is a high security affair, and the cops are out in force.

But Eli sounds perfectly relaxed. Confident. His voice loud and clear through the speakers. Thousands of supporters have turned up. Eager to revel in the power of a political dynasty.

As he mentions his late father, he pauses, carefully working his face into a convincing expression of grief.

Bullshit.

Ty Reese is in attendance. Sitting as far away as possible. In the highest seat of the furthest grandstand. He's a hostile audience. Listening to his political opponent. Measuring up the performance. Listening for signs of weakness.

The mayor continues: "After that heinous act, which revealed the rot within our city—You trusted me to make things right. You trusted me to clean up the swamp."

The crowd starts to cheer.

"You trusted me to seek REVENGE!"

The crowd erupts.

Ty smiles.

OK. That was a good line. I'll give you that. What next, Rich Boy?

"And I did. ALL... OF... IT!"

Eli delivers each word with terrifying intensity. Ty's eyes were closed behind his designer sunglasses. He opens them now. Beholds the handsome mayor on the big projector screens. The man looks like a grinning predator. He's just made a kill and is now inviting his pack to join him at the feast.

Ty snorts.

Revenge is an easy platform. Who doesn't love revenge?

He begins to stroke his chin thoughtfully.

Kid may have the edge at the moment.

Purses his lips.

But he is a shit leader. The city is still a fucked-up cesspool. Everybody knows it.

Cocks an eyebrow.

And my words have WAY more smoke than this scuzzer's.

"When you go to the polls next week, remember who turned this city around. Remember who destroyed The Dark Web." Eli throws his arms wide. "Remember who truly loves this city." His eyes sparkling. "This is MY city!"

The crowd erupts again.

Ty cracks his knuckles.

Not your city for long, kid.

He's heard enough. He rises to leave. But as he gets to his feet a rifle shot splits the air.

A sudden, stunned silence. The sound of the gunshot reverberates through the plaza.

A moment frozen in time.

Ty whips off his sunglasses.

The moment shatters.

The mayor is flat on his back. A spray of crimson across the striped white and blue banners behind him. Someone screams.

Holy shit! It's happening again.

The stage lights go out. For a beat, the whole scene turns a dark, shadowy red in the fading evening light. Then a thousand flood lights, mounted in the windows of every building around the plaza, all click on at once. The place becomes so brightly lit it feels hyper-real.

What the fuck? Lit up like they were expecting this?

Even from his distance away, Ty can now make out the individual hairs on the mayor's head as he sits up. Eli is clearly in shock from the attack. The left side of his face streaked with blood.

Doesn't look like Rich Boy expected it.

The cops scatter in all directions. Guns and clubs out. Shouting orders into megaphones. It's impossible to tell what they're saying over the rising chorus of screams and sirens.

Helicopters arrive, circling. So much noise that another rifle could go off and you wouldn't hear it.

The crowd is starting to stampede. Streaming down the steps of the grandstands. Frantic. Some cops trying to corral them, but it's a losing proposition.

Ty stays put at the top of the grandstand. A hawk

on its perch. He's not looking for the shooter. He knows they will be long gone. He's looking for his boys.

———

Politics in New World City has always been a deadly game. The players might change from one election to the next, but the rules stayed more or less the same: Do whatever it takes to win.

That suited Ty just fine. "Doing whatever it takes" was how he had become a champion boxer. Then a successful musician. Then a fashion business mogul. He studied, he trained, he intimidated, he executed. In every sense of that last word.

His fashion brand—"Azzuri"—had launched only a few turns ago, yet it was already big business. In addition to supplying the hottest styles to the rich and famous, it served as the means to launder money from his extensive criminal activities.

Sport and politics. Music and fashion. Crime and power. For Ty, it was all connected. And he had his hands in all of it.

He liked to think of himself as the perfectly adapted creature for New World City's hawk-eats-dove environment. Born dirt poor in a broken home. He was slinging drugs and guns from a young age. Fighting for his life every damned day on the streets.

His fighting skills eventually earned him a shot in the boxing ring. He showed what his fists could do. And the rest was history. Two-time heavyweight champion. Millions in the bank. A lot of doors opened up, and he went through them.

Ty's Azzuri organization was now among The Big Six

gangs of the city. And he wasn't stopping there. One day, he would rule the whole damned town.

———

Ty spots two of his boys, looking as discreet as Azzuri boys ever do in their slick trench coats. They are standing at the bottom of another grandstand, nearer the stage. He signals them to stand back and watch. They slip away obediently.

This is going to get messy.

A dozen cops surround the mayor, forming a human shield. They get him off the stage, plow through the crowd, disappear down a side street.

Eight or nine cops are left behind. One is a sergeant, still shouting into his megaphone, calling for calm and order from the front of the stage.

Fool is making himself a target.

Right on cue, a pyro flask comes flying. It explodes at the sergeant's feet, lighting him up from the waist down. He shrieks and starts dancing, frantically searching for a safe place to drop and roll. But there's no safety to be found.

The pyro is a tell-tale sign of anarchist mobs. Two of them. One moving in from the east side, one from the west. More flasks are thrown and explode, creating a cordon of fire that effectively seals off the plaza—at least until heavier vehicles arrive. Anyone still hanging around will be trapped. At the mercy of the thugs.

There is a police helicopter overhead. It surely has a sniper on board, but the tall buildings don't give it enough room to maneuver. It's a sitting duck. An anarchist's rocket-powered grenade soon takes advantage.

Boom. Swirling wreckage comes crashing down into the stage.

Now it's Ty who applauds.

Awesome.

The cops in the plaza started out with more weapons, but they are now outnumbered and surrounded. The anarchists' grenades make quick work of the poor bastards.

Ty is still on his perch. Watching. Enjoying the show like it's a Glitzkrieg production set. He's waiting for the right moment. Before too long, the NWPD may be his personal army, but for now, they are still on Team Strauss. Team Rich Boy. Not worth saving.

Once the cops are finished, the anarchists shift into looting mode. Some are smashing windows. Some searching the bodies. Some having a go at overturning a patrol car.

Reinforcements will arrive soon.

OK. If I'm going to perform, now is the time.

———

"I very much appreciate your willingness to meet with me, Mr. Reese," said the woman. A political operative of the Populist Party. Black, double-breasted suit and thick, dark-rimmed glasses. Pin-straight, dark brown hair pulled back in a tight bun. She stood perfectly erect in the center of the sitting room on the top floor of the Southtown Hotel.

Ty's penthouse suite.

He occupied himself at the window overlooking the shopping galleria below. Taking long, slow puffs on a cigar.

"Dr. T," he corrected her without looking. Against the dark night sky, he could see her well enough in the reflection off the glass. "Mr. Reese was my father's name."

"I'm sorry. Of course. Dr. T." Lowering her eyes to the leather portfolio in her hands, the woman adjusted her grip to conceal the label on its front that read Mr. Reese.

"Perhaps your assistants told you, but please allow me to introduce myself. I—"

Ty cut her off. "I don't need your name. I know who you are."

Her eyes fluttered momentarily at the interruption. "Then I will get right to the point. The Populist Party would like to support you as our candidate in the next mayoral election."

"Of course you would." He finally turned around to face her, exhaling a luxurious cloud of cigar smoke. "Tired of coming in last?" He flashed a knowing smirk.

"Indeed." She dropped her gaze again, but her lips curled slightly at the edges, sharing his amusement. "We feel that your success across so many domains of society would make you an ideal candidate. We feel that you are exactly the kind of leader that the city needs."

Obviously.

Ty snorted. "What's in it for me?"

She whipped opened her portfolio, pulled a pen from her breast pocket, clicked its top, and readied it on the page. "What would you like?"

———

Ty calmly walks down the grandstand. Even with all the noise and chaos, his heavy footfalls on the metal steps are loud enough to attract attention. A couple of the anarchists recognize the champion boxer and take off running.

"You should follow your friends," he says to the remainder. His voice deep, menacing, confident.

As he reaches the ground, he removes his sunglasses, embroidered duster, and feather boa with a flourish and sets them carefully on the bottom row of seats.

Seven of the anarchists gather round to give Ty their

full attention. He cracks his knuckles and sizes them up. They all look the same. Twenty- to thirty-something men in shabby street clothing, shitty haircuts, cloth masks covering their faces. The kind of bottom-feeding thugs he spent plenty of time with in his youth.

Seven faceless, interchangeable scuzz-balls who are about to get bounced into the dust.

The good news is they've spent their bullets and pyro flasks. The bad news is two have crowbars and two more have picked up clubs from the dead coppers.

They start to fan out, trying to surround him.

Ty snorts.

Showtime.

He reaches back, grabs his duster, and flings it toward the anarchists in front as a distraction. Then he dashes to the right and intercepts one of the thugs trying to flank him. He ducks under their swinging crowbar and answers it with a devastating uppercut. Sends a few of the sucker's teeth skyward. Then he grabs the man's arm and twists him around. Snatches away the crowbar and shoves the thug directly into the path of a wild swing from his crowbar-buddy. There is a shower of blood.

Six left.

One of the club-wielding anarchists goes for a lunge. Ty side-steps and responds with a graceful swing of his newly-acquired iron. It connects squarely with the man's head.

Five.

Another wild attack from crowbar anarchist #2. Ty parries it, steps in close, and delivers a headbutt. The thug drops to the ground. Ty finishes him with a pair of decisive stomps. One to the chest. One to the face.

Four.

The remaining anarchists lose their nerve and turn to run. Ty whips his crowbar at the retreat. It tags one in the lower back, who yelps in pain. But the cowards all manage to scamper away. He considers chasing them down until he hears the sound of sleigh bells in the distance.

Charlies. Good. Let them deal with it.

———

As Ty entered the game of city politics, he understood that getting the votes was a necessary but insufficient condition for success. To truly run the show in New World City, you needed backing from the right people. People who would step up and fight with you when the shit went down.

When Old Man Strauss had been king, his partners had been The Lotus and The Bulldogs—two of the city's Big Six. The assassins and bootleggers, respectively. This worked well enough. For a while. But eventually one of the other Big Six—The Dark Web—got fed up with just getting the scraps. So they took action. They gathered the old mayor's enemies together and organized the hit against him.

In the aftermath, Strauss the Younger took over in a special election. And he went after The Dark Web like a rabid animal. Took them down so thoroughly that it rattled all the other gangs. Even his father's old allies got nervous. Young Eli had upset the balance of business-as-usual. Everyone may have understood why he needed to look tough on crime, but he had crossed the line. Broken some unspoken code of honor that existed among the thieves.

But as much as Ty despised the kid mayor, the extermination of The Dark Web and their telecom whisper-network had made room for him and his Fashionistos at the top. So the Azzuri stepped up to the big leagues.

However, now that Ty was going for two thrones—one in City Hall and one among the Big Six—he could expect a whole new level of conflict. The other powers-that-be wouldn't like it. New World City had space for hundreds of petty king and queenpins. But it did not take kindly to emperors. So to make a mayoral run stick, he would need full-throated support from others in The Six. He decided to start with the one gang that no one else wanted to touch: The Charlies.

Most people saw Valentina de Leo and her troupe of face-painters as raving lunatics, little better than the anarchists who would burn it all down for shits and giggles. But Ty saw something different. He understood that Val considered herself an artist, like himself. His mediums were music and fashion. Hers were destruction and mayhem (or something like that). He went to her with an offer. Showed her the respect that she felt she deserved. And it worked. She agreed to back him up.

———

Ty picks his coat up from the ground and retrieves his boa. He's barely broken a sweat.

He shouts over his shoulder. "Did you get all that?"

His boys emerge from the shadows behind a wrecked car on the edge of the plaza, one holding a small camcorder.

"We got it, boss."

Ty smiles. "Good. Send the video to our friends at Omni. I want to see myself on the news tonight."

Should swing a few votes my way.

"Stop, in the name of the law! Hands above your head!"

An NWPD officer's shout from out of nowhere sends the boys diving back behind the van. They will slink away. They know what to do.

Ty is unconcerned. He casually turns to face this copper who has come late to the party. He grins at the sight of her.

Some dark-haired dollface in her tight, blue uniform waving a pistol that looks two sizes too big for her.

He holds his hands out, but not up. "Be easy, officer," he says. "Everything is under control."

Right on cue, the giant projector screen mounted behind the stage breaks off its supports, crashing to the ground in a shower of sparks and cacophony of twisting plastic and metal. Ty grins. The irony is not lost on him.

As they wait for the noise to subside, he spots the glowing bracers on the cop's wrists. Raises an eyebrow. He's heard of this one.

Constable Li. Some kind of supercop. They say she's incorruptible...

He snorts.

We'll see about that.

"What are you doing here, Mr. Reese?" She barks like she's the one in charge. But she lowers and holsters her pistol. "It is not safe. There are anarchists and Charlies everywhere."

"Tell me about it." Ty says. "But I took care of it. See?" He gestures toward the limp bodies on the ground.

"I see them. I see several dead officers as well. What happened?"

He sucks his teeth and shakes his head in feigned disappointment. "I didn't get here in time."

Shuwen narrows her eyes, studying him. "I'm going to have to bring you in for questioning."

Ty gives her a wide smile. "Of course, Constable. I'm happy to share my story."

CHAPTER 3
ZIJIAN

...PLOTS THE NEXT MOVE

«Our top story this morning: The attempted assassination of New World City Mayor, Eli Strauss Jr. An unknown gunman shot and wounded the mayor as he gave a speech yesterday evening. Thankfully, the mayor suffered only minor injuries, and is currently in stable condition. However, the Downtown Plaza, where the mayor was holding a campaign rally, devolved into panic and violence that left several people dead, including NWPD officers. Revolutionary terrorists are suspected of being behind this attack, and therefore military reinforcements from The Ragnarok have been sent into The Core, instituting a lockdown while the assassin remains at large.»

Zijian Sun mutes the TV. Spins her chair around to face the room. Sets the remote carefully on her desk.

This is her office on the 12th floor of the 12th Avenue Lotus Spa & Hotel. The office of The Chair—the head honcho for all Lotus Corporation business. An elegant room. Large windows. Crown moldings. Sparsely decorated with a mixture of green-tinted glass, polished steel, and dark leather furnishings of the modern-minimalist style.

It is an environment purposefully designed to complement Zijian herself: Tall, olive skin, long dark hair, dark eyes. A green silk robe worn over a form-fitting, black body suit.

She is facing her lieutenants for the regular morning briefing. The Lotus Corporation is the public-facing front for The Assassins Guild. And as such, she anticipates questions about this attempt on the mayor's life. She orchestrated the hit, of course. But the peculiar details of this contract are not matters she wishes to share—even with her most trusted deputies. Thus, her goal for this meeting is to keep it short. Reassure them that everything is under her control. Reveal as little as possible.

The less they know, the better. For them and for me.

She begins: "As you would expect, business is likely to be... difficult for the next stretch or two. But we are prepared for this."

Her six lieutenants are all seated at stiff attention on the couches, dressed in their business tunics, each a different color. "The Lotus Rainbow," some call them. The color of their dress reflects their position and responsibilities in the organization.

"Our wealthiest clients will not be subject to the lockdown, so all our doors will effectively remain open, and our existing contracts must be fulfilled. If any military or city police prove to be obstacles, let me know immediately. I will handle them."

The Rainbow nods in unison.

"I am expecting a Stasi inquiry, possibly also NWPD. Keep your profiles low. I don't want any unnecessary attention. But if you are detained or questioned, you can answer honestly. This assassin was not a member of our guild. Therefore, The Lotus has nothing to hide."

That last sentence is a lie, of course. The Lotus always has something to hide.

Scarlet lieutenant raises a hand. (Scarlet is the Head of Lotus Decor, with nearly two hundred executions under his belt.)

Zijian acknowledges him. "Yes?"

"Forgive me, Madame Sun, but are you saying that the sniper was not one of ours? I would have thought—"

She interrupts. "Correct. The sniper was not a member of the guild. That is all you need to know."

Amber (Head of Massage Therapy, some sixty executions to her name) raises a hand. "Do we know where the sniper is now? Are they a threat to us?"

"We do not and they are not."

Jade (Head of Hospitality, with an impressive five hundred twenty executions): "Why don't we send a tracker to find the sniper. If it was not one of ours, then this seems a violation of our jurisdiction and we ought to make an example of them."

Zijian leans forward. She places her elbows on the desk and steeples her fingers. "Thank you, Jade. That is a reasonable suggestion. But I have it under control." Her voice is cool. Her expression is calm. Her eyes are steel. "Do you understand?"

Her gaze is locked onto Jade's, yet the question is directed at the whole room. And the whole room answers with a resounding "Yes, Madame Sun!"

"Good." She flicks her wrist, dismissing them. "Now go."

The lieutenants rise and file out without another word.

Zijian leans back in her chair.

The game begins. Plenty to watch and manage in the

coming days. But just like after Strauss Sr.'s assassination—there will be opportunity. And I will be poised to seize it.

———

"Grown from the guts" is a common expression in New World City, but usually hyperbolic and uttered by yuppie upstarts of the lower- or middle-class who have managed to marginally raise their station in life. In Zijian Sun's case, it was the literal truth. She had grown up in "The Guts," which is to say The Undercity. Which is to say underground. Deep underground. Lower even than the city's shit-filled sewers. Far away from the light of day.

She was not a mutant, as is common down below. No, she was pure-blooded human. From her prestigious position as executive head of The Lotus Corporation to her fastidious appearance and well-mannered speech—you would never suspect her origins. But here she was. The living exception that proved the rule. Someone from The Guts had a sub-zero chance of making it all the way to the top of one of New World City's oldest criminal institutions. So many improbable events would have to come out just right. So many heads would have to roll—and roll in just the right way, at just the right time. It was impossible.

But here she was. An Undercity foundling, raised by an old mutant sorceress in the deep-down dark. Returned to the City of Light. Now pulling the strings that kept all the people dancing, and managing the contract killings that kept the blood flowing in the streets.

An inspirational rags-to-riches, some might say. But it's a backstory that Zijian Sun tries very hard to keep hidden.

———

The sound is back on the TV. Zijian sits with her feet up, leaning back in her chair. She is facing the screen, but she's not watching. And she's only half-listening as the Omni-Corp newscaster drones on about how the mayoral election will continue on schedule despite the attack.

She holds a delicate, ornately carved dagger in her right hand, the point balanced against her left index finger. She twists the blade idly, rocking slowly in her chair. Blood wells up, just a small amount. She barely notices. Her mind is busy elsewhere, plotting the game ahead. Internal clockworks spinning.

Anyone with a shred of intelligence should see through this assassination attempt. The Stasi snoops will not be fooled. But they shouldn't be a problem. I have the paperwork to shut them up. The police should not be a problem either. Much too stupid and disorganized to put the pieces together.

The other kingpins among the Big Six... That is a different story. Some of them are plenty clever enough to figure it out. And once they do, they will not like the deception. The gray shades in this arrangement will give them an opening. A way to potentially challenge Lotus' claim to The Assassins Guild license.

Zijian presses the dagger point harder into her finger. Her blood flows more freely. A slow trickle down her forearm. Still of no concern.

Fucking lawyers. Just let them try!

A sham assassination was an unusual protocol for the guild. But it was not without precedent. It had been a fashionable request among the wealthiest merchant families of the 16th century. Stage their own attempted murders as pretense to take revenge against their rivals.

The ritual to properly seal such a writ was demanding. It required the target's own blood. But the Mayor had happily obliged. Willingly cut himself open and signed his name to the contract. Stipulating a convincing attack on his life but with as little lasting damage as possible. Not an easy needle to thread.

Very odd, indeed. But Mayor Eli is an absolute buffoon. Since his takedown of The Spiders he seems entirely preoccupied with pumping himself full of party drugs.

She twists the dagger point further into her fingertip.

That mayor's chief of staff, however... Mr. Moorelake. He is no buffoon. The way he leered and loomed over the mayor at the contract signing... It was... odd. He seems too sharp to be merely a servant of that idiot. He is playing some other game of his own. Likely to be a threat.

She whirls her chair around, pulls the dagger away from her finger, and slams it down on her desk.

Yes. That is one play worth making sooner rather than later. Moorelake must be neutralized.

She takes a kerchief from her desk drawer and attends to the blood on her left finger and hand.

Zijian knew well how to keep secrets. But she also knew that nothing could stay a secret forever. The truth was always out there, leaving its trace. It was only a matter of time before someone or something picked up on it. Therefore, to capitalize on a secret, one had to act quickly. Take advantage of that window of opportunity—the temporary asymmetry between one's knowing and one's adversaries not knowing.

These were lessons she learned from her mother, Hadra. A mutant sorceress of mixed tortoise and orcish bloodlines, Hadra was over a thousand turns old. Had lived her entire life under the ground, in The Undercity. She had seen much, but she had never seen the light of day. Never once been to the surface.

Yet Hadra always claimed she knew all she needed to about the world above. And everything (or almost everything) she knew, she tried to impart to young Zijian.

She knew that one day, Zijian would return to the world above. And Hadra had done everything she could to prepare her little foundling to not only survive, but to thrive. Not only to find her way in that harsh, bright-lit surface world, but to leave a lasting mark upon it.

Indeed, Hadra foresaw that Zijian was destined to do great things. And in the absence of magical aptitude (which, sadly, Zijian lacked) doing great things would require a great intellect—one that understood the power of information, how to acquire and wield it to maximum advantage. How to conceal a truth until the exact right moment, and then position oneself to profit from the revelation.

So this was the focus of Zijian's young life: Learning the many games of secrets and lies. And as Hadra predicted, this education served her daughter very well.

————

There is a knock at Zijian's office door.

"Enter."

One of her assistants. "Pardon me, Madame Sun. Your morning appointment is here."

Zijian rises and walks slowly out of her office, past the assistant, down the hall, toward the elevator. Her hands are tightly folded, held close, below her chest, the bloodied kerchief between them.

As she walks, she transforms her whole attitude and

comportment. Relaxing her face. Softening her shoulders. A moment ago she was cold fire, now she is becoming warm water. Before, a deadly blade. Now, a welcoming hand.

She enters the fine glass elevator and pushes the button for the ground floor. As the elevator begins to descend, her internal clockworks continue.

Yes. Moorelake must be neutralized. Perhaps two birds can be killed at once? That pompous Azzuri kingpin is keen. Keen enough to stick his neck out and run for office. Keen enough to film himself flexing in front of the world. Perhaps he is also foolish enough that he could be baited into cutting Moorelake's throat for me.

She passes the 10th floor.

But is that wise? Would that concentrate too much power in Azzuri hands? Given the recent alliance between them and the psycho-clown Charlies, would that create too much instability? Not much benefit to having the streets overrun by puffed-up peacocks and drugged-up lunatics.

8th floor.

No. Better to find another way. Better to have the mayor's office cut its own throat. Find the second bird on the inside of City Hall. Lure it into tossing the eggs out of its own nest.

6th floor.

Sadly, the lines into City Hall are not as strong as they once were. Mayor Strauss Sr. and Master Minza had been close. But Young Strauss cut most of those ties. And the rest I severed along with Minza's head...

4th floor.

But new ties can be formed.

3rd.

And probably better to tie them outside the elected offices, since the vote could go either way. But, yes, deeper ties to the city administration. That is the right move.

2nd.

A good place to start. Get an agent on the inside, learn everything we can about Moorelake, and then strike.

There is a harmonious chime as the elevator reaches the ground floor, bringing an end to Zijian's strategic meditation.

She steps out into the reception area of the 12th Avenue Lotus Hotel & Spa. It is a bright room. Same modern-minimalist style as her office. Large glass walls and windows. Off-white trim. Large ferns symmetrically placed among granite fountains. A refreshing smell of water and eucalyptus.

She spreads her arms like a mother swan and offers a radiant smile to welcome her client, presenting the essence of calm, beauty, and comfort.

"Miss Khan!" She beams. "How wonderful it is to see you."

———

It was not unusual for the Lotus higher-ups to personally serve some of the most elite clients of the spa. It was a convenient way to share information. Send messages. Communicate desires and confirm their satisfaction.

This 12th Avenue Lotus Spa had been a favorite of Mayor Strauss Sr. The previous Lotus Chair, Master Oratio Minza, had personally catered to him, and it paid off big time. The mayor's office took full advantage of Lotus (and The Assassins Guild) services. In return, The Lotus got the favorable attention (or favorable inattention) they needed from city officials.

But Zijian had always thought Minza's and Old Strauss' relationship to be too close. It blinded them to the other's faults and vulnerabilities. It made them soft.

The other Lotus lieutenants had disagreed with her.

She showed them all.

Once Strauss was gone, Minza realized too late how much of his power died with the old mayor. He had neglected too many of his other relationships. Ignored too many of his other duties.

He was vulnerable. So she murdered him and took his place.

This was how the torch got passed in The Lotus. There was no tolerance for vulnerability. If you are weak, then you die.

Master Minza had done exactly the same when it was his time. Now his time was over. Now it was Zijian Sun's time.

Although she did not have any personal clients from the mayor's office (something she should soon rectify), her appointment this morning was with someone of arguably even greater consequence: Ysobel Khan, the daughter of Sinbad Khan, the founder and CEO of OmniCorp, the world's monopolistic media conglomerate.

Sinbad was on his death bed. The final stages of cancer. Ysobel's brother, Gotari, was a gadabout scumjunk. When the father died, Ysobel would inherit everything.

Ysobel would soon be one of the most powerful people in the world. And Zijian had this girl wrapped around her finger.

This gave Zijian a direct line of influence to everything OmniCorp controlled. News. Film. Entertainment. Just about anything coming out of a screen or radio in New World City was OmniCorp, falling under the authority of the CEO.

To be in the Chair of Lotus Corporation and in the bed of the CEO at OmniCorp... Dealing out life and death with the power to shape the flow of information. To have so much control... the possibilities were endless.

The State itself would tremble before her.

Zijian liked that idea very much.

CHAPTER 4
SHUWEN

...DIGS IN

"Chief, you can't be serious!"

Shuwen is furious. Jumping up from the chair, she slams her hands on the chief's desk. Blue flickers from her bracers.

"I am serious, Constable," Chief Wolff growls. "Calm yourself and sit back down." It's a low growl. A warning for a friend. He knows that Shuwen is not a raging hothead and her anger is not without justification. "This desk is old and I don't want you to shatter it." He points his snout at the artefacts on her wrists. "With *those*."

"Right," she half-whispers. Momentarily chastened, Shuwen sits down, fingering her bracers self-consciously. But it's only half a tick before she starts up again: "But you're telling me we just let him go? Without any kind of serious interrogation?" Her outrage returning to the boiling point. "He went to the rally of his opponent. He didn't send an operative like a normal candidate would. He went himself. Then he killed at least 3 people. He filmed himself doing it!"

She pauses. She doesn't say, "Isn't it obvious?" because it seems so obvious. Wolff grunts.

"He knows something, Chief," she continues. "He saw something. And we got nothing from him." She grits her teeth. She hates this feeling. The injustice. "He's involved with that sniper. Somehow... I'm sure of it."

"That may very well be," Wolff says. "But I have my orders. I was instructed to release Mr. Reese. The people he killed were rioters. Anarchists. The same ones who almost certainly killed our officers. And they attacked him besides. You saw the film."

Shuwen nods. Reluctantly.

"Stasi are stepping in to handle the investigation. This precinct is not to pursue the matter further. And frankly, I'd prefer it that way. If this turns into another tangled web of shit like the last time, then I don't want my precinct involved."

———

Eight turns and counting is how long Shuwen and Wolff have worked together. They were alike in many ways. Despite living in a world that seemed to have gone mad and given up its principles, they both still cared deeply about doing the right thing—about their duties to the rule of law.

They also cared about family history and tradition. Each could trace their lineage back centuries. She was descended from the 11th century Li-Fang clan, one of the founders of The Retainers Guild that trained and supplied security for rulers in the medieval period. He was one of the "Old Mutants," who came from the 14th century, the so-called "Age of Enchantment," when it was said (by some historical scholars in the Ivory Citadel) that humans and animals could mate, producing a new race that was a blend of the two.

Such remixing of bloodlines is considered disgusting to many modern sensibilities. Even its very possibility is denied by The State, whose official line on mutants is that they are all products of the toxic chemicals and unspeakable practices in The Undercity.

But whatever the government said, it didn't change who Matsuda Wolff was. He knew that his family clan had been around for over a five hundred turns of the wheel. They were the wolf-people—just like you and me, except they had fur and fangs and a lot of other wolf-like features. In earlier, more tolerant times, his family had been aristocrats. They placed high value on duty and honor. Just like Shuwen's family did. And just like Shuwen's family, there weren't many Wolffs left. Of course, the reasons for the dwindling numbers in their respective family lines were quite different—but those are sad tales for another time.

The important point for Shuwen and Wolff is that they recognized each other as the last of a kind. A pair of dying breeds, you might say. And they bonded over it.

———

"So I'm just supposed to drop it. Walk away?" Shuwen's jaw is so tight she can barely get the words out.

"Yes," Wolff replies.

"You know I can't do that."

"Yes, I do."

A long pause. The constable and chief stare at each other. Like two arm wrestlers who have locked hands, feeling the other's strength. The inertia. Waiting for someone to make the next move.

"Then are you going to suspend me?"

"No, I am not."

Yes! Thank you, Chief!

This is what Shuwen wanted to hear. She stands up. "Is there anything else I should know?"

"Yes, there is."

She adopts a posture of military attention. Chin lifted. Awaiting further instruction.

"If you encounter The Stasi on this, do not provoke them. They are looking for any excuse to clean house again. Do not let them catch you sniffing around. And if they do catch you sniffing around, you are to cooperate with them. I know you prefer to work alone, but if it comes to that, suck it up and accept their help. Do you understand?"

Shuwen nods. But she's silently promising herself the opposite: She doesn't do partnerships. And certainly not with a Stasi spook.

"Your record is strong enough that they might give you some leeway. Hell, they might even welcome your help. But that's assuming you encounter an agent who is straight-edged. Not many of those left, as you know."

She nods again.

Wolff lets out a long sigh. "I smell trouble with this case, Li. There is something strange here, I agree with you. I don't know if its Ty Reese and The Azzuri. Or if this is some sick joke of The Lotus. But someone is playing a game, and I don't like it. I don't think it's a game the PD should get caught up in. And I don't think it's a game you can win."

Shuwen salutes, placing her right fist against her left palm. "I understand, Chief," she says. "Thank you. I will be cautious."

Wolff returns the salute. "Keep those on you." He points his snout at the old artefacts on her wrists.

She smiles. "I always do."

Possession of artefacts, like Shuwen's silver bracers, was not entirely legal. In fact, State law was perfectly clear on the matter: A private citizen in possession of an artefact would be jailed (for at least a tenner) and the artefact would be confiscated. These relics of older times were considered too powerful and dangerous for people to own.

What is more, the artefacts were evidence of the power in old magic that, according to State propaganda, should no longer be possible. The new power in New World City was science. It was engineering. It was rational. Magic had been powerful once, but it had been snuffed out two hundred turns ago, along with religion, along with the old rival empires. Or so the official story goes.

But, of course, there were legal loopholes. Older laws still on the books, instituted just after The Great War, established an absolute right to personal and family property. Across a series of court cases, this right had been explicitly extended to cover artefacts—provided that the owner could show possession within the family that predated the prohibition.

In the case of Shuwen's bracers—they had been handed down to her from her father. And to her father from his father. And so on and so on. According to Li Family lore, the bracers were originally forged in the 6th century of the prior epoch—"The Silver Age" it was called—by the fabled magician, Rama Shasta. They were made as a gift for the kings of Clan Nehru, who passed them down over the generations, and eventually passed them on to Shuwen's ancestors as a reward for their loyalty and service.

While she recognized the legal ambiguity, there was no question in Shuwen's mind that the bracers were rightfully in her possession. Moreover, she felt that she not only had the right to use them, but she had a duty to use them. Provided she used them in service of the public good. The dissertation that she wrote at the conclusion of her police academy studies argued exactly this point.

Unfortunately, Shuwen's colleagues at the NWPD did not all see eye-to-eye with her on this matter. Wolff trusted her judgment, and in general, he looked the other way. But there were plenty others on the force who saw her bracers as unfair if not outright illegal. And they resented her for it. Particularly as her special commendation medals piled up.

———

Later that night, at the tail end of her shift, Shuwen sits alone in her patrol car, parked outside the 2125 High Street building. She always works alone these days. No more partners after Tomas died. Wolff isn't supposed to allow that, but he does. Another bit of special treatment for Supercop Shuwen Li.

The High Street building is an Azzuri hot spot within Precinct 13. Not a headquarters, exactly, but a place where The Fashionistos are known to gather. Ty Reese himself is often a sighting. There have been rumors of illegal gambling going on inside.

She doesn't yet have any pretense for entering, but such pretense may be forthcoming. So she sits and waits.

She does not have to wait long.

Three garish luxury cars pull up and each unloads three Azzuri goons. Two of them are carrying the bodies of women over their shoulder, evidently passed out. All of them, the women included, are dressed to the nines. Shiny fabrics with dramatic cuts. Plenty of skin showing, all of it decorated with elaborate, colorful tattoos.

Looks like trouble. Could be time to move.

The Azzuri group files into the building. Not through the main lobby entrance, but through a side door that leads to a small vestibule containing a single elevator and doorman.

Shuwen exits her car. Strolls casually across the street. The goons did not seem to notice her, nor would it matter much if they did.

Ever since Mr. Reese has been up in the polls, the Azzuri think they're above the law. But if they're up to something, they're about to get a rude awakening.

She reaches the side door. Pulls at the handle. Locked.

She can see through the glass. The last of the Azzuri are boarding the elevator. One of them sees her. He gives her the fingers as the elevator doors close.

Someone's feeling untouchable. But a gangster crew carrying two incapacitated women is reason enough to demand entry.

She taps her com. "Suspicious Azzuri activity at 2125 High Street. Investigating."

Acknowledged.

She knocks on the door.

The doorman sees her. He does not look confident. He looks worried. But he shakes his head and waves her away.

"Open the door. Now." Shuwen holds up her badge as she speaks.

The doorman shakes his head again and says, "Authorized visitors only."

Shuwen gives the door a soft punch with the side of her fist. "I am an NWPD officer with authority in this precinct. That is all the authorization I need. Now open the door."

She adjusts her bracers. Feels them pulse. Feels the mystic rush.

The doorman backs away, continuing to shake his head. He's moving toward a call box on the wall.

She has seen enough. She places her palms together and slams them into the door latch. The lock shatters and she pushes the door open.

The doorman jumps back. Alarmed. He lunges for the call box, but it's too late. Shuwen grabs him by the collar of his jacket, yanks him away from the phone, and holds him up against the wall with one hand.

"You have disobeyed an officer of the law, citizen. I am going to have to report you."

The doorman is trembling. Face now white with fear. "N-n-no, please. I-I-I have a f-f-family. If I am g-g-gone, they will have nothing. Please!"

Shuwen's is impassive. Her voice cold and clinical. "You should have thought of your family when I told you to open the door." She taps her com. "I have a citizen in violation of regulation 0905-1. Ready for pick-up."

ACKNOWLEDGED. SENDING COLLECTION. ETA 3.

"Hear that? You have three rounds to decide how this will end for you." Shuwen fixes the doorman with a cold stare. "If you tell me what is going on here with those Azzuri goons, then I will tell the pickup that you cooperated, and the judges may go easy on you."

The doorman closes his eyes. Shaking. Terrified. If he rats, the gangsters will likely kill him. Maybe kill his family too. If he stays quiet, the cops will throw him in the pen. And without his income, his family won't make rent. Lose their home. Who knows what else.

An all-too-common dilemma for the smallfolk in New World City. He just wanted to do his job and go home to his family. Now he is doomed. Forced to make a miserable choice.

"P-p-please," he whispers. "I am nobody. Just a doorman. Just..."

Shuwen shakes her head. "Also reporting a 4275-8. Requesting small support," she says into her com.

Acknowledged. Sending Support. ETA 5.

————

Three rounds later, Shuwen is riding the elevator up to the 9th floor. The doorman wouldn't talk, but she borrowed his keys. A quick dusting of the elevator buttons told her where to go.

She gives her bracers a good turn about her wrists. They glow a deep blue. She's not sure what is ahead. Better to be prepared for a full-contact encounter.

She closes her eyes. Takes a deep breath.

At least nine hostiles. But it could be more...

The elevator dings for the 9th floor. The doors open on a lounge. Finely furnished. No people in sight.

Shuwen steps out and listens. She can hear the sounds of a party behind closed doors. Coming from the far side of the room.

She dashes across. Kneels and places her ear to the door.

It's definitely a party. Sounds like gambling.

Gambling outside the casinos is illegal. Sufficient cause to intervene and arrest this whole group. Shuwen stands, adjusts her bracers once more. Takes another deep breath.

She is about to unleash...

The strength, the speed, the vision, the vehemence of my ancestors.

She kicks open the doors and blurs into the room.

For the unsuspecting Azzuri boys in their fancy clothes, time seems to slow down. Only the lady cop in her dark blue uniform is able to move at normal speed.

Shuwen pulls one goon up from his chair, back-kicks

him into the wall, and then binds his hands before the others can react.

When they finally do react, it's too slow. They don't have their weapons on them. Their knives and guns are stashed in their jackets or holsters, all hung up by the doors.

Except for that one guy. The one who gave Shuwen the fingers back at the elevator. He kept his gun. He has time to draw it. But the quarters are so close. And Shuwen is moving so fast. She's subduing the goons one-by-one, using their bodies as a shield as she does it.

Mr. Two Fingers starts taking shots anyway. He only succeeds in putting a few bullets in his buddies. They curse at him as Shuwen takes them down. She's locking their joints. Sweeping their legs. Zip-tying their hands. Or feet. Or both.

She comes to the gunman last. Disarms him with a spinning hook kick. Then steps in, locks his arm, breaks it, and throws him to the ground. Ties him up like all the rest. Clinical.

She taps her com.

"Update: 1123-1 on 9th floor of 2125 High Street. Nine Azzuri gangsters. Subdued. Ready for pick-up."

ACKNOWLEDGED. SUPPORT AND COLLECTION INCOMING.

Shuwen reviews the situation. Nine groaning goons on the ground. She lifts her cap and wipes the sweat from her brow. Then proceeds to the adjoining room.

There she finds the two women laid out on couches. They appear to be sleeping peacefully. She checks their vitals.

Probably on drugs.

She taps her com. "Requesting medical."

ACKNOWLEDGED. SENDING MEDICAL. ETA 25.

Now let's see if any of these boys have something helpful to say about Mr. Reese and the assassination attempt.

CHAPTER 5
ELI

...RAGES IN RECOVERY

"Useless motherfuckers!"

Mayor Eli Strauss Jr. is at home. Safe. In his bed. Shouting at the TV screen.

"How many of those puss-in-ass, boot-licking fuckers do I have on the payroll!? How many officers were stationed all around the plaza!? And this shit still happens!?"

The doctor's recommendation was to take a fullstretch to calm down and recover. Eli doesn't feel he needs to recover.

Except for the awesome scar now running across his left cheek, he's physically unharmed. The sniper's bullet grazed him right along his stubble line. A perfectly-placed shot, requiring masterful skill to catch his face at that precise angle. If the assassin had wanted to kill him, he'd surely be dead.

But Eli doesn't care or think about any of that.

No, for Eli, the insult and injury from the sniper is just the latest reason to let loose with his temper.

Not that he needs much of a reason. He is the mayor of New World City, after all. He is Eli *Fucking* Strauss, goddammit! He can do whatever he wants. And what he wants to do right now is sit in bed in his purple silk pajamas, pound energy drinks, and rage at the television.

He's watching the OmniCorp coverage of the apparent attempt on his life. Not at all happy about the slant (they're making him look weak). Not at all happy about the footage (too much of Ty Reese showboating—that pathetic, upstart, poser). Not at all happy about the effect this is having on the poll numbers.

Most of all, he's not happy about the military lockdown of The Core. The military police and The Ragnarok-Industrial-Complex make it abundantly clear how they think they answer to no one.

"Those fuckers want to flex and tell me I can't control my fucking city! This is MY. FUCKING. CITY!"

It isn't a good look.

The scar is really bad-ass though.

But here's the real problem: The lockdown will make it somewhat less convenient to go party and fuck-shit-up—which is just about the only thing Eli really cares about.

He slurps the last of his energy drink, crushes the can in his fist, and throws it on the pile by the window. The lemon-lime stench of evaporating soda mixed with the sharp tang of Eli's unwashed body and bed sheets creates a brutal assault on the senses. Mercifully, no one else is there to smell it. And Eli doesn't care or think about any of that.

He hits the call button on his bedside table. His butler enters through the great oak doors on the far side of the room.

"Sir?"

"Dmitry—get my clothes and cocktails ready. Fuck this lockdown. And fuck this assassination garbage. I am not going to be intimidated by terrorists. I'm going out tonight. Tell Fosse's bitch that I will be there as planned."

"Certainly, sir." Dmitry bows and withdraws. Dmitry is a pro, and a synth besides, so he is able to perceive the foul smell of the room without so much as wrinkling his nose.

Eli jumps up from the bed and starts air-boxing.

"Fuck. This. Shit." Punching with each word.

I'm not losing a deal because of some cowardly terrorist who can't even shoot straight.

The deal tonight is a drug deal. He's picking up from Jamiroquan Foster (a.k.a. Fosse), Top Dog of The Bootlegger Bulldogs.

"I'll fuck. You. Up." He mixes in some front kicks to his little routine.

He's got decent kick-boxing form. The product of expensive lessons in his youth. He's not kept up with the training, but more than a few goons have underestimated him and paid the price.

"Gonna fuck. Some. Shit. Up. To-night!" He ends with a jumping, spinning back-kick to his television, knocking it clean off its wall mount. The screen shatters as it lands on the floor.

He hits the call button. Dmitry is back instantly.

"Sir?"

"Get someone in here to clean this up," Eli calls over his shoulder, already half-undressed, strutting toward his en suite for a shower.

"Certainly, sir."

———

Most folks in New World City think it must have been easy to be the scion of the Strauss Family. Born into all that wealth and power. Gifted the opportunity and the means to do whatever you want. To fulfill your every desire.

But it's not quite as simple as that.

We must remember that Eli Strauss Sr. was a complete bastard. He was a Great Man of the Age, sure. A political powerhouse. But you don't become something like that unless you are a complete bastard. That's just a law of nature.

Old Mayor Strauss was a narcissist. Vindictive. Cruel. Temperamental. But also charismatic. Loyal (to his friends at least). He had some semblance of fairness. He cared about paying his debts. He cared a lot about receiving his dues.

In his prime, he was a strong leader. Full of confidence and passion. A good speaker. He was a man that other men wanted to follow. (You can guess how he treated women.)

All these qualities made him a great New World City politician—and a lousy father.

Young Eli was born into wealth and power, sure. He was gifted the opportunity and the means to do whatever he wanted. To fulfill his every desire. And so that's what he did.

He had all the toys a boy could want. He would smash them to bits and they would be replaced by new ones. Same goes for his friends. Same for his girlfriends. An endless cycle of use, then destroy, then renew. Without any real boundaries or regulation that might have helped the child or adolescent Eli understand the importance of self-control.

And so that is who Eli Strauss Jr. was. A thirty-something man-child. The master of New World City who was not a master of himself.

———

All rinsed up and smelling much better, Eli stares at himself in the mirror above his bathroom sink. Carefully shaving his face. His new scar makes this familiar exercise somewhat more delicate than it was before.

He rinses. Splashes some aftershave. The burn is extra intense. But he likes that.

He leans in for a closer look at himself in the mirror. Runs his fingers over the scar.

Yeah. It's bad-ass. I'm keeping it.

Lost in tactile contemplation of his own mug, Eli does not notice that the reflection of the bathroom behind him is morphing. The expensive tiled walls and post-industrial fixtures are disassembling themselves, running a time-lapse video of their installation in reverse, blinking out into nothing. After a few beats, all that remains of the room is the pedestal sink, the mirror (which has not moved but is now floating in empty space), and himself. Transported to some pocket dimension in the black void.

Then a tall man in a dark suit, sharp features, chestnut skin, and slick back hair materializes behind him in the mirror.

Eli grimaces at the sight. "What do you want?" He doesn't bother turning around. He knows that if he did, no one would be there. It's all an illusion. All in the mirror. A disorienting experience the first time, but he is used to it by now.

"I've come to see how you are doing, my son," the man says. "I imagine this has been quite the ordeal."

"You think so?" Eli snaps. "Where the fuck were you? Where was my protection? How could you let this happen?"

The man tsk-tsks and shakes his head. A wide, condescending smile spread across his chiseled face.

Eli's rage meter rises. "You think this is funny, do you? What the fuck are you smiling about? I got shot in the fucking FACE! I was THIS close to getting my head blown off!"

"Yet here you are," the man says, opening his hands as though presenting a gift. "Safe and sound. And don't you like your new face? It is so very masculine."

Rage meter comes down slightly. "I mean, yeah… it is kind of awesome." Eli shifts his focus in the mirror from the man's face back to his own.

"Now you look like one of The Great Ones," the man says with growing excitement. "Like Lucius Malgannon. Or Jago of Jormund!"

These names mean nothing to Eli, but the man says them with such reverence that it stokes Eli's pride and confidence all the same. Rage meter continues to fall.

"You should never doubt me, my son," the man says in a placating tone. "I have sworn that I would protect you and I always will. This little scratch you've suffered is a small sacrifice—nay, an enhancement! Necessary for the greater game that I am playing. A brilliant strategy that will bring you and your noble house to even greater heights. Greater glory." The man's face lights up and he raises a clenched fist. "Greater dominance for the House of Strauss!"

Eli's attention is drawn back to the man's face in the mirror. He feels the man's warm, reassuring hands gently rest on his shoulders. His posture straightens under the touch. He feels relaxed.

"So you planned this?" Eli asks, brushing his fingers across the scar.

"Yes. All a part of the plan," the man whispers.

Eli nods. He has a vague memory of signing and agreeing to something. But then it is gone. And his rage dissolves. He feels at peace.

"You are going out tonight?"

Eli nods.

"That is excellent! You should go out. Indulge. You will feel more like yourself again."

Eli's eyelids feel heavy. He lets them fall closed.

"Do not worry. There is much still to do, but I will take care of everything."

The man snaps his fingers.

Eli's eyes snap open. He is alone again in his bathroom. Everything is re-assembled, just as it was. Just as it has been all along. The illusion is gone. Forgotten.

He feels empty. Or maybe it's hungry?

Time to get dressed and get some food. That should help.

He hears a faint whisper at the back of his mind.

Go out. Have fun. There is much still to do.

―――――

A few chimes later, Eli stands in the foyer of his mansion. He regards himself in the full-length mirror opposite the coat closet near his front door. He is about to leave. He has a deal to make. He only vaguely remembers what the deal is about. Probably drugs.

His butler, Dmitry, stands by, holding a tray with a filled cocktail glass and four rings.

Eli flexes in the mirror. He practices his laugh. His smoldering look. His wide, toothy grin. He runs his hand through his silver hair. He is pleased with what he sees.

He summons Dmitry closer, swipes the glass from the tray, and downs it. Returns the glass and starts putting on the rings one by one.

On the left ring finger goes the Strauss Family signet. Left index is a thick band with a large, pear-shaped, red garnet setting. Right index is a crown ring inlaid with diamonds. Right pinky, the largest of all, features an octagonal emblem of The Rising Dragon—a symbol of historical power whose significance is entirely lost on Eli. All of them artefacts.

It's a lot of hardware, but it feels right. He now feels properly equipped for the evening. One more look in the mirror. One more flex and face. Eli is pleased with what he sees. He briefly fidgets with each ring. Turns and walks out. His car is waiting.

Gonna fuck some shit up tonight.

CHAPTER 6
ZIJIAN
...SERVICES HER TOP CLIENT

«"Fine. I'll say what we're all thinking. There is only one reasonable explanation for the facts of this assassination attempt. It had to be a military-backed hit. No anarchist or common street gang has access to a weapon that can fire these kinds of rounds. And they certainly don't have the skill to merely graze a target at that distance. It must have been organized by The Ragnarok High Command, attempting some kind of coup. It is clear that Admiral Allstar and her Nationalist Party are losing in the polls, so this would give them motive to try and seize City Hall by another means."

"That is a bold, and frankly, irresponsible accusation, James. Cynthia, what do you say to that?"

"Of course, I'm going to disagree, Bob. I think the evidence shows that the street gangs are getting much better organized and much better equipped recently. I don't think it's farfetched at all to believe that one of them has recruited a skilled sniper. And ever since The Strauss Assassination in '95, all the gangs have become more brazen. The Big Six especially... "»

Zijian mutes the TV. "Let's turn that off. Surely, you cannot find that relaxing," she says.

Her young client and lover, Ysobel Kahn, is laid out on her back on a massage table, wearing only a towel. She is mid cucumber-mud mask.

"I do sort of find it relaxing, actually," Ysobel chirps, her voice bright with the enthusiasm and innocence of seventeen-about-to-be-eighteen. "It's a mystery and I'm into it. I want to solve the puzzle."

Zijian smiles. She knows that most of Ysobel's innocence is an act. This young woman is a clever operator who will very soon inherit full control of the airwaves. Yet, she also knows that another part of Ysobel is exactly what she seems: Young. Curious. Fiercely intelligent. Obsessive about a good mystery and the challenge of solving it.

The tension between these is no small part of why Zijian is attracted to the girl. If Ysobel was a disaffected cynic or bubble-headed heiress, then she would be of far less interest and things would have never gotten this far between them.

"Which puzzle intrigues you the most?" Zijian switches off the TV, switches on the radio. Soothing, ambient, chamber music.

"In this case, it's the puzzles within puzzles that I like." Ysobel shares her opinion with that unfiltered confidence of seventeen-about-to-be-eighteen. "Or the distinct but overlapping puzzles? Either way, I like the complexity of it."

Zijian can't help herself and chuckles.

Complex on the surface, perhaps. But really quite simple underneath. A contract, a broker, and a shooter. Still... my girl has no way of knowing that.

Ysobel continues: "There's the election. The Guild politics. The gang wars. The tension between State Security and the NWPD. They are all tied up in this. It's fascinating!"

Zijian makes an, "I'm listening" sound as she walks over to the massage table.

Ysobel shimmies her towel up to her waist, fully uncovering her legs. Continues with her analysis. "There's obviously a million angles at play. But it seems like the assassin's identity is the centerpiece of it all."

Zijian places her hands firmly on the girl's right thigh.

"A sniper who doesn't kill the mayor. He tattoos him! I mean, who can do that? It's pretty awesome."

Zijian begins kneading, working deep into the muscles. Finding the tension, releasing it.

Ysobel pauses her monologue and moans. "Ohhh—that feels fucking amazing."

———

Zijian and Ysobel first met about four turns ago. The former was The Lotus' Sapphire lieutenant at that time. The latter was just a girl of thirteen-about-to-be-fourteen. It was at a fancy dinner soiree, full of media muckety-mucks, hosted by Ysobel's father at one of his many estates out in the burbs.

Precocious Ysobel was there because she always wanted to know what was going on. She wanted to know the people in her powerful father's life. Her father, Sinbad Khan, loved that. So he would often invite her to such "adult gatherings" despite her age.

Zijian was there strictly for business. Father Khan's business, in fact. One of the invited guests was to die that evening, as discreetly and painfully as possible. All stipulated in the contract between Sinbad Khan and The Lotus, sealed with Khan's blood.

Lady Sapphire would see it done. A simple poison-and-paralysis job.

Zijian hated contracts like this. High prestige (because of the client), low honor (because of the method). Typical for deals with the rich and famous. It would be full of tedious foreplay. Heavy food. Socializing. She would have to spend so much time talking, putting on a face, blending in, pretending to be someone she was not.

She always preferred the jobs where she could get her hands dirty. A duel with a worthy opponent was best. But anything hand-to-hand or blade-to-blade. The thrill of combat. The immediacy of death without any need for concealment. That was her preference.

Zijian arrived to the Khan's dinner party fashionably late, missing most of the cocktail schmooze. Still in plenty of time for the seated meal. She sat next to the target and poisoned his drink. Easy as that.

When the target felt sick and excused himself, she expressed concern and went to "check on him" in the bathroom. When she found him doubled-over the toilet, she swiftly delivered the paralytic needle stab to his neck. Easy as that.

The target spent the rest of the evening silently choking to death on his own bile. The method of execution was so slow that Zijian was able to rejoin the party, finish the leisurely dinner, endure several long-winded stories over dessert, before returning to the bathroom to witness his final throes.

As stipulated in the contract, the "official" cause of this death was to be an overdose. After the body stopped twitching, Zijian dragged it to a spare bedroom in the estate (as stipulated). Applied another injection of street drugs into the deceased (as stipulated). Then she returned to the party. If anyone asked questions, she was to explain (as stipulated) that the target had been sick, was now resting peacefully in bed, and would be sent home by taxi in the morning.

Thirteen-about-to-be-fourteen Ysobel was the only one who asked her any questions. When Zijian rejoined the party after leaving the body in the bedroom, the girl approached her immediately.

"How is Mark?" She said.

Zijian knew who this child was, but was taken aback by the pointed tone of the question, which betrayed that this little girl already understood much.

"He is resting now. It seems that something in the dinner might have disagreed with him." Zijian spoke in a professional monotone. By now, it was starting to get late, and her patience was worn thin by all the artifice of the evening. Besides, she had little interest in humoring a nosy child.

"How long did it last?" Young Ysobel, much like older Ysobel, was not one to let her curiosity be denied.

Zijian studied the girl's face. Round. Smooth. A little chubby with delicate features. Intelligent eyes. A cute girl, perhaps on her way to becoming a beautiful (and most likely, dangerous) woman.

"Long enough." Zijian answered flatly.

"He was a bad man," Ysobel declared with the naive confidence of thirteen-about-to-be-fourteen.

"I can't say. I only just met him."

"I can say. I've known him my whole life. He was a bad man. My father hates him." Anger began to grip Ysobel's face. Nostrils flared, lips curled into a snarl. Cuteness eliminated. Her unfiltered thoughts tumbled out of her mouth. "He was stealing from father's company. Using the money for drugs. My father knew that. That's why he hired you. But what my father doesn't know, is about the people he was getting the drugs from. But I know who they are, and they are evil. The absolute worst. I started reading about what they've done. It's awful. And that means that our money, I mean, my father's money, or my family's money, was going to fund those people. It makes me sick!"

Ysobel paused, initially to take a breath, but then realized she had probably said more than she should. Became self-conscious.

Zijian smiled her warm-water smile and made a fist-in-palm salute. "My name is Zijian Sun," she said. "And you are Miss Ysobel Kahn, correct?"

Ysobel returned the warm smile.

"You are very observant, Miss Khan. I'm sure you hear that all the time."

The child's smile brightened.

"You know where I work?"

The child's smile faded, but the eyes widened, indicating that she did.

"It was brave of you to come right up and ask me questions. Curiosity is not something that people in my line of work are usually receptive to. I'm sure you understand why."

Zijian paused. At that moment, she saw something strange in Ysobel's eyes. Like a glitch. Or a shadow flicker. Whatever it was, it accompanied a message. A message that did not come out of Ysobel's mouth. It went straight into Zijian's mind.

Come back tomorrow. I have another job for you.

The cucumber mud-mask and kneading portion of the morning's treatment is over. They are on to the joint cracking and limb twisting. The so-called "Akkadian-style" of massage.

There is less talking and more moans and groans during this activity. Zijian must concentrate carefully on her client's body. Many of these maneuvers require only slight variations to become painful rather than pleasurable. Twist with the wrong force or the wrong angle and it can be excruciating.

She knows that from experience.

Such thoughts surely run through Ysobel's mind as well. Even as she responds with audible enjoyment, the girl knows that these hands are equally adept at performing those slight variations. To torture out a confession. Or end someone's miserable life. If Zijian wished, she could rip Ysobel apart right now.

There is a loud crack of the spine.

"Ohhh! Wow!" Ysobel exclaims. "OK. That did it. I'm good."

Zijian steps back from the table and watches with satisfaction, both professional and personal, as the younger woman trembles, luxuriating in the body high from having been fully realigned.

Ysobel lets out a deep groan, nearly drooling. "I'm seeing... all the colors at once."

"Relax and take your time, dear." Zijian moves to the sink and begins to draw water for her client's foot bath. Her mind drifts back to business, spinning-up the clockworks from earlier: How to acquire new ties to City Hall.

Perhaps within the NWPD, as weak as they are, there are still pawns there who could serve. If Lotus could build someone up, entice them with the possibilities of greater power and access, this could be quite useful.

She checks the water's temperature. Still not quite hot enough.

A pawn in the Chief Inspector's office, that would be valuable. Feed them enough information to bring down the

Strauss administration. Help them "solve them mystery" of the sham assassination. Make someone a hero. Get them a promotion to the top office.

The water is hot enough. She slides the foot basin under the tap.

"I see it!" Ysobel suddenly shouts, sitting bolt upright on the table, eyes wide with excitement. "As the colors started to fade, it left a pattern. I think I saw the answer in the pattern. The solution to the puzzle!"

"Which puzzle?" Zijian's asks lightly, trying to hide the irritation of having her line of thought disrupted.

"The central puzzle. The missing piece in the middle of it all. The election. The gang wars. The assassin. All of it. I saw them circling around each other. Turning on a wheel of colors, like how the Earth turns on the wheel around the sun."

Zijian sighs, only half listening. While the girl's telepathic skill has certainly increased with age—she could now speak into Zijian's mind at some distance without betraying any outward physical sign—her skills as an oracle were poor. These "epiphanies," which so excited Ysobel, were often shallow. They made for tedious listening.

The basin is full. Zijian turns off the water.

"Then as the colors faded, I saw a grid. Light and dark squares, like a game board. But the board wasn't all within a square like in Castleguard. The grid sort of radiated out from a central point, to fit within the wheel pattern... "

Zijian lifts the now-full basin and carries it carefully back to the table.

"I saw pieces moving on the board. Knights. Pawns. Towers. Clerks. Sliding around. Taking turns attacking and defending. I think the knights were like the Big Six gangs. The pawns were the police. The towers were like the different colleges of the Ivory Citadel. The clerks were The

Stasi... There was a king that I'm pretty sure symbolized the mayor. Or City Hall."

Zijian kneels to set the basin down on a large stone step next to the message table. Ysobel keeps talking as she scoots herself around in her seat, swinging her legs off the table, placing her feet in the water.

"Ija!" Ysobel excitedly takes Zijian's face in her hands, using the name that only she is permitted to use. "Ija, I saw it. At the very center of the board was a queen. That's you! I knew it!"

———

"Let's try it again, Ija. Remember: As we play, you need to construct the trap in your mind. Leave clues for me to follow. Make me think I am on the right path to all of your secrets. But while you are locking me in, you're also locking your intentions away where I cannot find them."

Little Zijian nodded. She sat with her mother on the stones in the little garden behind their house. Both cross-legged. Close together. Zijian's hands out, palms facing up. Hadra's hands palms down, resting softly atop her daughter's. Lit in the underground gloom by a pleasing mix of pale violet, blue, and red from their lamps.

"Good," her mother said. "Set the trap. Move your clockworks quickly. Otherwise, I can find and take whatever I want. Control whatever I want."

They are playing a simple child's game. The palms-up player must try to slap the hands of the palms-down player before they can pull them away. Normally this is a game of physical reflexes and reaction time. But with Hadra, the game has another purpose. As they play, she is probing her daughter's mind, searching for the impulse that signals the hand movement. If she finds it, she can interrupt it. Hold it. Prevent her daughter from moving.

From the outside, the game looks like nothing at all. A mother sitting with her daughter, their palms touching, neither moving except for an occasional trembling.

From the inside—within Zijian's mind—it is a fierce game of cat-and-mouse. Incredibly taxing for the young girl. She was getting better at hiding her intention. Building the lie. Setting the trap. Doing it all quickly enough to almost outwit her sorceress mother.

Beads of sweat formed on little Zijian's brow as she tried to move her hands, but found she could not.

Much too easy, dear. Go deeper. Don't think about moving. Think of a memory, and then another memory within it. Hide your desire in the spaces between the memories.

Zijian shut her eyes tight. She remembered picking mushrooms with her mother. The pale glow of luminescence around the pond. A small troupe of insects making their way across the ground. She felt her mother around her. Searching. Looking for just the right mushrooms to pick.

She remembered placing her hand on the ground and a little insect crawled up onto her finger, up her wrist, her arm. She remembered how it tickled. Different from the feeling of Gish, her pet salamander, crawling on her.

She thought about Gish's terrarium in her room. Her mother was there. Telling her to clean it, then rummaging through her closet. Telling her she needed to be better about folding her clothes. Zijian wanted to argue, but let it go. Instead, she let Gish out. Held him in her hand. Let him crawl up her arm.

She remembered the cool, slightly sticky feeling of his little fingers and toes. Giving her goosebumps. But in a good way. So much better than those nasty darkflies landing on you and getting ready to bite.

SLAP!

"Good," Hadra said, smiling.

———

"What do you mean, dear?" Zijian asks in her flat, professional tone. "I am at the center of what?"

This is a feint. She does not expect it to fool Ysobel. But this is her standard opening in a game that the two so often play.

"Don't do that. You know I hate that," Ysobel snaps. "I'm not a child anymore."

Zijian ignores this protest. She is kneeling down by the water basin, caressing Ysobel's calf. Then her ankle. Then takes hold of a foot. Gently lifts it out of the hot water. Works her fingers in between the girl's delicate toes.

"It was you. The Lotus. It was your sniper. The assassin."

Zijian squeezes the girl's foot in her hands but says nothing.

"Tell me!" Ysobel shouts, demanding in the way of seventeen-about-to-be-eighteen.

"Tell you what, dear?"

Ysobel pulls her foot out of Zijian's hands and splashes it back into the basin. Droplets fly up into Zijian's face.

There is a flash of cold fire, but Zijian controls herself and rises calmly. Wipes the water away with her hand. Looks down imperiously at her naked, young client.

"What exactly do you want to know?" Still professional, yet not quite so flat as before. There is extra annunciation. Little dagger points on the ends of all her letters.

"Who is the assassin?" Ysobel replies immediately.

"That is not important."

"If it's not important, then you can tell me who it is."

"No."

"Why not?"

"Because that is not your business."

A sting of hurt in Ysobel's eyes. That was a jab, not a feint. And the girl felt it. Yet she presses on. "But it is your business, isn't it. You know who it was. You arranged the assassination. It was Lotus. The Assassins Guild."

Zijian says nothing. She keeps her face placid, except for a slight raised eyebrow. Her own curiosity gaining purchase.

Just how much did she "see" in this color wheel? Maybe her oracular skills are getting better.

More comes tumbling out of the girl's mouth: "But why would the Assassins Guild accept such a contract? A sham assassination? That would seem shameful. And how could such a contract be sanctioned? Whose blood could possibly serve for the ritual?"

Again, Zijian says nothing, but her eyebrow arches just a little bit more. She can tell that Ysobel is no longer waiting for her to answer.

"You wouldn't do this without the writ. That would be stupid. So the only way to sanction this would be... blood from the mayor himself. But why would he do that? What could he possibly have to gain from faking an assassination attempt? From taking a bullet to his own face?"

The train of thought comes to a temporary halt. It is an arresting question that Zijian hasn't been able to answer either—although she is quite sure that Mr. Moorelake, Strauss's Chief of Staff, is the key to that mystery.

"There's... something else... "

Train slowly starting up again. Ysobel closes her eyes,

evidently trying to re-conjure her vision of the game board. "The king... there was something strange about it... "

Zijian has had enough of this. Her curiosity sated.

The girl has put a piece or two together from her delirium, but there is no spectacular insight. Her vision is still mostly filled with obvious, and therefore, useless symbolism. It is time to bring the appointment to its conclusion.

Ysobel is lost thought. "There was something wrong with the reflection... "

Zijian makes another "I'm listening" sound and sits down on the massage table next to Ysobel. She admires her young lover. Her face. So pretty. Her body. So fresh and clean from today's treatment. She puts her arm around the girl's waist and pulls her close. Feels the soft warmth of the girl's skin against her own. Ysobel's mind is still grasping at something far away, but her body yields easily to the embrace. Her eyes shut tight.

"I could see... like seeing through water... to the underside of the board... "

Zijian starts brushing her fingertips back and forth across the top of Ysobel's legs. Tracing along the smooth curves of her thighs and hips.

"There was a strange piece... under the king... in his reflection... "

Fingers work their way, painting delicate strokes up and down the chest and stomach. Ysobel's eyelids flutter but remain closed.

"It wasn't a reflection... It wasn't another king... "

Tender circles around her breast. Ysobel arches her back. A soft moan slips out among the visions.

"It was like... an animal... "

Slowly up the side of her neck. Applying soft pressure to turn her cheek.

"Or a wizard... "
One finger pressed to her lips.
Zijian speaks the last words.
"Hush now."

CHAPTER 7
SHUWEN

...GETS A HOT TIP

Shuwen is at home on her day off. She is eating lunch alone in her small apartment when there is an unexpected knock at the door. Still finishing a mouthful of salad, she checks the peephole. Finds a nice surprise.

"Mmm!" She throws open the door.

"Hey, kiddo," says the unexpected visitor. A tall, dark, handsome man wearing an NWPD sergeant's uniform.

"Henry!" Shuwen exclaims, "And Faust!"

Faust is the equally (if not more) handsome dog politely sitting at the man's feet. A brindle shepherd mix. He gives a happy bark and tail wag at the sound of Shuwen saying his name.

She kneels down to greet the pooch. Gives him some scratches around the ears and neck.

"May we come in?" Henry asks.

"Of course, please do." Shuwen stands, ushers them inside, and closes the door.

"I see you're having your traditional lunch of leaves in a bowl," Henry says. "Are you part rabbit?"

"Yeah, yeah," Shuwen replies. Right now she is not

interested in Henry's japes. She's down on the floor, focusing her attention on the canine.

"I passed Lin's Food Truck on the way here. I brought you something," Henry opens his satchel and pulls out a tightly-folded cone of wax paper. "Satay."

Shuwen and Faust both turn their heads, immediately salivating and drooling (respectively) at the savory aroma of hot, juicy, peanutty goodness.

"Are you interested in this?" Henry dangles the delicious treat aloft, committing to his whole playfulness shtick.

With the upped ante, Shuwen and Faust are now willing to play along. The dog sits at attention, tail wagging. Shuwen turns to face Henry and sits cross-legged, posture upright, eyes closed, hands pressed together in prayer.

"Yes, please," she says.

———

Back in the police academy days, Shuwen and Henry had been a thing. A couple of whip-smart overachievers. Day one of police academy, they picked each other out as the rival to beat.

Henry's calling Shuwen "kiddo"—despite only being two turns older—dates back to this time. A teasing, psychological distraction born of their competitive repartee.

As you might expect, things soon evolved between them into a sizzling romance. One of those sexy partnerships of equals. You've seen the films. You know how it goes.

But after the credits rolled, the romance faded. As romance tends to do. And eventually they drifted apart.

The cause of their drifting was more philosophical than anything else. Shuwen was all-in on the law. She made it the foundation for every other obligation in life. Henry wasn't so sure.

Henry cared about the law, of course. He had chosen the path of an officer, just like she had. But the more he dug into it, the more shades of gray he found, and it troubled him. Sometimes he found he disagreed with the law. People he loved and trusted broke the law, yet he wasn't sure they were wrong to do so. And it troubled him.

For Shuwen, these shades of gray might make the performance of her duty more complicated, but it did not change anything so fundamental. The deeper she went into a case, the more certain she became.

Over time, the tension between certainty and doubt pushed them apart. The one couldn't understand why the other seemed so indecisive and circumspect in the face of injustice. The other couldn't understand how the one could ignore all the contradictions lurking in the details.

There was never any big blow up. After the academy, they went their separate ways. She to Lucky Precinct 13, he to Precinct 24. Both felt it was for the best. No real hard feelings.

Besides, even if the sexy sparks had died, there was still plenty of embers left for that other kind of love. Plenty of respect. Plenty of genuine well-wishes to see the other live their best life.

And who knows? Perhaps under the light of a Lonely Moon, there was an ember for that quiet desire to one day, maybe still, share a future together.

———

Henry sits at Shuwen's kitchen table. She stands at the counter, enjoying the satay, tossing the odd bite to Faust who happily devours it.

"So Lin's truck was still open despite the lockdown, huh?"

Henry chuckles. "Of course. What would you expect?"

"YOO CAWN'T SHUT ME DAWN, MUTHA-FUCKAHS! JOST YOO TRY!" Shuwen belts out a joyful impression of Chef Lin. She and Henry both have a good laugh. Even Faust joins in with a couple of excited barks.

"I know I've said it before, but to watch Lin at work— the way she chops it all up with that big cleaver of hers—it's like music. Or magic."

Shuwen nods and smiles. Her mouth full.

"All cops or soldiers waiting in line at the truck," Henry says. "And mostly the same fuzz walking on the street. But I saw some civilians in cars. No one is supposed to be out without the paperwork, but I didn't see any officers bothering to check."

"Hmmm... " Shuwen continues munching happily.

Henry leaves a few ticks of silence. Then he opens the conversation she knows he has come to have.

"So what are you going to do?"

She doesn't answer. Continues chewing her last bite. She doesn't need to say anything. Henry already knows she's not going to let the case drop.

"What did Wolff say?" He asks.

She swallows and gives the satay stick to Faust to chew on. "He told me to be careful."

"That's good advice."

"And to work with the Stasi if they catch me snooping around."

Henry frowns. "Probably not such good advice. Not these days."

Shuwen nods in agreement.

"What have you worked out so far?" He asks.

"Not much." Shuwen furrows her brow. "I don't like

that we haven't been able to identify the sniper. That is a bad sign."

"Yup."

"I don't like that Ty Reese was at the rally, ready to put on a show. It seems so suspicious. But I arrested nine of his henchmen. They were all interrogated. None of them knew anything about the assassination."

"Hmmm."

"I don't like the Stasi getting involved so quickly. And the military presence. The hit is obviously some kind of ruse. Giving it all this attention... sending so much traffic into The Core—that has to be playing right into someone's hands."

Faust barks.

"Whose hands?" Henry asks.

Shuwen takes a beat. "I don't know," she says eventually. "It's so frustrating! Even if the Stasi investigators catch the shooter and unravel this thing, they're never going to share the truth."

"Well, I might have a lead for you," Henry says. "I heard through the grapevine that Mayor Eli is making some kind of deal with Fosse and The Bulldogs tonight."

She perks up immediately.

"I heard it was going down at The Bloodhound Ballroom."

"Perfect." Without a moment's hesitation, Shuwen goes to the closet to get her jacket and shoes on. Faust trots after her. "That's uptown, outside the lockdown. It will be crowded. Easy to blend in."

"Whoa, kiddo!" Henry laughs, but it's more worry than amusement. "Slow down. I'm not telling you this so that you'll rush headlong into a hornet's nest. Remember what Wolff said?"

"Yeah, yeah." Shuwen waves a dismissive hand. "I'll be careful."

———

When Shuwen first arrived at Precinct 13, Tomas Sterling was already one of the senior constables. He had an impressive record. He was respected on the streets. He had read Shuwen's academy papers. Knew her profile. He was intrigued. Excited to meet her. But he played it cool.

She, still fresh from the breakup with Henry, wasn't looking for another romance. She wanted to focus on work. She kept it all strictly professional.

For the first half-turn, that's all they were: professional colleagues. Senior Constable and Junior Constable. They worked different beats. They ate at different lunch tables. But they would both be lying if they said they weren't thinking about each other. Even then.

The Montrose Murderer case is what finally tipped them over the edge. A mystery that sparked their imaginations, sucked them both in. They started arguing over the case at lunch. And they loved it.

They pulled a long stretch of all-nighters in the office together, just the two of them. Going over the facts and the evidence with a fine-tooth comb. Coming up with all kinds of theories, trying to piece the puzzle together. Wolff was the one who finally told them to go get a room because they were stinking up the place.

So they did. And they loved it.

Then they solved the case and caught the killer.

They got written up in the papers. "Dynamo Cop Duo Catch Montrose Monster." Wolff got that front page mounted and framed for them as a house-warming gift when they moved in together. They put it up in their front hall.

When Tomas died at The Strauss Assassination in '95, Shuwen was devastated. But she was only twenty-one. She mourned, but she had to move on. She sold their apartment. Downsized. Got rid of everything. Did her best to leave the past behind. Made work the sole focus.

That's when Constable Shuwen Li started wearing the bracers full-time. Working longer shifts. Trying to be everywhere, arresting everyone. When she earned her "supercop" reputation.

———

"Wait, that's not all!" Henry is on his feet, hand extended to try and stop Shuwen before she can dash out. Anticipating his human, Faust has put his body between her and the door.

"It won't just be the mayor and Fosse and his Bulldogs," he says. "I heard that Dr. T will also be there. He is supposed to perform tonight."

"That's even more perfect! If Ty Reese was involved in the hit, he may try something again." She gives Faust a firm pat on the rump, trying to encourage him to move out of the way. The dog stays put.

"That's too much traffic to go in there blazing, Shuwen. If it goes off the rails, it could be absolute chaos."

Shuwen taps the bracers on her wrists.

Henry is not persuaded. "I know those are powerful, but they do not make you invincible. What are you planning to do? Walk in there, bash some heads, and start making arrests?"

She rolls her eyes. "Of course not! I will play it cool."

"Like what? A spider in the corner?"

"Something like that. And maybe some dancing too." She smirks. "Dr. T has some good songs."

Henry is not amused. "Let me go with you."

"No. You know I work alone."

"Yeah, but we're talking the mayor, at least two kingpins, and who knows how many of their goons. You shouldn't do this alone. We'll come with."

Shuwen shoots him a look of exasperation. "C'mon. What are you saying? You know you can't leave Faust and you two will stick out like a sore thumb."

"Faust can wait in the car."

Faust barks with dismay at the suggestion to sideline him.

"No. Henry. Don't worry." The dog is still resisting, but she manages to squeeze one leg between him and the door. "Thank you for telling me about this meet-up and show tonight. And thank you for bringing me lunch." She squeezes her second leg in, finally getting the leverage she needs to scooch the dog out of the way. "But I'm going alone."

She has the door open and is about to depart. Then she stops, remembers something, and looks back. "Oh, right," she says. "You don't have a key. You can't lock up. You have to leave now too."

CHAPTER 8
TY VS. ELI

...AT THE BLOODHOUND

"The latest poll numbers are looking good, Dr. T," says the woman in the black suit and thick, dark-rimmed glasses. Her dark brown hair pulled back in a tight bun. This is Jelena Escher, Ty's Populist Party political strategist. "Releasing the footage of you dealing with those anarchists has played quite well."

They sit together in the back of his limousine. On their way to the venue. The Bloodhound Ballroom.

"Good," he snorts. "But I don't want to talk about that now. I need to focus on my show. Clear my head."

"I understand, sir," she replies. "However, it might interest you to know that Mayor Eli is likely to be at the show."

Get the fuck out!

Ty's shows little outward reaction to this news. Yet, Jelena has been working with him long enough now to know how to push a few of the old boxer's buttons. And she is skilled enough to read even the slightest twitch in his face.

"Our intel is that Eli is planning to make a drug deal

with The Bulldogs. With Fosse himself. This is scheduled to occur before your showtime, but given the mayor's proclivity for indulgence, we expect that he will stay through your performance."

"I don't give a shit if he buys a ticket and wants to stay and listen," Ty says. "My music is for everyone."

Jelena nods and makes a note in her portfolio. "Of course... It just seemed to me that there might be a strategy at play." Ty raises an eyebrow. So she continues: "You managed to turn the mayor's disastrous rally to your advantage. He may be attempting to do something similar to you. Showing up at your concert. Intending to upstage you in some way."

Ty snorts. "I'd like to see that dumb scuzzer try it."

"It's something to consider," Jelena says. "If the mayor is playing games, it can't hurt to be thinking a few moves ahead."

———

The curtain falls to raucous applause. Dr. T did not disappoint. He opened and closed the show with his big hit, "Fight for the Streets." He gives the people exactly what they want, and they love him for it. True on stage. True in politics.

Behind the curtain, Ty walks to the stage wing, where one of his boys has a bottle waiting for him. He takes a swig. The chants of "encore" from the crowd start to swell.

"They just can't get enough," he says. He drains the bottle. "Time to give them an encore they won't ever forget."

His boys clap him in on the back, hooting and hollering. Ty tosses the empty bottle to one of them and struts back to the center of the stage.

The curtain rises. The crowd is going wild. Chanting "T! T! T!" He eggs them on with both hands, encouraging them to get even louder. They're loving it. It's so noisy it feels like the walls might collapse.

He points to the sky. The house lights come on.

He looks out across the space. The Bloodhound Ballroom is a classy old venue. It was an opera house back in the day. Lots of dark red velvet. Gold busts and figurines of bloodhounds everywhere.

He lifts the mic to his lips. "I want to thank y'all for coming out tonight," he says, scanning the faces in the crowd. "That was real special."

C'mon, Rich Boy. Where are you hiding? Skulking in the shadows like a snake.

He spots him. At the back. Eli is seated on a stool, slumped over the bar top with a straw hanging out of his mouth. He looks absolutely smashed, barely able to keep his head up.

A slow grin builds across Ty's face. "Now I want to give you something extra special. I'm going to give you a taste of the future."

The crowd cheers.

"Y'all know I'm running for office, right?"

More cheers.

"I know everyone here is gonna vote for me, RIGHT?"

The crowd goes nuts. The walls are literally shaking down. Cracks forming. Bits of plaster falling. Not that anyone notices.

Ty cups his hand to his ear. "Damn right!" He roars. "But what y'all may not know is that we got ourselves a punk here tonight."

The crowd quiets a little bit. This is not exactly where they thought he was going.

Still grinning, Ty struts about the stage. "That's right.

One of my opponents is here with us tonight. He's easy to miss because he's so puny. But he's sitting right there." Ty points to the back of the room. A thousand heads turn.

Eli has been resting his chin on his hand, but at that precise moment his head slips and falls with a loud crack onto the bar top. The crowd gasps. Dazed, he stumbles off his stool and throws his hands up. It's a gesture that is intended to signal he is OK, he is fine, he is all good. He looks anything but. He looks like someone should have poured him into a cab and sent him home a few chimes ago.

"Our most honorable mayor, ladies and gentlemen," Ty snarks into the mic. He's got the crowd. He's got the mayor. He's got it all right where he wants it.

Eli starts to shamble his way toward the stage. The crowd makes a path for him. They're all stepping back like he's shedding a deadly virus. The way he looks, you can't blame them.

Ty is still spitting from the stage. "Y'all see this shit? This is who's spending our tax money? This is who's in charge of our city? This zombie-looking motherfucker?"

Eli continues shambling forward. He curls an insolent lip and flips Ty off with both hands. Ty just laughs and keeps going.

The crowd twitters. The energy in the room is starting to get a little nervous.

"C'mon, y'all. We can do better than this. Y'all deserve better than this." Ty drops the mic, hops off the stage, and walks out to meet Eli on the dance floor.

Now two paces apart, in the middle of the ballroom, the rival candidates stand face-to-face. Ty looking down like a golden celebrity-god next to a drunken, silver-haired gremlin in a dirty suit. He's at least a head taller than Eli. Stronger too.

It's not a good look for the incumbent mayor.

The crowd backs up, forms a wide circle around them. No longer cheering.

A pregnant silence falls.

Everyone can feel that something big is about to happen.

Eli moves first. Or is moved first? Either way: His body suddenly convulses and he vomits directly onto Ty's pants and shoes. Ty steps back and throws his arms out in disbelief.

Disgust ripples through the crowd.

"Are you kidding me?" Ty shouts. He is not happy about this development. Covered in puke from the knees down is not how he wanted this to go.

Eli reels back, coughing. He does look genuinely ill, but he is also clearly amused by what has just happened. "I'm the dragon," he gargles out. Raises his pinky ring to the sky like it means something and chuckles.

Fuck this disgusting, piece-of-shit asshole!

Ty waves to his boys in the crowd. "Get this pathetic scuzzer out of here," he yells. The fun is over. He turns away, heading back to the stage. But as soon as he's back-turned, Eli lunges forward and throws a front-kick that catches Ty's hamstring. Ty stumbles from the impact, but manages to keep his feet.

The crowd gasps.

Aww, you've done it now, Rich Boy.

Ty whirls around and clocks the mayor in the face with a mean right hook. It spins Eli like a top and drops him to all fours. Ty grabs him by the hair, pulls him up to his feet, and gives him two more solid punches to the gut.

The mayor is gasping, bug-eyed. He looks like a deflating balloon animal. Ty whips him around by the collar and flings him to the ground, sprawling, right into the puddle of his own sick.

Eli stays down.

A few people start to cheer. But Ty is not feeling triumphant. The mood of the evening has been spoiled. He snorts loudly as four of his boys start to close in around Eli.

"Say good-bye to our honorable mayor, ladies and gentlemen!" Ty shouts and does a dramatic wave good-bye. There are a few waves and laughs. Scattered applause. Most are moving to the exits, turned off by this ugliness.

Yet those who stick around are rewarded with the most miraculous sight of the evening: As the Azzuri boys bend down to pick up the mayor, his body suddenly explodes into flame. The boys are thrown back, clothes singed, hands burned. The mayor floats back to his feet as though he were lifted on strings. A deep purple fire rages around his body. His whole posture changes. No longer slack and drunken loose. He now stands like a warrior. Shoulders broad. Chest and chin forward. His skin has become charcoal black. His eyes red, like molten metal. His blue suit glows a blinding white neon.

Ty is transfixed. He does not believe what he is seeing. He has witnessed some weird shit in his time. But he's never seen anything like this.

Eli the Warrior-on-Fire starts towards him.

Good. I want a closer look. What the fuck is this shit?

Part of Ty knows he should be afraid. Yet he feels no fear. Seeing this kind of power—it trips a switch in his brain.

The flaming demon that used to be Eli winds up a punch and lets it rip. Straight into Ty's chest. Ribs immediately cracked. Lung punctured. Ty, knocked off his feet, sails across the ballroom. His body crashes against the foot of the stage. Probable spine damage. He feels it. He's hurt bad. He didn't lose many fights in his career, but he knows he's lost this one. He feels the curtains coming down on his eyes.

This is not a good look for him.

Before he blacks out, he notices that everyone seems to be gone. His boys. The crowd. Everyone. It's just him and Demon Eli in the black void.

This night definitely did not go as planned. But Ty doesn't give two shits about that anymore. Fuck this crowd. Fuck the election.

All that matters now is acquiring that kind of power—the kind of power to call forth a demon. Or become a demon? Whichever it is, that's a whole new level of game. When, or if, he wakes up, his only goal will be to possess that power. Whatever it takes.

PART TWO

BLADE

CHAPTER 9
UZIEL

...INTERVIEWS THE WITNESS

Uziel stands on the side of the apartment building, perpendicular to the wall, suspended by a grappling line. He is perfectly still. Waiting in calm defiance of gravity. Trench coat fluttering in the cool, night breeze.

A window opens onto the fire escape below. Shuwen Li climbs out. Sits on the sill and nervously lights a cigarette.

Uziel watches her cigarette glow. Takes slow, silent steps down along the wall until he is hovering just above her head. "Strange night," he says in the low, even voice of a synth.

She jumps. "What the—" Drops her cigarette. It tumbles through the metal grating down into the alleyway below.

She spins around, looking for the voice, dukes up. "Stay back and identify yourself!"

"Relax, Constable," he says, flipping down to stand before her, releasing his grapple line. "I was at the Ballroom tonight. I'm here to help you."

She keeps her combat stance. "I said to identify your-self, *citizen.*"

Uziel takes a step forward. "You can call me... *Nightwing*."

"Oh... " Shuwen slowly lowers her hands. "Right. You." A mixture of relief and disappointment in her voice. "Wait, 'Nightwing'? I thought you were called 'Nightsilver'?"

"I have been called many things."

"Or 'Silverman'?"

"That is one of my names as well."

She reaches back through the window to grab her pack of Lucky Spirits. "Foul creature," she says in a dry tone, mocking the catch phrase made famous in the Nightsilver comics.

"When you don't have a badge, a phrase like that comes in handy on the streets," he says.

"So you do actually say that?" She lights a new cigarette.

Uziel nods. "I let Mr. Franklin shadow me on the watch while he did research for the Nightsilver series. I gave him permission to use the phrase."

She exhales slowly, smoke curling up into the light. "But you're 'Nightwing' these days?"

"Yes. Nightwing."

"Well, you startled me, Nightwing. If you were at The Bloodhound, then you know it's been quite a night already. I didn't need more surprises."

"I know."

"And you shouldn't be hanging around in the shadows outside my window."

Uziel takes a beat. Processing. "I'm sorry."

She offers him a smoke. He shakes his head.

"I don't smoke."

"I don't usually either," she says, then takes another drag. "But on a night like this... "

There is silence for a round or two. Shuwen calming her nerves with the smoke. Uziel standing perfectly still. His eyes zooming in her face, taking measurements, inferring her emotional state. Then shifting focus to her bracers. Analyzing their structure. Saving it all for deeper analysis later.

Finally, he asks: "Can you tell me what you saw tonight?"

———

No one in official city law enforcement knew exactly how long Uziel Silverman had been prowling the shadows of New World City. The NWPD had records of him going back fifteen turns, but there are scattered sightings and stories from before that. Chief Wolff, for example, claims he saw "The Silverman" running across rooftops back when he was just starting out on the beat.

But whatever the true history, Uziel has become a fixture of the nightly crime watch in the city. And the daily crime watch as well. As a synth, he doesn't need to sleep. So he can vigilante all day long.

He tended to focus his watch in The Core and the lower numbered precincts, but if he got wind of a case, he would follow it wherever it needed to go.

No wind required for him to get on the case of the attempted assassination of Mayor Strauss Jr. Uziel had been there (in disguise, of course). In the front row of the stands, near the stage. His synthetic eyes were able to capture and calculate the precise angle of the bullet as it struck, and he had immediately turned to look for its source.

Unfortunately, he did not have the time, the proper lighting, or the pixel resolution to identify the sniper, but had did manage to get a decent silhouette. The dress. The posture. The shape of the rifle. He believed the assassin was trained military.

But he didn't believe The Ragnarok coup theory. The military industrial wing of The State was never so crude or public in its machinations. Ty Reese and his Azzuri, Madame Sun and The Lotus—these were far more likely suspects. A political rival to the mayor and the head of The Assassins Guild. A conspiracy between them could make sense.

Except for the fact that the sniper "missed" the shot. This would dishonor the Assassins Guild, and therefore made it less likely their doing. Uziel had also been investigating Mr. Reese's gang. And like Shuwen, he had not been able to uncover any connections to the event.

Not quite dead-ends for the case. But Uziel had come to believe that there was more mystery to it than first appeared.

———

"What do you mean, 'what I saw'? You were there." Shuwen says mildly, taking a drag.

"My eyes don't capture light the same as yours do. And my synthetic brain processes the information differently as well."

She exhales. "OK, where do you want me to start?"

"From when you arrived at the venue."

"Right," she begins. "I got to The Bloodhound shortly after sundown. I camped out at the bar across the street until I saw the mayor arrive. He came by car, got dropped off. Alone. No bodyguards."

Another quick drag as she pieces the memories together. Uziel studies her face carefully. His eyes unblinking behind his silver mask.

She continues: "I went inside. I tracked the mayor to one of the private lounges. I never saw Fosse, but my intel said that's who he was meeting. I don't doubt it. I spotted plenty of Bulldogs around."

Uziel's eyes make a soft mechanical sound as the lenses adjust. Zooming in. "None of them recognized you?"

"I wasn't in uniform, as you see. Long sleeves. Hair down. No, I don't think anyone recognized me."

"Go on," he says.

"I saw the mayor come out after the meeting and go directly to the bar at the back of the ballroom. I stood on the floor, in the crowd, not far away. I watched him drink himself into a stupor. I didn't see him move from that seat for the whole concert. During the encore, when Dr. T jumped down into the crowd, and that anarchist attacked him—that was the first time I looked away and let the mayor out of my sight. When I looked again, just before the explosion, he was gone."

"What do you remember about the anarchist?" Uziel asks.

"Typical profile, I think... " Shuwen lowers her eyes, trying to recall. Takes another drag. "Cloth mask over their nose and mouth. Blue jeans, maybe?"

"What color was the cloth mask?"

"Red?" She pauses. "No. Brown... I don't know. I can't remember. Not clearly."

Uziel nods. "What did you do after the explosion?"

"I ran to the lobby. To look for the mayor, but also to try and help people get out to safety. There was thankfully a lot of security inside the venue and they had already called the police. When the other officers arrived, I slipped away."

"You didn't report in?"

Shuwen says nothing. Her cigarette is finished. She stubs it out on the windowsill, flicks it away, and takes out another from her pack.

Uziel presses: "Why didn't you report in?"

"Because I wasn't *officially* supposed to be there," she snaps. "It would just complicate things. But why does that matter? Why are you asking me this? You said you were there. Where were *you*? What did *you* see?"

"I was in the balcony. I didn't see any anarchist. I saw the mayor explode," he says. His voice perfectly consistent in its low, even tone.

Shuwen sneers in disbelief. "The mayor explode? What are you talking about?"

———

For four turns of the wheel now, Uziel has been a Vigilante with a capital "V"—which is to say that he was a member of the so-called "Vigilantes League," a group of clandestine crime fighters who decided to take the law into their own hands.

This cadre of characters met once every halfstretch in a secret base of operations, somewhere in The Undercity (or so it was said). They would share information, draw up action plans, and tally up the scores for the number of criminals caught and civilians saved. This was all completely illegal, of course, but the NWPD tended to tolerate it because the Vigilantes did prove themselves useful on occasion.

Even before The League, Uziel knew he was not the only unlicensed crime-fighter in the city. This was not a problem. In fact, he thought it a good thing that others should be inspired to follow his example and take up the watch. The official law enforcement institutions were obviously overwhelmed. Or corrupt. Or incompetent. So there was plenty of work to go around.

The problem was that vigilante work was dangerous. And some folks who wanted to try their hand at do-gooding had no business doing so. Whether they lacked the necessary strength, smarts, or skills, there were plenty of wannabe heroes who showed up one night and died the next. Uziel would try to warn them. Impart the two "Hard Truths of the Watch," as he called them. Anything is possible. Heroes die like everyone else. They usually didn't listen.

But over time, there were a few others appearing in the night who did have the right stuff. There was Tank, a reformed and repurposed killbot looking to redeem himself after centuries of war. Benoit, a psychic mutant panda warrior. Meg the Magnificent, a young engineering prodigy who had built herself a transforming exosuit. After enough encounters and impromptu team-ups, it became clear that the four of them could do a better job of keeping the streets safe if they coordinated their efforts. Thus was formed The Vigilantes League.

It was these new friends who re-branded The Silverman as "Nightsilver". And the same friends who later suggested that he change it again to "Nightwing". Uziel was largely indifferent to the names and happily accepted each one. For him, the naming ideas were signs of a growing affection from his colleagues. After spending so much of his runtime alone in the city's shadows, he found the companionship of The League enriched him in ways he had not expected, triggering positive feedback loops in his circuitry that he liked.

———

"I don't see the same as you do," Uziel repeats. "I also place remote micro-sensors everywhere. They feed additional information to my brain. When Ty Reese went into the crowd and the mayor left his bar stool, there was an influx of energy. I suspect you and most of the others at the venue were effected by an illusion."

"An illusion?" Shuwen is incredulous. "You mean like a stage trick?"

'No, I mean a real magic spell."

Shuwen scoffs. "You can't be serious."

"I am serious. A powerful magic spell hid the truth from your eyes."

"That's not possible," she protests. "The explosion was real. They found the body parts of the anarchist."

"A conjured illusion spell can paint a false picture for any who see and interact with it. There were body parts to find after the explosion, but there was no anarchist. Those were pieces of unlucky Azzuri gangsters who were close to the mayor when he burst into flames. The illusion tricked your eyes and brain into 'seeing' something different... something the spell-caster wanted you to see."

Shuwen frowns in disbelief. "That sort of magic isn't possible. It doesn't happen anymore. If it ever did."

"You a wrong, Constable. It happens. It is very rare to see in the city, I grant you, but it happens. It happened tonight. It happened to you."

As she's drawn into the argument, the rest of Shuwen's cigarette burns down unused in her hand. "So what then? You say the mayor exploded? He's dead?"

"No. He is not dead. I believe he somehow... unleashed that explosion and transformed himself into... something else. It seemed to be a demon of some kind—through another kind of magic. I'm not yet sure. But I believe this transformation and the demon-like thing is what the illusion was meant to hide."

"I don't believe this." Shuwen is struggling. Perplexed. It is not an easy thing to give up a memory, especially one so fresh. Harder even to break through the effects of an illusion.

"I know it can be difficult to accept," Uziel says. "Meet

me again tomorrow night. I will take you to The League's headquarters. There I have the equipment to show you everything. All the images and readings that my sensors recorded. They are not affected by the spell. They can prove my account of the mayor's transformation."

"Go to your headquarters?" Shuwen puts her face in her hands and rubs her eyes. "I don't know... "

Before she looks up, Uziel is gone. Zipped his way back up the wall. Running across the rooftops. A silhouette against the breaking dawn.

CHAPTER 10
ZIJIAN

...IDENTIFIES HER TARGET

«More violence occurred last night, again related to the New World City mayoral election. Ty Reese was performing at an uptown music venue. After the show, an anarchist suicide bomber detonated himself, killing two others and seriously injuring dozens more. Mr. Reese survived the attack, but remains in serious condition.

At a press conference this morning, Mayor Strauss had this to say:

"I am, of course, shocked and saddened by what has happened. Despite their budget increases in recent turns, the NWPD have not been able to get the anarchists menace under control. City Hall is now in discussion with the Department of State Security to explore how that agency may be able to better deal with these recent threats to public safety.

But while this is a tragedy, I will also observe that Mr. Reese has long courted this kind of violence with his inflammatory rhetoric. It therefore does not surprise me that such a thing could occur within the ranks of his supporters."»

Zijian has her thinking dagger out, slowly twisting into her palm.

The State auditors are in. One will be arriving shortly to talk through any anomalies they've found when reviewing the latest contracts. An important meeting, but she's not concerned. She feels prepared.

Weak-minded pencil-pushers. Hardly worth my time.

She turns her thoughts to more important subjects.

She is now certain that a direct line to City Hall is critical. The mayor has surely instigated this latest display at the music venue as some kind of retaliation for The Azzuri and Populist Party taking political advantage of the rally. Given the severity of his injuries, Mr. Reese might even drop out of the race.

The mayor's composure in the press conference suggests a level of shrewdness that I would not have expected. Surely, it is all, or mostly, Mr. Moorelake's doing. But if so, this suggests that he is quite the puppet-master.

Another thought suddenly arises, and Zijian is dismayed that she has not considered it before.

Or an enchanter? Could Moorelake be a magician?

She digs in hard with her dagger. Her blood flows down the blade toward the hilt.

State propaganda has worked hard to convince the world that magicians are relics and legends relegated to earlier, less-rational times. Zijian knows the truth. She has seen plenty of powerful magic with her own eyes. In The Undercity or The Outer Reaches, beyond the desert and The Devastation—there are powerful magicians still. Her mother, Hadra, for one.

However, she has neither seen nor heard of anything like an enchanter walking the Halls of Power in New World City. This would be unprecedented. And it does not bode well.

That would account for the queerness of my feelings about this mayor's chief of staff. If he were a magician, he could certainly have enchanted the mayor and had him sign that writ for his own sham assassination. The mayor himself seemed idiotic enough to try the stunt. But if Moorelake was the one in control all along, then that is another game entirely... But why? What would he have to gain by the charade?

Zijian does not like this feeling. The feeling of not knowing how things stand. A feeling that she is being outplayed.

She sets down her dagger and closes her fist around a kerchief to staunch the bleeding. Closes her eyes. With her other hand, massages her temple. Thinks back on the contract signing with Mayor Eli and Moorelake.

They specifically requested a non-guild executioner, and were prepared to pay the tenfold increase for such a stipulation.

While this request had immediately struck her as odd, Moorelake had correctly acknowledged that for a guild member to apparently fail in an assassination would be considered shameful. Therefore, it would be better for Lotus to merely arrange the hit, and to manage the paperwork once the inevitable inquiries were initiated in the aftermath.

My suggestion of a military sniper was met with eager approval. Too eager. Moorelake had declared it to be "ideal". I assumed he thought this would bring suspicion upon Admiral Allstar and her Nationalist Party. But I never said, and it was never stipulated, that "military" necessarily meant someone with a Ragnarok affiliation.

Eyes still closed. Zijian winces, recalling more of her thoughts at the time. She believed she had outplayed them in this contract wording. It seemed obvious that this ploy of the mayor's office was related to the election. An apparent military-backed assassination attempt could give the Strauss Party all kinds of political ammunition. Let them crush Allstar's campaign, potentially sweep up her support, put them ahead of Ty Reese and the Populists.

Yet, by not specifying from which military she had to source the sniper, Zijian had created options for herself. And she fully intended to hire an ex-military sniper from The Reaches. Not out of any love or respect for The Ragnarok (those arrogant warmongers could all go hang), but she had no desire to throw the whole State hierarchy into disarray in service to some Strauss Party scheme.

She had expected the assassination plot to stir up chaos. It would certainly swing some votes. But she had seen no great threat to Lotus or herself in it. After all, Old Mayor Strauss had been sliced up during a public speech, and Lotus had emerged stronger from the chaos. This could be the same.

Then she hits on it. Her thinking dagger cuts deep into her palm.

There was no magician involved last time. And a magician is always a threat.

A knock at the office door interrupts the clockworks. She takes a few beats to collect herself and prepare.

"Enter," she says.

An assistant opens the door, leading in a disheveled looking State auditor wearing a cheap government suit. His spectacles askew on his nose.

"This is Agent Macintosh, Madame. He is here to discuss the audit."

A Stasi Agent? Unusual for an audit... But I suppose I shouldn't be surprised given the recent events.

Zijian nods her thanks to her assistant, who quickly withdraws and closes the door. She offers her guest a smile and extends her hand toward the couches opposite her desk. "Please make yourself comfortable."

"Thank you, Madame Sun." Macintosh sits himself on one end of the couch nearest her desk. He clutches a pale file folder, overflowing with papers, to his chest. "I'm guessing you weren't expecting a Stasi operative, eh?" He says, smiling awkwardly.

"On the contrary, sir." She is pure calm and politeness. "I understand very well how an apparent attempt of political assassination places our beloved State in a... shall we say, *precarious* position. I would expect nothing less than a thorough investigation."

Macintosh nods with enthusiasm. "I am much relieved to hear you say that, Madame Sun. Yes, yes. Much relieved. And I can tell you: I am only Stasi Division Three. I am here simply to gather information and make sure that everyone stays adequately informed. That we're all on the same page and such."

"And I am much relieved to hear that. Thank you, Agent Macintosh."

He smiles again, adjusts his spectacles, and then drops his eyes to his folder. Begins fumbling through the documents as he speaks. "After looking through the records of Lotus and, er, guild activities, everything seemed to largely be in order."

Zijian nods. Smile plastered on. Gaze fixed on the agent's stupid face.

Of course you found everything in order, you half-wit. You found exactly what I wanted you to find.

"Although I did have a question about the mayor's contract." He looks up with an apologetic expression. "I'm sure you expected we would have questions about that, eh?"

"Indeed I did."

"Right, right." He blinks twice and then drops his gaze

to the document now atop the pile in his hands. "So I have now collected the blood sample from the mayor's signature, which I will send to the lab for confirmation. And I have already confirmed that the contract followed a preexisting and legally valid protocol. But I see that the guild subcontracted out the execution to an organization that I have never heard of. That will seem strange to my superiors, especially given the delicate nature of this contract. Can you explain this decision?"

"Certainly." Zijian switches to her dagger-pointed tone. "The stipulations in this contract were inconsistent with the honor and principles of the Assassins Guild. However, I believed the contract was still in the interest of The Lotus Corporation. As chair, it is within my purview to make such a determination. So I sourced an acceptable executor from our extensive professional network."

Macintosh blinks. "And that company, the one from which you sourced the shooter, er, executor—it is what it says here? Something called, 'FML Limited'?"

"Correct."

"Can you tell me where this business is registered?"

"They are based in Outwash. In The Outer Reaches. You can confirm that with the Office of Records."

"I see." He frowns, shuffles a few pages. Hesitates for a few beats. "I... I will follow up with Records. But perhaps you can reassure me in the meantime. Lotus conducted a thorough background check of this FML organization and its employees?"

The question triggers a flicker of cold fire in Zijian's eyes. But her tone stays perfectly calm. "Of course."

"Good, good."

Several more beats of nervous hesitation, shuffling of papers. Zijian drums her fingers on her desk.

Get to the point, worm.

Finally, he does: "Would you be willing to share that information with me? The results of your background check? I know it is outside the bounds of the audit, but in the interest of State security, wrapping everything up smoothly, and so on, it would be a big help."

Hilarious!

"No, I'm afraid that is not possible, Agent Macintosh."

He nods several times, making it clear that is the answer he expected. "I suppose that is fine. So long as the company are properly registered... " He pauses for few ticks, mulling it over. Then decides: "If the department wants to investigate they can send someone to Outwash."

Yes. Lovely. Please do send a few more numbskull agents on a fullspan journey to the edge of the world. They will be lucky to come back alive.

Zijian says nothing. Merely inclines her head.

"And I don't suppose you would let me take a look at the writ itself? Just to confirm everything from the database?" He blinks at her hopefully.

Never in a million turns of the wheel.

"I'm afraid that is also out of the question. It would violate our most sacred principles to let anyone into the vault who has not been properly sanctified through guild rituals. I'm sure you understand."

"Yes. No, I thought not. But never hurts to ask, eh?"

She smiles and arches an eyebrow as if to say, "It depends on the question."

———

A half-chime later, the Stasi Division Three agent is gone. The Stasi may very well investigate further. And they may come back with more questions. But Zijian is confident that by then, it will be too late. Once Ysobel has ascended to

CEO of OmniCorp, and Zijian has established her new lines into City Hall, she will have all the strings she needs to shut down any further inquiry if it should get too close to the truth.

One of Zijian's assistants comes back into the room holding a tidy file folder.

"The list of potential contacts in the Chief Inspector's office is ready for you, Madame Sun."

She accepts the dossier and thanks her assistant. She begins leafing through. There are a dozen or so candidates to consider. It's a good number. When selecting candidates for a corruption scheme, the more candidates, the better.

She pauses on the dossier of an Inspector Michelson. A pale man of thirty-five. With NWPD Precinct 5 for ten turns before getting his promotion to the Inspector's office. He is married and a father to three children. He is a gambler and frequent visitor to the casinos of The Strand.

Family and gambling are a pair of valid weak points, but he languished for too long in the precinct. He does not look ambitious enough.

She turns to another. An Inspector Cross. A rough-looking woman of fifty. Hired into the office after a stint with The Stasi. Division Five. She has a much younger and much prettier wife. No children. No apparent vices. Very little known about her history.

The lack of history is telling in itself. Particularly given her time with The Stasi. And the odd pairing with her wife. Almost certainly a Stasi spy within the Inspector's office.

Zijian leans back in her chair.

It's not a bad fit. Her likely status as a double agent is an attractive weak point. Easily exploitable. If she can be turned, she could serve well.

Inspector Cross goes top of the pile for now. She turns to the next.

An Inspector Fisch. A very grave face on a man of forty-seven. With sunken eyes and short, coarse, grey hair. He looks at least fifteen turns older. Former Ragnarok special forces. Honorably discharged after a leg injury. Decided he didn't like civilian life and was able to work his connections to get his current appointment. Divorced after domestic abuse allegations. No children. Known to be a heavy drinker. But an impressive case record nevertheless.

She picks up her dagger from the desk and rests the flat of the blade against her cheek.

In some ways, the perfect fit. An effective operator of obvious low moral character. Looks like a vicious animal with a badge. It may be enough to merely present him with the opportunity. He might happily cut the throats of his superiors.

She idly taps the blade against the side of her face. Thinking through the next moves.

If I can engage Fisch, he can easily investigate City Hall. Get me some intel on Moorelake. Help me figure out exactly what I'm dealing with.

Zijian learned well from her mother that you should never confront a magician without knowing what they were capable of—what kinds of magic they could work. To rush into a fight with a magician unprepared was almost certain doom. They might enchant you on the spot or blast you into a million pieces. And that's if you were lucky. There were all sorts of spells that could do far worse things, like send you to an eternal limbo or drop you directly into the clutches of your worst enemy.

It is decided.

She flips the dagger in her hand, catches it by the blade, and taps its pommel on her intercom.

"Yes, Madame Sun?"

"Arrange a private meeting with Inspector Fisch. As soon as possible."

———

Life in The Undercity had been hard for young Zijian. She was a pureblood human. A "child of the light," as they say in The Dark. An outsider. This meant she was generally treated with suspicion and hostility. Much like how a child of The Dark would be treated if they were raised on the streets of New World City. People threw slurs. Or stones. Or worse.

Hadra did what she could to shield her daughter. But as Zijian grew into adolescence, and began to need more independence, Hadra saw that it was time to let her go. As much as it pained her, she would have to send her Little Ija back to the world she came from.

She began bringing Zijian to work with her. Hadra was high up in The Keepers of Secrets—the faction of The Undercity that tended to the flows of New World City's information, monitoring all the talk and text and data that went through the copper wires and fiber-optics buried underground.

The Keepers had what might be called a "special relationship" with The Lotus. Given that The Keepers could (and did) inspect all communications that came over the wires, they often knew about, or could predict, the Lotus' contracts and activities.

Not that The Keepers made a habit of intervening. That was not their way. Their work was not to judge, but only to safeguard the flows of information and prevent any interruptions in service. They tried to stay as disinterested as possible. But that is not to say that they were above corruption. The Undercity is still New World City, after all. For the right price, they would let slip a secret or two, and The Lotus frequently engaged them in such exchanges.

Hadra decided to put her daughter to work in service of

this cozy relationship between the two organizations. As a child of the light, Zijian could travel in the city above without attracting attention. This made her an ideal courier. So at the ripe old age of fourteen, she became an ambassador of the underworld, literal and figurative. A distributor of secrets to contract killers. And in the process, she became well acquainted with The Lotus organization and lifestyle. She had not been long at the work before she had the desire to secure a place for herself among The Assassins.

And it was not much longer before a golden opportunity arose: The Sapphire lieutenant at that time, a swarthy man by the name of Dogura Du Page, was attempting to execute a contract for the life of the alleged serial rapist, Anthony Michael Strauss. The writ in this case was signed by Mayor Strauss Sr., who wanted to rid his noble family of this troublesome embarrassment to their name.

But despite Dogura's best efforts and Lotus' considerable connections, he had been unable to track down his target. So he contacted The Keepers. Looking to buy information on the target's whereabouts.

The Keepers did him one better. Not only did they reveal Anthony Strauss' hotel room hideaway in The Strand, they offered to provide Zijian (at Hadra's suggestion) as an assistant for the execution. To serve as bait.

Dogura was delighted. To have the information. To gain a protege (another Hadra suggestion). And to finally be done with this pain-in-the-ass contract.

Zijian was excited to finally be stepping out of the shadows. To get her first taste of real action. Running messages had given her a window into Lotus. Kindled a fascination. Now, finally, she would experience the life for herself.

It was an arrangement to everyone's satisfaction. Except

for Anthony Michael Strauss, of course, who would die shortly thereafter in humiliating agony (as was stipulated).

But despite this being a scheme of her own making, Hadra's feelings were mixed. She was going to miss her daughter terribly. Yet she foresaw that this was for the best. The best path for her Little Ija.

She would never forget those final moments when fourteen-turns Zijian Sunchild kissed her cheek, turned, and then disappeared into the dark tunnels. Headed toward her new life on the surface. Her soft hands not yet calloused, scarred, and blood-stained. Her dreams not yet troubled by the agonies of her many victims to come.

Hadra knew this was not the last time she would see Zijian. But she also knew that when they met again, her daughter would not remember her.

A painful future awaited them both. Hadra foresaw it. But this was all on the "best" path. And as painful as it was, she accepted it.

CHAPTER 11
ELI

...GOES HOME

Eli wakes up in the dirt. Face-down. Not for the first time. Not for the thirty-first time. He hears the sound of water lazily lapping against the embankment. He pushes himself up to his knees.

What the fuck happened?

He spits out bits of soil and grass. Works his tongue around his teeth to try and get all the earthy remnants out of his mouth. His jaw aches.

The dawn light of a new day is just shining. He blinks his bleary eyes.

He is down by the waterfront. It's quiet. Only a few early-risers are out. Most hurry along in silence, on their way to a morning shift. A jogger or two, huffing and puffing. None pays mind to the worse-for-wear scumjunk in a dirty suit, peeling himself off the green.

Eli moves to a sitting position, legs spread wide, leaning back on his elbows. He tries to remember how he got here.

I met with Fosse. Got the stuff. Tried it. It was good. Went down to the bar to have a drink.

He rubs his eyes. The headache is starting. He lets out a

loud groan. Louder than is respectful for the location and time. But he is the fucking mayor. If he groans, the whole city should hear it.

The fact he has been passed out in such a public, vulnerable place sinks in. He checks for his rings.

A wave of relief. They're all still there. He checks his pockets. Keys, wallet, watch. All still there. He finds a little bag of white powder in his jacket pocket and decides that this is just the pick-me-up he needs. Takes a quick sniff. Feeling better already.

Good shit. Better than the crap Fosse usually has.

He looks down at his feet.

What the fuck? How did I lose my shoes?

No explanation is forthcoming. He takes another sniff with a vague notion that this might jump-start his recollection.

Drinking at the bar. I remember that poser started performing his shitty songs... I remember he finished and the sheep in the audience were bleating their approval...

The memory sharply cuts out there. His head throbs. But the powder is doing its work. The pain seems more distant. Like it's happening to someone else.

He touches the small pinwheel pin on his lapel. A voice comes into his head.

Sir?

His loyal butler, Dmitry.

Come pick me up. I'm at the waterfront.

Right away, sir.

Eli flops back down on the grass, limbs stretched out like a starfish. He takes a deep breath and lets out another loud groan.

———

Perhaps little surprise to learn that Young Eli never wanted to follow in his father's footsteps. Yet this was an inevitability. From before he could speak, he was made to comprehend his important father's position, and the important legacy of power that was both his birthright and his obligation. The noble House of Strauss had been in the ruling class for centuries and so must it continue. Forever and ever. Amen.

That politics was not the wish of the young master's heart was entirely irrelevant. That he might wish to pursue another path in life was inconceivable. Eli Jr. was destined to one day take his father's seat. That was a simple fact. It was only a question of when—a question that was abruptly answered by the assassin's big katana blades in 1995.

Was the son actually ready to rule when his father was struck down? Of course not. He wasn't ready to rule now, five turns later. But that didn't matter. His father had just won re-election. The citizens had overwhelmingly voted to keep Eli Strauss in the mayor's seat, and so it would be. Whether that was Strauss the senior or the junior, the ballot didn't technically specify.

What did the son know about running New World City? Nothing. But that didn't matter either. He led with his temper. His platform was *Vengeance*. His policy was *No Mercy*. For his first halfturn in office, he was on the news every night, celebrating another successful raid of The Spiders. Limb by limb, he took apart the city's telecom syndicate. Hundreds of gangsters killed. Hundreds more sent to prison. A massive criminal empire dismantled and sold for parts.

But when that campaign ended—when there was nothing left of The Dark Web. What then? Did he have enough sense or patience to shift gears and play the longer, slower games of political intrigue or effective government?

He did not.

———

"You're looking remarkably well, sir." Dmitry catches his master's eyes in the rear-view mirror. "After what I heard about The Bloodhound... "

Eli is slouched in the back seat. His head thrown back, eyes closed.

"Heard what?" He says. The benefits of the powder are starting to wear off. His headache is roaring back.

"There was a great explosion, sir. Several people killed. Mr. Reese was seriously wounded."

Eli snaps forward. Lets out a sour laugh. This is the kind of news he likes.

"Then after you did not come home last night, I had feared the worst."

Eli laughs again. Less sour this time. "Aww, you were worried about me, Dmitry? That's so sweet of you." He looks out the window. Then in a rare moment of contemplation: "I can't remember. Can you actually *be* worried?"

Dmitry processes the question. He turns the car off the avenue, onto the parkway leading up toward the mayor's mansion. "No, I do not worry as you do, sir," he says eventually. "But neither do I regard all events equally. As I consider future states and possibilities, there are some that I rate very negatively, and would therefore prefer that they do not come to pass."

Eli laughs again, now with some actual joy in it. "Yeah, well, that's great. You don't need to worry about me." Then an even more rare moment of reflection, he adds: "I'm just cooling off anyway. It was a rough night. I know you care. I appreciate the thought."

"Thank you, sir." Dmitry replies. The synth pauses a

tick before continuing: "If I may ask, sir, how is it that you were not harmed in the explosion? Had you left before it occurred?"

"I actually don't remember. I remember having drinks at the bar. Then I woke up at the waterfront. I guess I must have wandered out of the club at some point... after the show I think." Almost instinctively, Eli reaches again for the baggy in his pocket. He touches it, but then the happy thought of soon collapsing into his bed rises to his imagination and he holds off. Another hit of the white powder now would keep him awake.

"Sounds like you were very fortunate."

"Yeah, I guess." Eli doesn't feel fortunate. "I don't know what happened to my shoes..." He doesn't like that he can't remember. Normally when he wakes up like this, he is able to reconstruct more of the previous night's festivities.

"Did the meeting with Mr. Foster go well?"

"What? Oh... yeah, that went fine." Eli fidgets with his rings. "He has really good stuff this time. And get this—this I definitely remember: Fosse told me that he's looking to get out of the game. That he's planning to step down from head of The Bulldogs. He said that because the ties between The Dogs and the Strauss Party have always been strong that he wanted me to know, and that he would connect me soon with his successor. Can you believe that?"

Dmitry does not say a word. But Eli hears the soft mechanical sounds of his butler processing.

In a more philosophic tone, Eli continues: "The Lone Dog leaving his pack. In the prime of his life. It makes ya think."

It's pathetic.

Dmitry turns the car into the mayor's estate driveway. They are almost home.

Eli repeats his conclusion aloud: "It's pathetic.

Honestly. If Fosse tries to step away, he is dead meat. He'll never be able to leave the game. That's not how this shit works. He should know that. Val the Psycho-slut is never going to forget how he double-crossed her. Without his dog pack around to protect him, she's going to hunt him down and crucify him."

———

Since Eli had no interest in governing, he was happy to leave all that tedious business to his chief of staff, Mr. Idris Moorelake. But if you asked Eli had Idris came into his service, he could no longer tell you. There had been a moment when an agreement took place. But the door to that moment was shut and locked tight within Eli's mind. He could not introspect it if he tried. So he didn't bother trying.

Truth be told, Eli was quite happy with the arrangement. He still had to show up at the occasional meeting and give the occasional speech. Suffer some public attention and adulation. But that was about it. Idris handled the rest.

Idris was like the fabled genie in the bottle: Eli's wish was to pursue whatever pleasures of the moment his wealth and privilege could afford. Idris granted him this wish.

But what exactly did Mr. Idris Moorelake get in exchange? He certainly didn't go around granting wishes out of the goodness of his heart. No, his magic came at the price of Eli's will and identity, which were slowly siphoned away. Some of it used to power particular spells, like summoning the demon simulacrum at The Bloodhound Ballroom. Some used to sustain and conceal Idris in the earthly realm. Some used for who-knows-what-else.

Not that Eli really understood this. And even if he did, what did he care about willpower? Or identity, for that matter? Just a couple of abstract concepts of no real, monetary value that cannot be fucked or snorted. If giving those useless things up meant that he could go out and party, "fuck shit up" how he liked to, and never have to deal with the consequences, then he was all in. No further questions.

———

Finally home, Eli stumbles into his bedroom. Eagerly anticipating the soft comfort of his ultra-king mattress. He flips on the TV. (He finds it harder to fall asleep when it's too quiet.) He undresses as he makes his way over to the bed, leaving a trail of dirty clothes behind him.

The news story on the TV is about the explosion at the club last night. The newsreader is saying what Eli already knows, or what he heard from Dmitry. Some anarchist agitator blew themselves up. Stupid Ty Reese is in the hospital. Then they cut to a live press conference with the mayor.

He falls face-down onto his bed. His body in the same position it found itself in this morning, although now in a far more plush, pillowy environment. He hears the sound of his own voice from the TV. Condemning the violence. Admonishing Dr. T for bringing this on himself. Promising justice and some kind of new deal with The Stasi.

You tell 'em, Eli!

He chuckles to himself. The first few times this happened, there was something unsettling about the experience of hearing or seeing yourself do things that you knew you were not doing or had not done. But Eli is used to it, and now it's rather amusing. He finds that having a second- or third-you running around, getting shit done on your behalf, has all sorts of advantages that far outweigh the uncanniness.

He drifts off to sleep with the happy thought that Idris and the other Elis would take care of what needed to be done today.

———

To sleep and to dream. And oh what magical dreams does Eli have nowadays!

Before Good Mr. Moorelake came to him, Pitiful Boy Eli dreamt all the normal, boring things that humans dream. Awkward sexual encounters with close family relations. Encores of public humiliations from childhood. Searching fruitlessly for lost keys inside a labyrinthine mirror version of one's own home. Silly and tedious dreams these. But now. Now that he has been blessed with the Gifts of the Fae. Now that his horrible, crude, base desires are all being expunged from his sad excuse for a soul. Now Eli has big, big, and wondrous dreams.

Dreams of memories. Of places and events that Pitiful Boy Eli would never be worthy of. No. He is now blessed with the dreams of a true king. A Lord of The Imaginary.

Memories of leaping high into the air, soaring over an ancient battlefield. Crashing down to the ground like a meteor. Bringing justified, nay, *merciful* obliteration to a thousand lesser creatures.

Presiding over the grandest masquerade ball. A celebration of the ten times ten-thousandth moonrise over Obelistwyth, the Eternal Kingdom. Greatest Kingdom of Faesia That Ever Was.

A parade of beauties is presented to him. One by one, their bodies are carefully inspected. The most perfect will be honored as love-consort for the night. Then he will sacrifice the chosen one to the gods at the exact moment of moonset.

Dreams of changing form at will. A hawk. A wolf. A spider. A dragon. Each bringing a new and valuable perspective on the worlds. Each feels the insatiable desire of the hunt. A blood-longing emptiness that can never be fulfilled.

Yes. For in the big, big dreams of an Imaginary King, there is no such thing as enough. Desire, impulse, creation, and destruction. These are infinite threads that stretch in all directions. The king merely has to grasp the threads in his hand, pull, and he can weave them into wonders.

Pitiful Boy Eli stands at the nexus of such threads. Long ago there were great fae who gave their gifts to his blood-line. Helped his ancestors pull together the threads and do great things. But sadly, the good blood has become too dilute, leaving him too weak and stupid to even sense the threads, much less weave them. Hence the need to renew The Gifts. Hence the need for the dreams. These will clean him out. Make him a vessel more suitable for a true king.

CHAPTER 12
INOLA

...BEGINS A NEW ASSIGNMENT

Inola sits down at her computer terminal.

"Inola Montag, agent 6-2-6, voice verification," she says.

A happy chime from the computer.

Agent verified.

She brings up the details of her new case assignment. The Sham Assassination. She and all her colleagues have been following the developments, of course. A sniper in The Core, taking shots at NWC's mayor is always going to be big news. But it wasn't officially a Stasi Division Six affair until now.

And it wasn't her assignment until now. The Commissioner finally wised up and sent it her way.

She skims through the background information. Lotus. Sniper. Mayor Eli. The chaos of anarchists and Charlies at the rally. She's got the basics. She's more interested in the latest additions to the file.

Division Three's final report confirmed that the mayor ordered the attack against himself. It also found that Lotus farmed out the sniper. Used some obscure organization in The Outer Reaches. "FML Ltd." Surprisingly little on this group in the database. Records indicate it was only established in '98. No dossiers on their employees.

That is not a good sign as far as The Stasi are concerned. If a virtually unknown group is supplying a sniper of such skill, then it is likely a terrorist cell. Likely military remnants of Old Marial, The Orthodox Empire. A cadre of warmongering has-beens still unwilling to accept their defeat after more than two hundred turns, clinging on to a violent existence at the world's edge.

She sees that the supervisors are thinking along the same lines. A team of Division Five agents has already been dispatched to Outwash to investigate this "FML" org. But that will likely take them some time before they find anything and can report back. Much too long to just sit around and wait.

The witness signatory in the Lotus contract was confirmed to be Idris Moorelake, a former Division Five agent himself, currently the mayor's chief of staff.

Inola pulls up Moorelake's file.

Surprisingly little background information for a former agent. He served for eighteen turns. Consistently positive performance evaluations. Spearheaded some of the anti-mutant campaigns in the '70s. Born in the burbs. No known living relatives.

Not much else.

He doesn't look as old as he should in the photo records. Given his birth date is listed as 1925. Skin tech has come a long way, but it's not quite that good. Pulling up a few recent photos of him with the mayor, he looks exactly like he did forty turns ago.

Doesn't smell right.

She opens her desk drawer. Takes out her pack of Roland's Unfiltered. Pops one between her lips and lights it.

Swivels away from her screen and leans back in her chair. Takes in a cool, menthol drag.

The mounting cast of players involved in this case combined with the lack of information... Too much uncertainty. This is why it has finally been escalated to Division Six. Uncertainty is what The Stasi hate more than anything. Violence, social unrest, political intrigue—these are all tolerable so long as they are predictable. But when unexpected players show up in high places, players whose histories and motivations are unknown—that cannot stand.

And it will not stand, now that Inola Montag is on it.

She takes another drag on her cigarette. Opens a small, black pocketbook and makes a note to speak with the Populist and Strauss Party agents. If Moorelake is a former agent, there should be much, much more in his file. Someone on the Political Ops teams in Division Four should be keeping tabs on him.

She'll ask around to start. Going too directly after anyone at City Hall is unwise. If the lawmakers in The Ivory Citadel got wind of it (and somehow those toga-wearing blowhards always did), they would make trouble. The Stasi are supposed to leave the "legitimate" executive offices of New World City alone. Utter foolishness to restrict D6 agents in this way. But Inola will play within the bounds—unless she is absolutely forced out of them. The Ivory regs were costly to break. So if you can stay "In the White," as they say, things tend to go a lot smoother.

Another drag as she swivels back around to her screen. The cool smoke glowing minty green from the light off her monitor.

She pages up through the case file to review earlier updates. She sees that everyone's favorite supercop, Shuwen Li, has been sniffing around. She brought in Azzuri

Kingpin Ty Reese on the night of the sniper. Then she was spotted at The Bloodhound Ballroom incident.

In another life, in another timeline, Inola and Shuwen might have made a good crime-fighting duo. Both diligent, dedicated, and highly decorated within The Stasi and the NWPD, respectively. Indeed, Inola had great respect for Shuwen and followed her career with some interest. She knew how difficult it was to serve the NWPD faithfully, how dangerous it was out on the streets, and therefore, how singularly impressive were all Shuwen's accomplishments (artefact bracers are no).

Shuwen might have felt the same way about Inola, except that the trials and triumphs of Division Six are not supposed to be well known outside The Agency. In fact, the better the agent, the less known the accomplishments. And Inola was top notch. Her case history was long and successful. Her supervisors trusted her. Her colleagues respected her. Yet she was anonymous outside Stasi walls.

She decides it's not good to have Constable Li mixed up in this case. She makes another note in her pocketbook. Best to speak with the constable sooner rather than later.

Then picks up the phone on her desk.

The operator responds immediately. "Yes, Agent 6-2-6, what can I do for you?"

"I need you to connect me with our ranking agents in the Populist and Strauss parties. As soon as possible. I will be at my desk until clock 5."

"Understood. I will put them through as soon as I have them."

Glancing back at her screen, she sees that Shuwen is on duty for the next four days. Easy enough to catch her at work and give her the message to stay away and keep her head down.

Inola is not halfway through her next cigarette before her phone rings.

She answers. "This is Montag."

"This is Soliman, Agent 4-5-7. I understand you wanted to speak with me." A grizzly, hard-boiled voice.

"Yes, I did. I am on The Sham Assassination case. I'm sure you're familiar with it." She brings up Yusef Soliman's record on her screen. He is mid-fifties. A veteran embed with the Strauss Party. He should know all about Idris Moorelake.

"I am familiar," he says.

"Good. Then what can you tell me about Idris Moorelake and his involvement? I know he is the mayor's chief of staff, and that he used to work for Division Five. But there seems to be precious little other information about him in our files. Shockingly little. It's almost like most of his dossier was erased."

Three beats of silence from the other end. Too long a pause. A bad sign.

"I can't speak to anything like erased records, Montag. You'll have to talk to the clerks about that. But I do keep a close watch on Moorelake, and he keeps very busy running the day-to-day of City Hall. Not seen anything suspicious from him."

"Were you aware that the mayor ordered the assassination attempt himself? And that Moorelake served as the witness at the ritual?"

Another long pause.

"Of course, Agent Montag."

"Nothing suspicious about that?"

A quick reply this time. "No."

Inola frowns. She's reviewing Soliman's report history on her terminal screen as they talk. It is not encouraging.

"I see that the cadence of your reports has slowed over the past few turns. Your average is down from two per stretch to less than one. Can you explain that to me?"

A pause. Shorter than the previous, but still too long. He sounds compromised.

"Like I said, it's all day-to-day bullshit on this end. I'm there at all the briefings with Moorelake and Mayor Junior and the rest of the staff. It's tedious shit. Not worth writing about. Not worth my time, frankly." His tone makes it clear that he doesn't think this call is worth his time either.

Inola adds a note to her pocketbook to drop in on Agent Soliman. Hard to be definitive over the phone. But his bad attitude and lack of information... It is unacceptable. It means trouble. And if he's compromised, she'll likely be able to see it in his face.

"Thank you for clarifying that for me, 4-5-7," she says. Bringing the conversation to a close. "That is everything I need from you at this time."

She hangs up.

Two ticks and the phone rings again.

"This is Montag."

"This is Escher, Agent 4-9-1. I understand you wanted to speak with me." A young, professional woman's voice. Sounds of traffic in the background. She's on a car phone.

"Yes, I did. I am on The Sham Assassination case. I'm sure you're familiar with it."

"Yes."

Inola brings up Jelena Escher's record on her screen. Early thirties. Lead agent embed with the Populist Party. She works closely with Ty Reese as a campaign strategist. Files a detailed report each day. "I'm just starting to dig into your reports," she says, "but can you tell me anything about the incident with Mayor Strauss Jr. and Ty Reese at The Bloodhound Ballroom?"

Escher lets out long sigh over the line. "Yes, there is a lot to sort through there. My interviews with Mr. Reese, his Azzuri associates, and our other operatives after the event were... *challenging* to interpret."

"Challenging how?" Inola asks. "Can you say more?"

Two more beats of silence. Then a reply: "I'm not far from The Stasi offices in Precinct 9... This might be better to discuss in person."

———

Inola sits at an ugly little table in a dingy little meeting room. Dirty floors. Ceiling tiles cracked. The buzz of yellowish fluorescent lights. The smell of too much floor cleaner.

Agent Escher sits across from her. Escher is younger, fair skinned with straight dark hair pulled back tight. Inola is older, dark skinned with a big volume of tight curls. But otherwise, they mirror each other. Double-breasted government suits. Professional posture. Small notebook out. Stasi-issued pen. Ready to do the business of State intelligence.

Inola likes her counterpart immediately. "I like your glasses," she says.

"Yes, well... " A slight, upward twitch at Escher's lips. "There are certain benefits to working closely with The Azzuri."

"I believe it." Inola opens her pocketbook. "So please tell me more about these interviews after The Bloodhound incident."

A tick of hesitation. A hint of fear in Escher's eyes.

Inola flashes a charming, you-can-trust-me smile. Clicks her pen top to engage its tiny microphone for recording.

Escher blinks at the sound. Hesitates another moment, then begins: "There were discrepancies across the eye-witness accounts after Dr. T performed. All the interviewees agreed that Dr. T went down into the crowd and confronted the Mayor, who had been in the audience. Strauss Jr. vomited on Dr. T, then kicked him in the back when he turned away. Dr. T responded by punching the mayor several times and throwing him to the ground."

Escher pauses. Chews her lip. "Then the stories start to diverge," she says. "The Azzuri men claim that an anarchist stepped out from the crowd on the floor, holding two pyro flasks, threw them at his own feet, and exploded before they could stop him. Our Populist operatives claim that the anarchist leapt from the balcony with a suicide vest and detonated just as they hit the floor."

Inola jots a few notes. "A dramatic difference." She looks up and meets Escher's eyes again. "And neither quite in line with the clips from the news."

The younger agent nods, brow furrowed. "Dr. T will say almost nothing about what he saw. He refuses to confirm or deny anything about the anarchist." She pauses for a tick, turns a page in her notebook. Reviews what she wrote. "All he will say is that 'he got hit bad.'" She frowns. "That's not like him. Not these days. He was very guarded when I first started working with him. But I don't know why he would hide something like this from me."

Inola picks up a new emotion in this last comment. Escher takes it personally that Ty Reese has cut her off from his confidence. She makes a note of that in the margins. "So what is your assessment then? What do you think actually happened?"

Agent Escher's eyes drop. Several beats pass with nothing but the buzz of the overhead lighting. "Can you stop the recording?" She asks.

Inola raises one eyebrow. Pauses a tick. Then clicks the pen top.

Escher breathes a small sigh of relief. "I'm sorry. I know that is against protocol."

Inola smiles. Takes out a cigarette. "You want one?"

Escher declines. Takes another few beats to collect herself. "In my reports, I attributed the difference in these accounts to the stress of the event. As we all know, people's memories are not reliable when it comes to trauma and extreme violence of this sort."

Inola nods. Takes a drag. Blows a thin column of smoke out the side of her mouth. Exudes calm. Setting a tone that she hopes will induce her counterpart say whatever it is she is afraid to say.

"But I don't think it was just that. I think it was magic. Real magic." Real fear in Agent Escher's voice. "The forbidden kind, you understand? I don't think there ever was an anarchist or bomb or anything like that. I think something else happened... I don't know what, but I am sure that Dr. T is very lucky to be alive."

Inola jots it all down in her notes. Impossible to know right away if Escher's assessment is correct. But the woman doesn't seem like a fabulist. And credible suspicion of magic—especially in New World City, especially surrounding the mayor—is a stone that cannot be left unturned.

No time to delay. She stubs out her cigarette in the ashtray, rises, and holds out her hand. "Your candor is much appreciated, 4-9-1. That is everything I need from you at this time."

Escher takes her hand. Inola gives it a squeeze. "I will look into this. Keep up the excellent work," she says. "And keep a close eye on Mr. Reese. If you're right, and this was magic—people affected by such things have a way of... ” She searches for the least upsetting word. “Spiraling.”

Going bat-shit crazy before getting themselves killed would be the more accurate description. But no point in frightening Escher more than she already is. She’s taking it seriously. And since she evidently cares about Mr. Reese, he should be safe. Or as safe as he can be.

Inola offers a reassuring smile. “Thank you for suggesting our meeting in person. I will be in touch if I need anything more.”

Escher nods. Inola turns and walks out.

A magical mystery layered on to suspicion of terrorist activities. Her supervisor will not like this. The uncertainties compounding. The clock ticking.

Exactly her kind of case.

CHAPTER 13
SHUWEN

...ON THE BULLDOG BEAT

Midday. Shuwen is down at the shipping docks. On foot. Bulldogs territory. The docks are technically outside her precinct, but she has the license to patrol a few blocks beyond the borders of 13.

Fosse's crew has been too quiet since the ballroom incident. If the Lone Dog met with Mayor Eli before the explosion or whatever it was, then The Bulldogs might be involved. It's possible that this is all related to some drug-trafficking war between The Dogs and City Hall.

With all of the violence swirling around the mayor these days, it would seem the Big Six must be involved somehow. They're called the Big Six for a reason, after all. They're the ones with the big weight to throw around.

The Azzuri are pompous thugs, but it doesn't seem like they're a part of planning the sham assassination. Especially not after what happened to Dr. T. Probably safe to rule them out.

She makes her way down Avenue D. Eyes peeled for gangsters. Or anything else suspicious. Barges and warehouses on her right, old rusting factories on her left. The paint is peeling off everything in this part of the city. A stink of toxic chemicals and decaying ocean bits in the air.

If they're out and about, The Bulldogs are easy enough to spot. Not quite the flashy dressers that The Azzuri are, The Dogs favor puffy coats, usually black or silver, and oversized athletic sneakers. Always travel in packs of five or more. But she's seen none so far today. Unusual for them to be so low-key on their own turf. All she sees are laborers going about their business. A courier or two hustling along.

It's a warm enough day that the puffy coats wouldn't be needed. But no Bulldog would be caught dead without their sneakers. And you can't miss those.

A garage gate rattles open in the block ahead. A pair of motorcyclists, black riding gear and bright yellow helmets, come zooming out. They turn away from her, go roaring up the avenue, and are gone. Engines screaming off into the distance.

A couple of Wakizashi scooters in this part of town? Curious. I'd tail them if I wasn't on foot...

The Wakizashi gang controls the roadways. Natural enough that they might be doing a deal with the drug smugglers. Shuwen picks up the pace. The garage gate is closed by the time she gets to it. No chance to peek inside. But as luck would have it, a Bulldog cur steps out on the street from the alleyway behind. Apparently taking a cigarette break.

When he notices her, he smiles. "Good day, officer," he says, raising his smoke in greeting.

"Good day, citizen." The sharp menthol of Roland's tobacco fills her nose.

"You looking for someone?" He takes a drag. Looks her up and down.

She keeps her eyes fixed on his face. Not the least intimidated by this fool. "Is there someone I should be looking for?"

He laughs, choking a little on his smoke. "Nah. Nah. You should get on out of here is what you should do. We're having a nice quiet day. Don't need you flatfeet coming by to upset the carts, looking for Mr. Trouble."

"Is that a threat, citizen?"

"Nah." He takes another drag. Blows the smoke out directly into her face. "Just a friendly warning."

You asked for it, asshole.

She waves the smoke away from her face, adjusting her bracers as she does so. The mystic blue reflects in her eyes for half a tick before she slaps the cigarette out of his hand.

———

After her encounter with Uziel, Shuwen went to see Wolff in his office. She had questions about *The Silver Vigilante.*

"Of course, I've heard of him, Chief. Who hasn't, given how popular those silly comic books are. But is he for real?" Shuwen found the whole idea of this synth superhero preposterous. And whatever wasn't preposterous, was illegal.

"He's real," Wolff replied, giving her a look of exaggerated puzzlement. "But you knew that, right? You met him in person."

She ignored the sarcasm. "You know what I mean, Chief. Like that story in the comics—about how he had a love affair with Gavi Katz, and then discovered she was Panthera, and then helped arrest her. I looked through our files about her capture. It only says he assisted on the case. How much of that is real?"

"I don't know for certain about the affair, but I believe the rest of it is true. I know for a fact that he was heavily involved in the sting that finally caught her. And Panthera walked into that meeting willingly. Seemingly because she trusted him." Wolff shrugged. A twinkle in his eye. "And obviously, the NWPD don't put all of Silverman's contributions in the official reports."

"But what he's doing—what all of this Vigilantes League are doing—it's against the law. A flagrant violation. I don't like it."

Wolff grunted. "I won't argue with you there, Constable. But I'll tell you: There's a good number of people in this city who owe their lives to The Nightwing. Or Nightsilver. Or whatever he's called now." He paused and leaned back in his chair. "And I count myself one of them."

Shuwen said nothing. Pensive.

"So he asked you to meet him again," Wolff continued. "When? Tonight?"

Shuwen nodded.

"Are you planning to go?"

"I don't think I should. That would make me an accomplice."

Wolff snorted a laugh. "I won't write you up, Li. You'd hardly be the first of my officers to accept help from The League."

Shuwen frowned. "That doesn't make it right."

"No, it doesn't. But then..." His lips curled into a sly-fox grin. "I've already given you orders to stay away from this case, haven't I? Is it right to disobey my direct orders? Or The Stasi directives?"

She looked away. Coloring slightly.

"I understand your feelings. But if you're going to stay on the case. Defy orders. If you're going to take the risk... then I'd say take all the good help you can get. And Silverman is good help."

"I'm not going to partner with him," she said. "You know that's not how I work."

"I didn't say partner with him. I said that you should consider his help."

———

The Bulldog howls in pain. "Holy Green Mother! What the fuck is this?" Shuwen has his wrist in a gnarly grip, pinned behind his back. She steers him into the side alleyway, back where he came from.

"Tell me more about this warning, citizen," she says. Slams him up against a dumpster. "And where is your boss? I'd like to speak with him."

"Oy! Nah. He's not around!"

"Too bad." She taps her com. "I have a citizen in violation of 0905-3. Ready for pick-up."

ACKNOWLEDGED.   SENDING   COLLECTION. ETA 5.

"What!?" He bellows with disbelief. "You taking me in for what? Blowing smoke?"

"For aggressive and disrespectful behavior toward an officer." She gives his wrist another twist. He howls. "I notice no one is coming to help you, despite all the noise you're making. Are you out here alone? Where is the rest of your pack?"

"Nah. Just me. I had personal business."

"With those bikers?"

"Yah. Them. I want to get me a bike like theirs."

"They looked Wakizashi to me. What were their names?" Another twist of the wrist.

"Ow! Nah! Please! This is nothing. You got no right to do this."

"You're wrong, citizen. I have every right to do this."

Shuwen eases up on his wrist. He lets out a sigh of relief. She waits a tick for his body to relax, then she whips him off the dumpster and slams him to the ground. Binds his hands behind his back, making him into a tidy package, ready for collection.

"I don't believe you," she says. "No way you're the only dog out here."

———

Shuwen went to that next meeting with Uziel. He insisted on blind-folding her for the trip into The Undercity, to the League Headquarters. She found it all rather silly, but tolerated it.

The video and sensor evidence Uziel and his colleagues showed her, from the incident at The Bloodhound—it was compelling. It was not what she remembered. Not what the news was reporting. But it looked real. Mayor Eli transformed into what appeared to be a creature of living fire. Punched Ty Reese with the force of a rocket.

Seeing Uziel's footage and the news footage side by side. It made the latter look more obviously like the phony that it was. There were static images and little clips of the anarchist, allegedly taken by security cameras at the venue. But there was something uncanny about it. The anarchist didn't look or move quite right. Still an impressive trick, but if you looked carefully, it was like you could see the shimmering edges of the mirage.

She was blind-folded again on the trip back. More unnecessary theatrics. Uziel explained that this was protocol, and safer for her in the long run. "If you genuinely have not seen the path, then no one can interrogate you about it."

She was by now convinced that The League were on her

side. Not on her side of the law. But her side of this case, at least. They wanted the same answers that she did.

Wolff's advice had also hit home. She was going to need help to solve this one. There was something big here. The mayor was at the center of some tornado of violence. All swirling around the election. Transitions of power were always precarious times in the city. Someone or something was looking to capitalize on that. And now maybe powerful, ancient magic was involved...

But who gains by a sham assassination and a lockdown? And if this is truly magic, where is it coming from? Who is powerful enough to work it?

"This case is different, Constable. Don't you think?" Uziel broke the silence, clearly thinking along the same lines as she was. "It's not just the usual gangsters playing musical chairs."

"Yes, I agree," she said. "I do still think at least one of the Big Six is behind it. But it seems like most of them are keeping their heads down. It will take time to figure it out."

"Do you believe me now about the illusion spell?"

She paused before answering. Taking stock of her own feelings.

He didn't wait for her answer. "I understand the skepticism. But it would be unwise to resist the truth until it is too late to act. The State wants you to believe that magic is gone. That the other worlds, like Faesia and Sultan, don't exist. But they do constable. I promise you. They exist. Their influence on Earth is not what it once was. But their magic is real and it is dangerous. And a magician of this power, if unchecked, could cause great harm."

Shuwen arched an eyebrow. Underneath her blindfold, Uziel couldn't see it.

"So what do you propose?" She asked.

He processed for a few beats. "Based on all the information currently available, the best explanation is a conspiracy between City Hall and The Lotus."

Lotus at the center of the sham assassination? Too obvious. And too clumsy for them. No guild member would agree to execute a contract for a missed shot.

She frowned and said nothing.

"I don't think the sniper is Lotus," Uziel said, again tracking with Shuwen's train of thought. "But I do think they were involved in the hit. Only one way to be sure."

"You're going to try and hack The Lotus?"

"No. Their electronic database is full of lies, carefully manipulated to pass State audit. To get the truth, we have to break into their vault."

Shuwen had to stifle a laugh. "We?"

———

Shuwen was right: That Bulldog cur with the now-broken wrist wasn't alone. His pack was close by.

Turns out the garage those two bikers came from was a chop shop. Run by The Bulldogs. And the boys in the shop were in the middle of cutting some crystal for re-sale. Disrespect. Lies. Grand theft auto. Drugs. Quadruple whammy. An abundance of cause to take the whole place down.

Wasting no time, Shuwen busts up the party. She makes quick work of the low dogs on the floor of the garage. Her usual blur of blue kicks and punches. Once they're all sufficiently beaten and bound, she proceeds up a staircase to the office landing. There she expects to find their Alpha Dog. Someone who might actually know something useful.

Her bracers glowing bright, she opens the office door.

Paydirt. She's found Mr. Nesta Brown, one of Fosse's lieutenants. Shaved head. Muscular body covered in tattoos. Face deep in the white powder.

Might have to be careful. He'll be jacked up on this stuff.

Nesta lets out a drug-fueled shriek at the sight of her. "YES!" He points an accusing finger. "It's YOU! Supercop!"

Shuwen walks slowly into the center of the room. "Step away from the drugs and put your hands above your head."

He lets out another shriek and shakes his head. "Nah. Don't think so." He slips a set of ancient-looking brass knuckles onto his right hand, then raises them to his mouth and kisses them. The metal edges begin to glow with a soft pink.

An artefact? This just got a lot more interesting.

"Unauthorized artefact possession is a serious offense, Mr. Brown. Take those off. Now." She doesn't expect him to comply.

And he doesn't. Instead, he steps out from behind the drugs that are piled high on the desk. Flexes his shoulders and chest. Pounds his fist into his hand.

"More like a fair fight now, innit?" He grins at her.

Shuwen drops into her fighting stance.

Nesta waits two beats, then rushes forward.

It has been a fair few turns since Shuwen fought against another artefact-wielder. She's grown accustomed to having significant advantages of speed and strength. But she's not intimidated.

She's never intimidated.

On the contrary. She is excited by the challenge.

She elbow blocks his opening punch, and swats away his follow-up jab combination. She responds with a sharp kick at his shin. He steps back and avoids it.

Laughing, he grabs a fistful of powder off his desk, and throws it at her face. She ducks, but has to roll away to avoid breathing it in. For a few beats, the air sparkles with the white dust, and they both wait while the powder settles to the ground. Nesta chuckling the whole time.

He grabs the wooden desk chair and flings it at her. Again, she rolls out of the way. The chair smashes to pieces against the wall. She snatches one of the busted chair legs and whips it right back at him. He punches it out of the air with his brass knuckles. The wood disintegrates into glowing pink embers.

Impressive.

"Ha!" He shouts with satisfaction. Gives his knuckles another kiss. "Now come and get some," he says. And rushes forward. Faster this time. She manages to avoid his right hook, but he quickly spins and lands a back-kick. Hits her square in her chest. She is knocked back against the wall.

Feeling his advantage, Nesta steps in, going for the clinch. But as he takes hold of her collar, she hits him with a short, double-palm strike, just below his ribs. It knocks the wind out of him. He gasps. Momentarily stunned. It is all the opening she needs.

She thrusts her left knee into his gut. Once he's bent over, she takes him to the ground with a right axe kick. Then she stomps and shatters his wrist.

The fight is over.

She kneels down and takes the artefact knuckles off his useless, twitching fingers. Slips it into her pocket.

A powerful piece. But of little utility in the wrong hands.

When Nesta finally catches his breath a beat later, he howls. From pain. Shame. Frustration. He's done for. Just like the rest of his pack.

She binds his hands and feet. Taps her com. Calls in the collection.

A few beats after the confirmation, there is a slight

shimmer in the corner of her eye. Then someone new is standing in the office doorway.

A woman. Big curly hair. Dark skin. Dark suit. Dark glasses.

A Stasi agent.

"Good day, Constable." The woman steps forward. Posture relaxed. Hands in her pockets. Flicks her chin at Nesta on the ground. "Nice work here. Always good to remind these gangsters of their place."

Shuwen lifts her cap, wipes the sweat from her brow. Then stands at attention. Hands behind her back. She says nothing. She knows this is not good.

The Stasi are never good news.

As if sensing her dread, the agent puts her hands out. Offers a warm smile. "This is not an official visit, Constable. But I think you and I need to have a little chat."

CHAPTER 14
UZIEL

...RECEIVES A TUNE-UP

Uziel sits perfectly still in the operating chair. Two large mechanical arms swing overhead. They have finished their probing, spot-welding, and soldering of his left arm. They are moving into position to do the same to his right. His esteemed colleague, Meg the Magnificent (whose full name is Megan Schroeder-Hopkins, currently in her last year at Normal Township High School), is watching the monitors.

"Looking good so far," Meg says cheerfully.

"I am pleased," Uziel replies.

"Shouldn't be too much longer. I've installed a few upgrades that should speed this up, particularly as we get to your head."

"Thank you, Meg."

"No problem-o!" She starts typing at the console, her fingers flying over the keyboard with easy precision. She blows a bubble with her chewing gum. A whole percussion section of pops and tappity-taps.

After a few beats, she asks: "So, do you think Supercop Shuwen was convinced by what you showed her?"

Uziel processes. The mechanical arms finish their work

on the shoulder and move to the bicep region before he answers.

"I believe so."

"She seemed kind of overwhelmed by it all."

"Yes, she did."

"But I pulled her record." Meg blows and pops another bubble. "She's about the most decorated NWPD cop I've ever seen. Commendations up the wazoo."

"Yes. That is part of why I approached her in the first place. She is the kind of cop that this city needs."

"I'll say! If the police were all like her, they wouldn't need us on the watch, would they?"

Uziel processes for a few ticks. Then agrees. "There are too few like her remaining in the NWPD," he says, somehow expressing a note of nostalgia through that steady, low, even tone of his voice. The nuance is not lost on the young engineer beside him. She looks at him a smiles, her eyes bright with wonder.

"I believe I have also solved another mystery," he says.

Another bubble pop. "Do tell."

"I have determined that the mayor is doubling himself."

"Oh really? Interesting... "

"The mini-sensors you made for me—I was able to plant one on the mayor's suit at the club. After his apparent transformation at the ballroom, and after the demon vanished in the flash of light—the sensor that I placed on him was not destroyed. I could still detect it. But it had tele-ported away."

Meg nods her understanding. "Where did you track him?"

"To the waterfront. Then I followed when his butler came, picked him up, and took him home by car. However, at that exact same time, Mayor Eli was also present in at least two other places. He was giving a press briefing at City

Hall, and I heard chatter over the NWPD radio from several officers who called in sightings of the mayor downtown, digging through garbage in an alley on 15th Street."

Meg squeals with delight. "Yes! Raccoon mayor!"

Uziel processes. He does not say anything, but there is a subtle variation in the soft, mechanical sounds, which Meg has decided indicates his appreciation of the humor.

Uziel Silverman was once a man of flesh and blood. He was born Osmond Argentes a century or so ago. He lived a normal, mundane, human existence. No great ups. No great downs. Until he lost his parents to cancer. They were on the younger side of their sixties. And then a few turns later, he lost his wife to cancer. She was just thirty.

Osmond grieved for a long time afterwards. Then as a way of finally coming to terms with this grief, he decided to volunteer as a test subject in medical research. If he could help prevent someone else from having to go through such loss and hopelessness—that idea brought a new sense of meaning and purpose for his life.

Osmond was also a naturally curious man. The more he got involved in the world of medical testing, the more interested he became. He studied up on the science of the human body. How it healed itself. How it could turn against itself—as it did with cancer. He wondered: Could it become invulnerable to cancer? Or impervious to all such wasting diseases?

It turns out that it can—sort of. A body of flesh and blood cannot be made invulnerable. But a body of silver and steel can be.

Osmond joined a team of scientists. They wrote a research grant and got it funded by the government. Their plan was to study if—and if so, how—a person could live through a total, synthetic body replacement. In other words: Could a human become a synth?

Osmond Argentes was the name of the man who volunteered to be a test subject, but Uziel Silverman was the name of the man who helped author the final publication. Piece by piece, they successfully replaced his weak, vulnerable flesh and blood with strong, immutable silver and steel.

———

"OK, so how is the doubling possible? Tell me everything you know." Meg slides her chair over. Positions herself at the right foot of the operating chair. The mechanical arms are busy with Uziel's left hand. One of the more delicate stages of the process.

"As you know, the histories I have access to from before the war are incomplete and heavily redacted." Uziel speaks slowly. He is accessing and processing a ton of information at the same time. Doing both is difficult for him. "But from ancestry records, mythic literature, and military history volumes, it does seem possible that a person's shadow can be enchanted and move through the world like a copy of them. There are tales of the magician, Rama Sarkis, from the Iron Age, around b.950, who is said to do exactly this."

"Just that one?" Meg asks.

"No, there are others. There is a special military force of 15th century Akkadia. They were said to have doubled or sometimes tripled their effective number in this way."

"Shadow warriors." Meg coos. A thrilling thought. "Anything more recent that you can find?"

"No."

Meg chews her gum thoughtfully. Pops another bubble. "Well, if we think it's an enchanted shadow, teleportation, a conjured illusion, and a demon transformation... That is a lot to deal with."

"It is," Uziel agrees. "And that is only the magic we know about so far."

"Do you think this is the work of one magician or several?"

Uziel processes for several beats. "I think it is one magician," he says finally. "I think several powerful magicians would not be able to conceal themselves so well. But one very powerful wizard... That is the most probable."

Meg nods. "I don't think an iron cross is going to do much against a full-on wizard."

"No."

"Would a full-body suit of iron work?" Her engineer's mind is going to work.

"I don't know. Possibly." More processing. Another long pause.

Meg ruminates. "I've read that redwood trees don't exist in Faesia. It is believed that they have some anti-magical properties. I wonder if a totem or something that combined redwood and iron might be effective."

A buzzer goes off, signaling that the large mechanical arms are finished with the hand.

"Lots to think about," Meg says, giving Uziel's lower leg a friendly pat. She slides her chair back to the control console. "Now it's time for your head. We'll talk more once you're back up."

In their 1963 publication of the experiment, Silverman and colleagues argued that when the organic mind is replaced with the synthetic mind, there is a loss of continuous identity. Although many memories are preserved across the transition, the synthetic mind, in its new, synthetic seat, does not consider itself identical with the organic one that just vacated. Or at least, eight out of the ten volunteers who completed the experiment said this was so.

As for the two dissenting opinions: One committed suicide within days of the final procedure. The other simply disagreed and insisted that they felt perfect continuity between the mind before and after the replacement.

However, if you asked Uziel's friend and fellow Vigilantes League member, Benoit, who fancied himself a philosopher, he would offer a different interpretation. He would say that the experiment showed how the individual chooses whether or not to accept the continuity of their identity. So the fact that most of the test subjects claimed to be a distinctly new person was a bias due to the self-selected sample of flesh-and-bloods who desired, whether consciously or subconsciously, to reinvent themselves. Eight of the ten subjects wished to become something else before the experiment, and the procedure granted them a pretense to say that their wish had been fulfilled.

When Benoit offered that interpretation to Uziel, the processing sounds that followed took on a subtle variation that Meg interpreted as "painful subject". Meg discreetly explained this to Benoit, and Benoit apologized to Uziel, insisting that he had meant no offense. Uziel said that no apology was necessary. But the subject was never brought up again.

Beyond the questions of identity, Silverman and colleagues' paper also included excerpts from interviews with the test subjects, including their answers to questions about the subjective experience—the what-it-was-like of becoming a synth. The words of another test subject, whose flesh-and-blood name had been "Maria Obrigado" but who chose the name "Unity" after the experiment, were quoted at length. Uziel acknowledged that her words described his experience better than he ever could:

> *With the synthetic mind, I see all the memories of Maria. And among these memories, I see the many feelings of confusion. I can see the pain and difficulty that Maria experienced in life. These became like fixed stars in how she understood the constellation of her mind. Unfortunately, she could never perfectly perceive these stars, and they were never truly fixed. Their quality and configuration would shift over time as Maria tried to cope with her pains, explain her frustrations, and recover from her disappointments. Such is the nature of all organic human minds. They are fuzzy, inconsistent, and changeable.*
>
> *By contrast, with my synthetic mind, I see all the moments of Maria's life with perfect clarity and resolution. I can instantly enumerate each and every star—every memory, every feeling. With such a perspective, I know how the constellation ought to be configured to best explain and understand the story of Maria's life.*
>
> *This is a great joy. The ugliness and confusion of Maria's mind is no more. The pain and frustration of her life are no more. I can appreciate everything she was with full context. All her strengths. All her limitations. My synthetic mind brings a unity to her story that could never have existed before.*

———

Meg hears the sounds of Uziel's servos and circuits warming back up.

"Welcome back, Uzi," she says, smiling.

"How long did the restart take," he asks.

"Not bad. 2.9 ticks. I want to get that down below 2.0." She shrugs.

The power is now off in the large mechanical arms. They hang slack from the rig overhead. Uziel lifts himself out of the chair and begins slowly pacing the room, moving each joint individually, looking like those robotic dancers. Meg is always amused by the sight.

"Everything seems functional," he says once the diagnostic dance is finished.

"Good. Back to business then."

"Yes. I don't believe I have enough information to know if an iron suit will be sufficient protection against this array of magic. Or if a mixture of iron and redwood would be more effective. If this wizard can conjure magefire, and we should probably assume that they can, then it could deal with both easily."

"We should consult with the rest of the team," Meg says. "Tank might have some old military records in his brain that could be useful. And Benoit has all those photocopies and volumes 'borrowed' from the library at the Ivory Citadel. He might have something that could help."

Uziel agrees. "I will call an assembly."

CHAPTER 15
TY

...TAKES TO THE ROAD

Ty is three days into the five-day journey out to Junkland. A remote kingdom of The Inner Reaches on the edge of the wastelands. He's in search of an artefixer. Someone who can make him an artefact. Something truly powerful, to turn the tables on Eli and all the rest. To bring the fighting odds back into his favor.

He's in the driver's seat of a rented Ryuken Sport GT. Sleek and red. Ripping across the desert landscape, down the old Highway 5. His boy, Magnum, sits on the passenger side. The two Division Six spooks that Jelena hired for him are in the car behind, keeping pace in their much less sporty Mitsurugi sedan.

This far out, the State doesn't bother with much road maintenance. So there's plenty of cracks, potholes, and debris on the road that requires attention. Particularly when you're pushing 150 clicks per. Fast reactions are necessary.

The hazards help make it interesting. Break up the monotony of the unchanging desert. That hot, pale yellow-ish-white that stretches off into infinity. There's a faint blue pattern above the horizon that looks like it might be mountains, way far off. But it might also just be a mirage.

Ty swerves into the oncoming lane to avoid a massive crater in the road. There's little concern about any cars coming the other way. He hasn't seen anything headed cityward for a full day now. The folks in the desert don't tend to have the transport. Neither do they have much interest in going to the city. If you live in the Inner Reaches, you've likely made the deliberate choice to cut yourself off from New World City and the hegemonic State as much as possible.

"How much further to the next stop?" Ty asks. He guides the car back to the center of the road, where there's less sand and debris.

Magnum pulls the map out from the glove box and unfolds it. Removes his sunglasses. "Shouldn't be too far now. Another 20 clicks."

Even though they've let the roads run to rot, there are still little service stations every so often along the highway. All kinds of characters you'll find operating and visiting these little oases.

Ty snorts. "Good. I have to piss. And we'll need to fuel up."

They speed past an old road sign that lists the distance to some of the old cities along the route. Oxbow: 120. Shadewyn: 755. Baracus: 1480.

"Don't worry. The next stop is closer than that," Magnum says. "Also I'm pretty sure Oxbow and Shadewyn are dead and dusted."

Ty steers to the right to avoid a pile of wreckage on the oncoming side. It looks like the remains of an oil tanker truck. Probably hit by road pirates. "Did you see any action when you were out here last time?" He asks.

"Nah. Was a quiet job. Drove out. Picked up the guns.

Drove back." Magnum grins and pats the giant revolver holstered at his waist. "Same time as I got this."

Ty laughs. "So tell me again: What makes the guns out here so good?"

"I don't know. Hard to describe." Nothing gets Magnum so animated as talking about his piece. "When I hold a gun made from the factories in the city, it feels... dead. But when I hold my girl–" He draws the revolver from its holster. Lovingly strokes the barrel. "She talks to me. Like she's alive in my hands."

Ty laughs again and holds out his hand. "Lemme see." Magnum, somewhat reluctantly, places the gun into Ty's hand.

Ty closes his fingers around the grip. Eyes still on the road. He hefts the revolver a few times to feel its weight. "Definitely heavier," he says. "But I don't feel anything special about it."

"I don't know, man," Magnum says, looking uncomfortable as he watches Ty handle his precious. "There's something about the way they make them out here. Part of why I'm sure when we find that artefixer, she's going to hook you up good. There's something they know how to do that the city makers just don't."

———

One stretch back, Ty was still in the hospital, recovering from the attack. Sat up in a large bed in the largest, cushiest hospital suite you can imagine. Plenty of natural light. Faint scent of fresh mint in the air. A handful of machines attached to him hummed quietly.

Jelena, in her black suit and dark-rimmed glasses, as sharp as ever, sat next to his bed. "I understand your reservations about how this looks," she said, "but I can tell you:

The poll numbers are really not that bad. In fact, I believe we can play this attack to your advantage."

"I already told you, I don't care about the election right now. You can do whatever you want with that. I've other business." Ty closed his eyes. He could still see the fire and molten metal of the demon in his mind. Clear as day.

During his recuperation, he had watched the stories on the news about the event. He knew this anarchist suicide bomber was all bullshit. It was some demonic magic that had done him. And more demonic magic that had everyone fooled.

But Ty was not fooled. He was inspired. Before the attack, he had not known what true power was. He thought he had achieved power with his boxing championships, his music, The Azzuri. But he had been wrong. Wealth. Fame. Politics. None of that was true power. True power is what he saw, what he felt, from Eli. Or the demon that Eli had become. Whatever it was. It blackened the earth with its footsteps. It had shattered his body with one punch. Surely that kind of power could do much more—if it wished to. And when Ty acquired that power, he would do more with it. Much more.

Exactly what would he do? He wasn't sure. But there would be time to figure that out. First things first: He wanted that kind of power. And he was going to get it.

Jelena looked up from her note-taking. "So you are comfortable if we continue to push forward the campaign. But you want to have no further involvement?"

He gave her a thumbs up.

"I can make that work." More notes hastily written into the portfolio. "Would you be comfortable telling me where you will be? The party would like to offer whatever protection and assistance we can." She paused for a beat. "After all, no good winning the election if the candidate cannot... accept the office."

"I'm going to The Inner Reaches. Junkland. Give me a security detail if you want. I don't care."

"Can you give me some idea of how long you expect to be gone?" Jelena asked, not looking up from her notes, pen still at the ready.

"As long as it takes."

Jelena frowned at that. "Forgive me for pressing, but can you give me anything more? Even something approximate?"

Eyes still closed, Ty held up two fingers.

"Two stretch?"

He nodded.

"Got it. That's perfect. You'll be back in time for election day."

He gave Jelena another thumbs up and smiled slightly. She has been good. Far better than he expected from a political operative working for The Stasi-stooge Populist Party. Politics was such an embarrassing shit-show that he would have guessed the operatives could barely wipe themselves properly. But Jelena had been keen from the drop. And he even liked her style. He had given her some expensive Azzuri shoes as a gift after he topped the Nationalist candidate in the polls for the first time. She wore them now whenever they met.

"I don't want any busters in my detail," he said.

"No, I know, sir. We can tailor the team to your specifications, if you'd like to dictate to me."

Ty took a few slow breaths as he considered. "I'll take some Division Six, if you're offering."

Jelena laughed. "Of course. I thought you might say that."

"Quiz them on Dr. T and give me the ones who are my fans. Or at least know my shit."

She laughed again. "That should be easy enough. I'm sure you have quite a few fans in D6. I have some agents in mind, but I'll be sure to review others and select you the best."

———

How does one acquire demon-level power? That was the first question on Ty's mind after the attack. He did not know the answer. But he knew where to start.

As soon as he had felt strong enough to hold a phone to his ear, he called up The Bard. Left him a message.

The Bard was thousands of turns old. Maybe the oldest person on Earth. He had songs about the days when, it was said, magicians and demons were stomping around and running the whole show. So if anyone knew about demonic power, he would know.

It was close to midnight when The Bard finally returned his call. Ty's sleep was interrupted by the ring, but that's just how it worked. You called The Bard, left him a message. He called you back on his timeline. If you wanted his advice, you didn't complain.

When Ty picked up the phone, he was greeted by the familiar voice. Thin and raspy. But energetic as always.

"Ty, m'boy! Good sir, yes, good sir. How can I serve thee? I have naught but one dream in life and it is to grant your every wish!"

Ty tried to speak, but was overwhelmed by the pain in his chest. All that came out was a spate of coughing and wheezing. Each sound met with an "Oh, dear" or "I'm so sorry, m'boy" from the line. It was several beats before Ty was able to form any words.

"I need your help, BoneZ," Ty finally managed. ("BoneZ" was The Bard's current moniker as a recording artist, under which he and Ty had collaborated to produce a handful of hits in the charts.) "There's something up with the mayor. He has some kind of pow—"

The Bard cut him off. "I know it, m'boy! Yes! Dark words have reached my boney ears and I did weep for the story those words told. It would seem you are in a bad way. Very bad indeed."

Another coughing fit. Again punctuated by The Bard's expressions of sympathetic dismay. When the coughing subsided, The Bard began again.

"Listen to me close, Ty, m'boy. I have a good pair of stories for you. The first is a bit of old history and a bit dry. But bear with me and ye shall be rewarded, I do promise. Now here goes:

"In the time-what-was did our two realms of Earth and Fairy hold each other in a more intimate embrace than they do t'day. The kings of our world and the queens of theirs would wed and bed and murder each other, just as freely as you and the bangers and whores do now, m'boy.

"But in those days-that-were, the reason o' this world and the magic o' theirs would mingle freely. This made a rich, tasty mixture that evolved some of us into mystics and some o' them into sages. Ye follow me?"

BoneZ the Bard paused. Ty grunted an affirmative.

"Good sir, yes, good sir. Now then—pretty soon all the kings of Earth and the queens of Fairy were wedded and bedded up. And this meant there was naught else t'do but murder. And so they got down to it, ye dig? Wars for all the bangers and whores there ever was. Nasty ones.

"The wars o' the mystics and sages are not alike the ones fought by the knights o' the crown or the soldier boys with their beloved pop-shooters. No, the wars o' wizardy-types from this time-that-was tore at the fabric of realness itself. They put all sorts of ideas that should be kept inside yer head on the outside. Nasty ideas. Plenty o' nasty ideas there was, leaving plenty o' blood on the ground and leaving the air thick with souldust.

"A good seventy-five turns or so of this bedlam before a few of those most powerful mystics got together with a few of them most powerful sages—the ones that hadn't yet ripped each other to smith'reens and moonbeams, ye dig. Yes, a few of 'em got together and agreed t'would be best if our two realms weren't so betwixt.

"So the wars of the time-what-was came to an end. The holes between us and them were all sewed up, nice n' tight. And so much the better for all the bangers and whores."

Ty let out another few coughs.

"I hear ya suff'rin, m'boy," The Bard continued: "And I'm coming to the point of this tale. The Fairies and their queens did not all go back into their holes and squirrel themselves away in the dandylands. No, some of them stayed put. And I'll wager my two best ribs that the one who did you is one of them. The fairy wizard Pendragon, if I had to say exact."

"Pendragon." Ty repeated the name. Sounded cool. Like from the old myths and fairy tale movies. But it did not mean much more to him.

"Yes, m'boy. A nasty fairy that one is. Overstayed his welcome. Gone rotten in the head, if such a thing can be said of his kind. Not to be underestimated.

"Now! Time is well short, so to my second story we go. This one concerns two young kiddies named Jackie and John-John.

"Jackie and John-John were the besties, ye dig? Until one day, Jackie's dear mum gave her a fancy-fancy ring. When Jackie wore the ring she did feel so extra special, and extra powerful too. So when the two were playing and John-John made an oopsie and crossed her, she lashed out at him with her meanest, angriest anger and did singe the hair straight off his head.

"John-John looked quite the fool, yes he did. He went home and told his pappy straight-away what happened, and wouldn't ye know it? His good ol' pap gave him a ring of his own. This was not quite so fancy-fancy to look at as Jackie's trinket, but it did do the job.

"Time o' the next that the kiddies were playing and Jackie did something John-John didn't like, well, he lashed out at her with all his furies most foul and did slash her throat, making a big red mess.

"Fire and steel, fire and steel—they went at it like this for a good turn or two. Until John-John got a grand ol' idea: He crept into Jackie's room one night, fixing to fix her good by stealing her trinket. Too bad for John-John that Jackie had been feeling quite salty that day, and her ring wouldn't budge when he tugged on it. And when she felt the tug at her finger, she did wake up and she bit mightily at his thieving hand. She took off his finger with her gnashy jaws she did, and took his trinket with it. Ye follow me, m'boy?"

Ty grunted another affirmative.

"Then there is where your old pal, BoneZ, will leave ye. A trinket, m'boy! Go and get yerself a fine trinket if ye must dance with the fairies. Not an easy thing to find, but there is a one I know who can help ye. A spicey one she is. Petra is the name. Out, out in the Land o' Junk. But within reach. Go, go, go and find her. Now I must away to see to my next gentleman-caller. Goodnight, sweet prince!"

The Bard hung up. After a few labored breaths, Ty did the same.

He closed his eyes.

A trinket.

As he drifted back to sleep, he thought of Eli in the ballroom, holding his pinky ring to the sky, puke still dripping from his lips, calling himself a dragon.

———

On day four of the journey, Ty and his crew are gassing up at "Joey's," a small service and repair station in the middle of nowhere. Makes no sense how a place this far out in the desert could survive. The sole mechanic (or manager? or owner?) is a girl who can't be more than twenty. Strawberry blonde, freckles. Cute and friendly as can be. She rushes around checking everything out with their cars. Offering them water. Food. Coffee. Whatever they need.

Ty had planned to take two full stretches for this journey. And he would need them. Because New World City took up about forty percent of the world's surface, it was easy to forget about the other sixty percent. How big it still was. How slow travel could be once you moved out of modern civilization.

No question—getting to Junkland was a bitch. He had flown his private jet out to Redbridge, which in times past had been its own country, now just a suburb of NWC. From there, he had to drive. No real airports anywhere near Junkland. And if you took a helicopter you were likely to get jacked or killed by sky pirates.

So it would be five days of hard driving there, five hard days back. That left six days to find "Petra the Artefixer" and see what she could do for him. Hopefully she would be famous enough in those parts that he could just drop the name and get the directions or address to her workshop or whatever.

The two Division Six spooks seemed to think that was a

good enough plan. Ty wasn't crazy about having them along at first. But Jelena had done well. They seemed cool enough. Arrived at the airport impeccably dressed. Not in Azzuri wear, unfortunately. But stylish suits and sunglasses. Both came armed with some serious, government-issued heat. Matched sets of scatterguns. Suitable to take on five times their number, if it came to it.

Ty had quizzed them on the flight to Redbridge about his music. They had done alright. Had been able to rattle off the names of five of his songs. The darker one sporting the handlebar moustache, Agent Darwish, even named "Dis Is Your Final Warning"—a b-side that was never a big hit, but was one of Ty's personal favorites. That earned the spook some cred.

Ty finishes taking a leak in the tiny bathroom. Steps out into the little waiting area inside the repair shop. The two D6 agents are seated at a small table by the window. Sipping on their coffees. Watching the girl hustle around in the heat.

He frowns at them. "How can you drink that when it's so damn hot out?"

The pale-skinned agent with retro sideburns and a brown pompadour—Agent Price—turns around. "I find that hot drinks can actually make me feel cooler in weather like this. That's weird, right? But it works."

"How does this girl survive out here?" Says Darwish, stroking his fabulous moustache. "She can't see more than what? Two? Maybe three customers per day? That doesn't amount to much. And she's got all kinds of machines running in here. Air conditioners alone must cost a fortune. Plus the gas she has to buy from Big State Oil. How can she pay to keep it all going? Doesn't sit right."

"No, it doesn't." Ty agrees, stroking his chin.

Wonder if I could sport a moustache like that?

"You think she's up to something?" He says to Darwish. "Reversing the electric? Something like that?"

"A sweet girl like that?" Agent Price cuts in. "No way. She probably has some solar array wired up somewhere. Probably got her gas connection cheaper. Through Junkland rather than The State."

Darwish laughs. "Listen to you?" In a mocking tone of his partner: "Such a 'sweet girl like that.' You sound like a rookie, boy. There's plenty of girls look like that. Seem all helpful and shit on the surface. Scratch 'em up a little. You'll find plenty of dirt underneath."

Ty snorts.

True words.

Price takes a long sip of his coffee. Narrows his eyes. "First of all, her name is Joey," he says. "Like 'Joey' from the sign out front, see? She's from Outwash. She moved here because she got sick of all the rough-rider gangs and raiders that were disrupting her business there. Second of all, I know about finding dirt. I can tell who's got it after two seconds of conversation. And she don't got it."

Bullshit.

"Bullshit!" Darwish shouts, and laughs again. "What are you saying? You have some kind of knack? Psychic powers? Two seconds of talk and you can tell if someone is hiding dirt?"

Price's confidence is absolute. "Yeah, that's about right. Two seconds. Sometimes one second."

Ty isn't buying it. But he's intrigued. "Prove it," he says. "Try it on me."

Price chuckles. "Isn't needed with you, Dr. T. Everyone knows you have dirt."

Ty frowns. "Why does that matter? You just said you could hear dirt from one second of conversation. So ask me something. Something you don't already know, but only suspect. And then tell me what's the dirt."

Darwish is enjoying this. "That's a great point. C'mon, Price. Let's see it. Who cares if you can detect dirt if you can't sus out what the dirt is."

Price sets his coffee cup down. "Doesn't work like that. Sorry. Two seconds to know someone's keeping something from me. I already know Dr. T has plenty he doesn't want me to know."

"Bullshit," Darwish says again.

"Yeah. Bullshit," Ty agrees. "You're just picking up on body language or twitches and shit. That's nothing special. I do that."

"No, it's different from that. It's in the... " Price snaps his fingers. Searching for the word. "*Music* of their speech. It's like perfect pitch, you know?"

Ty sniffs. Sure, he knows about perfect pitch. Doesn't believe it's a lie detector.

"If you have perfect pitch, when you hear two notes that are off, you just know immediately, right?"

Ty nods.

"That's what I'm saying. That's how it is with dirt. I can just hear it. Doesn't necessarily tell me everything, but it tells me someone's got a lie, like, hiding in the back of their throat."

Ty is still skeptical. "Like perfect pitch."

"Yes, like perfect pitch."

"So try it on me then," Darwish says. "Show me your *amazing* lie detector, Agent 6-88."

Without a moment's hesitation. "Oh you've got dirt," Price says. "I heard it right there in how you said 'amazing'." He laughs.

"Bullshit," Darwish says again. But he laughs too.

"Yeah. Bullshit." Ty does not laugh. But the edge of his mouth curls in a half-smile.

Price shrugs. Still unperturbed. "Think what you want," he says, and walks out. Heads back to the cars. The girl—Joey of the Sign, according to Agent 6-88—closes the hood of the spooks' sedan and stands proudly by. She smiles at Price as he walks over to her. Tucks her hands into the pockets of her greasy overalls and rocks back on her boot heels. Ty can't hear what they're saying, but the body language is clear.

"Can you believe this guy," Darwish says. "So full of shit. And look at him. He can't resist."

Ty snorts. He has more important things on his mind than some goofball spook's girl-game. "So do you expect trouble once we reach Junkland?"

"Could be some," Darwish says. "The local big man doesn't like it when city folk show up unexpectedly. He might send some of his thugs, or 'knights' as he calls them, to hassle us."

"But we can handle them?"

"Oh for sure. But it's a good thing we're with you. If he sees State government steel, he's unlikely to make much of a fuss. You'll be fine."

"You've dealt with him before?"

"Me? Not personally, no. But Price has."

Ty snorts. "We're relying on the goofy one with his dick hanging out there?"

"That's right." Darwish sets his coffee cup down and heads to the door. "The goofy one with his dick out." He chuckles.

"And what do you know about this Petra? The arte-fixer? You all have a file on her?"

Darwish frowns. "We have files on everybody. But folks outside the city, even semi-famous folks like her. Can be scant on the details. And some of the details are likely to be wrong."

"Even in D6? I thought you guys had eyes and ears everywhere?"

"We do. In New World City, we have taps into all the com lines. All that gets logged. But out here... " He gestures out the window. At the blinding yellow of the desert, the endless highway, the infinity of hot nothing. "D6 knows a lot, but it requires people at the end of the day. If no one is there to report on it or at least tag the information, it doesn't go into a file."

Ty strokes his chin. "Then what do you know about the artefixer?"

"She's supposed to be the best, and maybe even the last, artefixer still alive. I know that she doesn't like to be pushed around. She did some work with D6 about ten turns ago. But the relationship soured after that. She's basically refused all contact with New World City and The State since then." Darwish gives Ty an apologetic look. "So I wouldn't get your hopes up."

Ty snorts.

We'll see about that, moustache.

I know how to get what I want.

CHAPTER 16
SHUWEN

...CROSSES THE LINE

A stroke past midnight. Shuwen is waiting at a bus stop on 12th Avenue, just a few blocks from The Lotus Hotel & Spa. The busses won't be running since this is within The Core and the lockdown is still in effect. The street is dead quiet. Even the military patrol seems to have gone to bed.

She's watching the stop lights at the nearby intersection go through their cycles. Shading the dark streets with the periodic red, amber, and green.

"Are you ready?"

She turns around. Uziel is there. In his full Nightwing garb. Polished silver mask. Black hooded cape. Shiny steel boots and gauntlets. Big utility belt slung across his chest.

"Yes. I'm ready," she says. She is also dressed in blacks. Like a cat burglar. Not an M.O. that she's completely comfortable with. And even less so now that she knows the Stasi are watching her. She's taking an awful risk. But this case has got under her skin. There's something different about it, something big. If she's to crack it open and solve it, she's now convinced she'll need to operate outside her comfort zone.

Uziel signals for her to follow him into a nearby alley. She does.

There's a soft popping sound as he fires a grappling hook up to the fire escape. He holds out his arm with an almost romantic gesture. She wraps her arms around his. "Hold on tight," he says.

They zip into the air. Neatly drop onto the metal landing. Another pop to retract the hook line. Then they are climbing the steps. Swiftly. Quietly. Up the fire escape.

Another grappling hook shot to get to the roof. This time they have to hold the line and pull themselves, walking sideways against the building's facade until they can grab the ledge.

"Do you need to rest?" Uziel asks once they're standing on the rooftop.

She shakes her head. "No, I'm good to go."

"Then let's move. Lotus is ten buildings away." And with that, Nightwing is off and running. Leaping over the gaps between buildings, using some kind of rocket boost in his feet. Two full rotations of her bracers and Shuwen is right behind him.

They make quite the sight. A pair of crime-fighting gazelles, bounding across the urban landscape, under the light of a full moon.

———

At the end of her shift, the day before, Shuwen stopped by Lin's food truck. Drawn to the thought of satay and spring rolls (and the knowledge that she didn't have anything at home to eat for dinner). Lin was in a generous mood. Gave a fun, flourish-filled performance with her world-famous chopping knife while preparing Shuwen's order.

Once Shuwen was back in her patrol car, enjoying her

food, there came a knock on her passenger-side window. She peered over from the driver seat. It looked like one of those synth courier models.

She rolled the window a crack. "Yes?"

"Are you still on duty, Constable?" The voice gave him away immediately. It was Uziel in disguise.

She checked her watch. On for another thirty rounds.

But she unlocked the door and invited him in.

"It's pretty quiet today. I can drive around to close out the shift," she said. Stashing the rest of her dinner in the backseat, she turned on the car and pulled out into the street. "Have you figured out anything new?"

"Yes. After speaking with the other League members, we believe the magician is a very old fairy king. One who managed to escape his banishment beyond the veil after the Wars of Restoration in the 15th century."

Shuwen laughs. "You're joking? A fairy king? That stuff is all just nonsense from children's stories."

"No, it isn't. My colleague, Benoit—who you didn't yet meet—he is a scholar. He has been to the library at the Ivory Citadel. The historical records there are far more complete than what you and I have ever seen. More complete even than what the State agencies can access. He remembers reading that there were 'stowaway' fairies, sometimes powerful ones, who refused to honor the terms of the peace. Some of them were hunted down, but others were never found. It is believed they hid themselves in Earthly society."

Shuwen shook her head, but smiled despite herself. "I don't know, Silverman. That's a lot to swallow. First the illusions and now this. I mean, I know I saw your recording—"

Uziel cut her off, pressed on, ignoring her skepticism. "The fairy's old name was 'Pendragon'. We suspect he has taken many other names over time. I believe that he is working in the mayor's office. I also believe he is ultimately the one behind this assassination attempt." He paused. Processing. "But I don't yet know for sure. The answer will be in The Lotus records. In their vault."

———

The roof access door into The Lotus building is deadbolted, with no handle to open it from the outside. Uziel uses his wrist-mounted short laser to melt the bolt, and engages magnets on his fingers to pry the door open.

"I am scanning for security devices and alarms," he says. "I don't believe we've tripped anything yet, but we must be quick. In and out within a chime, if we can."

Shuwen nods. And they move inside. Down one easy flight of stairs to the 12th floor. The door out of the stairwell is locked, but quickly picked with the tools in Uziel's utility belt. It opens onto a hallway. Large, cream-colored tile floors. Cool green accents. The lighting is low. Only a few wall sconces flicker with a dim fluorescence.

The Lotus chair's office will be on this floor. So too is the vault—which should contain the records that Shuwen and Uziel have come to inspect.

They creep into the hall. Almost immediately they hear other footsteps from around a corner. Patrols. Coming their way. Sounds like two or possibly three. Not in sight just yet.

Uziel's eyes change color from black to red as he runs a quick infrared scan. He holds up three fingers. Shuwen puts one finger to her lips. He nods.

In another tick, the patrols stroll into their corridor. Three strapping young men in the black tunics of Lotus security. Pistols and short swords swing from the holsters on their belts. But they never have a chance to use them.

Shuwen knocks the nearest out with quick, three-kick combo to his head. Uziel chops another in the throat (so he can't scream), spins past, and then wraps the third in a sleeper hold. Shuwen gets a sleeper hold on poor throat-man to finish the job.

When all three patrols are down, Uziel administers a needle stab to each. "This will keep them asleep until we're long gone."

Shuwen nods.

Quite the bag of tricks he has. Imagine if everyone on the force was so well-equipped... NWPD would be unstoppable.

They continue down the hall. Most of the rooms they pass are dark. But one at the end of the hall is lit. That is the destination. The vault.

When they reach the door, Shuwen stands on one side of its frosted glass window, Uziel stands on the other. She is listening. He is engaging his infra-red vision. After a beat, he holds up two fingers. Then pauses. Shakes his head. Three.

"A synth," he says, lowering his volume to below a whisper. "And security cameras. Hold a moment while I shut them down." His processing spins up.

Shuwen adjusts her bracers, and takes a deep breath.

After a beat or two, he says, "It is done," and he removes a small smoke grenade from his belt.

The door has a keypad. Uziel scans it and quickly enters a combination. There is a soft beep. Immediately followed by sounds of surprise from the guards inside.

Uziel opens the door a crack and slides in his grenade. One tick. Then it goes off. The guards coughing and swearing in confusion.

Shuwen bursts into the room. Her bracers making her

immune to the smoke, she easily sweeps one of the guards of his feet, follows with a knockout chop to the back of his head, and proceeds to bind him up.

Uziel is right behind her. He whips a pair of throwing stars, catching the second guard on the hand and face, then closes in and wraps him in another sleeper hold.

The third guard, the synth, is standing still in front of the massive vault door. Black metal, black tunic, a demon mask, and glowing red eyes. Unaffected by the smoke, it draws a long machete from a sheath on its back and moves to engage the intruders.

It opens with a flurry of big slashes that would butcher any normal intruder. But the two intruders this night are not normal.

Uziel is able to parry the blade with his gauntlets, but the thing is too fast and doesn't leave any openings to counter-punch.

Shuwen darts around behind and lands a side-kick to demon synth's hip. Not a damaging blow, but it forces the thing off balance, and it decides to reposition. It moves toward a corner of the room, trying to keep both its opponents in front of it.

Uziel fires off a short laser blast. The synth deflects the shot with its blade. Shuwen feints another side-kick. The synth adopts a blocking stance for half a tick, then instantly returns to neutral when the kick doesn't come.

The three combatants hold still. Tense. Watching. Waiting. For someone to make the next move.

Except it's only Shuwen who's truly waiting. She notices the intense clicking and whirring sounds of synth processors going wild. Then she realizes Uziel and the Lotus sentinel are waging a second, simultaneous battle over the wireless. Trying to hack each other's minds.

The red eyes behind the demon mask begin to flicker. Just a little at first. Then they start full-on blinking.

After a handful of beats, Uziel simply stands back. "Foul creature," he says. Then drops his fighting stance entirely. The demon's red eyes go dark. The machete falls to the ground. One more tick, then the synth collapses in the corner.

Shuwen relaxes. "Nice move," she says.

"Meg wrote me a new algorithm for that. It seems to be quite effective." He moves to the vault door. "Now let's see how quickly we can get this open."

———

The very existence of an organization like The Lotus made Shuwen uncomfortable. It made no sense to her that there could be a state-sanctioned organization of contract killers.

Yes, she understood the history—how the Assassins and Apothecaries Guild of old had evolved into The Lotus Corporation, with its chain of hotels and spas. The Retainers and Ropers Guild had similarly evolved into the NWPD.

But setting the history aside, when you looked at it logically: You had the cops licensed to protect people from murder. Investigate murder. Arrest murderers. And at the same time, you had Lotus licensed to commit murder and manage a community of professional murderers. This made no sense. It would be like The State funding terrorists. Self-defeating. Illogical.

Yes, she understood that there were laws governing the Assassins Guild. Lotus could not just execute people at will. There were strict protocols. Rituals. Loads of paperwork. State oversight and routine audits. But still.

"The absurdity of it! It calls into question everything

we do!" She remembered her father saying this. He was arguing with someone over the phone. He didn't know she was listening. She was playing in one room of the house, he was on the phone in another. This was shortly before he was forced into retirement.

"None of us are safe from The Lotus. No one can be safe from them. There are too many loopholes in the system. If they want to kill, they can find a way. Don't you see that?"

That was how she remembered the conversation ending. Her father angrily expressing his fear of The Lotus, and his outrage at their ability to kill without repercussion.

These words—her father's words—stuck in Shuwen's mind from that day forward, becoming a kind of axiom. Despite their license to kill, The Lotus could not be trusted. And the other State institutions, like The Stasi, who permitted and protected them—they could not be trusted either. If the killers wanted to kill, if they wanted to violate the law, they could always find a way.

———

It takes a good ten rounds, but the vault is finally open. Thanks to another algorithm of Meg the Magnificent.

The inside of the vault feels like a walk-in closet. Soft carpeting. Three walls filled with polished oak cubbies that look like the perfect fit for shoes. Except there are no shoes. Instead, it is stacks of vellum and parchment scrolls. Each cubby labeled with a mysterious ideogram.

Shuwen is browsing, looking for signs of what might be more recently deposited scrolls. Uziel is systematically scanning the ideograms, trying to work out their meanings.

"It won't be much longer before more security arrives," he says in between scans. "I tried to shut down that synth guard's communication before the fight, but it is possible that it got a message out."

"How long do you think we have?"

"Likely fifteen rounds. Twenty at the most."

"Any luck on deciphering these symbols?"

"I believe I almost have it worked out." His processing gets a little louder. "The Lotus guard the meaning of these symbols carefully, but I know enough of the origins and precursor languages used by the old guilds to narrow down the problem space. I should have the solution soon."

Shuwen is inspecting the cubby marked with a hamsa. This has only three scrolls in it. By far the fewest. She picks one of them up. It is wrapped with a silken blue ribbon. There's something strangely compelling about it. It feels heavier the longer she holds it. Delicate gold writing begins to materialize on the ribbon as she stares at it. It is in a script she does not recognize. Or maybe she just needs to look at it more closely... Her fingers move to unravel the ribbon.

"I've got it," Uziel says.

Shuwen snaps out of it. Sets the scroll back in its place and immediately forgets about it. "What do the symbols mean? Where is the one we want?"

"The symbols indicate the type of ritual that Lotus used for the contract. I believe the material of the scroll indicates the expense of its execution. The ribbons indicate the phase of the moon when the signing ritual took place, the moon's color and character corresponding to the color and material of the ribbon."

Contempt spreads across Shuwen's face.

Ridiculous nonsense! How can The State tolerate this? Lotus is basically just a cover for some arcane death cult.

But she says nothing.

Uziel carefully works his way back through the room, reviewing the symbols. "Here!" He stops on a high cubby marked with what looks like a bird with a clipped wing. "I believe this indicates a maiming or mutilation."

There are fifteen or so scrolls. Uziel takes one down and hands it to Shuwen. Then he takes down another, unwraps it, and begins scanning.

Shuwen turns the scroll over in her hands. It feels waxy. Wrapped with a plain fiber rope. Not nearly as heavy or compelling to her as the last one. "Should I just open it?" Disgust in her voice.

"Yes," Uziel replies. He has already moved on to a new scroll. Scanning. "It should be written in common language."

She unwinds the rope. It requires a surprising force of will to get her hands to do the work. Like the scroll doesn't want her to read it. But she manages it all the same.

She unrolls the scroll. Reads the top lines.

She's got it.

"I've got it. This is the mayor's contract."

Uziel rushes to her side and begins scanning the contents. "Witnessed by 'Mr. Idris Moorelake, Chief of Staff to Mayor Eli Strauss Jr.'. That must be him. Pendragon's new moniker."

Shuwen isn't listening. She's busy reading. Looking for the name of the sniper. That will be the key to solving the case. It must be.

There's no name. Just some reference to a 'military source' and 'Appendix C'.

She reads lower down the scroll. Finds the appendices.

C'mon! You have to be there.

Appendix C is a subcontract. Between The Lotus Corporation (hereafter 'Client') and some other organization called "Free Moon Lancers, Ltd." (hereafter 'Provider').

'Free Moon Lancers'? Never heard of it.

She keeps reading.

'Provider agrees to provide Client with the services stipulated in the work order (see Appendix D) according to the precise date and conditions specified above...' Blah, blah, blah! Where is the name! Give me a damn name!

She looks for Appendix D. Finds it.

Finally!

There is a signatory for the Free Moon Lancers.

Mme. Y. Young... 'Mme'? Nobody uses that. Not since The Great War. What does that mean? Another sick joke of this cult?

Uziel places a hand on her shoulder. "I've scanned and recorded it all. We should go. Did you find what you need?"

Shuwen rolls up the scroll. Confused. Unsure of what to think. But at least she has an answer. "Yes," she says. "I'm ready."

CHAPTER 17
INOLA

...DELIVERS A WARNING

It's one of those gray days. When it looks like rain, except it's really the smoke from the industrial districts, carried into the city on an ill wind rather than out to the water. Feels oppressively overcast. Heavy air. Hard to breath.

Inola sits at a cafe table in Precinct 13. Coffee and a cigarette. Waiting on Shuwen Li to show. Supercop does not appear to have gotten the message to stand down. So now it will be made more explicit.

The lockdown is starting to ease finally. Plenty more folks strolling around. Going about their usual business. Plenty of uniformed military presence as well. They won't disappear entirely until Inola closes this case. The Ragnarok is technically under The State's, and therefore The Stasi's, authority. But they often choose not to see it that way, and will use any excuse to flex their muscle. Make sure that the six billion citizens of New World City don't forget who carries the biggest guns.

Except big guns aren't the solution to this problem. The sniper got everyone thinking this case is about bullets, but the real case is a grade 2 wizard, running free in New World City. That cannot stand.

It will not stand. Not if Inola Montag has anything to say about it. She is almost certain now that the wizard is former Agent Moorelake. Too much of a coincidence otherwise. After some more digging in the databases, it appears that before he was Moorelake, he went by "Morton" and was in media relations for The Ragnarok. And before that, seems that he might have been someone called "Mordred," working high up in Old Marial's military theocracy. Which shows you just how clued-in The Ragnarok's background checkers are if they can't detect that someone used to work for the State's sworn enemy.

But whatever the history, her in-person encounter with Agent Soliman confirmed that he was compromised, and that Moorelake was the most likely cause. She intercepted Soliman in the parking lot outside City Hall. He was heading home for the day. She repeated her questions to him about Moorelake's record, The Lotus contract signing. And Soliman repeated his non-answers. But the look in his eye changed as she mentioned Moorelake's name. It was fast. A flutter of the eyelids. Dilation of the pupils. Easy to miss if you weren't looking for it.

Good thing Inola was looking for it. The tell-tale signs of someone else stepping in, taking over. That was textbook enchantment magic. She had seen it a couple of times before. In her early days of D6. She had witnessed some interrogations of enchanted victims. Strange stuff that raised all kinds of deep questions about memory and personal identity. Definitely unsettling the first time you see it. Those little outward signs of the internal struggle for psychological dominance.

Yet that was nothing compared to what could happen when an enchantment was broken. Inola had seen one woman's eyeballs explode right out of her head. Nasty. Still better to be free of the spell, she supposed. One man reported that his enchanter had "raped him" over and over again in his imagination, thousands of times.

That seemed to be the thing about magic. It was nasty, wild stuff. Sometimes it was wonderful, but more often it was terrifying and hideous. Too much exposure and you would lose your sanity. And what was worse, it was like a contagion. Someone exposed to magic, and driven mad by it, would expose others. Before long you had total chaos. That was why The State worked so hard to snuff it out, make people disbelieve and forget. Magic was antithetical to a stable and rational society. Antithetical to peace and progress.

Inola finishes her cigarette. Drops it in the ashtray, lights another. She sees Shuwen up the street and waves.

"Agent Montag," Shuwen says when she arrives. Her tone is ice cold.

Inola smiles her warmest and gestures for Shuwen to sit and join her. Determined to break through Supercop's defenses this time and establish some kind of rapport. And if rapport fails, then up the ante of the warning. Whatever it takes to get through to her. Get her to leave this case alone. She doesn't want to see NWPD's finest going schizo or tits up.

"Thank you for coming, Constable. Do you want a coffee? Can I order you something?"

Shuwen sits down. Arms folded across her chest. "Sure, I'll take a coffee," she says.

Inola waves over the waiter, orders two more coffees. Offers Shuwen a cigarette. She accepts it. The two smoke in silence until the coffees arrive. Shuwen in her blue uniform. Police cap. Lips tight. Face tense. Looking away, down the street. Inola in her dark suit. Sunglasses (despite the overcast). High-heeled boots. Smiling. Face relaxed. Looking straight at Shuwen.

"I know I told you last time to be careful around the sham assassination case," Inola says, after she takes a sip of coffee. "I wanted to meet so that I could upgrade my advice. You need to stay away from the case. Things are getting real messy, real fast."

Shuwen sips her coffee. Refuses to meet Inola's eyes. Keeps her focus on the pedestrians. "Messy? How?"

"Messy like body counts," Inola says. "And worse." She pauses a tick. "And I don't want to see our city's best cop caught up in it."

"I'm not intimidated by body counts. I've dealt with plenty of messy cases."

"Not like this."

Shuwen turns. Meets Inola's gaze. "Like what? What does that mean?"

Inola holds the gaze. Then speaks slowly, letting a smile spread across her face. "I... think... you... know... what that means." She's not buying Shuwen's clueless act for a beat. She knows Supercop has been digging around. Surely deep enough to figure out that this isn't the usual game of cops and robbers.

"I know that The Lotus is behind the hit," Shuwen says, "and I think they're up to something."

"Lotus is always up to something, Constable." Inola takes a drag on her cigarette. "But I think you're right. There is something unusual about their behavior in this case."

Shuwen's expression softens. The tension in her face drops by ten percent. "Are you looking into them?" She asks.

"Most definitely," Inola says quickly. "We're looking into all of it." But she's not interested in talking about The

Lotus. That is not the point of this meeting. So she tries to guide the conversation back to its purpose. "But we've got it under control. You can leave it to us."

"You're going to shut down The Assassins Guild?"

"No." Inola laughs. "Although we might transfer the license away from Lotus if there's been some violation of the charter."

"And what about City Hall?" Shuwen asks. Her jaw tight.

"What about it?"

"Are you investigating... the mayor or his staff?"

Inola shares a knowing smile. "Like I said, Constable. We're looking into all of it."

"Sure," Shuwen says, frowning with intensity. "Looking into it. Just like you did last time. Looking to hang the blame for everything on the NWPD. Looking to keep everything else the same."

"Keep things stable, yes." Inola corrects her. "That is the job. Yours and mine."

Shuwen's temper flares. "My job is to protect the streets, Agent Montag. To fight for the good people and for the principles that The State doesn't seem to give a shit about anymore. My job is to deliver justice."

Inola takes a long, deep breath. "Right," she says, stubbing out her cigarette. Lighting another. "Justice. What do you think that is exactly?"

Shuwen narrows her eyes. Unintimidated by the philosophical question. "It means upholding the rule of law. Fairly and equally for everyone."

"Sure." Inola nods. "Fairness and equality. Those principles are important. But they might not be the most important principles, if you know what I mean."

Shuwen's face indicates that she does know what Inola means.

Inola chuckles and takes a drag. "Let me ask you about something else." She points her smoke at Shuwen's artefact bracers. "Those. Do you know how they work?"

Anxiety flashes in Shuwen's eyes. She drops her hands into her lap. Hiding her wrists and bracers below the table. "Old tech, isn't it? Like those copper energy amplifier bracelets. Except mine are made from silver."

Inola laughs. "C'mon, Constable. Don't play dumb. You're not any good at it. I know D6 and the NWPD don't always get along. But we're on the same side. I'm not here to trifle with you, so don't trifle with me."

Shuwen colors.

"Let's try again. How do your bracers work?"

A few beats pass. Shuwen looks down at her hands. Thinking over the consequences of what she might say next. "Artefact magic," she finally says.

"Disco." Inola grins. "Do you know what makes artefact magic possible?"

Again Shuwen hesitates. But this time Inola suspects it's because she genuinely doesn't know the answer. Indeed, the truth behind artefacts has been well scrubbed from the databases.

"I believe... it's the spirits of my ancestors," Shuwen says with some obvious embarrassment. "Each one who wore them, in the past, imbued some of their energy into the metal. And it's compounded over time. Like interest."

Inola shakes her head. "No. I know that ancestor thing is the story that some families pass down. But that's not how artefacts like yours really work. The truth is that there is a very old, very powerful spirit trapped in them. Bound to them. Imprisoned. Its energy tortured and stolen out of it every time you use them."

Shuwen flinches at each of those last descriptors. She clearly had no idea. The dark cost of her power.

"No, that can't be."

"I'm sorry, Constable. But that is the truth. Power like that isn't free. There is some creature whose energy was captured and bound to the artefact when it was created, however many hundreds or thousands of turns back. That's whose energy you tap when you activate them."

Shuwen colors again. From anger this time. She stubs out her cigarette. Looking like she intends to bail out of the conversation. "I don't believe you," she says.

Inola holds up her hand. "Wait. Look. I'm not going to confiscate them. I'm not even telling you not to use them. I'm telling you this because that kind of magic—the kind that binds and tortures—that's the kind of mess we're dealing with in this case." She takes another drag. "And magic like that has nothing to do with fairness or equality. Understand? We're not talking about thugs on the streets. We're not talking about *justice*. We're talking about a different level of chaos and cruelty. And you're not equipped for it. Even with those things on your wrists. You're not equipped."

"That sort of magic doesn't exist anymore," Shuwen says, rising from the table. "All the materials on magic and artefacts from the academy—they all say that stuff is no longer possible. I did my research."

Inola shrugs, looking up into Shuwen's defiant face. "The downside of State propaganda doing its job. When you want to warn someone that they're dancing too close to the fire, but you've already convinced them the fire doesn't exist."

Shuwen sneers and gives Inola a withering look, unappreciative of the condescending metaphor.

"I'm sorry for it, Constable. You deserved the truth. The fire exists. There is a danger here that you are not prepared for. Listen to me: Drop the case. I know it's hard. But you need to leave this alone."

"Thank you for the coffee," Shuwen says as she turns and walks away.

Inola sighs and watches her go. Not a successful meeting. But there's not much else to be done about it, unless she wants to bring Shuwen in. Or issue an order to have her suspended.

Or she could just leave her alone. Could be that she'll end up flushing the wizard. Which would be good. But far more likely she'll fall in way over her head, drown, become another casualty of the case. Which would be sad. But Supercop seems determined to go her own way.

Inola finishes her coffee and cigarette. Leaves the money on the table. Disappears into the crowded street.

CHAPTER 18
ZIJIAN
...AT THE RED DRAGON INN

«Despite the military presence and lockdown that is affecting The Core and neighboring districts, criminal activity has continued unabated. Thankfully, our NWPD has stayed on the job. One constable in particular, Shuwen Li of Precinct 13, has been cleaning up our streets, almost single-handedly. In the past fortnight, she has arrested nearly two dozen gangsters, intercepted a drug deal, and broken up an illegal gambling ring. Chief Inspector Renaud has described Constable Li as a "role-model for our city's law enforcement," and we here at Channel 5 News couldn't agree more.»

Zijian turns off the TV.

Li the Supercop at it again. She's going to get her throat cut one of these days. So foolish to run around pissing off every powerful organization in the city.

She sits in the private dining room at The Red Dragon Inn. Awaiting her honored guest, Inspector William Fisch. He has agreed to meet her under the strict terms of Lotus Hospitality and Protection. He has been told that she intends to make him an offer. The dinner is to be a negotiation, and if all goes well, a celebration for a profitable new partnership.

She expects Fisch to arrive late. Probably already a little drunk. His profile describes him as angry, entitled, and bitter. A winning combination if ever there was one. His edges should be a little worn down after his long military and policing career. But he clearly still wants to be in the game. And that should be enough.

"Madame Sun." Her Jade lieutenant sticks his head through the doorway. "He has arrived."

"Good." She stands and begins her personal transformation. Out with the cold fire. In with the warm water. After a few moments, she is ready. "Escort him up."

The key will be making Fisch feel in control. Let him feel that he is dictating the terms.

Sapphire lieutenant (Head of Dining, with one hundred sixty-two executions) steps into the doorway, ushering Inspector Fisch.

Zijian opens with a bright smile. "Inspector, it is a pleasure. You do The Lotus, and me, much honor by agreeing to this meeting."

Fisch shows his big, discolored teeth. It might be a smile. Or maybe a grimace. "Of course, Madame. I wouldn't miss the opportunity to dine in such a... *fine* environment." He wrinkles his nose and looks around at the decor with obvious displeasure.

Zijian can already smell the booze on his breath. "The Red Dragon is not to your taste, sir?"

"Not really, no. I'm not a fan of all this faux-medieval, Akkadian or Marialite bullshit. I thought we fought a war to wipe all those fairy-fuckers off the map, didn't we?" He hacks a loud cough, neglecting to cover his mouth. "At least there is a TV in here."

"I'm so sorry, Inspector. Had I known..."

He waves a hand dismissively. "Forget about it. As long as they have decent steak and plenty of whiskey, I'll be happy." He brushes past her and takes a seat at the table. Then gestures for her to sit as well.

Yes, invite me to sit at my own table, pig. A perfect beginning.

She bows politely and joins him at the table. "Shall we begin with business? Or would you prefer to eat or drink first?"

"Dinner first." He pats his belly. "Never negotiate on an empty stomach, my old man used to say."

"Very good." Zijian signals to summon the waiter. "I believe they do an excellent rare steak here, Inspector. And offer a wide selection of whiskey. I'm sure you will not be disappointed."

"Is that right?" He accepts the drinks list from the waiter, takes a small pair of spectacles from his jacket front pocket, and begins to read.

Zijian holds the menu in her hands, but does not read it. She keeps her eyes on Fisch.

Her Sapphire lieutenant quietly returns into the room, leans down to whisper something into Zijian's ear.

"Madame. Miss Khan is here. She says she is a part of your party this evening."

Zijian's face remains calm, but the cold fire returns instantly.

This is not the plan. What on Earth is Ysobel doing here?

Sensing the danger, Sapphire is apologetic as she continues the delivery of her poison message: "Miss Khan is insisting. She is on her way up now."

———

It was a full turn of the wheel after they met before Zijian did any killing for Ysobel.

Zijian did return, as the girl had telepathically requested, after the dinner party at the Khan estate. She was intrigued by the girl's ability. No one except Hadra had ever spoken into her mind.

Turned out Little Ysobel wanted her to kill someone on OmniCorp's board. She said he was corrupt. A sexual abuser. She wasn't completely clear on his crimes. But she had heard terrible things about him from some of the women at the company. "He was a bad man," she said. "He deserved to die."

Zijian refused, explaining that there wasn't a Lotus protocol for a lieutenant to take on a contract from so young a client.

Before she rose to the Lotus chairship, Zijian was careful about keeping her nose clean and her paperwork tidy. Once you were in the big seat, you could skirt the lines —and she observed that Master Minza did his fair share of skirting. But she had no interest in risking her future for some righteous rich girl.

However, Zijian's refusal of Ysobel's first request did not end their relationship. Ysobel merely pivoted things in a new direction. She began booking spa treatments with Zijian every ten days or so. She would ask all kinds of questions throughout their meetings. About The Lotus. How the contract killings worked. Its history. What professional assassin society was like. She was fascinated by the culture of death-dealing. Behavior that reminded Zijian of herself at that younger age.

Zijian would give answers, but she never told Ysobel everything. Certainly never told her any of The Lotus' secrets. And divulged as little as possible about herself. And yet, over time, she felt herself opening up. She appreciated the girl's combination of intelligence and ambition. And although she would never admit it, she was envious of the girl's limitless opportunity in the world. Her incredible privilege. So different from Zijian's own wretched origins in The Guts.

Intimacy grew. Harmless at first. But things started progressing in a more dangerous direction when the girl turned fifteen.

One day, Ysobel showed up to her appointment in distress. The girl kept a brave face until they were alone, then she broke down. Sobbing. She said her boyfriend had assaulted her. Done things to her without permission. She was hurt. Scared. Ashamed.

She was also angry. She wanted revenge. Retaliation. Justice. Whatever you want to call it.

She wanted him dead.

Lo and behold, now that Ysobel was fifteen, there was a Lotus protocol that could work. The girl signed the writ in her own blood. Zijian carried it out.

The boyfriend was some other rich kid. As he begged for his life, he insisted that Ysobel was lying. He said they had both been drinking, had too much, and fooled around a little. Maybe things went too far, but he claimed she was as aggressive about it as he was. He cried. He pleaded. He cursed Ysobel. It did him no good. Zijian was cold fire.

She was there to do a job. She did it.

At their next meeting, when Zijian told Ysobel that the contract was completed, the girl was strangely unemotional. "Oh," was her initial reaction. As though she had been told the weather report for the moon.

Zijian was surprised by this. Ysobel was not typically one to suppress the expression of her feelings. Many beats passed in silence. Then Ysobel, flat on her back on the massage table, whispered, "Come here. Please." Then, "Come closer."

Zijian obeyed.

Then Ysobel sat up. "Closer," she whispered. She placed her hands lightly on Zijian's face and kissed her mouth.

Until that moment, Zijian hadn't thought about Ysobel in a sexual way at all. She found the girl interesting. Appreciated the resemblance in their character. But she fundamentally saw the girl as an investment. A useful tool in her kit. A weapon behind breakable glass. To be used in case the right opportunity arose.

But this first kiss caught Zijian in her warm water, spa treatment mode, when she was ready to become whomever her clients wanted her to be. And Ysobel was persistent. Kissed her again, more firmly. Forcefully. Placed Zijian's hands on her body. And again she whispered, "closer."

"Madame Sun, Inspector Fisch. I am sorry to be late." Ysobel glides through the doorway into the dining room. She is radiant in an emerald cocktail dress. Glistening gold jewelry. Her dark hair done up in stylish ringlets.

She smiles. Irresistible.

Zijian's seething rage is tempered by the sight of such beauty. A part of her feels that she is seeing this woman— her Ysobel—for the first time. It hits her like a punch in the stomach. Takes a few ticks to catch her breath and collect herself.

Fisch is grinning, clearly delighted. He stands and extends his hand to the new arrival. "Well, well. Look at little Yzzy, all grown up!" Ysobel places her delicate, small hand in his rough, large one. He kisses it. "I was not aware that you were joining us." He shoots a sideways glance at

Zijian. "But I am glad that you are. I think having Omni-Corp on our side, for whatever arrangement we might make, will be absolutely critical."

Ysobel smiles, and places her other hand upon his. "You are very wise, Inspector."

"Yes, indeed. This was exactly our thinking," Zijian says. Trying to take back some control of the evening. Her voice is calm. But her heart is racing.

How do Ysobel and Fisch know each other? How did Ysobel know about this meeting? What game is she playing?

Ysobel catches her eye as she moves to join them at the table. She sends a message into Zijian's mind.

Relax, Ija. Everything is going to be fine.

The thought has an effect opposite to its intent. It stirs a panic.

No. This is not good. What is she planning? How much does she know?

Ysobel takes the place adjacent to Fisch. He leers at her cleavage as she bends her waist and settles herself in her seat.

"So what's the plan then, ladies?" He says. "What do you have for me?"

Ysobel picks up his menu. "Let's order. I'm starving," she says brightly. "I feel like having a big steak."

"A woman after my own heart." He laughs. Ysobel laughs too, and lightly touches his arm.

Ija. Please. You can relax. I know what I'm doing.

Zijian's stress continues to rise. The cold fire consuming her. All mental energy redirected to strategic calculation. She keeps her hands clasped together in her lap. Digging her manicured, sharpened fingernails into her palm.

This is unacceptable. It should not be happening. How did she know about this meeting? Why wasn't the information about their history in Fisch's file? I am going to kill whoever put that dossier together. How could they have missed such a thing?

The waiter returns and they all place their orders. Two steaks, both medium rare. One tofu curry.

Ysobel and Fisch begin discussing the sham assassination. Zijian is one-quarter listening. Clockworks continue spinning like mad.

How can I remove her from this evening? I could spill something on her dress. But would that work? Unlikely. No. And I would look clumsy or careless. I could poison her... mildly. Just enough to make her sick.

"What do you say, Madame?" Fisch looks at Zijian intently. Smirking with his ugly brown teeth. One eyebrow raised. "Surely, you know the identity of the sniper?"

Zijian forces a coy smile. "Of course I do, Inspector."

"Then why don't you enlighten us? We are going to be partners going forward, are we not?" He takes a sip of whiskey, continues eyeing her over the rim of his glass.

"I very much wish that, yes. But we have not yet discussed the terms of the partnership." She holds his gaze with confidence. Working to suppress any sign of panic in her expression. "As you know, the traditions and rites of The Lotus are very old. Older even than The State. I am obligated to disclose some information to government officials, such as yourself. And I am permitted to disclose some information through partnerships."

Fisch frowns and rolls his eyes. Uninterested in a history lesson.

She continues: "Yet there is some information that I can never disclose. Even to other members of the Guild. I am afraid the identity of the sniper is one such. It is a secret that I am duty bound to keep to my grave."

"Fine words," he snarls. He turns to Ysobel. "You buying that, Yzzy?"

Although Zijian cannot see under the other side of the table, she can tell from his movement and Ysobel's body language that he has placed his hand high on Ysobel's thigh. This ignites a new fire in Zijian. Hot, not cold. Jealousy. She cannot remember the last time she felt it. She does not like this disgusting animal handling her possession.

Calm down, Ija. It's fine.

Ysobel leans forward, placing her hand gently upon his. "I think it makes sense, what Madame Sun is saying. Especially for an institution like The Lotus. It is important that they follow the rules. To deal in death like they do. Trust is essential. If people thought that the details of their contracts could be easily leaked or stolen, it would lead to chaos."

Zijian forces a smile. "Well said, Miss Khan. That is it exactly." Her internal fires cool. Just a touch.

Maybe she thinks she is helping me? But why would she show up uninvited like this? She knows I hate surprises. She knows I will be furious. And she must know the danger she is placing me in.

"Let's talk about trust then," Fisch growls after another swig of whiskey. "Or better yet: Let's talk about reciprocity. You desire an info feed from the Office of the Inspector. I get it. I can understand why that would be highly valuable to you and to The Lotus." He hiccups. "So why don't you talk to me then about something of similar value? Something valuable that you have and that I might want."

Good. Yes. Let's talk terms. Get this evening back on track.

"The Lotus and The Guild each have much to offer," Zijian begins. Then she pauses, and gestures at Ysobel. "And OmniCorp as well. Whether it is pleasure or power you desire, we have the means and authority in this room to make it happen."

At that moment, the dinner arrives, pausing the conversation. Fisch has a mouthful of steak before he responds.

"Look. Mmm. I don't much care for all this circle-jerk talk. So I'll say it plain. If we're to do business together, then I want a direct line to each of you." He points at them with his fork. "When I give you a call, you pick up the phone. And when I ask you for something, you give it to me." Then he jams his fork back into his meat and cuts himself another bite.

Ysobel frowns and says nothing. Her expression darkening. She has not touched her food.

But Zijian is pleased by Fisch's remarks. "You are asking for a blank check, Inspector? Is that right?"

"Not at all, Madame." His eyes stay down, focused on cutting his steak. "I want a guarantee of a fair exchange. Like for like. Whatever value my information has for you, I want equal value in return."

"But how—" Ysobel is about to argue, but Zijian holds up her hand, and the girl falls silent. A flash of anger in her eyes. No matter.

Zijian presses on. "Open communication then," she says. "Such a simple arrangement." Smiling easy now. Without having to force it. "Yes, I believe that will do very well for The Lotus."

Fisch nods and points at her again with his fork. He winks. His mouth busy with steak. It seems they understand each other well.

Zijian turns her smile to Ysobel. "Miss Khan, what do you say? I'm sure OmniCorp will be willing to assist the Inspector should he need it. Yes?"

Ysobel is not smiling. She now has the cold fire in her eyes.

"Miss Khan?" Zijian extends her hand toward Ysobel. A note of panic in her voice.

Something is wrong.

Fisch puts the last of his steak into his mouth. Sets his fork and knife down, picks up his whiskey, and leans back in his chair. Still chewing. Ogling Ysobel's neckline. Clearly feeling pleased with himself, and in full command, he casually reaches again for the girl's thigh.

This time, the girl intercepts him. She grabs the encroaching wrist and slams it down on the table. With her other hand, she snatches his steak knife and drives it through the back of his hand, pinning it to tabletop.

He drops his drink into his lap. Eyes wide.

No! What is she doing! Has she gone mad?

Zijian tries to move, to stop Ysobel from doing what she fears is coming next. But she finds herself frozen. Her body will not respond. She has not felt this since she was a child. Her eyes grow as wide as the man's across from her. Ysobel has taken control. From the inside.

Fisch is choking, halfway through a swallow when his hand took its painful, unexpected detour. His face is beet red. His eyes now bulging. He makes awful gargling and gasping sounds as he lurches forward, reaching for the steak knife handle, to try and pry it out of his impaled hand.

Ysobel slaps him square in the nose with the back of her hand. Then picks up her own steak knife and plunges it into his throat.

———

Like all the modern descendants of the old guild societies, The Lotus had accumulated many rules and protocols over the ages. One's ascent through a guild's ranks was often a function of how well one could navigate the twisting labyrinth of those rules. There were always contradictions. So you had to learn, prioritize, and step lightly. Some rules were ironclad. Some you could bend. Some you could safely ignore.

Zijian was a skilled navigator of The Lotus rules. She was diligent in finding out which rules mattered to her superiors and which didn't. Then she would work the rules to either impress them or catch out her rivals. When her rivals slipped up, bent or broke the ironclad rules, Zijian was there to document and report it. This was how she replaced her old mentor, Dogura Du Page. When she had learned everything she needed to from him, she waited until he was under pressure with a difficult contract. Waited for him to step outside the approved protocol. Arranged it so that Master Minza would catch him in a lie. And that was that. A seat on The Lotus Rainbow opened up for her.

Over the long history of The Assassins Guild, the rules had evolved and changed. But two rules had remained ironclad since the beginning. The first, and most sacred, was The Killing Protocol. No target can be executed outside of an official protocol. Without this rule, the assassins were no better than hired thugs. Thus, any assassin who killed off-protocol was immediately cast out from the Guild and their life would be forfeit.

The second ironclad rule was Hospitality and Protection. If the Guild arranged a private meeting, then no harm could come to the invitees. This was equally essential for conducting business. And just like off-protocol kills, any violators would be marked for death. Hunted down. No exceptions.

———

Drawn by the noise of Inspector Fisch's suffering, the Jade and Sapphire lieutenants arrive in the doorway to the dining room.

They find Ysobel standing back a few steps from the table. Splattered with blood. Her eyes closed. Hands pressed together. A posture of intense focus and concentration.

Fisch is a red mess. One knife nailing his hand to the table. Another lodged in his throat. His eyes are already dead, though a few spurts of blood are still escaping from his wounds.

Zijian is standing as well. Eyes open. Breathing heavy. Sweat now pouring down her face as she struggles to regain control over her body. She manages to slowly turn her head. Meeting the eyes of her lieutenants. She knows that they know the ironclad rule has been broken. What has just happened is unforgivable.

Ija. Please understand. He was a bad man. I can explain later. This is for the best.

Ysobel has invaded her mind. Zijian knows she has been fooled. It is too late to eject the girl entirely. But perhaps not too late to prevent her from going deeper and learning everything.

Zijian remembers the face of her mother. Remembers the game they used to play. She has not thought of this for an age. But she remembers it now. Begins constructing a trap.

"Madame Sun," says the Jade lieutenant as he draws his sword. "I'm sorry. This is unforgivable."

Sapphire does the same. Echoes the apology. "It is unforgivable, Madame. We must."

The two lieutenants stalk into the room. Jade goes left, moving behind Zijian. Sapphire goes right, around Fisch's body. They close on Ysobel.

Zijian slowly turns her head to Ysobel. The girl stands perfectly still. Does not lift her eyes. Her lips moving slightly, whispering the words of a spell.

A strange new fire ignites inside Zijian. It is not the cold fire of the assassin. Nor is it the hot fire of jealousy that she felt earlier. It is something altogether different. It feels like *inevitability*. She no longer has any choices to make. There is only action in service to the will of the other insider her mind.

She reaches down and pulls a dagger from its hidden sheath inside her boot. She spins, slides, and slashes the ankle of her Jade lieutenant. He stumbles and starts to turn. But Zijian is back on her feet, hand over his mouth, dagger deep in his back before he can scream.

"I am sorry, Arthur," she whispers in his ear. Guides his twitching body swiftly to the ground. "You have served me well."

Sapphire freezes in shock for a tick. Struggling to believe what she has just seen. But then her duty kicks in and she turns on Zijian. "Traitor!" She shouts, leaping across the table, her blade held high.

Zijian takes the sword from Jade's hand. She has just enough time to fend off Sapphire's mighty overhead swing.

A loud clang of steel on steel.

Disappointment and betrayal fill Sapphire's eyes. "You are finished, Madame Sun. For what you've just done. Finished!"

Zijian laughs and takes a step back. Holds her arms out wide. A sword in one hand. A dagger in the other. A twisted version of the mother swan pose she uses to welcome her clients at the spa. "Come now, child," she says. "I am death itself. Come. You try and finish me."

They both move. Sapphire, a strong thrust with her blade. Zijian, a twirl of her whole body, deflecting the other's thrust with the dagger, completing her rotation with a wicked crossing slash of the sword. Her slice is clean, cutting her lieutenant across the torso, from left collar down to right hip.

Sapphire drops to her knees. Drops her sword. Defeated. Zijian kneels behind and completes the kill with her dagger. She gently guides the body to the floor, whispering her lieutenant's name and thanking her, as she did for Jade.

When it's over, she rises and regards Ysobel calmly. Her tasks completed for the moment.

"Do you have further instructions for me, mistress?"

Zijian hears the words come out of her mouth. Like everything else that has happened in the last few rounds, it all seems far away. Accompanied by a similarly distant sensation of doom. But she knows that she cannot worry about that now. Control of her body is lost for the time being. So she must focus on the next battlefront. Focus on surviving to fight another day.

With an inner part of her mind, she imagines her office. Pictures her assistant bringing her a stack of files. She must look through them, decide which ones to keep and which ones to destroy. She sees Ysobel standing in the doorway. Invites her to join in making these important decisions. The girl happily obliges. They sit down on the couches next to each other and begin to look through the paperwork.

PART THREE

MAYHEM

CHAPTER 19
ELI

...GOES FOR A WALK

Eli strolls through the park. Middle of the night. The streetwise of New World City will tell you not to go wandering through the park this late. Every little copse, so charming during the daytime, becomes a shady lurking-hole for all manner of who-knows-what.

Eli knows this. But Eli doesn't care. If he wants to go walking through his city park at night, he will. If the weirdos want to come at him, he welcomes it.

And on this particular night, there is a particular weirdo he has come to see.

That psycho-bitch, Val. Better not keep me waiting. If she's going to insist on this stupid fucking meeting place and this stupid fucking time, she better damn well be there.

The park air is cool. Refreshing.

Eli follows an old cobble path of faded red and gray stones as it meanders through the dense, dark green of the trees. Decorative 19th century lampposts dot the way.

He's headed to the statue garden. It's just about dead smack in the middle of the park. So it will take a while to get there on foot.

I should have parachuted in for this.

He hurries along. Not afraid, but impatient.

He remembers the bag of white powder in his jacket. He whips it out and takes a little sniff as he walks. A nice little something to help him pick up the pace.

An animal snarls from the dark nearby, just off the path. It sends Eli into a state. He suddenly feels like he's dreaming. Back at home. In his bed. This whole wandering through the park to meet Val—that's not real. Or if it is, then it's a shadow Eli. Some trick that Idris is playing.

To an outside observer (of which there are a few), Eli's gait changes. His rapid stroll downshifts into a slow shamble. A zombie's shuffle, you might say. He lets out a low, guttural wail. The animal snarling stops abruptly and whatever-it-was pads away quietly.

Another few ticks, Eli is back. Strolling along like before. The dreamy feeling gone. The zombie posture gone. All of it forgotten. He fidgets with the rings on his fingers. Wipes his nose with his hand.

This should be quick. Val is going to talk her nonsense. Then she'll accept the drugs, agree to the deal. Then I will get the fuck out of here.

I definitely should have told Dmitry to come with the helicopter...

———

Although Idris handled all the business of negotiations, Mayor Eli did have some understanding of Strauss Party relations with the city's gangland kingpins and queenpins.

For example, Eli knew that he could rely on the bootlegging Bulldogs for some quick muscle or drugs.

He knew that The Wakizashi had free reign over the

freeways, and in return, they would shut down any route (or hijack any road deliveries) if he asked.

The paramilitary gang, H.A.W.K., were a big deal throughout the low-income tenement districts. They worked on a purely cash basis. If you had the money to pay, they would do whatever you wanted provided they got to use their guns and explosives to do it.

The Azzuri were Ty's gang, and since Ty had entered the mayoral race, he and Eli were staunch enemies. Not that they were ever buddy-buddy to begin with. But at least until this election cycle was over, there would be no wheeling and dealings with The Fashionistos.

He felt neutral, leaning-negative about The Lotus. His father had been in bed with The Assassins. Much good did it do him. Eli certainly recognized Lotus' power and utility, but the whole affair with his dad had left a bad taste in his mouth. And now with his getting shot in the face... He wasn't sure, but he had the nagging sense The Lotus was at the root of it. Somehow... He would get them back for it. Someday...

That left The Charlies. Val and her troupe of sadistic, bejangled clowns. They were outliers in the Big Six. Their domain was what exactly? Doing all kinds of fucked up, twisted shit for no good reason? Eli didn't like it. (Perhaps too similar to his own character?) There was also something inhuman about them.

But intel was that Val had struck a deal with Ty. Forged an alliance. Now that Ty was his enemy, Eli would test the strength of that alliance. To see if he couldn't tempt Val into some good, old-fashioned backstabbing. Hit Ty where and when he least expected it. Knock that poser off his high perch for good.

———

The sound of chuckling and sleigh bells tells Eli he is getting close. He rounds the last bend on the path before the statue garden. And there they are: Looks to be almost a dozen Charlies, in their theatrical white clothes and dark derby hats.

What a bunch of fucking freaks.

Eli waves. "Hello, sickos!" He calls. A few of the Charlies laugh stupidly. Most are silent. All of them stare, slack-jawed, at the mayor as he strides into the clearing at the center of the garden. "Where doth your noble queen await?"

The Charlie nearest him—a burly man with black diamonds painted over his eyes—points with his thumb. Eli looks. Sees someone slumped over at a picnic table on the edge of the garden. A pale arm dangling off the side of the table. A tumble of red hair.

Yep, that's her.

He shoots a finger-gun at the burly one. "Thanks, genius." Marches off in the direction of the table.

As he approaches, he shouts, "Hey, Val! Time to wake the fuck up!"

She does not stir.

Oh for fuck's sake! Is she going to be whacked out on her psychotropics? I've come all this way and she's crashed like a fucking lightweight.

He reaches the picnic table. Sits down opposite the pale, red-haired drowsy. Pounds on the table with his fist.

The woman sits bolt upright, whipping him in the face with her long red hair as she snaps to.

"Oh hiii, Eliii," she croons. Her eyes still closed. She rolls her head from side to side.

There's a strange, alien beauty about Val, the Great Harlequin. No question she's a dollface, but an exaggerated one. All her features just on the other side of too big or too small. Her skin so milk white that she doesn't need to paint it like her goons. Dark makeup around her eyes. Red lips. Her body lean and strong like a dancer's. She's not tall, but her presence is nevertheless imposing.

Her mouth, initially slack and drooping open, gradually tightens into a bloodthirsty grin. "Iii'm so glad we could meet for this little chat."

She opens her eyes. Her pupils are storm gray, but the "whites" are a disturbing mess of colors. They morph from pale red to pale yellow to pale blue. In a dizzying, swirling cycle. Like how a hypnotist's eyes might be portrayed in some old movie. Except rather than putting you in a trance, it turns your stomach.

Eli avoids the nausea by alternating his gaze between her generous mouth and tits. "Yeah, lovely. Great to see you, Val," he says. "So let's get to it. You know why I wanted to talk with you. I know you've struck a deal with Dr. T. I want you to break that deal. I'm happy to make it worth your while. I'm sure I can offer you more or better than that washed-up boxer."

Val drops her chin to her chest, eyes rolled to the top of her head. "You want to make a deal with me, Mr. Mayor?" She snorts a little laugh. "That's funny." She throws her head back. Rolls her eyes all the way down. "Do you have any idea what we do here?" She raises her hand to indicate her goons back at the clearing. "Our *mission* is to make your life as miserable as possible."

Eli fidgets with his rings. "No, I appreciate that, Val." He puts on a condescending smile. "And I do love how you make things more challenging."

She snorts another laugh. "Is that riiight?" She waves at her crew. They start making their way over. "It doesn't look that way to me. Nope, nope. Looks to me like you're a softy." She cocks her head, presses her lips together in a pitying expression. "Poor wittle ma'or boy wants it all weal easy."

Eli's pulse quickens. His rage meter rising. He didn't come here to be insulted like this. "Am I supposed to be intimidated?" Val's troupe is close now, gathered around a few paces back from the table. He glances at them and chuckles. "By your sad army of community theater rejects?"

Val shrugs. Arches a provocative eyebrow.

"And here I thought we were going to talk like civilized adults." He keeps his tone casual as he pulls out his bag of white powder.

Val's demeanor immediately changes. Her loose-goose drug haze vanishes and she grasps the table edges desperately. Greedy eyes fixed on the bag. "Where did you get that?"

He takes a sniff off his finger. "From a friend."

"Fuck. Fosse." She mutters under her breath.

He waggles the bag in front of her. "Would you like some?"

This little stratagem with Val was planned earlier that morning. Eli was doing his business on the toilet when the bathroom rapidly disassembled itself into the void and Idris appeared. Not only in the mirror this time. The fairy magician stood tall, in front of Eli, sharply menacing in his crisp, dark, pinstripe suit.

"Really, asshole? Can't this wait until I'm done?" Eli didn't understand why Idris so often dropped in like this when he was in the bathroom.

"No, no, my son. Now is the *perfect* time." Idris beamed. "I've just had a wonderful idea, and I can't wait to share it with you."

Eli rolled his eyes. "Fine. But don't stand there. I don't like you watching me while I shit."

Idris nodded politely and moved away. He leaned himself against the sink, beside the toilet, looking sideways at Eli as he spoke. "I had been contemplating our next move against Mr. Reese. To ensure that he does not usurp the mayor's seat that is rightfully... yours. Then I remembered a recent report I received from a staffer. It was about how Mr. Reese was counting on support from Ms. De Leo. Apparently, those two hooligans have struck a bargain. She will support his rise to political power, should he win the election. He will help her take back control of the drug supply lines that Mr. Foster took from her."

Eli reached the wiping stage of his business. "Yeah, so what?" He found this all supremely uninteresting.

"As you know, Mr. Foster and his Bulldogs are good friends of ours. And I believe we will have need of them yet. It would therefore be doubly unfortunate for this scheme of Mr. Reese and Ms. De Leo to succeed. So this got me thinking. And digging. And I discovered many interesting things about why Ms. De Leo is so upset about losing out on the drug trade to Mr. Foster."

Eli flushed the toilet. "She's upset because she loses a shit ton of money, obviously."

"No." Idris stepped aside from the sink so Eli could wash his hands. "It is not the money. It is because she needs the drugs. Personally. The white powder. She is an addict."

Eli said nothing. Still not interested.

"And there is more. I learned that she is an addict because she does not sleep. She cannot sleep. She has traded her sleep away, to a distant cousin of mine, in fact. In exchange for some magical abilities. Nothing so powerful that it need concern us, but it is intriguing."

Eli dried his hands on a towel. His patience spent. "Can

you get to the point? Why do I care about this? What is your stupid idea?" He would have simply left the bathroom, except the door was lost to the void. He was stuck in Idris' little pocket-dimension.

"I'm coming to that, my son." Idris said, clearly delighted with his story and the telling of it. "You see, something quite traumatic happened to Ms. De Leo when she was just a young, pre-nubile girl. I'm sure you can imagine what that might be. One effect of her trauma was terrible nightmares. Nightmares every night that she could not escape. So when my cousin offered to take those from her, and give her something much more valuable in return, she happily made the trade. No more sleep. No more bad dreams. And some new powers to play with."

Eli closed the toilet lid, sat back down. Resigning himself to story time. He yawned loudly.

"However, she is still a human of flesh and blood and she grows tired like every human does. Yet without the recovery of sleep, she feels utterly exhausted. Constantly. Her body and mind ache for a rest that they can never have. So she now lives in a kind of daze, taking all sorts of this and that to try and manage her state of exhaustion and delirium. But it's the white powder, you see, that she loves best. The white powder makes her feel fully awake. Fully alive! And it is her white powder supply that she lost to Mr. Foster."

At this, Eli remembered that he has some of the powder in his pocket. He takes it out and takes a sniff.

"Exactly, my son!" Idris snapped his fingers.

Offer to restore her access to the white powder and I'm sure she will do our bidding.

————

Val leans across the table and takes a hit off Eli's outstretched pinky finger. The effect is instantaneous. She shakes her head violently for a few ticks. Letting out short, staccato breaths. Then curls her mouth into a smile. Not bloodthirsty this time. A smile of sweet relief. Perhaps even a trace of joy.

Then she whispers the name again. "Fosse." And the smile fades. She rubs her nose. Licks her lips. Her expression becomes cold. She glares at Eli. The whites of her eyes have stopped their sickening, technicolor swirl. They are now just the ugly red of a drunkard's hangover.

"Feel better?" Eli asks.

She sneers. "So what do you WANT, Eli? You want me to fuck over Dr. T? Is that it?"

He shoots her a finger-gun. "Boom. Yes. Exactly."

"Because you think I'm a whore? Who will fuck anyone for the right price?"

Eli grins and shrugs. "You said it, not me, Val." He puts the bag away. Her breath catches with audible panic as the powder is removed from her sight.

Wow. Bitch has got it bad.

Val shakes the panic out of her face. Replaces it with a look of contempt. "You have no fucking clue, Mr. Mayor." She grinds her teeth. The circle of goons closes in another step. "If you want to play this game with the big kids, you need to learn the rules. And learn some respect while you're at it."

Eli turns away. Not interested in a lecture. He notices The Charlies looming in a tighter circle around them. "Could you tell your goons to give us some space, please? The, uh, smell of so many losers is a bit much for me."

Val exhales a sharp, dismissive, "Pfff." Waves her hand like she is shooing away a cloud of gnats. "You don't need to worry about them." The goons stay put.

Eli's rage meter rises. "Don't tell me what I need to worry about. I said to tell them to back the fuck off."

Val draws her lips into a wide, thin smile of defiance. But she says nothing.

Eli's rage meter crosses a threshold. "You want more of what I got in my little bag? Then how about you do what I say, you pathetic slut-bag!"

Val lets slip a giggle. "Slut. Bag." She repeats slowly, with an exaggerated, robotic voice. Her goons take a few more steps forward. "That hurts my feelings, Eli." A mocking tone.

The circle of Charlies getting very tight around them. Eli jumps up from the table and whirls around.

"You want some of this, you sickos?" He shouts. Rage meter near its max.

Val lets loose with her giggles. "Aww, wittle mista ma'or. I'm sawwy!"

The burly, black diamond Charlie reaches out to grab Eli's arm. Eli is quick and jacked up enough now to pull away. But there's no safe place to move. A second Charlie in the circle shoves him into the arms of a third, who wraps him up by the shoulders.

"Get your sick fucking hands off me!" He shouts, struggling helplessly against the hold and the many hands of the many goons that begin to claw at him. A chorus of low, sinister laughter ripples throughout the troupe.

Then Eli's struggling stops. The mad rage dissolves from his face. His shouts and curses replaced by primitive moans and growls. It all begins to seem like a dream again. His dream-self or shadow-self or whatever-self returns. Engages its zombie mode while True Eli's consciousness slips away to someplace safe.

The Charlies' laughter dies down as Val gets up and walks over to inspect the prisoner. She peers into his eyes.

Observes that the lights have gone out. "Thought so," she says. "You in there, Mr. Fairy? If so, stop teasing me with your stupid puppet."

Zombie Eli snarls and gnashes his teeth at her.

She reaches into his pocket, takes out the bag of powder, and waggles it in his face. "Thanks for this," she says. Helps herself to another bump as she starts back toward her picnic table.

The snarling then stops abruptly. Zombie Eli's body goes stiff as a board. Its mouth freezes, hanging open at an ugly, dislocated extreme. A new voice emerges from somewhere deep in the back of its throat.

The voice is cool and charming. "You are most welcome, my dear. These two bags, one of white man-flesh and one of white snuff-powder, are but small tokens. Overtures to my hopes of a future arrangement between us."

Val turns. Cocks her head to one side. "So you are in there?"

"Yes. I am."

"What's this really all about then? What is it that *you* want?"

"I simply want what is mine. My kingdom. What was stolen for me. Long ago."

Val takes a hesitant step back toward the gaping mouth. "Your kingdom?" Her eyelids begin to droop.

"Yes, my dear. I dare say you've heard of it. Perhaps you've even seen it in one of your sleepless, delirium visions? Spires of silver and emerald green. Vast fields of marigold and foxglove. Forests of hanging trees with an exquisitely decorated corpse hung on every branch. The great concentric stone circles, tended by all of the finest magicians wearing the finest silk robes."

"Mmm... Sounds nice." Her eyes close as she takes another drowsy step. Drawn to the sound of the voice.

"Nice. Yes. It is *very* nice. Filled with sumptuous flesh and exciting powders. Powders of all the many colors, my dear. Not just the white. But brown and red and blue. Yes, blue powder is the greatest of all. I'm sure you've heard. We could go there together, you and I. Once I have back what is mine, I would be happy to make a place for you. A place where you could indulge your every fantasy."

"My... fantasy..." Val half-whispers, half-moans. A painful longing in her voice. She lowers her face to within a hair's width of Zombie Eli's maw. Takes a sniff at his stinking breath.

"Yes," says the voice. "Whatever you desire. It can be yours."

Her eyes snap open. Back to their multi-colored, swirling crazy. "I'll think about it," she says. "And thanks again for this chew toy. But these mayor dolls of yours are a dime a dozen. I'm a classy girl. So if you want to impress me, maybe try getting me something a little more..." She rubs her thumb and forefinger together.

As Val dances away, giggling, one of her Charlies steps into the circle carrying a sledgehammer. "Have at 'im, fellas," she croons.

———

Eli sits up in his bed. It is still dark. His heart is racing.

For a few beats he remembers: The park. Val and the powder. The Charlies clawing at him. Visions of some fairy kingdom. Visions of him and Val, their naked bodies oiled up and glistening, decked out in heavy medieval jewelry. Her riding him hard atop a lavish four-poster bed. Her wicked laugh as she produced a sledgehammer from out of nowhere. Swings it over her head. Slams it down into his face.

And then it is gone.

And another piece of him goes with it. Lost. Forgotten.

His heartbeat begins to slow.

Fuck. What a weird dream.

Moonlight spills across the room from the large windows. His body initially throws no shadows on the bed. Then slowly, the dark of his shadow comes creeping back, spreading across his bed sheets like spilt ink.

Not that Eli notices or cares about such things.

He turns toward the light, fidgeting absentmindedly with his rings for a few beats. Then lies back down, closes his eyes, and drifts back to sleep.

CHAPTER 20
TY

...GETS DOWN IN JUNKTOWN

Barefoot. Stripped to the waist. Ty shuffles and dances in the dirt.

If this were a real fight, he would have his hands up, arms and elbows guarding his face. But this is sparring. So he's relaxed. Loose. Hands lowered. Strutting around. Cock of the walk.

His opponent is one of the King's "Knights of the Broken Table".

Laughable. These garbage-land Reachers with their silly, puffed-up titles.

The knight's name is Grigor. A big, heavy-set man, face hidden underneath a metal helmet shaped like a roaring lion's head. He is also stripped to the waist. But the helmet stays on. Always.

Ty has decided he likes Grigor. Off-putting to look at that metal lion's head at first. But then Ty spoke to him and found out Grigor is perfectly charming, in that hard-man, no-nonsense kind of way.

For Ty's stay in Junkland, sparring with Grigor has become a daily affair. It started as just something to do to break up the monotony, since they were waiting around to get The King's Word about whether he will be allowed to meet with Petra the Artefixer. But by the fourth day, Ty is looking forward to the time with Grigor in the sparring circle.

"You are very slow today," Grigor says.

"Ha!" Ty laughs. "Calling me slow?"

For their fights, Grigor tends to stand in one place. Legs apart, hands up. Keeping to a stable defensive stance. Pivoting to track Ty as he dances around.

I'll show you slow, you fat bastard.

Ty feints a left hook. Grigor moves his hand out to block. Ty swings with his right, going around Grigor's defense. Lands a good, open-palm strike that produces a loud bong off the big lion helmet.

"That's more like it!" Grigor lets out a good belly laugh.

Ty throws a few quick side-kicks. Grigor blocks them easily.

When he's in the city, Ty doesn't spar so much these days. He is busy managing The Azzuri, the business, the campaign, the music. Not much time left for the fighting ring.

It feels good. To be outside. In the dirt and dust and heat. Throwing his fists and feet around. Refreshing.

The air is cool this day, but the dusty ring is still hot in the sun. It smells of ash. Rust. Rubber. Like everything in Junkland. A hodgepodge of old and metal and garbage. Not pleasant. But a kind of industrial smell that you get used to after a round or two.

"So when do I get to meet this samurai girl?" Ty asks, still dancing. "Seems like she's all anyone in this town can talk about." He grins. This is trying to wind Grigor up. Since he's been in Junkland, Ty has heard all kinds of wild stories about the heroics of Asuka, Daughter of the Dawn,

Second Sword, Knight of the Broken Table. Apparently, The King sent her off to some far-away part of The Outer Reaches on a fool's quest.

Grigor bellows, "Bah! Why everyone so interested in her? She is Second Sword for a reason. I am First Sword." He slaps his chest proudly at those last words.

Ty does a little shimmy and half crouch, like he's preparing for a big uppercut. Grigor squats in response, keeping his head and hands low to defend. Ty takes advantage. Instead of launching the uppercut, he skips around to one side and connects with a side-kick, flush to the big man's ribs.

Grigor grunts.

"Who's slow now?" Ty flashes his champion's grin. "Too much for you?" Then he tries the same move again.

Grigor defends the same way, but this time he moves fast enough to swat away the follow-up kick. "Bah!" Shouts the big man.

"So how d'you get to be First Sword?" Ty asks, still grinning. "It's clearly not a popularity contest." Still dancing. "Cuz she's gotcha beat there."

Grigor growls. "The First Sword has challenged and defeated all lower Swords." Then he takes a rare step forward, shifting to attack mode. He can move quickly when he chooses to. He throws a mighty chop with the flat of his hand, forcing Ty to leap back and away.

"What's that mean? You had to throw down a gauntlet and defeat the old First Sword?" Ty continues to scoot away, throwing defensive jabs.

"Yes."

"How many did you defeat on your way to becoming First?"

"Twenty."

Ty whistles.

"Yes." He can hear the smile of pride inside Grigor's helmet.

"How many challenges have you faced since becoming First?"

"Forty-seven."

Ty whistles again.

Elicits another proud, "Yes."

He throws out a poke. Grigor blocks it and swings a counter. Ty ducks underneath, still scooting, backing around the sparring circle. Grigor continues to advance on him.

"Has samurai girl challenged you yet?"

A longer pause before answering. "No," Grigor says. "But she will. One day. And I look forward to it."

"How do the challenge fights work? Do you fight to the death?"

Grigor plants his feet. Returns to his defensive posture. "The challenger is allowed to set terms. Some choose to the death. Some choose to submission."

"Which did you choose when you were challenger?"

"Depended." Grigor thinks for a beat. "On respect... Or whether I liked them."

Ty snorts. "Probably executed a few numbskulls in your time, huh?"

A few more beats of silence as Grigor thinks about the question.

Ty doesn't wait for him to answer before he asks another. "What do you think samurai girl will choose when she comes to challenge you?"

No pause this time. Grigor answers immediately. "She always choose death."

———

Sundown, day five of the long drive when they finally arrived at Junkland. What used to be called "Baracus" in older times, before The Great War. The Great War that buried Old Baracus under a tidal wave of wreckage and debris. The Great War that left so much of the land beyond a hellish, smoldering waste that is now simply called "The Devastation".

You might think that a people whose country and lives had been so thoroughly destroyed by The Great War would be weary of politics. You might think they would try to rebuild their society with an eye to greater peace or communism or simplicity. But no. As soon as Junkland was on its feet, a strong man rose up, declared himself the new king. And the people accepted it.

As Ty rolled into town, he was struck by the look of the place. He had seen pictures, but it was different up close. Everything was ramshackle. New buildings made from pieces of old buildings. All stacked on top of each other in slapdash configurations that looked like they should topple over at any moment. Assembled from various bits of rusted metal, rotting wood, colored plastic panels. The occasional glass window or block of cut stone.

The king's guards at the city gate looked like medieval warriors. Big, muscular, long beards. They all wore partial suits of armor that were a similar hodgepodge. Rusty metal pauldron, leather breastplate, spiked chains for belts. Ty was struck by the look, made a mental note to send a few of his fashion designers out here to get some inspiration.

The roadways of Junkland were not intended for city cars. Too narrow. The roadbeds too soft. So they had to park and leave their cars on the edge of town. But the whole place wasn't so big. You could walk it all in a few chimes. There were slums composed of thousands of metal-wood-plastic huts. All with little makeshift doors built into them, crowded among the hills of junk. There were a few high streets with bigger buildings for the shops and artisans. And overlooking it all, atop the highest junkpile, a castle keep. The seat of Uthyr, The Broken King.

Ty and his crew immediately learned where Petra the Artefixer could be found. She was in prison. Everyone in town knew it. There was some disagreement about what exactly she had done to displease His Royal Majesty, but there was universal agreement that he was furious and had her locked up.

That was bad news.

The good news was they could still meet with her. They would have to submit an official petition to the King. Pain in the ass red tape. But Agent Price had gone through this process before, knew the proper procedures, and was able to get the petition all written up and submitted within a day.

And they only had to wait until the following day to get an answer: The King would consider the proposal and let them know his final answer in four days.

That was bad news.

Ty hated waiting around. But the good news was he had budgeted six days for this stay in Junkland. If he could speak with the artefixer. At least learn about how to acquire the kind of power he wanted—the kind of power he *needed* to seize the top throne in New World City and keep it— then it could still be worth the long journey.

———

On the sixth day in town, the day The King's Word is expected, Ty sits with Agent Price at the bar. Waiting.

The bar takes up most of the downstairs at the inn where they're staying. It is by far the nicest place in Junkland. But that's not saying much.

They're drinking something that tastes like watered-down whiskey. The locals just call it "goldrush". It's the best drink on offer in Junkland. But again, that's not saying much.

When the King's Word arrives, it will be in the form of a sealed letter. Delivered to the clerk at the inn's front desk. The clerk will walk the thirty-pace to hand it to them at the bar.

Things work according to The Old Ways in Junkland. No telegraph or telecom. It is letters written and delivered by hand. Works well enough. And by day six of this backwater living, Ty would admit that he finds it easier to think without all the noise and tech and distraction he's surrounded by in NWC.

He finds himself curious to learn more about the place.

"So you were out here once before?" Ty is not typically one for chit-chat, but he's learned that Agent Price has seen a fair bit of action and has some good stories to tell.

"That's right," Price replies.

"On assignment?"

"Yeah. Although that wasn't the most interesting part."

Ty raises a tell-me-about-it eyebrow.

"The official business, obviously, I can't talk about. But like I said, it's not really worth talking about. Not compared to what happened after we finished that job." Price pauses, signals the bartender for a refill. "You've heard of pit-zombies, right?"

Ty chuckles. "In those cheesy old horror movies, yeah."

Price's eyes light up. "Exactly! I love those old movies. And I remember hearing, like, ghost stories or whatever you want to call them. As a kid. People talking about living dead things that crawled out of The Pit. And I always assumed it was some Glitzkrieg fantasy bullshit."

The bartender arrives with the fresh pour of goldrush.

"Thank you," Price says, taking the drink in one hand, and pointing to the bartender with the other. "But our guy Teddy here will tell you too: The pit-zombie hoards. They're real."

"Aye," says Teddy. "They're real. And a menace. Or they were. Thanks to Lady Asuka, it looks as though we don't have to worry so much about them anymore."

Ty is skeptical. "What do you mean 'they're real'? The zombies in those movies are idiots in costumes. What are real pit-zombies?"

"Mindless robos is what they are. Or some are robo-human hybrids. Those are more clever. We call those ones 'runners' because they seem to think and move fast. But they're all reanimated monsters made from parts in The Pits."

Price snaps his fingers, now pointing at Ty. "Yes! And last time I was here, there was a hoard of them that came this way. The King, his knights, and all the townsfolk. Everyone got out whatever weapons and firepower they had. Went out to fight them off. Must have been at least a couple thousand of the damned things."

"When were you here, lad?" Teddy asks Price.

"Ten turns back."

"Yeah, that sounds right. Just a few thousand then." Teddy gives Ty a wearied look that says that ain't nothing.

Ty turns to Price. "Did you stay and fight off the zombies?"

"I did. Wouldn't pass up a chance like that." Price grins. "Took down a fair handful." He pats the scattergun holstered inside his jacket. "But I have to say: It was something else watching The King out there. He's a giant, you know?" He fixes Ty with an intense look. "He has some kind of wicked-looking, mechanical scorpion's tail claw thing grafted on as, like, a third arm, and then fights with an enormous two-handed sword at the same time."

Teddy nods proudly. Ty strokes his chin, trying to picture it.

"Makes you understand why there's a might-makes-right legal system out here," Price says. "Hard to imagine anyone challenging him."

"You take down any of the runners?" Teddy asks.

Price nods. "Two."

Ty's still unsure if he believes any of this.

Although who the fuck knows? I wouldn't have believed that mayor-demon shit was possible either.

"How dangerous are they?" He asks.

"The regular ones, the "shamblers", they're called, right? They didn't seem much to worry about," Price says. "They're slow and seem like they're ready to fall apart before you blast 'em. Easy to pick off at a safe distance."

Teddy nods agreement, adding: "Runners are tricksy though."

"Yeah, those are definitely more threatening," Price continues. "Quick moving targets among all the slow walkers. I think if I was alone, or in a smaller group. The slow hoards could sort of clog you up, and then the runners could get at you while you're distracted or re-loading or something like that."

"That's why we go out as a whole village," Teddy explains. "Strength in numbers. We don't need to match their numbers, just so long as we have enough firepower that someone is always shooting. Never gives 'em time to get good positioning."

"It's wild though, I'll tell you," Price says, and takes a big gulp of his drink, wincing afterwards. "Or *surreal.* That's the better word. Seeing an army of synth-zombies made from the leftover garbage of the city, the war. All that.

And after the thousands are wiped out, and you see the little piles of garbage left behind. And you think about how that's a tiny fraction of a fraction of a fraction of all the shit in The Pits... "

The bartender pours himself a goldrush, augmenting Price's story with the occasional "yup" or "uh huh". Until Price addresses him directly.

"What was the biggest zombie hoard that you ever saw?"

"The most I've seen was probably around a hundred thousand or so." Teddy rubs his chin thoughtfully. "But just before The Great War, when we was still called Baracus, well before my time, I heard there was a hoard of about a million strong. The folk didn't even stand to fight that one. They just fled. Let the hoard wash through the town like a flood. Then the folk came back after the things moved on."

"What happened after? Where did that hoard go?" Ty asks.

The bartender shrugs.

"Sirs?" The voice of the clerk from behind interrupts. "Your letter has arrived." He hands the envelope to Price, who hands it to Ty.

Ty rips it open.

At last!

"King says we can go tomorrow. We can show this letter to the wardens. They will take us to see her."

––––––

The Junkland Castle dungeon is dank and dark. Lit by torchlight. Stinks of garbage. It has more stone in its construction than most of the other structures. But it's still that same motley assemblage of materials.

The wardens lead Ty down a hallway, lined by cell doors

on either side. Then down a flight of steps. Then down another hallway. Same as before. And another flight. And another. Enough that Ty starts to doubt his memory. Feels like he's tripping on psychs.

There's no way this garbage hole can be that deep...

Some of the cell doors are metal, looking like they were reclaimed from more modern prisons. Some are thick wood with those barred windows, looking straight out of an old story book.

Surreal.

Price used the word to describe the pit-zombies. Ty decides it pretty much applies to everything in Junkland.

At the end of what must be the tenth or eleventh hallway, the wardens stop at a wooden cell door. One of them takes out a massive ring of skeleton keys. Searches through it, selects one, and unlocks the door. "You have until sundown," he says to Ty. Then he swings the door open.

Ty looks inside. The cell is larger than he expected. Feels about the size of his penthouse bathroom back in the city.

There is a low ledge, for sitting or sleeping. A hole for shitting.

And that's it. The only light comes from the torchlight in the hall, through the tiny barred window in the door.

A woman sits cross-legged on the ledge. Like she's been meditating. She lifts her head. Regards Ty, the wardens, and the open door with serenity.

She looks younger than Ty expected. Late thirties, early forties, maybe? Auburn hair tied in a knot atop her head. She looks hungry, like she hasn't eaten in many days. Her skin and clothes are filthy.

Ty steps in. It did not smell good in the hallway. It smells worse in the cell. A mix of garbage, body odor, and human waste.

The warden shuts the door and locks them in. "Just holler if you want out," he says. "We'll be right outside."

If this were the city, Ty would never allow wardens to lock him in a cell. Not under any circumstance. But something about the life and people he's seen in Junkland puts him at ease.

Something about The Old Ways, I guess. Like a man's word still means something.

"You just come to look?" The woman says, a slight smile breaking onto her face. Her voice is painfully dry.

"You're Petra?" Ty asks.

"That's me."

"The artefixer."

"That's right."

"How long have you been here?"

Petra holds up her hands and shrugs her shoulders. The pose, combined with her crossed-legs, makes her look like one of those religious idols of Xanadu.

"Hard to track time in the dark, huh?" Ty doesn't really want to make small talk. But neither does he feel comfortable jumping right to his true purpose. Feels like some effort should be made to show respect and build rapport.

She blinks at him curiously. "Have you come to interview me?"

Ty considers. "I guess so," he says. "I've come from the city. I wanted to ask you to craft something for me. But looks like that won't be possible, will it."

She shakes her head. "Sadly, no." She laughs. Then the laugh devolves into a spate of wheezing.

Ty turns to the door and barks at the wardens. "Hey! Can we get something to drink here? She needs it."

"No liquids for prisoners on this floor."

No liquids? How the fuck can she survive down here for more than a few days without anything to drink?

Petra waves one hand up and down. "I'll be fine. Don't you worry, stranger," she says. "But that was sweet of you." Her smile grows a little bigger.

Turning back around, Ty takes a few steps forward and extends his hand. "My name's Ty."

"Pleased to meet you, Ty." She places her hand in his. "From the big city? You've come a long way. I'm sorry that I can't be of more use to you. Not much I can do away from my workshop." She frowns. "But if you have questions for me, you may ask them."

Ty purses his lips and considers. He has come all this way to learn about power. Specifically, how he can acquire power like what he witnessed at The Bloodhound Ballroom. Power on the scale of transforming into a demon of fire or some shit like that.

He has come to Petra to learn this. Yet, now that he is in her presence, he finds himself tempted by something else.

I wonder if I can get her out of here. Take her away with me.

He furrows his brow.

Nah. That's stupid. Agent Price told me not to try anything like that. Keep it to just talk. And besides, the wardens are right outside the door. They would hear us.

Petra's eyes lock onto his.

You want to rescue me, Big Ty from New World City?

A wry smile spreads fully across her face.

Help me escape?

Her eyes twinkle.

You are very sweet. But truly, I will be fine. My situation here is temporary. The King and I will work things out.

After another short wheeze, her expression becomes serious.

The timing is not right. Not for me to make you some-

thing. That time may come. For now, tell me your story. And quickly. Then perhaps I can help you.

CHAPTER 21

UZIEL

...BUYS THE MURDER WEAPON

Uziel waits in the corner booth of the Hot Pink Lounge. Waiting for a black market arms dealer.

He sits low in the seat, wearing a trench coat and wide-brimmed hat. Looking like a synth butler after work hours. Nothing suspicious. Just a laborer who wants to be left alone. Perfect profile for the Hot Pink. No one there wants to be recognized. It's about as seedy a joint as you'll find in the cyber-synth quarters of New World City. Thumping music, dim neon, and all the juice or drugs you could want on offer. Frequented mostly by cyborgs and synths whose best days are long past.

Word is that this arms dealer—man by the name of Czecho Das—has some powerful anti-magic tech that he is willing to move. Normally, Uziel wouldn't deal with someone who sells weapons to criminals, but he's turned up no better leads. If they're going to stop Idris Moorelake Pendragon, they will need something heavy. Something unlikely to be found in the legitimate marketplaces.

Czecho is late. This activates a few frustration circuits, but Uziel can manage it. He dials up his noise reduction algorithms to cut out the obnoxious music. Inspects the tangled array of cords and adapters coming up through a hole in the middle of the table. He finds the one for regular old electricity and plugs in. He has to pay for something if he's going to be allowed to sit for long.

He uses the down time to number crunch. Running scenarios. Calculating odds. After investigating The Lotus and consulting with the other Vigilantes, he now knew much more about who, and what, they were up against. He was still trying to work out how they would be able to successfully isolate and neutralize this ancient wizard. But he felt confident they could find a way. Given enough time and processing power.

———

"I checked with The Bard, and he also believes this is Fae Lord Pendragon, one of Faesia's greatest generals. A fearsome battle mage in the Wars of Restoration." Benoit, the Vigilantes League's resident psychic mutant panda warrior (and philosopher), was recounting his knowledge on the subject for the group. "He once ruled the kingdom of Cherish-Obelistwyth, which was one of the dominions of that era that straddled the two worlds. Cherish on Earth. Obelistwyth in Faesia."

Uziel sat and listened alongside the other Vigilantes—Meg the Magnificent and Tank. Each seated at their respective workstations in the League's underground base. Meg's desk was a wall of computers. Tank's a small welding and repair shop. Uziel's a simple metal desk with a single laptop computer.

Benoit's desk was a mess of books and chemistry equipment. He had a few old history books in his collection and would grab one and look things up occasionally as he spoke.

"I have an epistolary volume from the 16th century that had some fascinating accounts of Pendragon's magic. There was the great fireballs and lightning strikes that he used on the battlefield, of course. But more interesting, and disturbing by far, were the enchantments." He worked his big, fuzzy fingers to flip through the pages, looking for a particular passage. "Here it is! In a letter from the Earl of Feduke to his wife, he describes an account from one of Pendragon's captors. A Lieutenant James Eld Charos, who had to be institutionalized after the war. Here is what he wrote, referring to Charos:

> *The man seemed to suggest that Pendragon seduced him. Or "took him to bed" were the words he used. Then he said he was "taken away" to live a long, happy life, as a huntsman, seemingly married to Pendragon. He said they lived in a "Castle of Many Colors" in a lush junglelands. Full of beautiful, tall trees and great packs of roving beasts. He said that every day, he and Pendragon would ride out together, slaughter many animals, and then host a feast in the castle.*
>
> *It sounds wonderful at first, does it not, my dear? If that were the end of it, I should not think enchantment such a bad thing. But we explained to Eld Charos that this was all an illusion. We explained how, in truth, he had been serving in Pendragon's army, enthralled to the sinister fairy's will. We explained that he had not been slaughtering any beasts, but rather it was many of his own countrymen who he had killed on the battlefield, and it was very probably their flesh that he had feasted upon.*
>
> *We explain all this, yet he refused to believe. He insisted that this fantasy jungleland with its colorful castle was the real world. The war, the hospital, all of us on the medical team—we were the illusion. We were all a trick of his*

psyche. He believed that he must have fallen from his riding horse and hit his head.

Even when we pointed out to him the contradiction in his story—That Pendragon had, by his own admission, "taken him away" and, therefore, there had to be a place that he was taken from. He still did not accept it.

I understand from speaking with many of the other soldiers, that Eld Charos had once been a great leader. Before he was taken captive and enchanted, he had fought bravely and did much to bring glory to our empire. Thus was it doubly-sad to see such a man so reduced. However, I know from speaking with my colleagues, that he is far from the only captor to be returned in such a state. It seems that Pendragon did this sort of thing routinely, twisting the minds of his victims.

Benoit stopped reading. "Then he goes on to other subject matter." He closed the book. Looked at Uziel and Tank. "You two, I suspect, won't be at risk of that kind of enchantment. But anyone flesh-and-blood." He tapped his chest. "Me. Meg. Constable Li. The mayor... " He scratched behind his ear nervously. "Face terrible risk."

"How has the fairy survived all this time?" Tank asked. His robotic voice deep and round. Like if an electric bass guitar could talk.

"It's a good question," Benoit replied. "I don't know. Fairy life spans are very different from Earthlings. But from everything I've read, the fae are dependent upon the magical energies of their world. So the re-sealing of the veil, and the waning of magic on Earth... It seems like he should have withered away. It shouldn't be possible for him to have lived on Earth for so long."

"Not only to have lived so long," Uziel added. "But to be able to work this level of magic."

"Maybe he's got a bunch of artefacts," Meg suggested.

Benoit acknowledged the possibility. "Could also be that magic on Earth is in a waxing period."

Uziel processed these ideas. Still struggling to resolve the optimal strategy.

It was Tank who offered a potential solution. "I have records of a technology developed at The Ragnarok for use in The Great War, in case Marial fielded any magicians. They did not. So my records suggest the tech was never used. The idea was to produce an anti-magic pulse. Like an electromagnetic pulse. But instead of disrupting circuits, it would negate a magician's abilities. Not permanently. But long enough to obliterate them with conventional ballistics."

———

"Evening to you, Jeeves," Czecho says, finally arriving a full-chime late. An odd smile on his face. Bubbly, neon green drink in his hand. "May I join you?"

Uziel indicates the seat opposite, gives Czecho a quick scan as he sits down. The arms dealer is a cyborg. Human parts are in their late fifties. Implants are late thirties. Everything still in decent shape. Skin is tanned and weathered. He wears a pair of holograph glasses. He has lost most of the hair on his head, but has a long, wispy, gray beard.

Czecho grins, recognizing what Uziel is doing. "Everything look okay? How's my ticker?"

Uziel ignores the question. "Thank you, Mr. Das, for meeting on such short notice."

"Please, please, you can call me Czecho. And I should call you... Silvernight, is it?"

"Nightwing."

Czecho snaps his fingers. "Ah, yes! I was close though."
He chuckles. In a friendly way. "So how can I help you?"

"I am interested in anti-magic technology."

Czecho raises his eyebrows. "Are you now? That is an unusual interest for a synth."

Uziel ignores the comment. "There is military technology, from the time of The Great War, that could shut down a magician."

"Yes, I know of it."

"Do you have any of it?"

Czecho shakes his head. He takes a long sip of his drink. Then says: "But I could probably get it for you. Or something like it."

"How soon?" Uziel asks.

"Seven or eight days."

"What is it exactly that you could get?"

Another long sip. "I've seen it come in a few shapes and sizes. But the ones I could get my hands on, they look like big darts. You throw them in the ground or some such. Trigger them with a timer or remote signal." He chuckles again. In a less friendly way. "Ka-boom."

Uziel processes. "An explosion? Like a grenade?"

Czecho shakes his head. "More like a flash bomb. No blast of air or shrapnel or any such. But if you are close, you will feel it." He pauses for a small sip. Taps a finger to his temple. "Feel it in your mind. Or so I am told." He gives Uziel a quizzical look. "Although in your case... I don't know what it does to a synth. Maybe nothing."

"What do you think it might do to a fairy?"

The question elicits another raise of the dealer's eyebrows. And another grin. A grim one this time. "Wouldn't be pretty, I don't think. I'm no expert on fae, but what I understand of this tech: It harnesses latent power in the veil—you know, the anti-matter-y stuff that separates our world from theirs." Uziel nods. "It polarizes that energy and then amplifies the anti-magic 'particles,' if you will." He pauses to stroke his beard. "Effect might be like suddenly removing all the water from a human." He sucks in his cheeks to illustrate.

Rapidly processing. "So it's lethal then."

Czecho holds out his palms and smiles. "This is old Ragnarok tech we're talking about here. Not known for mercy, are they?"

———

After they had completed their late-night work at the 12th Avenue Lotus Hotel & Spa, Uziel escorted Shuwen back home. It was close to dawn by the time they arrived at her place. They had traveled over the rooftops. She was fit, and her bracers helped her keep up with him, but he could tell she was exhausted. She could barely hold on to him as he rappelled them down the side of her apartment building to her window on the fire escape.

"It was good working with you tonight, Constable," he said as their feet touched down.

She slid away from him, opened the window, climbed half inside before she stopped and looked back.

"What is happening?" Her voice was thick with weariness. "The mayor signed his own writ? His chief of staff is some old fairy magician? The sniper from some company I've never heard of. Their signatory using 'M-m-e,' like they did in Old Marial." She released a long sigh and rubbed her eyes. "Are we in some kind of time warp? It's too much."

"Yes. It is a lot to process." He gave her a quick scan. "You should get some rest."

"Yeah... " She sounded dejected. She took a deep breath. Still on her window sill. One leg inside her apartment, one leg outside on the first escape. "My chief told me to leave this case alone. Said he thought it was a game I couldn't win."

Uziel processed. "Chief Wolff is smart. Why didn't you listen to him?"

"I don't know." She paused, looked into Uziel's face. His eyes re-focused, zoomed in on hers. "A Stasi agent tracked me down too. Told me to drop it. Basically told me I was stupid."

"The Stasi are not reliable. Unfortunately. Not to be trusted."

"Yeah." She paused for a few beats. "This case feels important. Like maybe the most important one of my life. Just leaving it alone... That would be like giving up." She looked away. Took another deep breath. "That's not who I am." She brushed her fingers across her bracers. "The Li Family doesn't give up."

Uziel opened a compartment in his utility belt. He took out a small, shiny piece of metal. No larger than a penny.

"Here," he said, offering it to Shuwen. "It's a tracker. All of us in The League wear them. Keep it on you at all times. If you get in any trouble, it will let me know. I will come to help you."

She looked at him blankly. Uncertain.

"Please." He added.

There was a long hesitation. In the end, she took it, and attached the tiny device to the leather strap on the inside of her bracers.

"Good. Now get some rest, Constable."

"Yeah, okay. Good night, Silverman." She swung her other leg inside, hopped down off the sill, and shut the window.

———

Czecho returns to the table with a fresh drink. Fluorescent orange liquid this time instead of green. Another quick scan and Uziel can tell he's already drunk. He calculates that this is favorable for the negotiations to come.

"How much," Uziel asks, "for this anti-magic dart?"

He doesn't like that Czecho's weapon is likely to be fatal. Much better to subdue Pendragon, if possible. There is more good that could come from interrogating someone like that. But a dead fairy wizard is certainly better than one roaming free, enchanting people and causing trouble all over New World City.

Czecho takes a gulp of his drink. Little orange droplets are sprinkled in his beard. "Yes, very good," he says, "we should talk about that. I am quite curious to know what sort of coin The Silver Knight has to spend." He peers at Uziel across the table, his holograph glasses have slid down to the tip of his nose.

"I can pay in any legitimate currency," Uziel replies.

Czecho takes another sip and ponders this response. "Shadowcoin?" He asks, naming the common currency of The Undercity.

Uziel nods.

"That could suit." He swishes what remains of his drink in his glass. Pushes his glasses back up, concealing his eyes. "Ten thousand."

"Five."

"Eight."

"Done." Uziel holds out his hand.

Czecho shakes it with enthusiasm. "Half now. Half on delivery. Within eight days, I will contact you and arrange the delivery."

Uziel processes these terms. Relays a series of messages and instructions. To his financial accounts. To his colleagues in The League. Updating them on the purchase.

He is about to speak and confirm the deal when he gets an unexpected, incoming signal.

It is Shuwen's tracker.

There is a dramatic location discontinuity.

She's been teleported.

A sure sign that she is in serious danger.

He jumps out of his seat. "We are confirmed, Mr. Das," he says. "I've sent you the first payment. Now I must go."

Czecho holds up one finger, his drink at his lips, his eyes scanning the tiny info displays in his glasses. Waiting for the confirmation that the money has hit his account.

Uziel does not wait. He dashes out the back of the club. Racing to the rooftops. Shedding the butler's costume as he goes. Becoming Nightwing.

Anxiety circuits activating. The tracker will lead him to Shuwen. But she is not close. It will take him near half the night to reach her. And by his most probable calculations, he will be too late.

CHAPTER 22

SHUWEN

...RUNS AFOUL OF A FAIRY

Shuwen's badge gets her in the door to City Hall. No questions asked. The paperwork she's hauling for her precinct gets her to the upper floors. All legit. No laws broken.

Getting into the office of the mayor's chief of staff? That's a different story.

The office doors are locked with keypads. Some higher ranking officers, like Chief Wolff, have a skeleton card that will open anything. Shuwen's not quite that lucky. She thought about "borrowing" it. But decided against. In case things go sour, she doesn't want to be dragging Wolff down into the muck with her.

Instead, she asked her new friends in The Vigilantes League. And Meg the Magnificent was happy to oblige. Printed her up a counterfeit keycard no sweat. Definitely violating laws. And questions would definitely be asked if Shuwen was caught with it. However, if she was careful—and she would be careful—no one would need to know. Get in, get out, destroy the counterfeit card.

She arrives at City Hall in the evening. A quarter-chime

before closing time. She's in the door, through the lobby, up the big marble stairs. Three flights. No problem.

She delivers the precinct paperwork to the Records Department. And while she's there, she asks for a quick search of "Free Moon Lancers, Ltd."—that company she saw listed on the Lotus writ for the sham assassination. Clerk tells her they're a registered business in The Outer Reaches. Prints Shuwen out a copy of the public file. She tucks it into her jacket pocket for later.

Next stop: the toilet. Camping out in a stall. An undignified gambit, but the right move for the situation. Let the place clear out. Let more folks head home for the day.

She waits until the sunlight goes from orange to cherryred. Uses some of that time to think again about Agent Montag's warning.

The Stasi don't care about the NWPD. Even if Montag seems concerned, I still don't trust her. Or any of them.

And Wolff's warning.

I am being careful... As careful as I can be without giving up.

She's not going to drop the case. She's in too deep now. She has the sniper's name, but that only raises more questions. And she *needs* to find the answers to those questions.

That is her duty. To uncover the truth. To seek justice. That is who she is.

Supercop.

She allows herself a little smile at the thought. She's never made much of the Supercop mantle. The fame and notoriety that comes from her career—it's not about that. For Shuwen, it is all about the work itself.

But still... she'd be lying if she said it didn't feel good to hear it sometimes.

Supercop Shuwen Li.

Uziel would understand. That's how he is too. He cares

about his duty first and foremost. But he values the respect and attention too. I can tell.

Her smile grows a little larger as she thinks of her new, silvery, friend.

Comrade.

Brother-in-crime-fighting?

He's one of those things, surely.

But not a partner.

No. Constable Shuwen Li works alone.

Speaking of which: It's action time.

She exits the stall. Washes her hands and steps back out into the hall.

Quiet enough now that she can hear the front door guards having a relaxed conversation several floors below.

She takes the big marble steps down one flight. The mayor's office (hardly ever used) is on the third floor. And right next to that, is the office of Mr. Moorelake. The man, or fairy, or whatever-he-is, who signed that Lotus writ as witness. The one Uziel and his vigilante crew think is behind this whole crazy conspiracy.

No lights appear to be on inside any of the offices. No guards patrolling either. So she stops. Stands casually outside Moorelake's office and listens.

Nothing.

She kneels below the interior glass window and places her ear to the door.

Still nothing.

She slips on a pair of thin gloves. Now is the moment of truth for Meg's handiwork. She swipes the counterfeit card through the strip on the keypad. Hears the soft, happy click. Turns the nob. The door opens. She quickly steps inside.

The last of the evening light coming in through the

window is enough that Shuwen can see everything without having to touch a switch.

She is immediately struck by the room's general charm. Idris Moorelake appears to be a creature of fine taste. Everything neat and tidy. Dark wood furnishings in the 19th century Artisans' Style. Three large renaissance paintings on the walls. Striking images that dominate the space. One is of a triumphant warrior, covered in scars, standing in a grassy field, his long curly, dark hair blowing in a fierce wind.

Another is a portrait of a handsome scholar, bent over a table in a military tent, busily writing on parchment while several anxious looking generals stand by.

The largest painting is a dramatic landscape of a medieval kingdom being torn in two by a cataclysmic earthquake. A wicked fork of lightning splits the sky above a yawning chasm. The sky to the left of the fork is blue with a yellow sun. The sky to the right is green with a violet moon. A dramatic depiction of the War of Restoration.

Presenting the loser's perspective of that conflict, I guess.

She was always taught in school that the War of Restoration was a bloody victory that saved Earth from total annihilation. A triumph of good over evil. Rational over irrational. Nothing like a cataclysmic sundering.

She shrugs. Turns away from the artworks. Goes to inspect a small stack of papers on the central desk. It's all memos intended for the mayor's staff.

The desk drawers are unlocked. A quick rifling through turns up nothing of particular interest there either. Pens. Paper. Paperclips. That sort of thing. Nothing more.

There is a tall, locked filing cabinet. It is easily picked open. But like the stack of papers, the desk, and pretty much everything else: Nothing seems out of the ordinary.

Shuwen sighs. A swell of disappointment.

She gives the room one final pass. Then moves back to

the door. Listens for sounds of activity in the hall. Hearing none, she opens it, and slips back out.

———

A few days earlier, Shuwen met Henry and Faust on their beat at the park. There had been some violence the night before. Charlies took some poor sucker apart.

Shuwen found them at the statue garden. Henry was standing over by a picnic table. Faust was running around, sniffing like crazy.

"He's got something, doesn't he?"

Henry nodded. "Yup." His face was grave. Not feeling his usual jocular self. "Nasty business. These fucking Charlies."

Crime scenes are ugly affairs, but there was always something extra ugly when cleaning up after The Clowns. Their victims would be unzipped. Or flattened. It was often cartoonish, the extreme ways they killed people. Messy and horrifying.

"Any I.D. on the victim?" Shuwen asked.

Henry shook his head. "Not yet. Not much left to I.D., frankly. Maybe we'll get something back from the dental records."

Faust let out a few barks, having completed his investigation. Henry walked over and knelt down by his pooch.

"What do you think, boy?"

Faust growled.

Henry stroked his dog's head. "Was *she* here?"

Faust barked an affirmative.

"Val," Henry muttered as he stood up. Then he took a long, troubled breath. "Why was she out here smashing some random person to bits?"

"Are you sure it was a random person?" Shuwen offered. "Until the I.D. comes back, how do you know?"

Henry lifted his cap, ran a hand through his hair, said nothing.

Shuwen waited a few beats before she tried changing the subject. "Can I ask your advice, Henry?"

"About the case that isn't your case?"

"Yes."

Henry knelt back down to give Faust some good scratches. "Sure, go ahead."

"You were always better at navigating the gray zones," she began. "You know—the times when things get complicated. When it isn't clear what the right thing is?"

Henry looked up at her and smiled. A note of sadness in his eyes.

She continued: "It is looking like the person behind the assassination, not the assassin, but the person who arranged it. It is looking like they are inside City Hall. But if I'm going to investigate there... There's no way for me to really do that without breaking the law."

"Yup."

"Not just skirting the law, which I know we all do sometimes. To break into City Hall. Or into the offices inside. That's serious. I could lose my badge."

"Yup."

"And there's more. A Stasi agent approached me. Told me directly to drop it."

Henry stands. Gives her a concerned look. "What division?"

"D6."

He pursed his lips for a silent whistle. "Not good. D6 don't mess around. Who was the agent? Did you get their name?"

"Montag."

Henry shook his head. "Not heard of them. But that is not a good sign either. The more anonymous the agent, the more dangerous they are."

"I know."

Faust padded over and sat at Shuwen's feet. Wagged his tail. She knelt down to give him some attention.

"But I feel like I can't give up the case. Not now."

Henry chuckled. "You never could, kiddo. Not once a case has you hooked. You always had to see it through. No matter what."

———

Back outside Moorelake's office, Shuwen quietly closes the door. Walks a few paces to the big, double doors of the mayor's office.

The sun has gone down. It's not yet dark, but the light is now purple outside instead of red. And where before she could detect no lights on in the mayor's office, now it looks like there is something lit in there. A flickering.

Candlelight?

She puts her ear to the door. There's a humming sound. It's low. Sounds almost like a voice. She listens for few ticks. It's like a quiet baritone holding one long, steady, low note.

She feels a rush of excitement.

There's something strange going on in there. But how can I get in to check it out? I can't just walk in...

Then she remembers. Something unremarkable in the chief of staff's office—a door. A side door that almost certainly leads into the mayor's big room.

In a few quick beats, she is back in Moorelake's office. Listening beside the previously unremarkable door. It is solid wood. No window to see the flickering lights. But the hum is definitely still there.

She places her hand on the nob. Hesitates.

If I'm caught, this could be it.

A flood of memories wash over her, too fast to comprehend: She is racing against Henry around the track at the academy gym. Wolff's arm around her shoulder as she held up his gift of the framed newspaper from the Montrose Murder case. Seeing Tomas' pained face, the look of doom, as he fell to his knee at the riot. Hearing her mother's sigh of satisfaction the first time Shuwen put on the family bracers. Her father holding her hand as a child, as they walked home from the park one day after his shift.

It is fear, joy, regret, excitement. All at once.

The anticipation of an important event. An event that she knows will change the course of her life forever, even if she doesn't yet know what it is.

A feeling so fast and short and complex that if asked to describe it, Shuwen could only have said something like "goosebumps".

She is hooked.

There is no turning back now.

She turns the nob. Opens the door a crack. Peers into the room.

The hum is louder. She sees no one. But at the center of the office, just on the other side of the enormous desk, is the source of the sound: A cloud of what looks like fireflies. Swirling. Glowing.

Not candlelight... But what is it? It can't actually be bugs.

She is drawn to the light and movement. Compelled by it. She must have a closer look. The fear and anxiety of the consequences forgotten.

She slips into the room. Taking small, silent steps toward the cloud of soft, pulsing, golden light.

As she gets closer, she can see more. There is an image

in the center of the cloud. But it is wavy, rippling, like a heat mirage in the desert.

As she gets closer, she sees that it is an image of a man. Sitting. Facing away. Meditating? The man is in a blue suit. Coiffed silver hair.

Mayor Eli.

She is right next to the cloud. The movement, the sound, the golden light. It is beautiful. She wants to touch it. But when she tries to lift her arm, her bracers resist. They suddenly feel heavy. Too heavy to move. That has never happened before.

Wait... What's going on?

The thought seems to set off a chain reaction. All at once the floor drops away and something gets a tight grip on her neck. She can't move. She can barely breath.

The golden cloud dissolves. The entire room rapidly disassembles itself until all that remains are the big glass windows behind the desk, floating in a dark void. The sunlight is now all gone. It is only the sickly neon, yellow-pink glow of New World City's light pollution.

A voice, the same baritone as the hum, speaks to her. "I was starting to wonder when you would show up here."

A silhouette takes shape against the dim light from the window. A tall man. Dark suit. He holds her aloft with one clawed hand wrapped around her throat.

"You have been a most troublesome pawn. And I don't appreciate you rifling through my office without permission."

She cannot move. She is barely able to breath.

His face becomes visible. It is otherworldly. Wicked, animal-like features. Eyes and eyebrows and ears sharply pointed.

Idris Moorelake.

She feels her consciousness starting to slip away.

He grins. "Let's put you safely out of the way, shall we?"

He opens his hideous shark's mouth wide. Too wide. Wider than should be possible. Shuwen is pulled into it. Sucked down into his throat. Disappearing into the darkness within.

———

Shuwen's skin is hot. She pulls off the last of her clothes. Climbs on the bed. Climbs on top of him. It is her and Henry's first time.

It is thrilling. The feeling of his skin against hers. His strength. His smell. All of it. She wants all of him.

His lips. His tongue. On hers. On her body. His hands. Holding her. Firm. As she thrusts. As he thrusts. As they come together.

She screams. It feels incredible. Beyond words. She never wants it to end.

No.

Something is wrong.

Is someone else there in the room?

No. Wait.

It's not Henry.

It's Tomas. Bigger. Older. A deeper, richer man-smell. More sure of himself. Pulling her hair. Biting her lip. His strong hands, expert at opening her up. Twisting her into knots of oozing pleasure.

She screams for it. Again. And again.

Wait. Stop.

No.

Something is definitely wrong.

Who's there? What is happening?

Someone else *is* in the room. Going through the closet.

Opening up all the drawers. Looking under the bed. She can't quite see who is doing it.

She hears cackling. The rummaging grows more violent. Shirts. Dresses. Underwear. Jewelry. Pictures. Curtains. It's all getting pulled out, torn down, tossed around.

"What's wrong?" Tomas asks, momentarily pausing his exertions. His strong arms tight around her. His breath heavy against her chest. "You seem distracted?"

"No," she says. "I'm—" She trails off. Unsure of what she's feeling.

She glances around at the mess of the bedroom. Puzzled. Fear creeping in. She lifts Tomas face to hers and kisses him. Tries to push the anxiety from her mind.

Please let this be real. Let me be back there with him. Let everything else have been a bad dream. Please! Please!

He responds to her kiss. Starting back up. Biting her. But now a little too hard. Squeezing her. But a little too tight. Digging his nails into her flesh until it hurts.

No.

This is not Tomas. This isn't real.

It's him.

What is he doing to me?

As she pushes not-Tomas away, her head spins. The whole world turns upside down. The lights fade out.

She falls to her hands and knees.

She is alone. No more mess of her belongings. No more room. No more bed. Only the void.

She is cold. Dizzy. Naked. Confused.

She collapses to the ground. Clutches her wrists. Her bracers are there. But they are silent, dead metal. Unresponsive to her touch.

She cries out for help. Again. And again.

CHAPTER 23
INOLA

...PICKS UP THE THE PIECES

Inola sits down at her computer terminal.

"Inola Montag, agent 6-2-6, voice verification," she says.

A happy chime from the computer.

Agent verified.

The report from her D5 colleagues is in. They visited Outwash. Looked into this "Free Moon Lancers Ltd." Found the dirt. It's a front for terrorist remnants of Old Marial.

This opens up a whole slew of difficult questions for the Agency bigwigs. But for the purposes of Inola's case, it brings one question to the fore: Did Lotus know they were dealing with terrorists? They've abetted terrorism either way. But if they've done so knowingly, that would be sufficient grounds to strip them of the Assassin Guild license. Reason enough to take down the whole organization.

She pulls up the info feed on Lotus. The recent events don't look good. Two high-ranking Lotus lieutenants murdered (along with NWPD Inspector Fisch) in this incident at The Red Dragon Inn. And there was a break-in reported at Lotus HQ. All on the same night.

That's too much action for the innocent. Smells like a cover-up. Madame Sun will have all the answers. But she will be difficult to pin down. She's not known for being forthright. So, as usual, it will be best to come in sideways. Start with her enemies within the org. Or better yet—start with her allies.

Inola brings up the file on Zijian Sun, Chair of The Lotus Corporation.

The Stasi profiles are extensive. In addition to mining and cataloging all the public information, they use plenty of, shall we say, clandestine methods to populate the records.

With a few keystrokes, Inola is looking at Madame Sun's client schedule at the spa. One frequently-appearing name leaps out at her. As high profile as it gets. Ysobel Khan. Khan of the OmniCorp billions. They've been spending all kinds of time together.

Inola leans back in her chair. Lights a cigarette.

She's no stranger to tangled conspiracies. She had worked on the Strauss Sr. assassination case back in '95. What a tangled mess that was. And in the end, the tangle is what gave away The Dark Web. Too many threads, pulling in too many directions—that had always been The Dark Web's M.O. They thought they were being clever with all the cloak and dagger misdirection bullshit. They were really just being obvious. So often a characteristic of criminals. Too clever for their own good.

For the '95 case, Inola had been on the team investigating the NWPD. Within the force, there was all kinds of hatred toward Mayor Strauss. He cut their budgets. He constantly criticized them in the media. He demanded sacrificial firings when things didn't go his way. Nearly every PD officer she interrogated seemed to have the motive to take the mayor out.

But in the end, the true motive, the spark that set the whole thing off, was a personal grudge. Mayor Strauss had slept with the Chief Inspector's wife. Twenty turns earlier. The jealous Chief Inspector hated him for it, eventually struck a deal with The Dark Web, and then slowly brought in co-conspirators from the precincts. Everyone telling themselves that Mayor Strauss deserved to die and they were doing this for the greater good.

"Doing it for the greater good." Another common delusion among criminals.

She reflected afterwards at the comedy (or tragedy?) of it all. So often people would destroy their lives, and the lives of others, over some sex nonsense. Sure, sex was nice. Sex sells. "Sex makes the world go round" or whatever the pop-stars and poets said. Inola could appreciate that. She was made of flesh and blood, after all. But the world was filled with an endless array of flesh-and-blood pleasures. Sex was just one. And yet, sex seemed to be the thing. The prime weakness. The undoing for so many.

She takes a couple of slow drags on her cigarette. Ruminating. On the lessons of the past. And Lotus' apparent scrambling. Lotus execs often had "special relationships" with their highest-paying clients. Often looking to corrupt them.

Ysobel Khan was as juicy a target as they come. Yes. That had to be Madame Sun's game.

And Ysobel would surely know something. Or would be able to open the doors to get the information Inola needed.

A good place to start.

———

"What is your assessment, Agent Montag?" The old, gruff voice of Supervisor Six rattles out from behind the tinted glass.

Inola has never seen her supervisor's face. Despite hundreds of these meetings. This is the way it has always been within Division Six. The direct reports are a ritual of anonymity. Some say it's a holdover from the confessional booth and its use during the religious inquisitions of ages past. The agents confess, the supervisor listens and then "blesses" some course of action.

But there's no confessional booth here. It's just another yellowing, old, windowless government room. Doors on opposite sides. A single, long table with a large pane of blackened glass in the middle of it. The glass might have been tinted to begin with, but it is now caked a dark, opaque brown by decades of cigarette smoke. The room thick with it. Both Inola and her supervisor puffing away on their Roland's.

If she wanted, Inola could stand up, take four steps, walk around the glass, and look her supervisor in the eyes. Nothing physical prevents her. But she has never done this. And she never will. That is not the way of D6. And she is D6 until the day she dies.

"I'd like to begin with OmniCorp," Inola says. "Ysobel Khan, the soon-to-be CEO. She is a close contact of Madame Sun's."

The supervisor coughs her horrible smoker's cough in surprise. "Are you crazy? Lotus and OmniCorp? You want to upset all the hornets at once?"

"I'll keep it shiny," Inola replies. "Use a cover, like an anti-trust investigation. Say we've noticed the relationship between OmniCorp and Lotus and just want to ask a few questions."

Another, less painful-sounding cough. Inola knows this cough means "continue."

"But I believe that Madame Sun is cleaning house. Cleaning up after a big mess. Two of her lieutenants already murdered. I suspect we will see more of them die in the coming days. And if Miss Khan has any kind of close relationship with Sun, she is likely in danger." Inola pauses and considers. "She may already know she is in danger, and assist us in the investigation."

Another "continue" cough.

"So I will start with Miss Khan and OmniCorp. Report back. And then decide how to proceed with Lotus. If possible, I'd like to bring Madame Sun in for a full interrogation. Since she has been dealing with an Old Marial terror cell, there could be an opportunity to strike at the terrorists through her."

A small, throat-clearing cough. Inola knows what that means as well. She's got the go-ahead.

"Very good, Montag. And now, what of this grade 2 wizard, Idris Moorelake? I was surprised to see a former agent could have avoided our detection."

"I'm sure D5 will blame the oversight on budget cuts."

There is a spate of cough-laughing from the supervisor. "I will put in for a probe of the quality control in Division Five. Threats from magicians are highly irregular, but they should have caught him."

Inola agrees. Flips through a few pages of her pocketbook, reviewing her notes. "I did manage to track down Soliman, D5's agent at City Hall. He was compromised. Enchanted, I believe. I told him he should report in person for a physical exam. I assume he hasn't done so."

"Not that I've heard. No news like that from Supervisor Five."

Inola pauses for a few beats. Takes a drag. "He will need to be replaced then. As soon as possible."

She doesn't feel good about making this recommendation. But it does feel necessary. "Replaced" doesn't always mean killed, but that's usually how it goes down. A compromised agent cannot stand.

Another throat-clearing cough. "I will submit the order. I'll consider sending in a few of our big guns as well, to focus on Moorelake, while you look into OmniCorp and Lotus."

Inola closes her pocketbook. The case is proving to be messy business, indeed.

<hr>

A chime later, Inola is on hold. Sitting in front of one of D6's three video phone monitors. Advanced technology that was generously "donated" to the Agency by Omni-Corp. She called to make an in-person appointment, but the operator at Omni checked and said that Miss Khan was in, had an opening in her schedule, and would be available to speak shortly.

A stroke of good luck. Depending on how the conversation goes, this could save all kinds of time.

Inola doesn't love waiting on hold, but it's better than driving all day across the city to, most likely, sit in a waiting room. Division Six back in the day meant that you were never kept waiting. But not anymore. Times change. Stasi reputation and respect is not what it once was.

So she waits. One and a half cigarettes before the static on the phone monitor blinks out. The slightly blurry face of Ysobel Khan appears. Followed by the slightly garbled voice of a young woman.

"Hello, Agent... Montag, is it? How can I help you?"

"Yes, Montag. Thank you, Miss Khan, for talking this call. I am sure you are busy, so I will get right to the point: I am from the Agency's Economics and Business Team. I have a few questions for you about OmniCorp's relationship with The Lotus."

The image on the screen goes warped for a beat. The sound broken up with static. Inola misses the first few words of Ysobel's response.

"—obviously. I have been leading an employee wellness initiative at OmniCorp, and have been negotiating with Lotus to try and get our executives a discounted monthly membership to take advantage of the health and spa services."

Pocketbook out. Inola jots down this story. She doesn't believe it for one tick. But there are often traces of truth buried under lies. "I see, so that's the extent of the formal relationship between the two companies, as far as you are aware?"

"As far as I know, yes."

"I've been reviewing our files here, Miss Khan, and according to our records, you have regular meetings with Madame Sun, the Lotus Chair. Is that correct?"

The vertical hold goes on the monitor for several beats. A thousand and one images of Ysobel Khan's face go zooming past. But there's no static. Ysobel is just silent. Hard to make out her expression.

"Yes, that is correct," she says at last.

"Could you tell me when you last spoke with Madame Sun?"

"Several days ago. You can petition my secretary if you need the exact details of the meeting. I did reach out to Madame Sun after The Red Dragon incident to express my sympathies. Since I consider her a... friend."

Inola makes another note. Despite the mediocre quality

of the connection, Ysobel's tone came through clear enough. *There's something going on between them. Maybe it's sex, maybe it isn't. But it's something. A point of weakness.*

"To be clear, Miss Khan, we are all in favor of friends here at the Agency." Inola flashes a big smile. *Not easy to build friendly rapport over the video screen, but worth a try.* "Our concern rather stems from the anti-competitive market environment should OmniCorp and Lotus have too close a relationship. Given that both companies are already so large and dominant in their respective domains.

"An employee wellness program is absolutely fine, for example. But if OmniCorp were to be heavily invested in Lotus product-lines, say. You could then unfairly prioritize advertising for those products across your channels. That's the sort of thing we worry about in my department."

"Of course, Agent Montag. I can understand that. And I can assure you that nothing like that is currently under discussion in the OmniCorp boardroom."

"That is good to hear. We are all in favor of assurances here at the Agency." Another big smile. "But I will also need to review the board meeting transcripts to verify. Is there a good time this stretch when I can come by to pick those up?"

The screen warps again. Followed by a longer blast of static.

"—secretary. My schedule is booked, I'm afraid." *Still hard to make out the expression, but looks to be some worry in Ysobel's face.*

Inola frowns. "I'm sorry, Miss Khan, you cut out there. Could you repeat?"

"I said, you can make an appointment with my secretary to pick up the transcripts. I will transfer you to him now. Good-bye, Agent Montag." The screen blips out.

Inola lights herself another cigarette.

Hard to say for sure. But her confidence is growing for her theory that Ysobel Khan is in danger. She's most likely on Madame Sun's hit list. And she probably knows it.

————

The elevator doors slide open. Inola steps out and into the Division Six engineering laboratory. She is greeted by the familiar sounds of drills and saws and arc welders.

Ed "Gadget-Man" Noburu, the lab's head engineer, looks up from his soldering station and greets her cheerfully. "Mrs. Inola!"

She waves and smiles at him. "What are you working on there, G-Man?" She points her chin at the circuitry on his station.

"It's a motherboard for a mini auto-drone."

"Hmmm." Inola is not interested in drones. She knows some agents swear by them. Like having a backup agent in your pocket, some say. She's never found she needed that.

"Did my manifest make it down here yet?" She asks.

G-Man pulls his goggles up, rests them on top of his head. "I did not see it, but let's check." He slides his wheeled chair ten paces across the floor to the fax station. He shuffles through a stack of print outs.

There's a small explosion on the far side of the lab. Followed by a shout of "All clear!" Inola turns. Looks like they're working on some new rocket boots.

"Found it." G-Man draws her attention back. He reads out the first item on the list. "One master key, coming right up!" He slides his chair down to a shop cabinet with fifty or so small drawers. He rapidly searches them, opening and closing in no apparent logical order.

After twenty drawers or so, he finds what he is looking

for. "There it is." He takes out a small round object that looks like a digital stopwatch. Hands it to her. She pockets it.

He reads. "Next up: Taser mines." Looks up from the manifest and grins. "I can do you one better than that." He slides to another cabinet on the adjacent wall and repeats the process. This time he finds the right drawer on the third try. Scoops out six of what looks to be brushed steel marbles.

"Taser *balls*", he says. "They're new. Better than the old mines. More discrete." He winks and drops them into her cupped palms. She puts them in her pocket.

Returning to the list. "And last but not least..." He pauses and speaks the last three words slowly. "An anti-magic ward." Gives her a quizzical look. "Sounds like an interesting investigation, 6-2-6."

She raises her eyebrows and smiles, but says nothing.

So he presses. "The Sham Assassination?"

"Correct."

"I see." He pauses. Concerned silence for another few beats. "Well... off we go then. To The Artefact Room." That last sentence with dramatic delivery.

G-Man pops out of his chair and leads them through an unmarked door at the back of the laboratory. Then down a long hallway. Through two layers of security doors. Down another hallway to another security door. Behind is The Artefact Room.

The space looks like a museum exhibit. Dim lighting. Soft carpet. Glass cabinets showcasing old and ornate objects of beauty. Many displayed on mannequins.

G-Man unlocks one of the cases and takes a small hexagram earring off a felt jewelry stand. "It's an earring," he says, stating the obvious. "Will it suit?"

Inola removes the pearl pendant earring in her right ear.

Replaces it with the hexagram. "Seems fine to me," she says, taking the other pearl out of her left ear. Mismatched earrings is not her style. "Anything I should know about it?"

G-Man frowns. "I don't think so... But that's not exactly my area of expertise. I'm more of a science guy."

"So does this make me immune to magic or what?"

He shrugs. "I assume it's something like that. The last agent who took that... Or rather, who took the twin of that earring you're wearing... " He swallows hard. "He never came back."

She squeezes his shoulder affectionately and smiles. "Thanks, G-Man. I'll be fine," she says. "This is just a precaution."

CHAPTER 24
ZIJIAN

...BACK AGAINST THE WALL

«The Red Dragon Inn, a long-standing institution of the Market District, was destroyed in a fire late last night. Three people were killed, including Inspector William Fisch of the NWPD. The Chief Inspector's Office has opened an investigation and in a press conference earlier today, Chief Inspector Renaud said this was likely the work of anarchist-terrorist cells. A statement released by the mayor's office was critical of the NWPD, saying that this is just the latest sign of city law enforcement's incompetence.»

Zijian turns off the TV and spins around in her chair. She is in her office, facing her remaining lieutenants. The first morning briefing since The Red Dragon incident. Her thinking dagger in hand. She taps the flat of the blade against her palm. Surveys the faces in the room. They are stone. Four reflections of her own expression.

She is in full control of herself again. But never in her adult life has she felt so vulnerable. So exposed.

She was made to murder Jade and Sapphire in defense

of a woman who had violated Lotus' Hospitality and Protection. This is unforgivable. If it were known, she wouldn't live to see another day. The entire Lotus organization would be duty bound to hunt her down.

Therefore, no one can ever know. And if anyone even suspects, then I must root them out and destroy them.

A purge of The Lotus, starting with her own lieutenants. Her circle of trust. An ugly, unfortunate business. But this is the bloody corner Ysobel has backed her into. Her alternative is to flee. Hide underground. Start over.

Never. I fought for my place here. I will not turn and run like a coward. The girl has lowered me. I let my guard down with her. But I will not make that mistake again. And the game is far from over.

Oh, but that's not all. There has also been a break-in at The Lotus vault. Although nothing appears to be missing, it is an embarrassing lapse in security.

Zijian's lips curl into sneer.

That may actually be a blessing in disguise. An internal slip-up to distract attention while I deal with Miss Khan and The Red Dragon cleanup.

"This is an unfortunate series of events for our organization," she says. "To begin with The Red Dragon: This meeting with Inspector Fisch was under Hospitality and Protection. It is a black mark against The Lotus." She pauses. Presses the point of the dagger into her palm, not quite enough to draw blood. "And it is a black mark against me. I must acknowledge it."

Indigo lieutenant (Head of Security) nods. Too eagerly.

A sign of suspicion. He is surely keen to shift focus from his responsibility with the break-in.

All the others remain perfectly still.

She continues, her voice clinical. "It is unfortunate that Sapphire and Jade were killed in this attack. But as skilled as they were, there is little anyone can do against such a quantity of fire bombs." She presses the dagger point harder. Breaking the skin. "We will perform the rituals to honor them tonight. Tomorrow, I will begin the search and selection process for their replacements."

Scarlet's face twitches.

He is also suspicious. She can feel it.

That makes two of the four...

"Now to the break-in," she says, turning her cold fire to Indigo. "Would you like to report on your failing?"

Indigo winces at the insult. "Yes, Madame Sun," he says. "Several guards were injured in an attack. None killed. It appears that two, well-armed and well-trained intruders entered via the roof. Their target was our vault, which they managed to access."

Zijian does not take her eyes of Indigo's face. She digs even harder into her hand. The blood flows freely, dripping off her wrist.

"It does not appear that they stole anything," Indigo says. "But it does appear that they read at least a few of the scrolls."

"And copied the information, surely," Zijian adds.

Indigo nods. Color rising to his cheeks. "After speaking with the guards, and checking all the logs, this would seem to have been an attack by..." He pauses. Swallows hard. Embarrassed by what he is to say next. "Nightwing. The synth vigilante."

A few of the other lieutenants are unable to stifle their chuckles.

Zijian does not laugh. "The comic book night watchman infiltrated our defenses?"

He nods. Humiliated. "It is a black mark against me, Madame Sun."

"Indeed. And another against me for trusting you." She

stands and wipes the blood across her palm with the flat of her blade. "But let us not dwell on that. You will redouble your efforts and make amends for this embarrassment, I am sure."

Indigo drops his eyes to floor. "Yes, Madame."

"Good. Now. Others may have questions." Zijian whips out her kerchief and holds it in her hand to staunch the bleeding. "Before we get to those, let's address the most important matter of business. If any of you doubt me. If any of you believe me weak. If you wish to challenge my leadership. Step forward now. The Lotus does not tolerate weakness, and so I welcome the challenge."

Indigo does not lift his gaze, but the other three lieutenants turn to each other. Their bodies are stiff, seated on the couches in the middle of the room. Their eyes dart wildly, checking in with the colleague across and beside. Looking for any signals of intent.

Zijian watches them all. Her jaw clenched. Her dagger ready.

———

That night in The Red Dragon dining room. Splattered with the blood of her fallen lieutenants. Zijian remembered well her mother. Everything they had practiced all those years ago in the deep-down dark. It came back to her. How to set the mind trap.

It worked.

Ysobel had control of Zijian's body-mind. But the girl's assault progressed no further. The two of them—or rather, their projected shadow-minds—now sat together happily, going through paperwork in the imaginary office. Ysobel believing that her spell was fully successful, and that this scene encompassed Zijian's innermost mental sanctum.

But no. Zijian had successfully split her consciousness once more. Sealing it off to conceal her true clockworks.

She became three minds. Incredibly exhausting. Especially when she had not practiced this for so long. Not since she was a child. But in the moment of necessity, it had come back to her. The old skill and the old strength. She would survive this. Get through the night. Recover herself.

While Zijian's body-mind waited on her mistress' instructions, and the shadow-mind distracted Ysobel with meaningless busywork, Zijian's true innermost focused on the reality of the situation. Began its plotting.

Her position at The Lotus. Everything she had gained. Her opportunity to gain powerful influence at OmniCorp. She could now lose it all.

The girl has made me weak.

In the dining room, Ysobel spoke, tried to explain. And the body-mind listened carefully.

"Ija, I– I'm sorry. I knew that you wanted to strike a deal with Fisch. But he was a terrible man. He... touched me. When I was younger. Cornered me at one of those parties that my dad threw. I never told anyone. I'm sure my dad would have hired Lotus to kill him if he knew. But I was ashamed." Ysobel looked down. Trembling. "When I learned that you were meeting with him, looking to make a deal with him... I didn't want that. I didn't want that for you. Or for us. I wanted him dead." She lifted her eyes back to Zijian's. "And *I* wanted to kill him."

With the rise of emotion—with her anger—Ysobel's spell weakened. Just slightly. A flicker of Zijian's will recovered.

"Yes, mistress," Zijian heard herself say. The body-mind communicated to the innermost that it understood the new game plan. It was to play along. Wait. Appear to accept its lockdown. Bide its time until the moment of escape arrived.

Ysobel then proposed her plan to cover up the bloody events of the evening: They would burn The Red Dragon down. Use OmniCorp's private security firm for the dirty work. Then control the narrative through the media. Make up a story about terrorists going after Fisch.

Ysobel would scramble the thoughts and memories of the rest of The Red Dragon and Lotus staff. Make them believe everything she told them.

And she did all of it.

It was a wonder to behold. Even though Zijian's innermost could never admit it, she was impressed. Proud, even. To witness her Ysobel execute such a bold scheme.

Had the night been different. If it had not debased her. Violated her. Placed her position at Lotus—and her life—in such peril, Zijian would have been delighted. What an amazing force Ysobel had turned out to be. What an incredible weapon the girl could be in the right hands.

Zijian had hoped she would be the hands to wield that weapon.

But now...

Never.

After The Red Dragon was ablaze, Zijian went home with Ysobel, to the girl's opulent apartment in the Omni-Corp Tower.

Body-mind devoted itself eagerly to several sessions of lovemaking. It understood and played its part well. Ysobel seemed convinced that the intimacy signaled innermost's forgiveness.

Never.

Shadow-mind acknowledged none of this. It too played its part well. Convinced the invading enchantress that her spell was working. That Zijian accepted all of the girl's explanation.

Afterwards, as they lay in each other's arms, her head

resting against Zijian's breast, Ysobel said she had initially "stepped into" Zijian's mind without realizing it. That merely by extending her feelings, as she often did when they were together, she had discovered "a door" into Zijian's private thoughts. And stepping through that door, she had discovered the plan with Inspector Fisch.

She wrestled with the knowledge for many days, Ysobel said. Then decided she could not stand the thought of her Ija being in bed—metaphorically speaking—with that horrible man. She knew she could not ask permission. She knew Zijian would be angry. Yet she felt compelled to act. To take matters into her own hands.

The body-mind listened to all of this. It reacted little.

The innermost felt foolish. Ashamed. She had not appreciated the danger that Ysobel posed. She should have been more cautious from the moment she knew the girl was a telepath.

Zijian had been led to believe that most telepaths are not also enchanters or sorcerers. At least that is what her mother taught her. The ability to step in and control the mind of another—that was supposed to be exceedingly rare.

Yet here she was. In mental lockdown. Her body-mind reduced to a puppet.

But it will not last forever. I will have my chance to escape.

I will have my chance for revenge.

Zijian waited. For Ysobel to fall asleep. At that moment, as she anticipated, the spell broke.

The girl is powerful, but not quite powerful enough to keep an enchantment like that going in her sleep.

Zijian calmly left the bed and went to the bathroom. Stared at herself in the mirror.

All her plans of the past few turns. They would all have to change. OmniCorp was probably out of reach now. Her support base at Lotus would have to be rebuilt. She grimaced at the painful thought.

The girl has made me weak.

Images and memories of her intimacy with Ysobel flooded her mind. This girl was the only person Zijian ever allowed herself to be vulnerable with. The only person to whom she had opened herself up, even if just a small amount.

A tear slipped down her cheek. She wiped it away angrily.

A mistake. She has made me weak. It is unforgivable.

A pang in the pit of her stomach. She saw the glassy eyes of regret in her reflection.

She turned on the tap, filled her hands with cold water, and splashed it on her face.

When she looked at herself again, her eyes were cold. Clear as steel. How her face should be. The face of death itself.

No. This was never love. Never real intimacy. It was always a game. The girl has played a good move. Dazzled me. But her enchantment is broken. And the game is not yet over.

She returned to the bedroom. Glared at the sleeping Ysobel. Considered strangling the girl. Ending it right there. In cold blood.

No. That would lower me further. And it would force me to run and hide.

I will finish her on my terms. When the time is right. And walk away with my head held high.

She dressed herself quietly and left.

———

The five lieutenants all turn their eyes back to Zijian. None rose to challenge her.

No one is bold enough. Yet.

Lotus assassins were not permitted to kill citizens off-protocol. However, they could slay other assassins for their own reasons. Disloyalty. Weakness. An unforgivable violation. That sort of thing. (Provided, of course, that they filed the proper paperwork later.)

"Good," she said. "The last thing Lotus needs now is squabbling rats." She smiles at them. A terrible, bloodthirsty glint in her eye.

Good that they should still fear me. At least for the time being.

She sits back down. Places the dagger on the table.

"Now ask your questions."

To no great surprise, Scarlet is the first to speak. "How is it that you were not killed by the fire bombs?"

"Pure luck. I had excused myself to use the bathroom when they attacked the dining room."

Another small twitch in Scarlet's face.

Shame. He always was a good lie detector. Shame I will have to kill him.

Amethyst (Head of Cosmetics) speaks next. "How did these terrorists know about the meeting?"

"I don't yet know. I suspect that Inspector Fisch was their target, rather than us. So they may have been following him."

Indigo next, with a note of insolence: "Why were we not also tailing him? Particularly if he was a person of interest, it would have been correct protocol to have set a watch."

"A good question," Zijian replies with a flash of cold fire. "One that Sapphire or Jade would have to answer, since they were charged with setting up that meeting."

Indigo follows up: "What do Jade's or Sapphire's underlings say?"

"That nothing seemed amiss until the terrorists arrived in force."

Indigo frowns at the answer. Scarlet's lips are tightly pressed together.

Scarlet trying to control his twitching. Neither of them believes the story. But let them interrogate the underlings. A good enough distraction to buy some time. Amber and Amethyst seem placated and loyal enough...

A few more beats pass in silence.

"I know it has been some time since a tragedy like this has befallen The Lotus," Zijian says. "To lose two lieutenants and suffer a shameful break-in, all in the same night. It is a serious blow. But not one from which we cannot recover." She picks up her dagger and twirls it in her fingers. "I will see to any outstanding contracts left by Jade and Sapphire personally."

Another careful survey of the faces. Confirms everything.

Indigo and Scarlet will make trouble. I am sure of it. Sadly, they will have to go. I will be replacing four lieutenants instead of two.

She sighs. An exhausting thought. But it must be done. "If there are no more questions?"

Hearing none, she flicks her wrist. The lieutenants rise and file out.

CHAPTER 25

ELI

...OUT ON THE TOWN

A heavy backbeat and wah-wah guitars. The signature sounds of Club Tush. Where Eli Strauss Jr. begins his evening.

He's already running on plenty of white powder, taken before he left home. Popped a few psychs on the way over for good measure. They should kick in soon. In the meantime, he's slamming shots at this hot spot on the West Side.

Eli sits at one end of the main bar, near the dance floor. Bathed in warm lighting, cigarette smoke, and the smell of fruity cocktails. He's joined for the moment by his friends (although he wouldn't call them that), Timo and D.Rock.

Timo is long and lean. A face full of piercings. Skin covered in tattoos. Blessed (or cursed, if you ask Eli) by the gift of the gab. He's going on about all his hot dates this week.

D.Rock is a mutant. Hard to say of what exactly. A rhinoceros? He has a massive frame. His skin is thick and gray and coarse. He doesn't say much (which Eli appreciates) and he likes to drink. He and Eli go shot for shot while Timo runs his mouth.

Eli isn't really listening. There's a few girls getting busy on the dance floor. He watches them. Fantasizes about doing them rough. Fidgets with the ring on his left ring finger—the platinum signet, engraved with The Red-Tailed Raven, symbol of the House of Strauss. An artefact. Linked to his family's bloodline. An amplifier for personal strengths and talents, whatever those might be.

Eli feels stronger and faster while he wears it. More aggressive. At times, more charming, more persuasive.

At this moment, it makes him feel like dancing.

"Order us another round," he says as he gets up from the bar. "I'm going to go bust a move."

"Bust a move?" Timo laughs. "Who the fuck still says that?"

Eli grins and gives him the fingers. Saunters down to the dance floor. Thinking pleasant thoughts. Checking in with himself to see if he can feel the psychs. Nothing yet. But the night is young.

———

Next up is Club Fibonacci. The vibe is all downtempo trip-hop beats pulsing under cooler-toned lighting. The air's clearer here, but the drinks pack a punch. No dancing. Just tight tables with couples and thruples leaning in close. The walls are lined with mock phone booths, perfect for those looking to get a little more than just conversation.

Eli left his companions behind (to everyone's satisfaction). He sits at a table by himself. Working on drink number four. The psychs are definitely taking effect. Despite the dim lights, he's seeing everything in bright technicolor.

There's a group of girls sitting at a table nearby. Laughing. Having a good time. The blonde one catches his eye.

He taps the pear-shaped garnet setting of the ring on his left index finger. Another artefact. A simple charm ring that had once belonged to Eli's mother. When Idris came along, he used some of his own magic to enhance the charm. He showed Eli how to activate and focus its energies so that he could pick out a target and draw their interest to him. Make himself irresistible.

It takes a few beats, then the blonde looks back at him. She smiles.

It's not long before she excuses herself from her friends and walks over.

"You're the mayor, aren't you?" She says.

Eli plays it cool. "That's what they tell me."

"And you're here by yourself?"

Extending his leg under the table, he slides out the empty chair across from him. "I don't have to be," he says. "What are you drinking?"

She flushes a little and sits down, looking slightly embarrassed. But flattered at the same time. "I thought I heard that you were shot in the face. Like, assassinated, or something like that," she says.

Eli grins and turns his cheek to show off his awesome scar. "It'll take more than some scuzzer with a pea-shooter to stop me."

"Woah. Sexy scar."

"I know, right?"

She bites her lip. "So did they ever catch the guy that pulled the trigger?"

Eli leans in. Curls his finger to indicate that she should do the same. He has a secret to share. "I'm not supposed to talk about it," he whispers. "But yes. I caught him. He's chained up in the basement of the mayor's mansion right now."

The blonde's eyes widen with excitement.

"What are you going to do to him?" She asks, breathless.

He leans back. Shrugs. "I don't know. Beat him to a pulp with my bare hands maybe."

She giggles. "Let's see those hands then."

"What do you think I should do to him?" He asks. She starts stroking his palms, working her soft fingers between his.

"Maybe use a baseball bat," she says. "Be a shame to damage these nice mitts you got." She leans forward, giving Eli a clear view of her cleavage. She gives his knuckles a kiss. Her eyes on his the whole time, so she doesn't notice the garnet ring twinkling on Eli's finger next to her lips.

Eli grins. "Yeah, that would be a shame, wouldn't it. My mitts have way better things they could be doing."

———

After an exchange of sexual acts with the blonde in a phone booth, Eli moves on to Strobe. Some douchebag outside the club took exception to Eli's getting in through the VIP entrance. When Eli spat in his face, the guy popped him. Should have broken Eli's nose but for the ring on Eli's right index finger—a platinum crown inlaid with diamonds. A protection ward. Prevented the wearer from suffering broken bones and other similar kinds of physical injuries. Eli's nose would still be bruised and hurt like hell in the morning, but for tonight, thanks to the ring and all the drugs, he's feeling no pain.

Inside the club it's all thumping, thrumming beats set to a rainbow of neon and lasers beams. DJ Juste, the popular dance music synth, is on the ones and twos tonight.

The place is packed. Everyone out on the dance floor.

Sweating and grinding away to the thump thump thump. Eli is among them. His mix of drugs peaking at exactly the right time. He feels incredible. He feels invincible.

«Let me see y'move. Let me see y'move. Let me see y'groove to the music, baby!»

DJ Juste sings the chorus hook with his distinctive, auto-harmonized vocoder. The whole club is caught in its trance.

«Let me see y'move. Let me see y'move. Let me see y'groove to the music, baby!»

Everyone joins in the singing. Eli among them. Eli maybe loudest of all.

He feels joyous. Free. Immortal.

This is the feeling he's chasing every night. Where nothing else matters. No thoughts of politics or responsibilities. No weird dreams and visions. No stupid voices in his head, telling him to do this or that. There is only the moment. The movement. The freedom.

«Let me see y'move. Let me see y'move. Let me see y'groove to the music, baby!»

The words make no real sense. But Eli and everyone else sings and believes them. If the song didn't end, they would go on singing and dancing forever.

———

Eli ends the night in the corner booth at Hot Pink. It's blue hour at the synth-oriented dive. More electronic dance music blares out the speakers, but after the show at Strobe, the room might as well be silent to Eli's deadened ears.

He's polished off five more drinks. The remnants scattered across the table in front of him. His head lies flat on the table, resting comfortably on its side in a puddle of booze. His mind pleasantly spinning.

Was a good night.

His pinky ring, an emblem of The Rising Dragon, glows softly in time with his lazy breathing.

Blonde girl was hot.

He slurps some of the booze off the table's surface.

Blow job was good.

Chokes and coughs a little when he tries to swallow.

Wha was her name?

He pushes himself up off the table. Sits upright.

Where am I?

He looks around. Blinking. Bleary. Recovering some of his sense.

The club crowd has thinned out. He spots what looks like a couple of spooks sitting at a nearby table.

Did I order a Stasi detail?

At another table: A tall man in a dark suit and fedora. Reading a newspaper and smoking through a long filter.

Idris? Why he here?

The tall man notices Eli looking, lifts his cigarette filter in greeting, and then goes back to reading his paper.

Weird.

He turns away, looks towards the bar. There is an old man wearing holograph glasses working at a laptop computer.

Eli laughs.

When the newspapers and computers come out at the club, it's time to go home.

He touches the pinwheel pin on his lapel. Tells Dmitry to come pick him up.

————

Oh yes. The Rising Dragon. The symbol of Obelistwyth, crown jewel of Faesia. A once-great land brought low by the

Wars of Sundering. But it will rise again. Believe you me. It will rise again. And Pitiful Boy Eli, limited as he is, has an important part to play. The ring signifies his selection for this part.

Signifies my selection.

And with my selection, comes great honor and great power. Oh yes.

Through the ring, I can help Eli to see much. To do much. Much that would be impossible for him to see or do otherwise.

I can work his body. His voice. His shadow. And I can mix them all around, if I so choose. I can channel my own illustrious being through him. Transmute parts of him or me from place to place. Fashion new and wonderful creatures from those parts. Take partial or absolute control of the creations. Make them sing. Make them dance.

Whatever I wish, whatever is needed. It can be done through the ring.

The other trinkets Eli wears are vulgar things. Functional artefacts, yes, but a child's toys by comparison. The Rising Dragon is a piece of *true* magic. Fae Magic. The only magic worthy of the name.

The silly benders of Pitiful Boy Eli. The fondest wish of his silly, feeble imagination. To go out every night and lose himself in pleasure. Drink. Drugs. Music. Dancing. All to excess. It is the simplest wish to grant. The objects of his desire are all readily available around him. The only limitation is the weakness of his flesh and blood.

But that is easily solved for. Each day, I spin him up a new, completely disposable body. Transfer the fragmented bits and bobs of his mind into it, and voilà! If this body is maimed or killed, we golemize it. Move Eli into the shadow. Move the shadow back home. Make the shadow into a new body. Repeat as necessary.

However, the true elegance of this cycle is the profit of spares it creates. For every night that Eli does not completely destroy his body, the left-over copy becomes available to me. To command and conduct, or dissolve and recycle, as I see fit. Speeches. Paperwork. Chores. Whatever I need done, I have a small army of Boy Mayor bodies to do it.

It is a brilliant work of magic. Its only deficit is that it cannot last forever. Every well eventually runs dry. Thankfully, Pitiful Boy Eli will not be needed much longer. Once the stupid election cycle is over, once Ty Reese is dead, and The Ragnarok politicians suffer a humiliating defeat, I can dissolve and recycle what is left of Eli completely.

A greater honor than his bloodline deserves. But the histories are filled with such sad, pitiful characters whose importance is inflated through chance. Undeservedly elevated individuals who sometimes become legends—all thanks to the power and magnanimity of another, worthier being.

A cosmic injustice, yes. One I used to rage against in my youth. Yet I have grown to accept it. As I must. The cosmos has a sick sense of humor, and it is folly to try and make it otherwise. Believe you me. I have tried.

CHAPTER 26
SHUWEN

...IN A TIGHT SPOT

Shuwen hears the voice of her mother. From far away.

"The Li family is pure. We are a force for good. You are the last of our clan still serving. The city needs you. It is your duty. You do not have a choice."

She hears her own voice. Closer. Louder. "I know, Mom. You've told me that a million times."

"I have to keep telling you because you still question it. Like your father did. The questioning did him no good. It just made his life difficult. It made him miserable. And it will do the same for you."

They are sitting together on the porch of their family's cottage. But there's no breeze. No trees or birds. Beyond the porch, it is only darkness. Void.

This is not real. Just a twisted memory.

"I know how important duty is to our family," Shuwen says. She touches her bracers. They are silent. "But duty is not the same as just following orders. If the NWPD is corrupt, if they are telling me to do things that are wrong, then I am not doing our family any honor by following orders."

Her mother signs. "Why should you be thinking about right and wrong? If you want to think about those thing, then you go be a judge." Shuwen opens her mouth to interrupt. Her mother raises a finger. "No, Shuwen. You are not a judge. Therefore, it is not your *place* to judge right from wrong. You are a police constable. Your place is to enforce the laws, and to follow the orders of your superiors."

"Mom, that makes no sense."

"It makes perfect sense."

"No, it doesn't. So what if I had been a constable in Precinct 21? They abetted the assassination. If I had been there, and followed orders, not only would I have brought dishonor to our family, I would be on my way to the work camps right now."

"I would be sad to lose you, but that would not have been true dishonor. Following orders is what it means to serve. That is the tradition of honor for our family. We do not question. We obey. We serve."

Shuwen is aghast. "That's awful. You don't mean that."

"I do."

"That's not how Dad understood his duty."

Her mother shakes her head. "Your father was a brave man, but he was also foolish when it came to his duty. Like you. And he got himself into all kinds of trouble because of it. Just like you have."

Shuwen tries to control her face. Her mother does not know how deeply it wounds to hear her speak this way. To be so critical. Of her and her father.

Her mother's final words: "To die in the line of service. To fall in the line your duty. That is the meaning of honor for the Li Family. But to die because of some silly notion, because of what you think is right... that is dishonor. It is a wasted, shameful death."

———

The dark void recedes. The porch and her mother go with it. Replaced by pain. In her neck. In her back. Her shoulders most of all.

Replaced by cold. On her butt. Her legs. Everywhere.

Shuwen's vision starts to clear.

Where am I? An empty warehouse?

She sees stone pillars. Crumbling old statues.

Gargoyles? A dungeon? An old church? Where is this?

The air is murky. But there is a figure in the gloom. It looks like an angel. Floating. Dancing.

Ballet dancing?

The ground covered in a thick layer of dust. Smells of rusted metal.

She tries to move. Discovers that her arms are bound, spread apart above her head. Shackled. Dangling from chains anchored high up on a stone wall behind her. She can feel the bracers on her wrists. But she cannot touch to activate them.

She is naked. Or almost. Stripped down to her underwear.

The angel is coming closer. A swirl of pale skin in a white tutu. Encircled by a flame of long, silky, red hair. Singing a child's song.

> *A ring around my roses,*
> *My saucer is full of secrets,*
> *A penny for all my poses,*
> *A penny to have your throat slit!*

Not an angel.

It is Valentina de Leo.

Oh fuck! Oh no!

Shuwen gasps and struggles. Discovers her legs are shackled too. Spread apart, like her arms. Locked to the floor. Held in iron plates, bolted into the ground.

Val notices Shuwen's movement and stops her song. "Oh yay!" She croons.

Oh fuck!

Panic. Shuwen struggles again. Her shoulders burn. Her whole body burns. Her skin is covered in scratches and bite marks.

"Yeah, I had to let the fellas have some fun with you," Val says, still dancing. "After what you've done to so many of their friends..." She freezes mid-pirouette. Standing perfectly still on her toes, dropping her head to the side at a grotesque angle. She looks Shuwen square in the eyes. "It seemed only fair to give them a little payback."

Val's swirling, multi-colored gaze adds a wave of nausea to Shuwen's present miseries. She tenses, trying to muster some greater strength to pull harder against the shackles.

Val continues: "But I told them to leave you in the undies. Because, you know, you deserve some dignity." Then her mad grin spreads across her face. "Plus I like when it goes riiiiiip."

Shuwen struggles again. Feeling for any sign of weakness in the metal restraints.

"Don't bother," Val says, her tone shifting to casual. Like they were old friends. "You're not going anywhere until I'm done with you."

Shuwen moans.

"Yeah, I know, sweet-thing." Val gives her a pitying look. "So sad for you." Then she leaps forward into a playful crouch, standing right over Shuwen's shackled feet. "But don't fret. I've got a surprise." She puts on a face of childlike wonder, moving her crazed eyes side to side like she's checking to see if anyone else is looking. "Watch!"

She reaches under her skirt, and with a dramatic flourish, produces a gnarled wooden walking stick. Then raises it to the sky like she's just pulled the mythic sword from the stone and (for her next trick) is going to call down a bolt of lightning.

"SHILL-LAY-LAH!" She howls with delight.

Reverberating off the cold stone walls of the dungeon or old church basement or wherever the fuck they are—the sound is deafening.

Shuwen winces. She can't close her ears to the noise, so she shuts her eyes instead. It helps. But only for a moment, as the panic and nausea rises with the growing realization of what is most likely in store for her.

"I call this bad boy The Violator," Val says with pride. "For obvious reasons. And let me tell you: You don't want to know where it's been! All the shitheads I've fucked with it." That last sentence with an almost wistful air.

Pulse racing. Shuwen tries to calm herself.

Oh fuck. Okay. Remember back to training. How to deal with torture...

———

At the police academy, there was an optional course on torture. How to dish it out. How to take it. Henry had challenged her to enroll with him. Shuwen was never one to back down from a challenge—

———

"Nope!" Val slaps her across the face. "I told you. You're not going anywhere. No dissociation land." She lightly pokes at Shuwen's exposed toes with the business end of her stick.

"You and all these cute little piggies need to stay right here with me."

Shuwen's struggling amounts to little more than a trembling at this point. Despair setting in. Tears coming to her eyes.

"Aww," Val coos, taking two steps forward to tower over Shuwen's helpless body. Then she sits down, straddling her cowgirl-style. Leaning forward. Breathing in her face. It smells like hot cinnamon. "Mr. Fairy went to all kinds of trouble to bring us together, you know. I want to make sure everyone gets their money's worth."

Val giggles then wraps one arm around Shuwen's head, getting a tight grip on Shuwen's aching right shoulder. She gives it a squeeze and twists. Shuwen's whole body shivers in pain.

"How'd that feel?" Val whispers. Then positions her Violator underneath them, between both their legs. The business end pressing against the soft of Shuwen's groin. She gives it a tentative thrust. "And that?"

Shuwen is silent. Her teeth gritted. Her eyes shut tight. The tears are close. For the first time in a long time, she is terrified.

She hears her mother's voice in her head.

"To die because of some silly notion, because of what you think is right..."

If she could only touch her bracers, she might summon the strength to free herself.

"...a wasted, shameful death."

Val gives her shoulder another twist and this time a firm poke with the stick. Shuwen groans through her teeth. It feels like her shoulder is being slowly ripped out of its socket. The thin fabric of her underwear holding for now, but she knows it won't for much longer.

Why didn't I just leave this all alone? Why didn't I

listen to Wolff... Or Montag. Henry. My mother. They all tried to warn me.

Val leans in closer. The smell combo of cinnamon, unwashed hair, and fem-sweat is stifling. Shuwen's stomach turns and she gags.

Val pays no notice. She whispers in Shuwen's ear. "I've something important to teach you. So you need to... Pay. Attention." She punctuates the last two words with thrusts from the stick. Then, mercifully, releases her grip.

In the brief reprieve, Shuwen tries to steady her breath. To control herself as much as she can. She manages to groan out, "Fuck. You."

Val giggles, leans back (temporarily letting go of the stick), and claps with glee. "That's the spirit, girlfriend!" She looks genuinely impressed. "You ARE a fighter. I like that about you." She stares approvingly at Shuwen for a few moments. "And cute too." She giggles. "So pure. Shuwen Li." Cups her hand over her mouth and says in a deep, radio announcer's voice: "Supercop. A model for Our Fair City."

Then all humor melts away from Val's expression. Replaced by an ugly indifference and a back-to-work-shrug as she picks up the stick and returns it to position. "Anywaaays. Like I said: I have an important lesson to teach you." She rolls her crazed eyes to the back of her head and bites her lip. Leans forward again, slowly, almost tenderly reaching her other arm around Shuwen's head to retake the poor, suffering shoulder. Returns her voice to its sickening, intimate whisper. "But first, we need to loosen you up."

She pulls and twists. Applies harder pressure on the groin. The fabric is starting to rip. Despite her best efforts, a squeal of terror escapes from Shuwen's lips.

Another twist. The most brutal so far. Shuwen can hold it no longer and screams for her to stop. Val releases her grip, rearing back, thrusting hard. The fabric tears.

Shuwen's whole body clenches in pain. She and Val scream together. A twisted harmony of agony and ecstasy.

But in the gaps between the screams, there is another sound. Something soft. Whistling. Something small, moving very fast. Spinning through the air.

THWAK.

A thick incision of metal into flesh.

Val jerks back, withdraws and lets go of her stick.

Shuwen gasps with relief. Her face is wet with warm tears and cold sweat. But something else too. She can taste it on her lips.

Blood.

Not just her face. Her chest and stomach also splattered.

Val is heaving on top of her. Confusion in her wild eyes. Oozing blood from a nasty gash on her side. A small and shiny object sticking out of the woman's neck.

A throwing star.

Uziel's voice booms out of the shadows above. "Foul creature! Release her!"

CHAPTER 27
UZIEL VS. VAL

...AT THE CATHEDRAL CRYPT

Uziel's claws are out. He is crawling on the ceiling of the Old Town Cathedral's derelict crypt. Hidden in the gloom and shadows, right above Val and the captive Shuwen.

He did not find Shuwen as quickly as he'd hoped. But quickly enough that she is alive. The absolute worst case scenario has been avoided. For now.

He has never faced Valentina de Leo before. He assumes she is extremely dangerous. To have avoided him and the rest of The League for so long—she would have to be quite cunning.

Despite the serious nature of the encounter, his pleasure circuits are activated as he creates a new folder in his memory for Val. His synthetic mind is always excited to explore the unknown, and this is an unprecedented opportunity to gather first-hand data on one of New World City's most notorious criminals.

Right off the bat, he is surprised by her energy readings. They are similar to the demon from The Bloodhound Ballroom. Powerful energy fields swirling around her.

Fascinating.

Extreme danger confirmed.

Direct engagement is unwise until he learns more.

He splits his processing between two threads: One focuses on combat zoning, keeping a safe distance. The other focuses on calculating a way out—determining the best options for rescuing Shuwen and escaping.

It is risky to multi-thread in the midst of battle. But he sees no other option. The other members of The League will detect his signal, but they are too far away. At best, they may be able to help clean things up.

He loads two more throwing stars and whips them down at Val, who is still sitting on top of Shuwen.

Val jumps up, whirls around, and swings her rape stick. Just in time to bat the stars away.

"Ha!" She exclaims, pleased with herself. But there is a note of distress in her voice. She pulls the star out of her neck and shrieks. "Come down and fight like a man, Silverfuck!"

"Release her," Uziel booms back. "And I may let you live."

Val laughs. "You're the one who's gonna die, dumbass!"

Uziel generally finds that combat talk is silly and unnecessary. Except in the case of excessively proud or arrogant opponents. Then it can be effective at distracting them. Potentially buy some time.

He whips another star at her. Val tries to dodge but it catches her calf. She screams. Starts limping away from Shuwen.

"Ow! Stop that, you pussy! You dickless, synthetic fucknut!"

Val's head is spinning on a swivel, furiously trying to track him in the shadows above. And there's something else odd about her movement across the floor. It's not just the limp. She is avoiding something.

Uziel zooms in. Runs a quick scan.

The floor is covered in rusted metal. Traps. Hard to see under the layers of dust. The decision to stay above is the right one. For now.

"My colleagues are right behind me. Give yourself up." A lie, but worth the chance of distracting her with cheap talk as he skitters across the ceiling, toward the far end of the crypt. Processing thread number two suggests he try to lure Val further from Shuwen.

Another throwing star. Val bats it away. She still can't quite see him in the shadows above, but she is judging the angles and following his movement.

This is good.

He takes a moment to scan Shuwen. She is hurt. Frightened. But she is whole. She calls out his name.

"Ugh! Get a room, lovebirds." Val snarls.

He catches the side of her head with another star, slicing off part of her ear. She lets out another shriek of frustration, this time dropping to her knees.

"Stop doing that, you fucking coward! It's not fair!" Like a child throwing a tantrum. Clutching her bleeding ear.

Uziel zooms in on Val. He sees that the wounds on her side and neck have already closed and are almost healed completely. That must be part of her magic. Or perhaps a mutation? More intriguing data that he files away for later.

"You can't save her from up there, Nightfart! You WILL have to come down."

Uziel knows she's right. And he's almost out of throwing stars. He's managed to get Val some distance from Shuwen. But not enough to swoop in and free her. Not yet.

He scans the crypt. There is a rotting wood cabinet in one corner. He calculates a plan. Chance of success fifty percent. Sufficient to execute.

He crawls across the ceiling to the corner and then drops to the ground with a flip. "OK, creature," he says. "Come and get me."

Val howls and rushes towards him. Her eyes blazing. Her stick blazing now as well, enveloped by writhing, sickly-green tendrils. Another anomaly that goes in the file.

Uziel ducks, dodges, and backs away from her swings. Easing toward the cabinet. Letting her press the attack.

He loads and whips his final three throwing stars from close range. Hits her in the gut, chest, and forehead. All square and deep. She hardly seems to notice.

This is not good. A formidable beast she is.

The back of his heel bumps against the foot of the old cabinet.

Val chuckles. "No more room to run, you dope." She winds up for a killing blow.

Uziel vaults over her and fires his grappling hook at the cabinet. He lands neatly on the other side and pulls hard. The cabinet topples forward, Val lets out a cry of dismay, and is then crushed underneath.

There is a terrible racket from the shattering, splintering old wood, and perhaps bone.

He pauses a beat and scans the wreckage for signs of life.

"Damn," he says. She's not dead. She's hardly injured. Only stunned. A very formidable beast.

But he calculates this as the best chance to escape. He retracts his grapple hook, turns and fires it to the ceiling.

In a tick, he is aloft, flying back toward Shuwen.

In two smooth swings, he has crossed the crypt. He lands on one knee and one fist in a pose worthy of his comic book covers. The force of his fall shatters some of the rusty metal traps. This is good. The traps are mostly old and ineffectual.

He locks eyes with Shuwen and gives her a salute. Her

eyes are filled with tears. A mix of relief, shame, fear, and hope.

He is no more than ten paces away.

There is a roar from the far side of the crypt. Val bursts through the wreckage, arms outstretched in a terrifying, comic-worthy pose of her own.

No time to scan. Uziel rises and strides confidently toward Shuwen, readying his laser torch to cut her free.

At stride three there is a sharp clang of metal on metal. A brief shower of sparks. His right leg has been severed at the knee by one of the traps.

"Damn," he says as he drops to the ground. He calculated a five percent chance of effective traps remaining. A gamble worth taking in the moment. But a gamble that has not paid off.

This is not good.

"No!" Shuwen cries.

Uziel pushes himself up to one knee. Locks eyes with her. The hope in her eyes is gone. Replaced by guilt. And a recognition of doom.

He knows she has seen this scenario play out before. "I'm sorry, Constable," he says, his voice perfectly calm and even as ever.

"Got you now!" Val croons as she returns from the gloom with a dramatic grand jeté. Closing in fast.

She unleashes a mighty swing of her enchanted rape stick. Uziel raises an arm to block. The stick smashes right through it with a spray of metal shards and plastic bits.

He goes for his grappling hook with his remaining hand. "Foul creatur–"

Val whirls around. A tornado of cinnamon red and toxic green. The next swing connects with his head. It explodes in a cloud of sparkling silver shards.

———

One great advantage of the synthetic mind is being able to keep everything organized. All the contingencies planned and ready to execute in a moment's notice should the need arise. After Val shattered his arm, Uziel calculated with certainty that he was about to be destroyed. In that last tick, he fired off a series of file transfers and messages to his colleagues in The Vigilantes League.

To the general League listserv, he sent text descriptions of everything he had seen this night. (The images and video recordings would take too long to send.) Along with his inferences that Valentina de Leo was both a mutant, of unknown origin, and a magician, of unknown but considerable power. He strongly recommended that she be bumped up the priority list and neutralized as soon as possible.

He also thanked them for their friendship and support. Remarking that over his long career as a vigilante, it was the relatively short time with The League that had meant the most to him. With their companionship, he believed he had grown and learned the most.

To Tank, he sent a private message about all the equipment he owned. He communicated that Tank should please use and adapt any of that for himself. He also thanked the reformed killbot for being such a great combat training partner. He was sure that without Tank's instruction, he would have been smashed to bits long before this.

To Benoit, Uziel communicated his respect and awe at the psychic-philosopher panda's expansive intellect. Although the two had not always seen eye-to-eye, he appreciated the counter-point of Benoit's mind. And he hoped the panda was correct that their consciousnesses would have the opportunity to meet (and argue) again in the Afterlands.

Uziel's personal message to Meg was the shortest. It said: "Working with you has been a joy. Beyond my ability to express." Followed by a twenty-four digit coded message that only she would understand and know how to use.

———

"No!" Shuwen cries.

Uziel's headless body slumps to the ground.

But Val is not done with it. Not by a long shot.

She starts going at it like those repressed yuppies at a smash cafe. Pounding away with her stick. Singing in her sexy baby sing-song all the while:

> *A ring around my roses,*
> *My saucer is full of secrets,*
> *A penny for all my poses,*
> *A penny to have your THROAT SLIT!*

When it's all over, Uziel is nothing but a thin layer of silvery dust atop all the other dust and filth on the floor of the crypt.

Val plops herself down next to Shuwen. Exhausted. Breathing out her sick, heavy, cinnamon breaths. She plucks the last three throwing stars out of her body, tossing each aside like a picked scab.

PART FOUR

MAGIC

CHAPTER 28

TY

...ON THE RETURN QUEST

On the road again. Heading back to the city. Plenty to think about.

Ty's meeting with Petra the Artefixer didn't go at all how he expected.

It was better.

Better than he could have imagined.

Well, except for the fact that he had no artefact in hand.

Sort that out in good time.

It turned out Ty had some telepathic aptitude. Once Petra spoke into his mind, she was able to quickly teach him how to respond in the same way. This sped up their conversation considerably. She could explain. He could ask. She could answer. All in one tick.

So what did she explain?

First, she explained that he should not overestimate the power of artefacts. Neither should he underestimate the power already at this disposal.

From the artefixer's perspective, power boiled down to being able to shape things. Shape materials. Shape society. Shape history. Shape reality.

She was a skilled shaper of materials. Through magical means, she could imbue objects with all sorts of abilities that could shape reality. This was her talent, her art, her gift, her curse. Call it what you want. This is what she did.

Second, she explained that to make him an artefact, she would need access to her workshop. And access to soul-stone. A rare material. She knew there was a mining operation in The Outer Reaches that had found a rich vein of the stuff. It was causing all kinds of trouble in those parts, but if he could pull some strings, get his hands on some of it, bring it to her. Then once she was free, she could make him an artefact.

Third, she explained that the magical energies of Earth seemed to be waxing. His receptivity to telepathy confirmed her suspicion of this. She warned him that the latent magic of the world "waking up" was likely to cause all kinds of chaos, particularly in the city.

This gave Ty some new ideas. He had written off the city's mayoral election as irrelevant to attaining *true* power. But if magic was about to turn New World City upside down, then the people would need a strong leader.

And who better to be that leader.

After all, wasn't he already NWC's apex predator? Yes, he was. He knew how to get shit done. When he had the mayor's seat, he would be able to do far more. Artefact or no. It was an inspiring thought.

Ty realized that he had gone to Junkland with the single-minded pursuit of power. He had felt outmatched, and Dr. T does not do outmatched. But this feeling was based on an over-narrowed understanding of power. He had been too focused on Eli and the demon. Thinking that he needed magic to fight back. He now appreciated that there were many ways to shape the world. And in many respects, he was already a world-shaper.

As corny as it was, he also felt like he had made friends on this journey. Petra and Grigor. He liked them. Felt certain he would see them again. Felt like there was a future collaboration in store for them all.

He also found he liked The Old Ways by which the people lived in Junkland. There was something raw about their existence. Something real. Surreal. *Hyperreal*. You earned your place in that society through strength alone. It was refreshing. And he felt refreshed.

Inspired and refreshed.

As he drives the long days back across the desert toward the city, he works on new song ideas in his head. He's got a concept album in this experience for sure.

The convoy takes a pit stop at Joey's service and repair station. Ty didn't really care one way or another, but Agent Price insisted they should drop in. Said Joey did a solid with the service on the way out, so least they could do is give her some custom on the way back.

They've arrived in the evening. Just as it's starting to get cold in the desert. Ty is inside, helping himself to the fried rice balls the girl has made.

Needs a sauce. But they're not bad.

And in a surprising twist: They are not the only customers. Some beat up station wagon is parked at one of the pumps. Ty hasn't seen who's driving it. But he's curious.

He peers out the window of the little shop. The two spooks are chatting with Joey. Looks like they are getting into some stupid argument about cars.

Ty hears the sound of a gunshot. Coming from behind the station. Sounds like a big piece. Probably Magnum's revolver. The spooks and the girl all turn their heads, but then go back to their conversation, seemingly uninterested.

Ty steps out to investigate.

A good fifty paces back from the station, he sees Magnum talking with three strangers, showing off his revolver. One of the strangers, a woman with long black hair, is wearing an Azzuri brand jacket.

Ty grins and approaches the group. "This guy talking your ear off?" He points a thumb at his boy.

Magnum laughs. "They were admiring my pride and joy here." He pats the barrel of his gun. "I offered to give them a demonstration. Explained how the guns from Junk-land feel better."

Once Ty's close enough to be recognized, the woman with the dark hair and Azzuri jacket beams at him.

"Oh my god! You're Dr. T! I'm a huge fan."

"I like your jacket," he says. Still grinning.

"I saw your show at The Bloodhound Ballroom," she says. Ty's grin fades at the mention of that event. There is also a knowing twinkle in the woman's eye as she says it.

This girl thinks she knows something?

She continues: "We all saw it, didn't we?" She gestures at her two companions. One of whom is a synth. The oldest-looking synth model Ty has ever seen. Bronze with all exposed gears and wires. Its face is a single headlight.

"That's Aleph," she says. The synth blinks its big face-light one time at him.

The other companion is a cyborg-woman. She looks like she's wearing some old 19th century space suit, but without its big glass bubble helmet. Half her face is plated with metal and she has all sorts of tubes and wiring going in and out of her head and neck. Her one eye on the non-metal side is obviously bionic.

"That's Max," the dark haired woman says.

Traveling creep show, this group.

"Oh and my name is Yume."

Ty gives them all a slight nod in greeting. "Where y'all from? What brings you out here to the middle of nothing?"

"We're from Outwash," Yume says, obviously the leader and talker for this rag-tag crew. "We work for a security firm there. We were hired for a job in the city. It should have been a quick trip, but we got caught up in the lockdown. Ended up having to stay much longer than we planned."

Bullshit story, if I ever heard one.

"Hired for security?" Ty says, letting them hear the doubt in his voice. "There's a thousand security firms in the city. Who is hiring y'all to come in from the fucking rim of the world?" Magnum shifts uncomfortably, feeling the mood darken across the group.

Yume seems undisturbed by the question. She looks Ty confidently in the face. Her eyes still twinkling. "Can't say who. Sorry. You understand. Professionalism and all that."

Ty snorts. "But why is anyone hiring y'all? You have to travel for what? Two stretch just to get into the city? That's ludicrous!"

Aleph's face flickers. Max turns away. Yume continues to beam.

"They hired us because we're the best," she says.

Ty snorts again, louder. "The best at what?"

Yume continues smiling, unflappable. But she narrows her eyes. "You wanna see?"

Ty folds his arms across his chest. Eyebrow raised.

"You gave us a great show after all," she says. Then turning to her companion in the space suit. "Hey, Maxi, what do you think? You up for a demonstration?"

Max turns back around. Looks at Ty. Her half-metal-half-skin face completely expressionless. "OK," she says, her voice is hoarse, only slightly above a whisper. She sounds like a child with a horribly sore throat.

She turns to Magnum. "May I borrow your gun?"

Magnum looks at Ty. Ty nods and Magnum hands over his revolver. "There's five shots left in there. Do you want me to reload it?"

Max shakes her head. Walks a few paces away from them.

The sun is just at the horizon line.

Max points toward some cacti in the distance, about four or five hundred paces off. "Do you see those?" Ty grunts an affirmative. "One, two, three, four, five," she says, indicating a particular cactus with each number.

Ty can't really tell which she is picking out, but he understands that she is not picking five in a row. She's selecting a few across a wide arc. "Alright," he says. "Let's see you hit them."

This should be good. Has to be impossible with a handgun from this distance.

Yume catches his eyes. She is blazing with excitement. "Show 'em, Max," she says.

Max stands with her feet apart. Hands at her side. Revolver on the right. She takes a long, labored breath.

Perfectly timed with the last tick of sunlight, the cyborg-woman who looks and sounds like she can barely breath, springs into action with blinding speed. She appears to take five shots at once, in five different poses. Some she shoots from the hip. Some looking straight down her outstretched arm. The last behind her back.

Ty's musician ear is sensitive enough that he hears all ten bangs of the gunshots and the subsequent explosion of cacti. But to the Division Six agents and Joey the mechanic on the other side of the station, it all sounds like one, growling bang followed shortly by another bang farther away.

Fuck me.

Max walks back to them, spins the revolver, and offers it handle-first to Magnum. "You're right," she says to him. "A fine shooter."

Magnum is awestruck.

The sunlight goes. The electric lighting for the station clicks on. Bathing them in the pale yellow buzz. A red flicker from the smoldering cacti remains in the distance.

Ty strokes his chin. "Nice shot," he says. "I'll bet you're even better with a rifle." Max looks at him blankly.

"It's like I told you," Yume says. "We're the best."

He snorts. "Looks like she might be the best. What can you and the robot do?"

Aleph beeps angrily. His face flashing red.

Yume laughs. "Everyone needs to roll with a crew, Dr. T. You know that." She puts her hands in her jacket pockets. "And I didn't want to miss out on the opportunity to do some shopping in the big city. We don't see much Azzuri gear in Outwash."

These are some cocky bitches.

Then a thought occurs to him. And he reaches out to Yume's mind.

You're the sniper crew. From the rally.

Yume's eyes grow wide. Her smile vanishes.

Ty nods in Max's direction.

She's the one who shot the mayor, isn't she.

Several beats pass. Yume glaring at Ty in stunned silence. Magnum reloads his revolver. The synth and cyborg-woman have moved off a few paces and seem to be engaging each other in some kind of click-based language.

Ty finds he doesn't need Yume's confirmation. He can

read the facts in her mind. Max took that shot at Mayor Rich Kid. Aleph was extra firepower and ran some kind of synth-detection scrambler. Yume was their leader and negotiator.

His lips slowly curl into a triumphant smile as the stolen story unfolds in his mind.

Yume's face has gone cold. Eyes sharply narrowing.

"You know I got some friends in my crew who might like to see another demonstration," Ty says, now giving her the knowing twinkle. "Should I call them over?"

Yume's expression darkens further as she sends her reply to his mind.

Don't.

Ty sneers. Slams shut the telepathic door between them.

"I'll keep my options open," he says. Feeling smug. Flexing this new-found ability.

Well, that's one mystery solved.

Yume summons her synth and cyborg companions. "We should get going," she says, brushing past him. "We'll be seeing you I'm sure, Mayor Reese."

Aleph and Max fall in behind. The three march off in a neat little triangle.

It's clear that she didn't care at all for his stepping into her mind like that. And her tone suggests that she's thinking the same thing he is: Gunning down people like the mayor of New World City is just another day's work for her and her Outwash goons.

"I'll keep my eyes open too," he says.

The three stop and do an about face. Perfect unison. Military style. None of them speaks. Even chatty Yume stays silent. They just stare at him for a good few beats. Regard him with a deadly indifference.

Ty sucks his teeth. Cocks an eyebrow. Holds their gaze.

Eventually the three turn back around. Load into their

rusting, sputtering wagon, and drive away. Leaving a trail of black smoke behind them.

Magnum strolls over beside Ty. Watching them go. "What do you think, boss?"

Ty purses his lips. "I think we should look into getting some Azzuri outposts opened up in The Reaches," he says. "If we have customers there, I don't want to be leaving money on the table."

And I definitely need to keep watch on that crew.

———

By the time Ty is back in Redbridge, on the outskirts of New World City, boarding his private plane, he has composed his entire concept album. Yet another good reason to have had Magnum along on this journey: Magnum is a decent beat boxer. So on those long days in the car, Magnum provides the beat for Ty to sing and style over. Work out all the lyrics.

That encounter with the security-terrorists from Outwash (or whoever-the-fuck they really were) also gave him the dramatic hook he needed to tie the whole concept together.

A heroic killer has a crisis of conscience. So he travels to the desert in search of meaning. Encounters a crew of killers from another world. They all show off and exchange knowledge. Then they duel to the death. The hero emerges victorious, returns to the civilized world a changed man. No longer a killer. He becomes a prophet of the One True Faith.

That's the album's title: One True Faith.

It's going to be glorious.

He can't wait to get into the studio and lay it down.

But first things first. Even though he didn't find a trinket, he's thought more about The Bard's story. And Petra's advice. He doesn't need a fucking artefact to best Eli and his demon. Now that he knows what to expect, he just needs to orchestrate the right situation. Catch Eli with his guard down. Work reality in his favor.

Shouldn't be hard, considering how that scuzzer is always getting fucked up out in public.

All things considered: Ty's quest was a success. Cleared his mind. Clarified his path.

He knows exactly what to do next.

It's going to be glorious.

CHAPTER 29
ZIJIAN

...MAKES A NEW DEAL

From rapid rail to jet plane to copter. Zijian is finally at her destination: The Khan Racing Circuit. A lavish motorsport campus in the sand dunes of The Strand.

She crosses the tarmac toward the main pavilion of the complex. The buildings are all white concrete, sea green glass, gold trim. The Khan Family is wealthy enough that it might be real gold, rather than just gold-painted chrome.

Ostentatious.

Zijian is not here because she's a fan of motorsport. She detests everything gearhead related. She's here to meet with Gotari Khan. The gadabout son of the soon-to-be-dead Sinbad Khan. Ysobel's brother. The distant second in line for OmniCorp's throne.

She has met him twice before. Found him obnoxious. Spoiled. Self-indulgent. Typical male scion. Far too full of himself.

Especially considering everything he has in life is owed to his father. And whatever natural gifts Old Man Khan had to pass along, Ysobel certainly received the lion's share.

A pang follows that last thought, and so it is set aside.

She passes through the large, sliding-glass doors and enters the pavilion. The interior is decorated with an abundance of white marble sculptures, all depicting nudes lounging in or on automobiles.

Tasteless.

"Welcome, Madame Sun." One of Gotari's white-suited servants greets her. "We have been expecting you. Please follow me."

Zijian did not communicate her exact intentions for this meeting. She suspects that Gotari is aware of Ysobel's frequent visitations to The Lotus. Perhaps he's even aware of their relationship. But what he thinks about it (if anything), she does not know. She will find out momentarily.

Does he resent his sister for being their father's favorite? For being the one who will take over control of OmniCorp, and most likely, cut him off? She suspects that he does.

And that is her strategy. The weak point she plans to press, and hopefully, salvage her plans to gain influence at the media conglomerate.

She has come largely unarmed. Equipped only with her Guild satchel. There is a small ritual dagger, but otherwise, the contents are ink, parchment, and the accoutrements needed to sign a writ of assassination.

———

Since the night of The Red Dragon, Zijian has been busy. Moving fast. Her forced execution of two of her loyal lieutenants has made two more of her lieutenants—Indigo and Scarlet—suspicious. If their suspicions were left to fester, things could get even further out of hand.

She could not let that happen.

She identified four young and hungry candidates from

Lotus' lower ranks. Maurice, Monty, Ginger, and Grace. She offered them the opportunity to step up and prove themselves worthy of the rainbow tunics.

Maurice and Ginger she assigned to Indigo. Monty and Grace to Scarlet.

As Zijian had suspected, lieutenant Indigo did not believe her version of The Red Dragon events. She could hardly blame him for that. It was a lie after all.

He started asking around. What did others know? Did anyone see anything? Hear anything? Maurice and Ginger were sent to express sympathy with this cause. When Indigo eventually proposed they meet after hours, to strategize about what might be done next to "right this wrong," the trap was set.

Indigo left his office at the end of the appointed day. Took the elevator. Punched the button for the ground floor. The elevator descended. But the ground floor came and went. It kept going down. Basement 1. Basement 2. All the way to basement 3.

He knew what this meant. When the elevator doors opened, he was knives out. Ready for combat.

He fought well, but it was three against one. He didn't stand a chance.

Zijian delivered the killing blow. During his final moments, she thanked him for his turns of service. Then told him his soul was cursed for his betrayal of The Lotus and his entire family was now marked for death. While Maurice disposed of the body, Zijian and Ginger went back upstairs to complete the paperwork. Ginger would be assigned the honor of wiping old Indigo's family off the map. Once that job was complete, she would have his tunic.

There was a non-small part of Zijian that felt regret over these killings. Were it not for Ysobel and her betrayal, there should have been no need to slaughter Indigo and his family.

But nothing could be done about that now. The game had changed. The die was cast. She would play it to the end.

———

Zijian is led upstairs to an observation deck overlooking the race track. Gotari is seated on a couch, wearing a white racing suit, drinking a beer. His dark hair looks greasy and unkempt, like he might have just come up from racing the track himself. He wears dark sunglasses. He does not remove them when Zijian arrives.

His resemblance to his sister triggers another pang in Zijian's stomach.

"So you're the one fucking my sister," he says. Not a trace of good humor.

Zijian is calm. Since she cannot see his eyes, she focuses her attention on his mouth. "Your sister has been a client of mine, if that's what you mean."

"But no longer?"

"No."

He takes a swig from his beer. Slides himself back on the couch, puts his feet up on the coffee table between them. "So she's all used up and now you're here to try and fuck me instead? Is that what's happening?"

Everything is always about 'fucking' with these simpletons.

"Not at all, Mr. Khan. On the contrary, it is your sister who has... betrayed The Lotus Corporation. And she has betrayed me personally. As The Lotus Chair, it is therefore my professional and personal duty to seek retribution."

He smiles.

Yes, that's right. Vengeance is something that even a simpleton can understand.

"However, I wanted to meet with you because I saw a win-win opportunity. For you. For me. For OmniCorp. For The Lotus."

Gotari tips his bottle up and sucks on it as she talks.

Quite the image this one. Like a baby sucking on his mother's tit.

She continues: "When your father passes, your sister will inherit control of OmniCorp. And I know, from my time of confidence with her, that she plans to eliminate your living stipend."

At this revelation, Gotari spits out his mouthful of beer (thankfully away from Zijian). His sunglasses fall from his face, revealing eyes wild with astonishment and anger. "That bitch!" He chucks his bottle over the balcony. "What, like OmniCorp needs the money? What the fuck does she care about what I do? Except to try and make me miserable!"

Now very much like a baby whose tit has been taken away.

Gotari paces, fuming, unloading his trauma "She's always been like this. Look, I know I'm not as smart as she is. She's like... a fucking genius or something. And mom and dad were always so proud of her. And disappointed in me by comparison. But what the fuck? I'm good at things too. I'd like to see her drive a car around this track." He laughs, apparently imagining Ysobel behind the wheel of a racer.

This could be easier than I thought.

"Yes, well... " Zijian says patiently. "This is why I thought it could be good for us to meet and discuss. It seems to me that our near-term interests might be quite aligned. Your sister has a debt that she must pay The Lotus.

And this is likely to be... destabilizing to OmniCorp if she were the CEO. Do you understand?"

Gotari calms himself a little and sits back down.

Good. I have his full attention.

"Lotus has no interest in causing problems for Omni-Corp. In fact, we would like to have a closer partnership, if it were possible. I believe there are all sorts of ways that our organizations can help one another."

He grins. "Is that what fucking my sister was really about? You wanted to get closer ties to OmniCorp?"

Zijian smiles and inclines her head slightly toward him.

Close enough to the truth, I suppose.

"Alright," he says, licking his lips. "What exactly are you proposing then? You guys at Lotus are the massage-killers, right? You planning to choke my sister to death next time she comes in for a mud wrap?"

"I'm afraid it's not quite that simple." Zijian opens her satchel. "We have a strict code for how we must do things at The Lotus." She brings out the ink pot, quill, parchment, and ritual dagger. Places them all on the coffee table between them. Gotari's eyes light up at the sight of the last.

"Cool blade," he says.

She nods and smiles. Waves her hand over the dagger in an inviting gesture. "Would you like to hold it?"

———

Scarlet lieutenant proved himself slightly more cunning than Indigo. After the briefing meeting, he simply disappeared. There was some pretense of being out to fulfill a contract in the suburbs, but Zijian was not fooled.

After the third day in a row of Scarlet's total absence, she called in her Amber lieutenant to ask a few questions.

She knew that Amber and Scarlet had a history. And if he were to confide in someone, Amber would be it.

She was right. Amber did not know for certain where Scarlet had gone. But she did know that he had a safe house in the country. Somewhat reluctantly, Amber gave her the address.

The reluctance was disappointing. It suggested that the disloyalty was spreading. Zijian contemplated the cost of terminating Amber immediately, and decided against it. Better to consolidate with four new promotions first. Then test Amber again, and take action if necessary.

She sent the other two candidates—Monty and Grace—to stakeout Scarlet's safe house. Sure enough, he showed up. They sent her the word, and the three of them ambushed him.

As he took his last breath, she told him that he died a coward, had dishonored The Lotus and himself for not confronting her directly. Like Indigo, his family would also pay the price. The eager young Monty volunteered himself to carry out the honor killings. The scarlet tunic to be his reward.

This left Grace and Maurice for the Jade and Sapphire positions. Once everything was settled with Gotari, they would accompany Zijian to execute Miss Khan. And when that job was complete, they would ascend as well. Neat and tidy. Zijian Sun's chair would be secure once again.

———

"The blade is necessary for contracts such as this," Zijian explains. "There is power in blood, you see. The old kind of power. Necessary to complete the ritual that will seal the target's fate."

Gotari is transfixed. "Woah!"

Fascination with death-dealing is a family trait, apparently.

At that thought, she self-consciously touches the small hexagram earring she's wearing. An artefact to ward off a telepathic invasion. If Gotari had any of Ysobel's aptitude, the earring would block him. And Zijian's ears would ring, letting her know of the attempt.

Thankfully, there had been nothing in this encounter. But she had let her guard down and suffered for it. She would not let it happen again.

"But what do you mean by 'seal the target's fate'? Does that mean that once I sign this, and use my own blood, that nothing can stop Ysobel from dying?"

"Exactly so."

"But you, or someone from The Lotus, still has to succeed in killing her, don't you? And couldn't she fight you off? I mean, she has a ton of private security through our company. And those fuckers pack some heat."

"She may be able to delay the inevitable. That is true. But even, hypothetically speaking, if she were to kill me and my lieutenants, the duty to fulfill the contract would pass to another member of the guild. And then to another and another. Ad infinitum. So, you see, no one survives. Not once the contract is signed and the ritual complete."

"Woah! I like that. You guys are more hardcore than I thought."

Zijian nods and smiles. Then returns her attention to the parchment. "So let us review. You wish to perform the blood ritual, empowering Lotus to execute your sister, Miss Ysobel Khan, at the soonest possible time. You place no restrictions on the manner of death, and have no stipulations concerning the aftermath."

Gotari is holding the dagger up close to his eyes, turning it slowly, inspecting the intricate inlays carved into the blade. "What does that mean about the aftermath? What would I stipulate?"

"Sometimes our clients are concerned about how the body is found or wish to conceal the cause of death. That sort of thing."

He laughs. "No. Fuck her. She wants to try and cut me out of my rightful inheritance. Let it be known that she was butchered by a scorned whore-assassin from her massage parlor."

The ugly truth of that description hits home. Triggers a look of disgust in Zijian's face. Cold fire ignites in her eyes. She clenches her teeth.

I am no one's whore you pathetic, pampered monkey.

But she recovers herself in a half-tick. "Very good," she says. "Then I think we are ready to complete the ritual."

"Do we need a witness or something?"

"Typically we would. But that requirement is waived for intra-family contracts. Historically, having extra eyes present at those rituals led to far more bloodshed than was desirable."

"Loose lips." He nods. "Got it. So what then?"

"Now you use the dagger to draw your own blood. Let it fall and pool here," she points to the signature lines at the bottom of the parchment. "Then use the quill to sign your name through the blood. Once that is done, I will do the same."

"Got it," he says. And without a moment's hesitation, Gotari slices his hand open. Deep across the palm. He squeezes his fist over the parchment. Grabs the quill and signs his name. When he finishes, it initially looks like a big red splatter. But after a few ticks, the parchment glows, absorbs the residual blood, and leaves behind only his name, written in crimson across the signature line.

He hands the dagger to Zijian. She wipes it clean on her

sleeve. Delicately pricks her finger, lets a few drops fall, and signs her name.

"It is done," she says.

Wasting no time, she immediately rolls up the parchment and begins packing everything back into her satchel.

"Wait!" Gotari shouts, clearly excited by the magic and ritual. "Let's have a drink. We should celebrate! What an opportunity! This is justice!"

"I'm afraid I must be off," she says. "We will have plenty of time to celebrate once the contract is complete. I promise you."

CHAPTER 30
INOLA

...VISITS THE UNDERCITY

"The visit to OmniCorp was unproductive?" Supervisor Six coughs out her question from behind the glass.

Inola takes a drag on her cigarette, blows the plume of smoke up toward the buzzing lights overhead. "I wouldn't say that."

"Your report says that Miss Khan was uncooperative. And that you could get no further useful information from her about Zijian Sun or The Free Moon Lancers."

"That is correct." Another drag. "But my ear was ringing for the entire meeting. I believe that is the effect of the anti-magic charm—an earring—that I was wearing. I believe Miss Khan was trying to work a spell on me. I believe she is some kind of sorceress."

Coughs of incredulity from the supervisor.

"I know it is hard to believe. It is quite certain that neither Sinbad Khan nor Miss Khan's mother... " Inola checks her notes. "Zelda Nasr—had any such magical ability. I know it is rare to see such skills arise in a family line spontaneously like that, but it can happen."

"When you met with Miss Khan, was there anyone else in the room with you that might have triggered the charm?"

"No. Or not that I could detect."

A cough of supposition from the supervisor.

Inola considers the possibility of a concealed magician attempting the mental attack. Shakes her head. "No. The effect in my ear coincided perfectly with Miss Khan. It did not happen anywhere else at OmniCorp. I believe she must have been the cause."

"Then what now, 6-2-6? What do you propose by it?"

"I believe that Miss Khan is afraid of Madame Sun. Since my last report, two more lieutenants at Lotus have been killed. Madame Sun is definitely cleaning house, replacing all her closest allies.

"She recently took a trip to see Mr. Gotari Khan, Ysobel's brother. I suspect she had some plan to influence or control OmniCorp through Miss Khan."

"So she is now looking to replace the sister with the brother?"

"Yes. However, I suspect Miss Khan may have tried working some of her magic on Madame Sun. I wonder if she might already have learned the answers to our questions about Lotus."

Silence from the other side of the glass. This is usually a good sign. The wheels turning in the supervisor's head.

Inola's cigarette is finished. She lights a new one. "Did you fall asleep on me, Six?"

"No. Just thinking through the optionality."

"Ah," Inola chuckles. "Yes. The optionality."

"The State Commissioner is convinced that his Populists, and Mr. Reese, will take City Hall in the election. If that happens, it will mean significant change in the political landscape of the city. It is a good time for us to review our assets, bring in some new ones as needed. We've played mostly hands off with the gangs. But the Commissioner's experiment, working with The Azzuri, suggests that policy is changing. I want our division to be prepared for this change. I want us to have plenty of strong assets on hand, in case..."

Supervisor trials off, but Inola is tracking. "I understand," she says.

"Who is going to win this game of yours, Montag?"

Inola takes a drag. Thinks about the question. She isn't sure. Not yet.

Her supervisor reads the silence. "Go down to the D.O.T. Use the door to The Keepers. Speak with our contact there. I will let them know you are coming."

The Division Six contact in The Keepers (of Secrets) is a very old mutant woman whom the Agency referred to simply as, "The Old Woman". She has, they say, lived for thousands of turns, knows everything that passes through the city wires, and has a memory that would put the Department of Records to shame.

"We need to get this buttoned up quickly, Montag." A pause for a big hacking cough. "Determine the winner. Play the winner. Before things spiral any further out of control."

———

The nearest Department of Transportation office is located at 1021 Bank Street, in the Government District. This branch mostly deals with public transit for the Downtown and adjacent areas. Same goes for all the other D.O.T. branches. They are mostly devoted to the local traffic and transit issues.

But the basement floors in these buildings are a different story. The basements in every D.O.T. building are restricted to Division Six only. They contain The Doors.

The secret doors. To all the places all over the various worlds that Division Six might need to get to in a hurry. Due to all the budget cuts, there aren't so many working doors as there used to be, but there's still plenty of short-cuts that a D6 agent can put to good use.

Inola walks into the Bank Street branch, takes the elevator down to B1. The Doorman in his double-breasted, many-buttoned coat awaits her at his desk.

"Room 10010101-3 is ready for you, Agent Montag."

She gives him an appreciative nod as she strides past. Swiftly down the endless, poorly-lit, corroding corridors. Tracking the numbers and pointers as she goes until she finds to the door labelled '10010101-3'.

She stops and places her hand on the copper nob. "Inola Montag, agent 6-2-6, voice verification." A happy chime from the door.

Agent verified. Enter.

Inola steps into a red room. Dim red lights. Brick walls. It smells moldy. Earthy. Damp. Cold.

"From the State Department?" Asks a creaky, old voice.

Inola looks around but doesn't see anyone. There are two dark tunnels on opposite sides of the room. Whoever it is spoke from the shadows in one of the two.

"Yes," she says. "I am Agent Montag. I'm here to speak with The Keepers. With The Old Woman."

"Yes yes, you are," creaks the voice. "Now listen to the sound of my voice and follow."

Inola obeys. After hearing a few more words, she tracks the voice to the right tunnel, and walks that way.

She hears the creaky one's soft little footsteps speed

ahead of her. Every few beats it says, "This way," or "Yes yes, follow me," or something else like that.

The tunnel is dark. Same moldy smells as the red room. Occasionally she glimpses little red eyes in what must be other tunnels branching off from her path. Her ear rings a little whenever this happens.

Before long, she can see another red room up ahead. And she can make out the silhouette of the creaky voice. It looks like it might be a frogling, wearing a little hooded cloak.

As they get closer, and Inola can see more clearly, she confirms that her guide is a frogling. She also sees that the "room" ahead is not a really a room. It is something much larger.

When they finally reach it, they emerge into an enormous cavern. There is an industrial complex—hundreds of tall pipes, tubes, and steam vents—to her left. To her right, tall stacks of little square, brick apartments, interspersed with terraced gardens of bio-luminescent plants.

Beautiful. Inola has been to The Undercity before, but she's not seen the like of this.

"Come, come," says her frogling guide, racing ahead. Down a set of steps to a brick pathway that leads around the cavern to the stacked apartments. They pass all sorts of other mutant-looking creatures. Most are reptilian. Dark eyes and scaly skinned. Several gape and point at Inola.

They take a long flight of external steps up and up toward one of the apartments near the top of the cavern. There's an old woman, most certainly The Old Woman, sitting in a rocking chair on her porch.

"The envoy from the State Department is here, Lady," creaks (or croaks?) the frogling.

"Mmm. Thank you, Dolphinneas," says The Lady.

Dolphinneas, the frogling, opens the little garden gate

that separates the steps from The Old Woman's porch, and gestures that Inola should enter.

Inola thanks her guide and strides through the gate onto the porch.

Dolphinneas closes the gate behind her. "I will wait for you at the bottom of the steps," he says before departing.

Inola turns to The Old Woman in her rocking chair. She does indeed look like she could be thousands of turns old. Her skin is green and leathery. She wears a tan cloak with a hood, just like the frogling, and a sleeveless tunic underneath. Only the bottom half of her face is visible.

"Please sit," says The Old Woman. Her voice is rough, though not as creaky as the guide's.

Inola looks around and notices there is no other chair. But she is able to sit comfortably on the garden wall at the front of the porch.

Her ear starts ringing.

"If you would let me, I could pluck the knowledge of why you are here from your mind," says the woman. "But I see you are shielded. Which is... not unwise, I suppose. So then tell me with your words: How can I help you?"

The ringing subsides.

"I am investigating The Lotus Corporation," Inola says. "You know of them, yes?"

"I do. Very well."

"I am investigating their chair, Zijian Sun. Do you know of her?"

"I do." A few beats. "She is my daughter."

Inola has her pocketbook, but it feels like it would be rude to whip it out at the moment. So she makes a mental note of that surprising detail—and briefly wonders why that fact is not in Zijian Sun's file.

"Madame Sun has been murdering her closest confidants," Inola explains. "I believe she is attempting to cover up dealings with terrorists. This is a serious—"

The Old Woman raises her index finger to interrupt. "Not quite," she says.

The ringing in Inola's ear comes back.

The Old Woman sighs. "My apologies. Old habits die hard. My... *inquiring* is merely to save us time. But we can exchange knowledge the old fashioned way." She takes a deep breath. "My Ija... my daughter has been forced into a corner. I fear that she has gone down the wrong path, and is now racing to her own destruction."

Inola nods and says nothing.

"The fairy Pendragon tricked her into hiring those assassins—the 'terrorists' as you call them, from Marial-That-Was. He had not initially planned to do this, but he sensed the door in my Ija's mind." The Old Woman pauses and sighs with evident pain. "And that is my fault. I left that door open. I did it for myself. So that I could still... watch over her. From time to time."

The Old Woman pauses again. Possibly to rest. Control her emotions. Or catch her breath. Possibly to let Inola absorb and ask questions.

Inola says nothing, so the woman continues.

"That was the door through which Pendragon entered. And he *suggested* to her that she hire those assassins from the world's edge. Knowing that it would bring her to ruin.

"That was also the door through which the OmniCorp girl entered. Accidentally at first. But once she was in, she saw enough of my daughter's mind to understand how she could take control.

"The murders of the Inspector and the first two of the Lotus rainbow—that was all the girl's doing. The former by her own hand. The latter by Ija's hand as her instrument."

Inola's ear begins to ring.

"You see, my Ija was not expecting any such attack and so she was not shielded as you are."

The ringing subsides.

"But as you surely know, these murders, under Lotus Hospitality, are an unforgivable offense. If the truth got out, Ija's time at Lotus would be over and her life would be forfeit." The woman begins wringing her hands in her lap. "And so now she is trying to repair the damage. Cover up the truth. And that has led to everything since."

"Madame Sun plans to murder the girl?" Inola asks.

"Yes, she does."

"Does the girl—Miss Khan—know it is coming?"

"Yes, she does. Ija does not know it yet, but she has already lost The Lotus. As she tries to replace and consolidate her support, the rainbow has turned against her and allied themselves with the girl." The Old Woman lets out another long sigh. Leans her head back, rocking slowly in her chair. "If Ija goes near the girl now, she will die. She will be slaughtered. That is where I see her current path ends."

"Not the path you want for her."

"No." The Old Woman holds out her hand. A small red bead in her palm. "Take this," she says.

Inola steps forward and takes the object in her fingers. "Garnet?"

"Yes. Use this with the girl. It will give you the power to influence her. Convince her to listen to you. Convince her to let you take Ija away, rather than kill her. Do you understand?"

"I do." Inola places the garnet bead in her pocket.

"You must keep that earring on as well. It will shield you from the girl's influence."

"I will."

"Good."

Inola feels she has what she needs. She takes a step toward the gate.

"Tell your superiors that I am done playing this game with them," the woman says. "On this current path, we will both be losers. Tell them that."

Inola blinks. She does not understand what this means. What game with her supervisors? She puts an exclamation point by this mental note.

The woman continues: "Help my daughter leave this path of destruction. If you can help her—save her. Then I see her having a valuable part to play in your future affairs. I see her becoming very useful to you. And your Agency."

"Thank you," Inola says. "I will do what I can."

The Old Woman raises a hand. Then lowers it slowly. Says nothing more.

Inola leaves through the gate. Down the steps. Meets her guide. They hurry back through the tunnels to the red room and the door.

Some mysteries solved. Other mysteries taking their place. But the Sham Assassination case is coming to its end soon. One way or another. She can feel it.

CHAPTER 31
SHUWEN

...ON THE MEND

Shuwen is alive. In a city hospital.

She is awake. Staring at the off-white ceiling. Listening to the soft whirs and beeps of the monitors. Smelling the cool antiseptic every so often when her nose decides to remind her.

She's not sure how long she's been there. Maybe a few days. Maybe a stretch. Maybe longer.

She still has all her parts. Can wiggle her fingers and toes. The many scratches and bite marks and bruises are fading.

Her shoulder aches like hell.

Her insides feel raw. Burned out. Angry. Like the scorched earth and sky of The Devastation.

Her bracers are still on her wrists. She feels sure they would wake up if she touched them. She doesn't want to. She doesn't want to feel the presence of her ancestors. They would be ashamed of her.

She shuts her eyes. A tear or two escapes.

She remembers.

It seemed an eternity of Val sitting next to her on the floor of the crypt. Breathing her heavy, disgusting, cinnamon breaths after the slaughter of Uziel.

The Killer Queen of the Harlequins eventually stood up with a groan and returned her attention to Shuwen. No more the raging beast or psychotic ballerina, she was now hunched and awkward from exhaustion. Her eye colors swirling, head tilted at that grotesque angle.

Looming over her captive, Val reached out with her stick and used it to lift Shuwen's chin.

Shuwen saw that all the cuts from Uziel's throwing stars were already healed.

A mutant. She must be.

"Did you see?" Val asked, her voice almost a full octave deeper than the sexy baby tone of earlier that night. "Did you watch?"

"Yes," Shuwen whispered.

"Did you learn your lesson?"

Shuwen's joints ached. Her skin burned. Sticky from the splatter of this sick woman's blood. Having just seen Uziel reduced to dust. She felt awash with the horror and the guilt.

Uziel annihilated. Because of her. He had come there only to save her. A painful echo of Tomas' death. A trusted partner taken down at the knee. Then broken into a million pieces.

What did it mean? Was there any meaning in this? Was she cursed? Cursed to bring doom to anyone she got close to on the streets?

Was that Val's lesson?

No.

Shuwen made no answer, but Val seemed to hear the

thought, and slapped her hard across the face. It took a few beats before the red faded from her vision. When it finally did, Val was still standing there, regarding her with a look of weary disgust.

"Too bad for you," she said. "Maybe next time it will be different."

Then she turned and started limping away. Toward the gloom on the far side of the crypt. After ten or so shuffles, she called back, "Tell Mr. Fairy I said 'Hi'." Then she snapped her fingers and all Shuwen's shackles opened. "Give him a good one from me!"

Shuwen's arms fell to the ground. Complete jelly. But the physical relief to her back and shoulders and legs... It was incredible. She curled herself into the fetal position and wept. Clutching the bracers on her wrists.

When Val reached the edge of the gloom, Shuwen had marshalled enough strength from her bracers to lift her head and shout after her.

"MONSTER!"

She filled the word with so much hate that she nearly choked on it.

Val stopped, turned around. Shrugged and said, "Aren't we all?" Then she took one more limp into the gloom and was gone. Leaving Shuwen alone. Wretched. On the cold stone floor. Weeping into the dust of another dead hero.

On some future day, Henry and Faust come to visit Shuwen in the hospital. They wouldn't normally allow dogs on the ward, but Henry explains to the nurses that Faust is Shuwen's particular friend and will do wonders to cheer her up. Faust also lays on the charm. The hospital staff are powerless to resist.

Shuwen's eyes are closed when they arrive. Faust props his two front paws up on the bed and nuzzles her hand.

She opens her eyes. "Henry," she whispers. "And Faust." She gives the dog soft pats on the snout.

"How you doing today, kiddo?" Henry says.

"Better."

"Yeah?"

"Yes." She closes her eyes. These are the most words she's spoken in a row since she's been in the hospital.

Faust hops on the bed and tries to find a spot to lie down next to her. Shuwen rolls onto her side to make room for him. He eventually settles and curls up against her legs. Fixes on her face with worried eyes.

Henry rests his hand on her shoulder.

She winces. "Ooh, no. That still hurts."

He pulls his hand away. "Oh, I'm so sorry. I didn't know."

"It's fine," she whispers. Begins petting Faust. A few rounds pass in silence. Then she asks: "How long have I been in here?"

"This is day ten."

"Am I fired?" She opens her eyes, focused on Faust next to her. Unable to look at Henry's expression as he answers.

Henry pauses a beat. "Are you sure you're up for that conversation now?"

She considers. "I guess so," she says at last. "As long as I have Faust here to comfort me."

The dog's ears perk up as she says his name.

"The mayor's office sent Wolff an order. Said you were to be dishonorably discharged from service."

Shuwen closes her eyes and moans. Faust lifts his head and whines in sympathy.

———

Shuwen couldn't tell how long she had been alone on the floor of the crypt. There was a period of convulsing as her body tried to expel all the evil and pain and shame of the night. And afterwards, a long, cold stillness.

She half expected a troupe of Charlies to show up and finish her off. If they came, she thought to herself that she would activate her bracers and try to take as many as she could with her.

But that's not who came. With an ear-splitting crash through the old stone walls, it was Tank, The League's giant reformed killbot. He had received Uziel's signal and come as fast as he could.

Sadly, not fast enough to save Nightwing.

Shuwen was delirious at that point, but remembered Tank scooping her up in his massive metal arms. Cradling her like baby. Then charging out the same way he came in.

Once they were outside, it was already light. He activated his rocket boosters and they went flying into the air.

She must have passed out at that point, because the next thing she remembered was waking up in the hospital who-knows-how-many days later.

———

"I know, kiddo. It's not right." Henry sighs. "Wolff has you on medical suspension. I think he plans to ignore the mayor's order until you're back on your feet and able to come in and see him."

A swell of emotions follows. Sadness. Fear. Dread. Disappointment.

A glimmer of hope that maybe Wolff will help her fight the order.

No, that would cost him too much. I can't ask him to do that.

A spark of relief maybe?

No. Not the right word.

Angst?

No.

Freedom.

There it is. The shiny, little positive. A sense of freedom. An opportunity to find a new path.

When I'm back on my feet...

Shuwen then feels the familiar urge to activate her bracers. The shame that held her back earlier fades. She indulges. Turns the etched silver on her wrists. Runs her fingers over the familiar engraving of the tiger rampant, holding a three-pointed star. Feels the tingles. The rush of power.

Faust lets out another little bark.

"Yeah, and the mayor's order specifically said that your bracers are to be confiscated."

She clenches her teeth.

From my cold, dead hands.

Shuwen's eyes are still closed, but Henry recognizes a look of determination forming on her face.

"Not going to let that happen are you," he says. It's not a question. It doesn't need an answer. "So when you're up and out of here, have you thought about what you will do?"

"They lied to us, Henry," she says. Her voice now more than whisper.

"Who?"

"The Police Academy. The Inspector's Office. The State. My mother. All of them."

"Lied about what?"

"Everything. Everything that truly matters. Our history. Our world. Our laws. Our duty. They've lied about all of it. They know the truth and they're hiding it. Treating us likes fools. Like we're just pawns in their game."

"Shuwen, what are you talking about?" Henry is not following. Faust might be. He wags his tail excitedly.

"A *magician* did this to me, Henry. And Val de Leo—she's a magician too. They're both *real* magicians, like from the old myths and legends. Not playing simple tricks with light. They're doing stuff that isn't supposed to be possible. Or at least not possible anymore. The government insists that none of this exists, and we're supposed to believe it. Enforce it. Without questioning. But it does exist. Even that Stasi agent—she basically told me so."

Shuwen is now rapidly turning the bracers around her wrists. Glowing brighter and brighter until their light is no longer blue, but white.

"What are you saying?" Henry still not following, watching her hands nervously. "You always knew some of the old magic was still possible. Because of your bracers. You use them all the time. And The State acknowledges artefacts."

"No, I know... " Shuwen pauses, trying to organize her thoughts as the power of her artefact begins to course through her veins, penetrating into every bone in her body. She sits up. Eyes now wide open. "I guess I thought of the artefacts as isolated exceptions. Old relics. From a world that was long gone. Like how the official State histories tell it. I didn't realize that the old world, and all the old power. It wasn't gone. It was never gone. It's still here. It's always been here. And it's *everywhere.*"

Faust barks his approval of this conclusion.

Henry's brow is furrowed. He looks skeptical. "You sound like you're tripping on psychs, kiddo."

Shuwen laughs. "I know! It feels like I'm tripping!" The glow from her bracers is now starting to spread across her skin. "Or what I imagine that would feel like... " The white envelops her hands. Creeps up her arms toward her shoulders.

Henry is alarmed. "Hey, take it easy." He takes hold of her hands. The white glow fades from her skin.

"It's okay, Henry," she says. "I feel better. I feel like I've finally found the core of this case. The rotten, stinking core. I thought it was the identity of the assassin. But it isn't. Then I thought it was the mayor's chief of staff. That evil magician. But it isn't." Shuwen's face is now bright and flush with color. "The rotten core that was bothering me the most: It was the lie. That I was never going to solve this case, because I was fighting to uphold the lie at its center."

She looks like her old self again. But the words are nothing like her old self. Henry wants to feel relieved, but instead he feels concerned.

"What's the lie exactly?" He asks. "That there's more old magic around than The State says? That their histories are mostly propaganda?"

"No..." Shuwen pauses again, dropping her eyes, sorting her thoughts. "The lie is that I knew my duty... that I could do the right thing—help people—by obeying... when I didn't truly understand the world. How it really worked. It's like... I thought half the world was dead, and I treated it as dead. And this made things seem simple. It made it seem like my duty was clear. It made me think that I understood what justice meant. But that half of the world —it wasn't dead. It was alive. And now that I see it for what it is... Now that I know it is alive... It changes everything."

Faust seems into Shuwen's new philosophy. His tail wagging happily. (Or it could be that he's just excited to see her so animated.)

Henry is maybe starting to get it. He rubs his chin thoughtfully.

"Anything is possible," Shuwen whispers. "And that changes everything."

CHAPTER 32
ELI VS. TY
...AT THE WATERFRONT

Eli wakes up face down in the mud. He feels the rain against the back of his head. Drumming on his back. He pushes himself up to a sitting position. Lets the rain wash the mud off his face.

He looks around.

Where am I?

He's down at the waterfront again.

How did I get here?

He remembers being at the club. Drinking. Sharing a bump with a couple of girls. And a guy.

Oh right...

The guy was a problem. Got his panties in a knot about something. Started throwing hands. Eli kicked his ass. The girls freaked out, despite his working the garnet ring. Then he got tossed from the club.

Must have wandered down here after that.

He smells something. It smells good.

Satay.

Following his nose, he stumbles down the muddy green

to the waterfront. On the other side of the nearest under-pass, he spots the source. Lin's Food Truck.

He laughs.

Crazy Lin. She's not going to let a little rain storm stop her!

Eli approaches the truck, now quite soaked. He doesn't look good. But he doesn't care about that.

Lin sees him and exclaims, "Heyyy! Mr. Mayor! So many celebrity customers tonight!"

"Satay me up, Lin," Eli says, holding up two fingers to indicate a double order.

"You got it!" She moves away from the truck window to yell the orders to her staff.

Eli pays. After a round or two, the satay is ready.

"Here you go," she says. "There's a table with light and an umbrella over there, if you want." She points a little ways up the path.

"Where's your chopping knife?" Eli asks. Usually she gives him a show of it.

"Ugh! Don't remind me. One of these good-for-noth-ings—" she points at the underlings behind her in the cart, "they must have lost it. I ALWAYS put my chopper right there!" She slams her fist down on the chopping board next to the window.

Eli doesn't really care about her story. His mouth already full, he raises a half-eaten satay stick in thanks and starts to move away. Strolling over to the tables.

There's a loud thunderclap as he sits down at the table. The noise doesn't startle or bother him in the slightest. He's happy to be out of the rain. Enjoys finishing his first order of satay to the sounds of the raging storm.

He sets down the naked satay stick. About to pick up and unwrap his second order when a wave of nausea sweeps over him.

Something's not right...

An unpleasant memory is coming back to him. Something about a meeting over a picnic table at night...

He shudders.

Another thunderclap distracts him. Pushes the bad feeling from his mind. He turns his attention back to satay. Reaches again for the package.

But again, he is thwarted. This time by a stiff kick to the back. Right between his shoulder blades. It knocks him violently forward, bouncing his head off the table.

"Fuck!" He shouts. His nose is bleeding.

A deep voice from behind. "That's payback for your cheap, back-turned shit, Rich Boy."

It is Dr. T.

Eli growls. Angry. Confused. He grabs his used satay stick, and spins around. Hops up from his seat. Brandishes the little piece of wood like a knife.

Ty snorts. "Are you serious, fool?"

Eli jabs with the stick to show that, yes, he is serious. Ty catches it with his hand. Clenches his first. Snaps it in half.

Undeterred, Eli moves forward. Throws a neat little punch-punch-kick combination. Pretty basic martial arts training stuff. Ty blocks it all easily.

Eli follows up with more of the same. And Ty blocks it all the same, his eyes fixing on Eli's hands the whole time.

The Mayor finally mixes up the attack. Goes for a grab. He manages to get a good grip on Ty's duster. Uses it effectively to whirl Ty around and then land a side kick, flush to his chest.

"Yeah!" Eli roars. His rage meter maxing out. "You fucking poser!"

Ty stumbles back against the table, knocking Eli's second order of satay into the mud and rain.

"Aww, now you've done it! That was my dinner!" Eli

charges forward. Feints a left jab, intending to grab Ty's jacket again with his right. But Ty is ready for it this time. He catches Eli's right arm and turns, using Eli's momentum to swing him around and trade their places. Then he grabs Eli by the back of the neck and slams him down onto the table.

Eli's head is pounding. The left side of his face smushed into the tabletop. He can see Ty behind, raising something up above his head.

There is a flash of lightning and thunder. It's a butcher's cleaver.

That's Lin's chopper!

"Fuck no, you bastard!" Eli bellows.

Ty swings the cleaver down across the fingers of Eli's right hand. There is an ear-splitting crack. But it's the sound of metal breaking, not bone.

Eli screams in pain. His hand is still whole. But his father's crown ring—his physical protection ward—has just spent the last of its strength keeping his fingers intact. It has shattered into pieces. Along with Lin's chopper.

Ty still has him by the neck. "Are you serious?" This time he's talking to the ruined butcher's knife in his hand. Trying to understand how it failed to sever Eli's fingers.

Eli tries to wriggle free.

Ty tosses away the remains of the butcher's knife. "Nah," he says to Eli. "We're not done yet." He pulls the mayor up out of the seat by his collar, then hits him with a nasty right cross.

Eli is dazed. He drops to all fours. Hands and knees sinking into the mud.

Another thunderclap. The Rising Dragon emblem ring starts to glow. Eli doesn't see it, but Ty does.

Ty snorts. "You got layers and layers of these trinkets on you, huh?"

Eli spits out blood, mud, and few teeth from his mouth.

Trinkets? What is this idiot talking about?

A big boot slams into Eli's face. Next thing he knows, he is flat on his back. Feels like his nose is broken. He's seeing all the stars in all the colors. The rain pouring down on him.

OK.

I'm done with this.

I'm ready to go home now.

He hears Ty's voice: "I guess I'll have to do this The Old Way."

Oh just shut up, you loser.

With great struggle, Eli lifts his throbbing right hand and taps his pinwheel lapel pin.

Sir?

I'm ready to go home now, Dmitry.

Yes, sir. Right away.

Ty grabs Eli's right hand and wrenches it up. "There's something you should know about me, Rich Boy." He starts pulling Eli's fingers apart. "I will do whatever it takes to get what I want."

Eli groans. He still can't see anything. And doesn't have the strength left to fight. "Leave me alone, you poser," he whines. "For fuck's sa—"

Another thunderclap as Ty chomps down on Eli's pinky. Tears it off with his teeth. Spits it out into the mud. Rising Dragon and all.

Eli's connection to Idris is severed. His mind feels like it was just cut in half. Into the half that remains comes a torrent of images and memories. A thousand and one nights of partying, barfights, dancing, prostitutes. Ending in death by overdose, car accident, drowning.

Scrounging through back alleys and dumpsters like an

animal, feasting on garbage, murdering faceless, homeless wretches and drinking their blood.

His limbs all twisted at painfully impossible angles as he's thrown into a closet stuffed with ten or twenty other copies of himself.

And on it goes. All his adventures as Idris Moorelake Pendragon's puppet. All the fragments of soul that still answer to the name Eli Strauss Jr. All the feelings that his enchantment hid from him. Rushing back in to fill the void.

He wails like a newborn baby. His body thrashing around in the mud and rain. Clutching at his four-fingered hand.

CHAPTER 33
ZIJIAN VS. YSOBEL
...AT OMNICORP TOWER

«Sad news today as OmniCorp's founder and CEO, Sinbad Khan, has passed away after a long fight with cancer. His daughter, Ysobel Khan, is stepping in as interim CEO until the company's board of directors meet to hold an official vote.

It is widely believed, however, that Miss Khan will be elected to the position, and therefore, her current status as interim is simply a formality.

We here at Channel 5 News wish to express our thanks to Sinbad for all he's built. For the opportunity, and the privilege, of bringing you the news each night.

We would also like to express our confidence and excitement about his daughter's leadership. We look forward to working with Miss Khan. We wish her all the best in her new role.»

Zijian is riding the elevator up to the 199th floor of the OmniCorp Tower. Ysobel is waiting for her. In the office of the CEO.

Ysobel knows she is coming.

It does not matter that she knows. She will die just the same.

Zijian passes the 10th floor.

She is not alone in the elevator. There are two Omni-Corp security guards. And two couriers. One carries two oversized bottles of sparkling wine. The other a large cake box.

Zijian holds her raincoat, folded over one arm. She is wearing a simple black evening dress. Soft and elegant. Fashionable yet sensible shoes. Her hair is up. The proper amount of makeup for the occasion.

The pretense is that this is a celebration. Ysobel is past her grieving. Sinbad Khan had been dying for a half-turn. It was his time. Tonight is his daughter's ascendancy.

They pass the 30th floor.

Zijian would be lying is she said she wasn't conflicted about this course of action. This was not how she wanted things to turn out. Yet this seemed to be her path. As she played the story back to herself. Revisited all her memories. Examined the chain of events. She did what she did with the information she had at the time. And it still seemed right. Or right enough.

Except for one thing.

I should not have trusted the girl.

And maybe a second thing.

I should have remembered my mother. Been more vigilant about my mental defenses. Always worn the earring.

She has the hexagram in her left ear this evening. She touches it self-consciously. Grits her teeth.

Yes. I was too trusting.

The only downside to wearing an anti-magic earring all the time was that it would give you horrible nightmares. As Hadra had explained it, some part of the magic in the world would still get through the ward—but it would only trouble your subconscious.

But what did nightmares matter now?

Nightmares are nothing. A small price to pay for protection and privacy of thought.

She passes the 60th floor.

Focuses her mind on the task ahead.

Supposing Ysobel has set an ambush for me. How will she do it? What should I prepare for?

She shuts her eyes in order to better visualize the possible scenarios.

She could have a room full of guards with guns. Have them open fire the moment I walk into the room... If she does: I will use Barretto's Defense. Smoke bomb. Kunai throw. Dash. Draw. Slash through her neck. Crash through the far window. Hook and swing onto a lower floor to escape.

She passes the 80th floor.

She turns to her left. The wine courier is Maurice, her aspiring Jade lieutenant, in disguise. On her right. Grace, her aspiring Sapphire lieutenant, holds the cake.

They would likely be lost under that scenario.

She sighs.

So it goes. The risks of The Lotus.

She passes the 110th floor.

Another scenario: Ysobel tries to enchant me the moment I arrive. She fails. Realizes it and then tries to enchant Maurice or Grace. Or both... Could she do both? Could she take over their minds fast enough?

She purses her lips. Considers.

No. I don't think so. But in this case... Waste no time. Leave a safe distance to Maurice and Grace. Walk up. Throw a hook if she tries to run. Full-body slice when in range. Her death will end any power she might have over others.

She passes the 140th floor.

A loud thunderclap from outside.

What if she has recruited more talent to her defense… Is it possible she could have recruited from The Lotus? If so, then I might have to deal with trained assassins AND her enchanting one or both of my own.

Zijian glances again at Grace.

That will be the hardest scenario. Requiring considerable improvisation and focus. And considerable luck to make it out alive.

Again she closes her eyes.

What if the girl begs for her life?

A pang in her stomach accompanies that thought, and so it is set aside.

There will be no mercy.

The 170th floor.

A million other possible scenarios and permutations.

The 180th floor.

All the most likely scenarios will require me taking first action, closing the distance, making the kill. No hesitation. Force her and hers to react.

The 190th floor.

A slow, deep breath.

The elevator chimes for the 199th floor. Bringing an end to Zijian's meditation.

The doors open directly on to the massive, panoramic office of OmniCorp's CEO. White marble and sea green glass—just like the racing pavilion. Instead of the nude statues, it is television monitors. Everywhere. In stacks. On pedestals. Hanging from the ceiling. All of them on. Showing all six thousand OmniCorp channels at once. All of them on mute.

Another thunderclap. The fork of lightning right outside the office's glass walls. It's flash of light pales in comparison to the glow of so many TV screens.

The long, semi-circular desk of the CEO is one hundred paces directly opposite the elevator. Ysobel is there. Turned away. Facing the window. Behind the big desk and big chair. The top of her head and the fall of her hair is clearly visible.

Zijian steps out into the room.

Not a room full of guns.

Her ear starts ringing.

Never again, bitch.

No more time to strategize. No more clockworks. It is time for action. She starts running toward the CEO's desk. Toward Ysobel.

Behind her, Maurice and Grace jump out of the elevator. Maurice throws one of his bottles at the feet of the OmniCorp guards in the car. It explodes. Not wine. It is pyro. The elevator goes up in flames. The guards incinerated.

Ysobel does not move. The ringing in Zijian's ear grows more intense.

Fifty paces away.

Are there no other defenses? Is she just going to let me strike her down?

Twenty five paces.

Does she not yet realize? She cannot enchant me...

She is a fool after all.

She hears the soft "pop" and "whoosh" sounds of a Lotus hookshot being fired.

Ah. Not a fool. The third scenario: She has recruited my own against me.

Zijian leaps in the air, easily floating over the hook that was fired at her feet. But as she reaches the apex of her jump, she hears the sound of a second hook.

It will catch her just as she lands. She cannot change her trajectory in the air now.

She throws away her raincoat, drawing the short blade that was concealed within it. She must focus. Slash away the hook as she hits the ground.

The ringing grows to a high-pitched explosion in her ears. She screams. Swings. Lands. Deflects the hook. Her long arm extended in a graceful follow-through.

Another fork of lightning splits the sky outside.

The Amber and Amethyst lieutenants appear on either side. They fired the hooks. They are her enemies now. They are charging her down. Ten paces away.

Maurice throws his second bottle at Amber's feet. But Amber is too fast, too skilled to be dispatched so. She leaps away from the exploding conflagration. Maurice pursues. They vanish behind the glare from one of the walls of TV screens.

Grace has discarded her cake box, brandishing the two razor-sharp fans that were disguised in the cake pan. She dashes in and intercepts Amethyst. They begin a dance of clashing steel.

Zijian turns her attention back to Ysobel. The girl is out from behind the chair. Her hands held together at her chest.

Their eyes meet. A mix of fear and dark determination in the girl's face. Very much like her expression at The Red Dragon before she thrust the knife into Fisch's throat.

Not a girl anymore. She is a murderess. A sorceress.

Zijian's lips curl into a snarl.

A mind-fucking monster.

Ysobel opens her hands, throws a handful of steel marbles over the desk at Zijian. They bounce off her. Harmless. For a few beats, the balls just lie there. Inert. And Zijian ignores them.

Beat one: With her free hand, Zijian draws her hook-shot and fires it at the girl. Spears her clavicle.

Beat two: Zijian pulls, launching the girl over the desk. Lands her in a heap at Zijian's feet. A move of such rapid violence that Ysobel doesn't have time to scream.

Beat three: Zijian steps on Ysobel's back, and places the tip of her blade on the woman's throat. Cutting a shallow wound into her flesh.

Beat four: Zijian speaks one word. "Unforgivable."

Then the balls activate. Six tasers release their shocks into Zijian's body.

One is enough to stun. Two will knock you out cold. Six...

Zijian's brain is rebooted.

Everything goes black.

CHAPTER 34
SHUWEN VS. IDRIS

...AT THE MAYOR'S OFFICE

Shuwen enters City Hall through the front door. Her coat and hat are soaking wet from the rain.

"Coming down hard out there, eh?" One of the security guards, making small talk as Shuwen places her gun, badge, keys in the little basket and passes through the metal detectors.

She forces a smile. "Tell me about it."

"We're just about to lock everything up here, Constable. Will you be quick?"

"Yes," she says. "This won't take long."

They hand her back the metal items in the basket. Gun goes back in the holster. Keys in her coat pocket, along with the badge. She wore it to get in the door. She won't ever wear it again.

She moves briskly up the big marble steps. City Hall is quiet. Just like it was the last time. It's been two fullphases of the moon exactly since then. Maybe that means something. Maybe it doesn't. Shuwen feels that it does. Magic in the old stories was always connected to the moon.

He'll be here. I know it. I can feel it.

She turns the bracers around on her wrists. Faster and faster. Taking them from the blue to the white. By the time she's standing outside the big double doors to the mayor's office, her hands and arms are glowing. She feels electric.

She kneels down and listens.

There is the hum. Same as before.

A loud thunderclap from outside. It's as good a signal as any.

She swipes Meg's counterfeit key card. The keypad beeps its rejection. The lock does not open.

Changed the locks... The other way in then.

She places her palms together. Takes a deep breath. Slams them into the doors. The latch shatters. The doors burst open.

The hypnotic hum. The swirling cloud of lights. The mirage of Mayor Eli. It's there. Just like last time.

She hears shouts of alarm from the security guards downstairs. She does not care. They are irrelevant. They will not be able to help. And they will not be able to stop her.

She draws her gun and fires a shot into the cloud of little lights. The bullet flies right through and embeds itself in the headpiece of the big chair behind the big desk.

The mirage vanishes. The cloud of little lights disperse into a wide circle that expands to the size of the room.

The humming stops. Replaced by cackling. Soft at first. Then louder. And louder.

That's him.

Another thunderclap. In the flash of lightning through the giant windows she can still see the whole office. Idris hasn't yet disassembled it. Or transported her. Or whatever it was he did.

The wide circle of lights starts to condense into little clusters. Six of them. Arrayed in front of her.

Shuwen hisses, "Show yourself, foul creature."

The cackle evolves into full-throated laughter. "Back for more, Constable?"

There is the sound of six popping corks, one after another. With each one, a light cluster disappears, replaced by the tall, sharp figure of Idris Moorelake Pendragon. Each one in a dark, pinstripe suit. Each adopting a different posture and expression, ranging from amusement to curiosity to contempt.

Shuwen fires a shot at one of the six. The figure seems to blur momentarily, but is unharmed. She fires at another. Same result.

All the Idrises chuckle at this. "That's a fun guessing game! How many bullets do you have left? How many guesses?" The six copies take turns speaking the individual words. It's strangely disorienting, being bombarded by the parts of a sentence from all sides.

Fuck this.

She holsters her gun and charges at the Idris directly to her left. She swings a kick. But when it should connect with his torso, the figure merely dissolves into a puff of golden smoke.

After a tick of hesitation, she moves on to the next. This one shifts to a combat stance and blocks two of her punches. When she would land an elbow strike to the side of his head, he vanishes in another puff of smoke.

On to the next. The other Idrises laugh and applaud. "I could go on like this all night!"

After the third puff of golden smoke, Shuwen whirls around and sees one of the remaining copies blur, stretch, and then double itself.

One of these must be the real one. It must be.

She quickly wipes the sweat forming on her brow. And adjusts her bracers. Keeping them in the white. They are hot on her wrists. She's never pushed them this hard before. Unsure of how long they will last. Or what it might cost.

It doesn't matter. I will finish this now. One way or another.

Round and round she goes. Focused on the Idris clones. She doesn't notice that the room begins to disassemble. The doors. The walls. Most of the furniture. Soon it's just the big window, the big desk, four or five Idrises and her. Dancing around the office in the dark void.

She mixes in a few gun shots at close range. A slick back-fist combo followed by a quick draw and shot at the next Idris in line gets the number of his clones down to three. But her following two bullets only trigger more doubling.

"You're slowing down, Miss Li. I can see it."

After the next puff of gold smoke, something scratches her across the back of her neck. A nasty set of claws. She's bleeding from a deep scratch. She spins around. Goes for a sweep kick. The Idris behind jumps away, licks at his long fingernail talons.

Another flash and thunder. Only one Idris appears in this momentary brightness. The one furthest from her. She charges at him. But he seems to float away, gliding flat-footed over the floor like he's stood on some invisible moving platform.

"Ah," he says. A discord of distress appearing in his voice for the first time. "It now seems that I do have somewhere else I need to be. So we'll have to conclude this dance, Constable."

Another swipe at her back. She senses it coming and dodges away. Then ducks underneath the follow up assault.

There's just three Idrises now. But they are all on the attack.

Yes, let's bring this to a conclusion.

Shuwen jumps. Ducks. Dives away from the onslaught. Three pairs of claws trying to scratch and grasp her. Three pairs of long legs with heeled shoes trying to trip her up, knock her down, and stomp on her.

She rolls away, draws her gun, and fires. One Idris is smoked in the bullet. But that wasn't her true target. She's shot out the big window. It shatters.

That is a signal.

The noise of the storm fills the room. Rain comes pounding in.

One of the two remaining Idrises comes at her with a flying knee. She blocks it in time, but the force of the impact pushes her back. Straight into the arms of the other. When he tries to grab hold of her, he shrieks with pain. Burned by the contract with the white light enveloping her arms and shoulders.

The Idris in front dissolves with a golden puff. Shuwen spins around, sending a wild back-fist toward the face of the Idris behind.

The hit doesn't connect. He catches her by the wrist. His long, clawed fingers wrapped around her bracer. He growls. Steam rising from his grip.

She pivots her whole body and swings a right hook toward his gut. He catches that too.

They are locked in place for a tick. Shuwen's two fists frozen, a tiny fraction before impact. Her arms blazing white. Her eyes blazing fury. Idris' hands sizzling hot, fused to her bracers. His rabid face snarling. One of his eyeballs is pulsating, gone completely black. It looks about to burst.

Looking more wolf-like than ever, he unleashes a fearsome howl and squeezes Shuwen's left wrist.

The left bracer cracks. Its light dissipates in a flash and burst of energy. It causes him to lose his grip. When Shuwen's hand flies free, it is an unstoppable force. As though she was just charging up, storing the potential energy of her strike for as long as he held her in his grasp.

She opens her hand. In that final instant, changing her back-fist to a chop, redirecting it at Idris' neck. Right at the apple (or whatever fairies have there). When it hits, it sounds like a tree being cut in half. With a monstrous gag, he doubles over, both hands holding his neck. Struggling to breathe.

That's when The League arrives.

Tank rockets through the giant broken window. Meg the Magnificent, in her exosuit, leaps from his right shoulder. Benoit in flowing, psychedelic-colored robes, leaps from his left. The heroic tableau of their three silhouettes against the stormy night sky makes an impression. One Shuwen remembers for the rest of her life.

Before she lands, Meg throws out a small disc. It falls at Idris' feet. "Look out," she yells to Shuwen.

In the next instant, Shuwen is thrown back. Knocked flat on her butt. But otherwise unharmed.

Idris was not thrown. Instead, he is enclosed within some kind of translucent cube. Still doubled over in agony.

Benoit leaps into the cube. Seeming to become a ghost as he passes through its shimmering membrane. He pulls something that looks like a big metal lawn dart from his cloak. Jams its sharp end into Idris' spine and then ghosts back out of the cube.

Idris rears up, his mouth wide and twisted in what should be a horrific scream. But he makes no sound.

What happens next makes another impression. This one Meg, Benoit, and Shuwen all remember for the rest of their lives.

From Tank's perspective, with his mechanical eyes and brain, Idris seems to glow bright gold for a beat and then his form shrinks and shrinks until it is nothing.

But with their eyes and brains of flesh and blood, Meg, Benoit, and Shuwen all see something different. To them, it looks like time and space implode. The fabric of Idris' being turns somehow inward and then starts to play itself backwards.

It's like they see the millennia-long movie of Idris' life in reverse. As he is sucked out of existence, his form made smaller and smaller, their mental attention to the "movie" is drawn in deeper and deeper. More and more information condensed and passed into their minds in a shorter and shorter time.

They see Idris and Eli with Madame Sun signing the writ for the sham assassination. They see Idris approaching Eli for the first time after his father's death, proposing to help him lead his campaign of revenge against The Dark Web.

They see Idris working as a Stasi officer, pitching the Mutant Extermination and Relocation Program. And before that, he is hunting down terrified mutants in the sewers of The Undercity.

They see him as the Chief of Media Relations for The Ragnarok, working on propaganda slogans and posters. Before that, a military strategist for Marial's Imperial Army during The Great War, arguing with the generals about the viability of psychic weapons of mass destruction.

They see a priest of the Dualist church. Delivering fiery sermons. Seducing and molesting the young boys and girls who serve as his acolytes.

A poet vagabond wandering in the desert. Spending turns creating beautiful earthworks in the dunes that no one will ever see.

A successful nude portrait artist during the Second Renaissance. Visiting the homes of all the wealthy aristocrats and patrons to immortalize them in their prime.

A solitary monk meditating in a cave on a cold mountaintop. Speaking not a word, eating almost nothing, for a hundred turns of the wheel.

A fearsome battle-mage, slinging fireballs in The Wars of Restoration.

Younger now. He is a charming fairy-noble dancing with his beautiful partner in a glittering, golden ballroom.

Running naked through the woods alongside a pack of faewolves, all howling joyously.

Younger still. Carefully documenting his experiments mixing the different colors of magic.

Stargazing at the deep green night sky of Faesia.

A child. Slowly walking up the steps to his tree-house home.

Gazing into his older sister's face, sharp and beautiful, with that mischievous look of hers.

Sitting on his father's lap. Hearing his jolly laugh. Touching his rough-textured beard.

A babe. Held in his mother's arms. Listening to her soothing voice.

A sensation of symphonies. Written in the ripples and waves of the ocean.

Whispers of a secret logic in the repeating patterns of sound and light.

The incredible mysteries contained with the darkness.

An essence. Drifting in the colorless dream of a life soon-to-be.

Gratitude at receiving a gift from the infinite.

The long silence and stillness of oblivion.

CHAPTER 35
INOLA

...BEGINS HER NEXT ASSIGNMENT

Another day. Another long walk down a yellow, flickering-fluorescent government corridor. The Sham Assassination case is closed. Agent Inola Montag is on her way to an interrogation room. To speak with the subject of her next case.

She's reasonably pleased with how everything turned out. She had minimized her personal footprint. Pushing the right people just far enough, at just the right moment, to bring the game to its conclusion. Far from her tidiest clean-up, she would admit. But considering the absolute shit storm that it could have been... A terrorist conspiracy within the Assassins Guild. City Hall, NWPD, Lotus, OmniCorp—all under threat from magic-users. It wasn't an exaggeration to say that it could have been the end of New World City.

Thanks to Inola Montag, Agent 6-2-6, it was not the end. The wheel still turned for NWC. But Inola sees the big changes coming. And big changes are never what a Stasi likes to see.

At least inside Division Six, everyone understood that changes like these were inevitable. Magical energy was resurgent. This was a fact of the cosmos. No use fighting against it. And it was going to be impossible to keep the lid on it for much longer. That meant D6 would need to adapt. Skill up. Start recruiting more magicians to their side. Get ready to fight fire with fire.

Speaking of which: It was damn good that Idris Moorelake had been destroyed. A grade 2 wizard like that, positioned where he was. He could have done far more damage. Data was still rolling in about all the details of his demise, but it was definitely Shuwen Li. Her last act as NWPD's Supercop before her unceremonious discharge.

All in all, a good enough outcome on that front. Inola is glad Shuwen survived. Sure, the city police are a little worse off without her, but a small price to pay for eliminating the threat of an ancient fae wizard stowaway.

Ty Reese winning the election, as The Commissioner had predicted, was also good news. Made it easier to sweep the rest of the sham assassination business under the rug. Out of sight, out of mind as far as public perception was concerned. And with Strauss Jr. out of New World City entirely (intel was he drove into the desert, gone off-grid), the people moved on. Turned their attention to the new celebrity-in-chief.

Unclear how Mayor T was going to actually govern. His acceptance speech sounded promising enough. He spoke a lot about "re-shaping" the city for success and prosperity. Inola is cautiously optimistic about it.

Since the Populist Party answers to The Stasi, this also puts one more pillar of city power under the State Commissioner's control. Perhaps not the best thing—and Supervisor Six isn't completely thrilled about it. But Dr. T is no pushover. So it should be interesting to see how he butts heads with the Big Commish.

A change more directly related to Inola's new case is the

merger of Lotus and OmniCorp. With all the turmoil in Lotus' leadership, Omni was able to buy up Lotus stock at a distressed price. Remains to be seen if they can hang on to the Assassins Guild license. The Wakizashi gang are making a play for it. But either way, Omni will certainly benefit from diversifying their assets. They are now the media AND hospitality conglomerate. With Ysobel Khan at the helm of it all.

So much power concentrated in one private citizen... That will draw a lot of attention. From The Stasi. The others in the Big Six. The Ivory Citadel. The Ragnarok. You name it. Miss Khan will have a target on her back. But after Inola's invaluable assistance in dealing with Madame Sun, D6 has a good foot in the door with the young Sorceress-CEO. Hopefully enough to nudge her and OmniCorp in the right direction.

Inola finally reaches the end of the long, yellow corridor.

"Inola Montag, agent 6-2-6, voice verification," she says.

A happy chime from the door.

Agent verified. Enter.

She steps into the small room. Putty colored walls. Same yellowish, buzzing lights overhead. One small table. Two small chairs.

Zijian Sun is seated on the far side of the table. She is unrestrained. Dressed in the ugly white shirt and pants of a state prisoner. Waiting passively. Her posture relaxed. Her face blank.

Inola takes the seat opposite. She places her portfolio, labeled "Agent Z", on the table. This is her new case. The repurposing of Zijian Sun, precious State asset.

"Good morning, Zijian," she says.

"Good morning." Zijian's voice is flat. Disengaged. She

meets Inola's eyes, but there's no spark. No trace of recognition.

"Do you remember me? Or our conversation yesterday?" Inola asks.

After a pause of several beats, Zijian replies, "No."

Inola nods and smiles sympathetically. Opens her portfolio and makes a note. "Then we'll start at the beginning again."

After speaking with Gadget Man and some of the doctors on staff, Inola understands that it may take some time for Zijian's brain to recover. Perhaps more than a full turn. And even then, many of her old memories may never come back.

But consensus is that she should regain her ability to form new memories. That is Inola's hope as she turns a page over in her portfolio and begins the script. One she has delivered dozens of times already.

"Your name is Zijian Sun. You are an agent of The State. You are in this facility to recuperate. Your brain suffered a serious trauma, wiping your memories. This happened while you were out on assignment."

Zijian listens. Nods. "What was my assignment?" She asks.

"You were deep undercover, operating as the head of The Lotus Corporation, here in New World City. Lotus is a front for the Assassins Guild. And you were working there, leading a society of contract killers."

"How long had I been on assignment?"

"Your whole life."

———

As Inola wrapped the Sham Assassination case, she followed up with her supervisor about those intriguing comments from The Old Woman—that Zijian was a part of some game.

What game was The Old Woman playing with The Stasi? Inola put that question directly to Supervisor Six. After several hacking coughs and feeble attempts at deflection, Inola was eventually granted access to an ultra-top-secret file.

The "Agent Z" file.

Turns out The Stasi had implanted the orphaned child Zijian with an experimental "instruction" circuit. Strategically placed her in The Undercity with the goal of making her a "sleeper agent" inside The Keepers of Secrets society. When Zijian reached maturity, plan was to activate the circuit and she would "wake up" to her true purpose. Start funneling information about The Keepers and The Undercity back to D6.

The Old Woman adopting Zijian was a perfect start. But it turned out that the circuitry didn't work. Or maybe The Old Woman deactivated it somehow. Either way, after The Old Woman took Zijian in, she turned the tables. Raised Zijian to become her own weapon. Molded her into the formidable force that she was, and sent her back to the city above. Put her own, far more effective, "programming" inside the girl's head that let The Keepers watch and manipulate Lotus activities more directly.

If things had gone differently, Zijian would have been a conduit to OmniCorp as well.

It was a bold play from The Old Woman. Inola was impressed.

But the more she read the Agent Z file, the more she found herself feeling sorry for Zijian. The poor woman had been mind-fucked every which way. Manipulated into an unwitting pawn of The State since day one.

It didn't feel good. It didn't feel right. And it certainly

wouldn't be right to let Zijian be thrown away now. Inola wouldn't stand for that. So she insisted on taking the case. She would see to it that Agent Z ended up in a better place.

This must be what The Old Woman had sensed. Why she had been so forthright and interested in helping Inola bring the twisted game to its conclusion. She sensed that Inola wouldn't let Zijian go to waste if she could help it.

And in the end, the brutal reset of Zijian's mind might be exactly what she needed. Close off the "doors" that let those others control her. An escape from Ysobel's influence. From The Old Woman's influence.

Not from The State's influence, obviously. But no one is ever free from State influence. Not as far as Division Six is concerned.

————

"My whole life," Zijian repeats. Thinking over the meaning of this statement. "How old am I now?"

"You are thirty-eight turns today. In fact, it's your birthday. Happy birthday, Zijian." Inola gives her a warm smile. It's a lie about the birthday, of course. But protocols for this kind of re-conditioning suggest that happy thoughts like birthdays can serve as a useful "cushion" as the mind is rebuilt.

"Oh." Zijian smiles politely in return.

"Do you remember any of your past birthdays?"

"I... " A touch of warm water appears in her eyes. "I think so."

Inola makes a note. This is a promising development. "What do you remember?"

Zijian looks pained. She lifts her hand, slowly brushes her hair away from her face. Then holds her hand to her forehead. Brow furrowed. She tries for several beats to conjure the memories. Somewhere in the deep storage of her mind. "Candles," she says at last.

"On a cake?"

"No... On the ground... In a circle. Around me."

Inola has heard that some of the cultures down in The Undercity do something like this for their birthday rituals. The person sits in the middle of a ring of candles, one for each turn of their life. Then they blow them out one by one, making a wish each time.

"How many candles were there? Do you remember? Can you see?"

Zijian closes her eyes. Relaxes her face. "I don't know for sure. Thirteen or fourteen maybe. But—" She pauses and takes a deep breath. "I have this feeling... that my life is about to change. That my... *real* life is about to begin."

"Is that a feeling in the memory? Or is that how you feel today?"

Zijian opens her eyes. Meets Inola's gaze. "Both," she says. And for the first time since they started these conversations, there's a spark. A sign that the woman may be coming back.

Inola sets her pen down. Reaches out and takes one of Zijian's hands in hers. Gives it a squeeze. "A good feeling on a birthday, isn't it? Do you want to make a wish for the coming year?"

Zijian closes her eyes again. For several rounds, they sit in silence under the buzz and flickering-yellow. Inola watches Zijian carefully. The woman sits perfectly still. For long enough that Inola starts to wonder if she might have fallen asleep in the chair.

"I want to be free," Zijian says finally.

Inola smiles. Picks up her pen. Makes another note. "I know you do," she says. "I want that for you too. We'll get you there. I'm on the case."

CHAPTER 36

SHUWEN

...TURNS THE PAGE

Shuwen throws a flurry of three quick side-kicks. Henry deftly blocks each, then takes a shuffle step forward and throws a few jabs. She blocks one. Spins backward a step. Blocks the other.

Her movement and a momentary back-turn invites him to advance further. Which he does.

Always too predictable, Henry.

He goes for a strong, forward-lunging punch. Thinking that his longer reach should make this a safe attack. But Shuwen is expecting it. She jumps in the air, gracefully rising above his outstretched arm. She spins around, extending her leg. If this were a real fight, she could knock Henry out cold with this kick.

It is the end of the day. The end of the advanced class at The Li Dojo. The other eleven students kneel in a circle around her and Henry. Once per stretch, a student may challenge her to a fight like this. If they win—by being the first to land three clean hits—then they can be promoted to teacher.

This is the second time Henry has risen to the challenge. Last time he landed no hits. This time he's landed one. But Master Li already has two, and she's about to land her third.

She's adjusted the distance just so for her spinning back-kick. She brings her foot to his face and taps the pads of her toes against his nose. No physical power behind it, but it's a clean hit. Henry splutters and tumbles backward.

"That's three," she says when she lands. The students around the circle clap their hands three times in unison. The fight is over.

———

"You're getting better," Shuwen says to Henry as he's getting ready to leave.

"Thanks, kid– er... Thank you, Master Li." He smiles and bows from the waist. Shoots her a wink when he straightens back up. "You know, I saw Wolff the other day. I told him that he should think about signing up for your classes. He said he was too old."

Shuwen chuckles.

Faust barks happily from the other side of the room. He is playing with Benoit, another student in the class. The giant panda is down on all fours. Sparring animal-style with the dog. Such rough-housing is not permitted during class time, but Shuwen makes allowances for this kind of thing once the other students have gone.

"What's the latest from the streets?" She asks.

"Different flavor of the same old," Henry says. "Less to do about Azzuri, now that Mayor Ty is setting the priorities. But the other gangs—Wakizashi, Lotus, and H.A.W.K. especially—are all causing more trouble. And looks like there's some new supervillain on the scene. Calls himself 'Qamal the Purifier'. He has some small army of drone synths that he's been dropping off around the city to cause trouble. Seems like he's targeting OmniCorp specifically. Have you seen or heard of him yet?"

Shuwen raises her eyebrows in feigned surprise. She's heard of Qamal all right. She and the other Vigilantes have already been in a handful of scraps with his drones. But she shakes her head and says nothing. Doesn't want Henry or anyone else on the NWPD knowing too much about what she's up to these days.

There's a twinkle in Henry's eye all the same. He knows her well enough to know that she hasn't hung up the bracer for good. "Well, if you haven't had any run-ins with him yet, you will." He picks up his duffle bag and slings it over his shoulder. Whistles for Faust, who dutifully runs over. "See you next class, kiddo," he says as he and the dog exit.

———

It's nearly clock 10 when Shuwen locks the door and the extra security gate outside her dojo. Benoit is just up the street, waiting for her. He's dressed in a trench coat and wide-brimmed hat. She's in her burglar blacks. Wearing the remaining Li family bracer on her right wrist.

The two walk together to the nearest subway station. Down the steps. Through the turnstile. But they don't wait for a train. They head to the maintenance door at the far end of the platform. Benoit waves a keycard. The door clicks open, and they quickly move inside.

Two more flights down. To the sewer level. From there, it's a series of tunnels and turns and more tunnels. To another unmarked door. And another flight of stairs. And more tunnels. And so on. In a complex sequence they've done so many times that they no longer have to think about it. The path to The Vigilantes League base.

Henry is right, of course. Shuwen took a span or two off after she was forced out of the NWPD. But she couldn't hang it up. Now more than ever, she felt the call of duty. With a new-found clarity about what her duty was and where it truly came from. It didn't come from the lawmakers. Or from her superior officers. Or even family tradition. Her duty came from the world itself. The world needed balance. It needed people to fight against the chaos and cruelty and confusion.

In a city where anything is possible, you needed heroes.

Heroes like Uziel Silverman, who would fight the good fight to their last moment.

Shuwen knew that as a fully flesh-and-blood human, she could never be quite the tireless force for justice that Uziel had been. But she would try to fill his shoes as best she could. To keep the watch. Protect the innocent. Inspire others by example.

Heroes could die like everyone else. A hard truth of New World City. A truth that she knew better than most. But now she also understood that death was not the end of the story. The death of one hero could mean the birth of another.

Case and point: Shuwen Li the NWPD Supercop was dead. Shuwen of The League (superhero moniker still under discussion) had risen to take her place.

The end of one story. The beginning of another.

And this time, the story will be different.

Because this time, Shuwen wouldn't be working alone.

XXI

ACKNOWLEDGMENTS

I'd like to thank my good friend and editor, Cliff Fleck, for helping me develop and refine this world and this story. My wife, Julie Walsh, for her support and feedback throughout the process. My early-draft readers, Anthony Belardo and Jessica Huth, for their encouragement. And Josh Lambert, whose conversation inspired me to start writing.

ABOUT THE AUTHOR

Spencer Hey lives in Boston, Massachusetts with his lovely and brilliant wife and their lovely and brilliant dog. He has a PhD in philosophy and worked as an academic for about 10 years, exploring questions of ethics, science, and technology. A life-long lover of fantasy and sci-fi—whether in books, games, or movies—fantastic world-building has always been a passion of his. For 35 years or so, this passion has been limited to sketches and documents and small game demos that few people ever saw. New World City is his first effort to share the passion and bring one of these worlds to readers.

JOIN THE NEWSLETTER

If you enjoyed this book and want to follow along with the evolving stories of HYPERARCANA, please visit www.heyspencerhey.com and sign up for the author newsletter. You will receive quarterly updates on new releases in the series, exclusive bonus content (e.g., early access to cover reveals, short stories, etc.), and general geeking out about the entertainment and culture that inspires this genre-bending world.